Donate
Emma Ellis

This is a dark novel. Readers should know it contains references to abortion, miscarriage, and self harm.

Donate is written in British English

Chapter 1

Part 1

The Society is safe for all of its citizens, as all citizens help to keep it safe.
All Eyes Are Our Eyes.
Manifesto pledge of the Eyes Forward.

***

Mae walks home past the houses with coloured window frames: pinks and yellows and sky blues, old paint peeling off in coiled ribbons, pastel shades, complimentary. The flakes sprinkle on the pavement like dandruff. Window boxes filled with multi-coloured stones, glassy and shiny, attract her attention like she's a magpie. Anything to keep her mind occupied. Thoughts lead to more thoughts. Darker ones.

What are we going to do—

Thoughts.

I'm not ready for this—

Thoughts.

A trickle of panic slithers down her spine. Not the kind of panic when she's running late for work. More of a guttural panic. Primal, raw. The sort of panic that glues her to the spot, stops her breath yet races her heart.

She looks straight ahead, her eyes blurring out the houses and street furniture, the lines of people meandering their way around each other. Slow lanes of pedestrian traffic mix with the fast lanes, yet it doesn't bother her like it usually would. Her mind is too disordered to accept order. She considers carrying on, past her address and further — wherever the road leads. She's never walked that way, not that far, not in a long time anyway. The road goes on forever, and it would be a long run to nowhere. There's no escaping her own mind.

Storm clouds collect overhead, dulling the shine from the glassy stones. The wind blows the painted dandruff into eddies around her feet, like it's trying to be pretty, like the world isn't really this dark. Then she remembers his smile, his excitement. Soothing, supportive. She puts one foot in front of the other again, not just because of the bottleneck of pedestrian traffic building up behind her.

'Excuse me.' One gruff-voiced man shoulder-barges his way past her, his face less polite than his words. He looks old though. She can forgive that. He's not the worst of them.

She realises the traffic lights must have changed from the torrent of bikes that race down the street, spraying her ankles with mucky puddle water.

Brown stains on her cream tights like crap on paper. Sums up her day well.

She curses and kicks off the bulk of it. She should really hurry home, dry her feet, shower, piss, face the music.

She stands on her front porch for a while. A length of time that will draw attention, curtain twitchers, phones ready. Society Police are rife in Berkshire. She'd do the same if she were them. Her Life Score isn't high enough for her current lifestyle, let alone the one that could come. A few extra points would do nicely.

Can she report herself? She wonders with a laugh, allowing her mind to drift again, just for a moment, until her lust for procrastination wanes. She enters and plods up the stairs to her apartment.

'So?' Pasha grins as soon as she walks through the door, his eyebrows raise above his mop of hair, face full of delight she was struggling to find.

'I haven't done it yet.'

'Well, get on with it. I'm dying to know,' he says, hopping around like he's the one needing to pee. 'There's the announcement in a minute.'

'I know. It's not going to be good news. I can feel it.'

'Just go do it! I can't wait any longer.' He manages to relax his smile enough to kiss her on the mouth, though her frown remains steadfast. He shoos her to the bathroom, his eyes glinting, hers low with guilt.

She should be excited rather than full of dread. This should be a happy day.

She side-steps into the bathroom. Only a couple needed, such is the cramped space in their apartment. Ridiculous to think a whole other human could fit in there.

'Turn it up, will you. I can't hear it,' she says through the closed door.

'You're only peeing on a stick. How loud can that be?'

'Just turn it up. I want to listen.'

'I'll Bluetooth it to the speaker in there. Turn it on.'

She reaches above the cabinet, standing on tiptoes and the news comes blasting through. The excitable newsreader's voice recites the headlines like a kid waiting for Christmas.

'I hate that guy,' she says as she reaches for the test kit in her bag.

'Well?' Pasha pokes his head around the door.

'Clearly I haven't done it yet.'

'Sorry, I'm just excited.'

'No shit. Go away and wait outside. Allow me a bit of privacy.'

The Prime Minister says significant progress was made at the conference, with every country in the world in agreement on how best to proceed.

'Is the speaker working okay?'

'Yes, it's fine.'

And now we go live from Downing Street.

'The PM looks wiped out,' Pasha says. 'No easy job arguing with every other country in the world about how to fix the population.'

'Shh. I don't need a visual commentary. I'm trying to listen.'

'You should be peeing.'

'I'm reading the instructions.'

Good morning, people. It has been a tough couple of weeks while the entire world makes decisions as one on how best to proceed. But this is a momentous day, as all countries have come to an understanding. The population crisis is being tackled globally, with every single nation in agreement. A truly historic moment in human history. Never before has such cooperation been achieved.

'I can hear you peeing.'

'Shh.'

Our own efforts to curb humankind's population growth have failed. As we hit the twenty billion milestone, it is clear that every country has failed in this task — our Great British Society included. Our incentives for not having children have proved ineffective. The hormone additives in our food have not stopped backstreet fertility treatments from working. We have tried a softer approach, and it has not worked. This is not a problem we can overcome individually. We must act as one planet for the common good.

'You've stopped peeing.'

'I am well aware of that.'

'Well?'

'Just wait and be quiet.'

We know that the Society will be a shining example for the rest of the world. Our Society, inclusive of all regardless of Life Score status, is the envy of the world. Each county is a slice of the Society—

'Eurgh, he's using food metaphors again,' Mae says.

'Makes me hungry.'

—And each slice must do its bit to support every county. The entire Society. We have drafted up a list of global laws to be adhered to by every person in every nation. These laws will be implemented immediately.

These new laws are as follows: On the matter of the pharmaceutical, Pres-X, its global legality is still up for review. The pharmaceutical's creator XL Medico will update us on its figures. Pres-X will not be available on the National Health Service, and we shall be monitoring its use. International governments are doing the same.

'Well, no surprises there,' Pasha says. 'The wealthy in charge want to live another seventy years and stay young. I'll bet he's had a treatment. A man that age looking that young?'

'It's probably just makeup.'

'Mae! Since when do you give them the benefit of the doubt?'

'Since I need you to be quiet.'

That will come as no surprise to any of you. But the huge jump in life expectancy is not without consequence. So we move on to the issue of creating life. Pregnancy registration will continue, but will be closely monitored. All must be registered immediately. Anyone found to be deliberately not registering a pregnancy will be punished with imprisonment for up to eighteen years.

'So, do we have one to register?'

'I said wait!'

The next steps are going to be harder to hear, but will be fully implemented. Tough decisions have had to be made. As of now, anyone over ninety years old will no longer have access to any medication except for pain relief.

'Shit. Did you hear that?' The energy in Pasha's voice gives way to alarm.

'I did. God, that seems harsh.'

She opens the door with a trembling hand; the stick lying on the floor, its result making her muscles go limp.

Every pregnancy registered after midnight tonight may only be brought to term by sacrifice.

She doesn't need to say anything, the look on her face clearer than words. Perhaps unspoken words can undo the truth. No chance. As Pasha's jubilation restores, he picks her up and swings her round. 'We're really having a baby!'

'Yeah. I guess so.' She fidgets free from the tangle of his arms. 'Just wait. We need to listen.'

'Who cares about that? We're having a baby.'

'Pasha, shut up. What did he say about sacrifice?'

This means that for every child born, an elder citizen must volunteer to be euthanised in their place. If a volunteer is not found by the eighth month, the pregnancy will be terminated, or else the would-be parents will be prosecuted.

'Shit.' Mae's knees go weak, and she sits, the sofa's exposed springs digging into her thighs. The room spins as her shoulders curl forward like she's been punched in the gut.

He sits next to her and takes her hand. 'Did he actually just say that?'

Younger people with life-limiting conditions can also volunteer for euthanasia. We will use the latest nano technology to ensure a peaceful end. The nan-E medication will be administered at time of registering for sacrifice and will be timed to activate an hour after birth. Giving the volunteer an hour to enjoy the new life they have enabled to be born.

'They can't be serious,' Mae says, a sandpaper roughness to her voice.

'They are, though. What time is it?'

She checks her watch. 'Six-thirty.'

'I'll get the laptop.'

He opens it and logs in, deft fingers flying over the keys. The news website has a link to the registration form. He clicks it and waits. 'Here,' he passes her a tablet. 'You try too. My laptop's being slow.'

She takes it and tries the link again. 'The website's down.'

'Oh, you're kidding me.'

'Thousands of people trying to register, I reckon.'

'I doubt thousands have just found out they're pregnant. Bet they've known for ages and are now panicking.'

'It's okay.' She takes a breath. 'We've got a few hours. I'll make a cuppa.'

'Can you drink tea in your condition?'

She scowls back from the kitchenette and puts the kettle on.

'There's a phone number too. Shall we try that?' He's dialling before she's even answered.

'Sure.'

He puts his phone on speaker. *You are number ten thousand five hundred and fifty-two in the queue.* 'Dammit.'

'Keep trying. It'll be okay. We still have plenty of time.' She checks her watch again. Taps her foot. Five hours. Ages.

After an hour, she makes another tea. The phone chiming every minute with a ridiculously cheerful announcement. *You are number ten thousand four hundred and twenty-four in the queue.*

'Maybe we should try somewhere else, go to a café or something?' she says as she paces in circles. She doesn't need caffeine. She needs something relaxing, camomile, maybe. Like that stuff Moira makes when she tells Mae she needs to sleep some more, after she critiques her dark circles and dull complexion. Moira is not who she needs to be thinking about right now. Calming thoughts. Happy thoughts. Thoughts to stave off panic rather than add insecurities into the mess.

'Maybe our internet is being slow?' she says. A useful comment. Productive. Helpful.

'Look at this chatter online.' He points and glares at the screen, as if a stern gaze can make the internet work faster. 'Loads of people can't get on the site, the thing has crashed.'

'I'll bet those with a better Life Score get through. They get all the bandwidth. Our Score doesn't even allow us to buy a new bloody sofa.' Her tone smacks of bitterness as she reaches for a cushion to sit on. An old red one from a thrift shop, an eyesore against the peach sofa. The sort of velvety texture that reminds her of the curtains in an old folks' home. Pasha's uncle, Charlie, hands them one when they visit, like he's doing them a favour, before he starts his bigoted rant and general moan. She ignores the colour clash and perches on top, tucking the cushion underneath, and feels no more comfortable.

The news is still playing, just a background hum she's been ignoring. But rolling across the screen are updates on the announcement, the reactions, polls done already. Seventy-five per cent currently in favour of the new measures. No age breakdown as yet. No doubt that will come later. The same, overly ecstatic news reader takes calls from irritated soon-to-be parents, and Mae turns up the volume.

And we have Kyle on line two. Good evening to you, Kyle.

Bloody awful evening, actually. How are we meant to register when the site is crashing?

Plenty of people are getting through. When is your little one due?

Three months.

Well, the registration process has been live for some time. Silly you for leaving it too late.

'Look Mae, there's an exemption list.'

'Really?'

His finger scrolls across the screen, picking out every word. 'It says if both parents are orphans, it may be possible to get an exemption, depending on how many exemptions are awarded.'

'Well, let's not rely on that.'

'Too right. Although, this is the happiest I've ever been about my parents being dead.'

'Bit harsh, but me too.'

Four more hours pass. The bottle of wine on the counter starts calling her, and she curses her condition. Condition is a good word for it, she thinks with more than a pang of guilt. Illness. Disorder. All words that relinquish control, designed to describe her body as a biological entity rather than a person, and say that she is at the mercy of mother nature. That would usually be bad enough. But now she is also at the mercy of crappy internet and world leaders with power-mad ideals. The wine calls louder. The one time she really needs a drink, and she can't have it. She checks the bottle as Pasha tuts from the sofa. The sort of judgy tut that gets her back up. She tuts louder, like some passive aggressive game of disapproval. He's right, of course. One per cent alcohol is still alcohol.

The phone chimes again. *You are number eight thousand and twelve in the queue.*

'This is hopeless,' she says, her voice its own special brand of pathetic. 'One hour left.'

'The site loaded up the next page, then crashed.'

She leans back on the sofa, the refresh screen on the tablet frozen in limbo. She looks away, out the window, outside of the shrinking space of her apartment. The moonlight kisses the buildings. Far away a vixen screeches, screaming for her mate, for her body to be allowed to do what she wants it to do. The vixen demanding what she wants when she wants it. Announcing she is ready. Bloody foxes have more rights than people.

Mae looks at the clock. Ten to twelve. Ten minutes left.

'I'm in! I'm in!' Pasha says as he air punches. Always such a kid.

'Finally. Thank God.'

'Shit, the details needed on this form are insane. What's your national insurance number?'

'Here, I'll fill in my details, then you do yours.' She takes the laptop and begins. 'Why on earth do they need my grandma's maiden name?'

'No idea. You done yet?'

'Almost. Obviously, they want our Life Score.'

'Can't even go into a pub without declaring that.'

She fills in her numbers and hands him the laptop.

'Income, family.'

'Just two minutes left, Pasha.'

'I know I know!' He smashes at the keys. 'Parents' occupations, my degrees, fuck's sake. You'd think our Life Score would be enough. They're the ones that say that number tells them all they need to know.'

'Pasha, hurry!'

'I am! Who's our bloody doctor?'

'Doctor Hookway.'

'Done. Submit. Done. Phew.' He wipes his brow and sinks back on the sofa. The laptop pings and he reads, 'Confirmation email received. Form submitted at precisely. . . Shit.'

'What?'

He doesn't answer straight away. She checks the time, then looks over his shoulder and struggles to find breath.

'It says twelve-o-two.'

Chapter 2

Mae opens the wine bottle and selects the two least chipped glasses, placing them on the counter too firmly, causing a fresh crack on the base. She fails to care. What does it matter? Everything is broken. All their plates have blemishes, every teacup is damaged, every surface has a mark. Sums things up nicely, she thinks. A small broken shard pings away and disappears into the gaps in the tiled floor, hiding in the shadows where the dim lighting can't reach. The agreeable *glug glug* sound of pouring wine masks her thoughts, just for a moment, drowning out the telly, at least. The symbol of the Eyes Forward party. A large eye with walls, either side spinning on the screen while their manifesto pledge plays to music in the background. The manifesto reminds everyone that the days of left and right are over. Now they look only in one direction, forward. Blinkered more like, Mae thinks as she turns her back on the telly. The sound of wine is definitely more pleasing. White noise to obscure the dark. Entranced, she over fills. Red wine pools on the counter, a little stream of claret meandering towards the splashback.

'Baby brain affecting you already?' Pasha asks as she hands him a glass. He raises his eyebrows at her, and not in the excited way he did earlier.

'It says it's organic, hardly any alcohol, and has "herbal relaxing ingredients".' She makes air quotes before taking a large sip, then wipes the counter. 'I'll bet stress isn't good for pregnant women.'

Pregnant women. She stops wiping for a second and allows that label to permeate, collecting in chilling pinpricks across her scalp. *Pregnant.* She looks at the wine bottle again, re-reading the disappointing alcohol content and wishes she could have something stronger. A lot stronger, strong enough to make her forget this day, to reset. Or strong enough to give her the bravado she needs, the *I'm not ready* thought still the most dominant. She shivers as beads of sweat form across her hairline, and she rubs it dry with her hand.

'It'll be fine,' he says with an air of nonchalance, like they hadn't just witnessed the same news bulletin. 'I'll think of something.'

The surface looks clean, but she keeps wiping anyway, her eyes seeing stains that aren't there, stains imperceptible to most, but she knows they must exist. She takes the bottle of olive oil and the mugs from the side, then places them on the floor, wipes around where they were, freshens the cloth and starts again. Inside the cupboards now, her scrubs get faster and harder, scuffing away at the surface, removing the day's tarnishes. Rubbing away any evidence of the last twenty-four hours. She moves the tins out the way, counting as she does. Sixteen tins. She squeezes out the cloth so tightly it tears, then scrubs again until she is sweaty and her arm cramps.

Then, on her hand is another. He stands next to her, his strong hand gripping hers, wringing out her worry. 'Hey,' he says as he leans in. 'It's clean. You know it's clean.'

She hasn't realised she is shaking until his stillness is so close. A sturdy rock in a rushing river. She nods and after a breath, releases the wet rag, letting it fall to the floor.

'I said I'll think of something. I'm not going to let anything bad happen. You trust me, don't you?'

She nods again, feeling the warmth from his hand tickle up through her arm. A cushion all around her. She leans into the soft but solid support of his body, and his other arm wraps around her. He still holds her hand.

They slump back on the sofa, where she rests against him for a while, allowing him to take some of the weight. She yawns, then wipes a sleepy tear from her eye. The skin of her stomach collects in small folds at her waist, like some empty fabric, devoid of stuffing.

'How about we kidnap one of the old homeless people on the street corner and coerce them into dying for our future baby?' Conviction in her tone, like it wasn't the worst idea she's ever had.

He gives her the side-eye and sips his wine. He still hasn't released her hand.

'There must be some grace period,' she says, though her voice cracks with doubt. 'It's not our fault the site crashed.'

His hold tightens. 'Don't you worry. I don't want you stressing.' He puts his glass on the floor, then bends to kiss her tummy, lifting up her T-shirt like he was unwrapping a delicate parcel. 'And don't you worry, little one. Everything is going to be okay.'

She pushes him out of the way, his hot breath on her skin more intrusive than reassuring. 'Don't do that.'

'What?'

'Talk to my tummy.'

'Well, there's a baby in there.'

'Hardly.'

'Come on, Mae-bug, be excited. We're having a baby.'

She rolls her eyes at her pet name. His smiles come too easily, delight always barely a sentence away. 'I'm pregnant, Pasha. There's a difference.'

He reaches for her as the apartment closes in, the tiny space getting smaller with every worry. Those worries that creep over her and give her gooseflesh. She pulls her hand free, then wriggles further along on the sofa, away from him, away from his pity stares and expectant affections. He never understands her desire for space. Her lifetime of solitude is unexplainable to him. She could be in a room with a hundred people and still be alone. Not by choice. By conditioning. By awkwardness. Always on the other side of some wall, breathing different air. The world looks so different through her eyes than his. She gives him

her best *leave me alone* look and squirms around the springs,
plumps up the extra cushion to sit on, then scrolls through the
tablet. The site has new documents uploaded, the new rules,
terms and conditions, like getting pregnant was now supposed
to be some contract with the government.

'It says we have eight months to find a volunteer,' she says. 'If
we don't get certified as exempt.'

'It's just bollocks, though. There must be thousands of people all around the world in this situation. It was just an IT error.
It'll be okay.'

The creases in his forehead are saying what his voice fails
to convey. She's so bad at reading people's expressions usually.
Everyone's but his. He is so simple to decipher, like an easy
maths sum, and she knows the formula. She reaches over and
strokes his hair, rearranging the shaggy mess so it covers his
brow. Now she can believe his voice instead. She loves his hair
more than anything. It's the only mess she can ever tolerate.

'I'm worried about your nan,' she says as she finishes her glass,
relaxing herbal ingredients clearly not up to the job. Eleven
pounds that bottle cost. What a rip-off. 'What meds is she on?
She's ninety soon. They're all going to get stopped.'

'She's a tough old bird. She'll be fine. She'll probably hack
some system and change her identity to make herself younger
or something.'

Mae chokes back a laugh. 'She is pretty resourceful.'

When she and Pasha first got together, old Iris had dug up
details of each of her past relationships, her education, every

address she'd ever lived at and her mobile phone plan and gym membership. Not out of malice or even curiosity. Just for something to do. Exercising the hacking skills she had used for so long, like an itch that needs scratching. 'Use it or lose it,' she had said, her sleek grey hair adding an air of elegance to her words, implying she meant something more than just knowledge of tech. The methodical brain she has is calming, Mae always thinks. She's one person Mae doesn't feel awkward around: kindred spirits. If you need information, if you need answers, it's there. A few clicks, some coding. Strings of numbers and symbols. That sort of prying makes sense. Ambiguous questions and unreadable expressions are so much more of a puzzle.

'Listen,' Mae says, taking his hands now, her eyes piercing his. 'Maybe I should just have an abortion. It's not like we were even trying to get pregnant. This is just an accident. Nothing has to change. There's that foetus donation thing for science. It pays well.' She places careful emphasis on the *nothing has to change* part.

'No way! No. Come on, Mae. I've — *we've* always wanted a baby.'

Mae flinches at his words. Her earlier *I'm not ready* thoughts are still knocking around her mind. More percussive than the hurt in his voice. More obstinate than his reassurances.

'So, this will be fine,' he continues.

That damned F word. Mae wonders how many times he has to say it before even he believes it's true.

'I'll think of something,' he says. 'Let's go to bed. It'll all seem okay tomorrow. It's Saturday tomorrow. What do you want to do?'

A Saturday with no plans is usually a treat. No work to do, no friends demanding her time to celebrate some mundane non-life event: new job shower, new apartment shower, come have dinner to look at my new carpet event, celebrate my Life Score going up five points, new puppy shower, painting the kitchen colour reveal party, new furniture reveal party. Their apartment isn't even in need of a deep clean. Nothing to do. Only now, some ridiculous excuse to occupy her mind would be welcome. Now she craves a distraction.

She thinks for a moment. 'Brunch? Maybe go sit in the park for a while, take a book?'

'Sure. Perfect.'

The doorbell rings, and they look at each other, brows knitted. Mae checks the time. One a.m. 'You expecting anyone?'

'No. Certainly not at this time. Probably some drunk.' He gets up, then presses the intercom. 'Hello?'

The video screen shows not a person, but a thick black disc with red laser eyes. The voice comes through, grainy and robotic.

Pregnancy registration drone. Open the door, please.

'Mae. It's a drone for you.'

'A what?'

'Apparently we have pregnancy registration drones now.'

'Shit, you think the neighbours heard?'

Pasha buzzes the street door open, then opens the apartment door just a tiny bit, peeking through the gap. Cool night air blows in and Mae tightens her cardigan, a chill creeping up her neck, the hairs on her arms standing on end. The smell of cooking oil wafting up from the takeaways down the street makes her swallow back a mini sick. She's never noticed before how strong that smell is.

The whirring buzz of the drone coming up the stairs echoes through the hallway. It's one a.m. Mae reminds herself. Most will be in bed. Surely no one is listening. However, footsteps from the apartment opposite inform her otherwise. A latch clicks open from the apartment two doors left. A sliver of light slices through the hallway from the open crack, while the light of a phone camera shines through a hallway window, and whispers bounce up from below. The sensor lights flick on as the drone approaches, and across the hall, blinds and curtains jerk side to side.

The drone looks bigger than on the video screen. Its shiny body is so dark, it's like a black hole. Its red laser eyes full of scrutiny.

The pregnant person must put their arm by the red light, it says with a mechanical, emotionless tone, too loud for this time of night, shamelessly spilling their secret.

Mae steps around Pasha, and the drone repeats its message. She hushes it, feeling stupid for hushing an insentient machine. Before it can speak again, she holds her forearm in front of its eyes.

'Ow!' She snaps her arm back, a raised red mark now on her skin.

This will be synched with your donor once they are found.

She tries to hush the drone again, instincts overtaking common sense.

Their nan-E will be coordinated with your birth hormones. Have a good day and congratulations.

'You okay, Mae?' Pasha's voice is filled with worry as he closes the door, then turns his wide eyes on her.

She blinks hard, like she's trying to undo what just happened, but when she looks at her arm, the red mark is still there. 'What the hell? I've been tagged? Are they trying to harm the pregnancy?'

'I don't think they're doing abortion injections just yet.' He takes her forearm and kisses the red mark. The touch of his lips melts her coolness, just slightly.

'Come on,' he says and takes her hand. Not even a shake. Her sturdy rock in a rushing river. 'We'll figure this out later. Let's go to bed.'

***

Mae's lips recoil as they walk past some homeless people begging for change on the street corner on their way to the café. The acrid smell of urine irritates her nose, and she fights back a gag. There never used to be this many homeless, they never used to have to hop over people when walking down the street. She steps around wider, leaving Pasha between her and them. Where she scrunches her nose, his mouth upturns, where her eyes narrow, his moisten.

'Sad world for so many,' he says.

It wasn't right, her reaction. Hormones, senses in hyper-drive, stress. Her mind attempts to excuse herself, but her smattering of freckles isn't enough to disguise the shame flushing her cheeks. She rummages in her handbag for her bank card, then swipes each of their pay machines, holding her breath as she approaches.

'Maybe hold back a little on the spending?' Pasha almost whispers.

'It's only donations.'

'Let's get to the café. Come on.' He takes her wrist and drags her away before she gets to the last in the row.

They pass seven cafés by the time they find one suited to their Life Score with seats to spare. Mae's hunger instantly diminishes when a heavy waft of eggs and grease blows by. Bile burns the back of her throat. Pasha makes a show of being chivalrous by taking her peacoat to hang, then pulling out a chair for her. She obliges and swallows back the hot wave of nausea, hiding her greening complexion behind a menu.

'You're eating for two now, remember?'

'I don't think that's really a thing.'

He's wearing a yellow T-shirt, the colour of hope, she thinks. Or summer. Too bright for this time of year. There's a small stain close to the neckline that draws her gaze. Her skin is tight, itchy, like she's a snake about to shed. He just didn't notice the stain this morning, she tells herself. It's not his fault. The washing machine didn't clean it properly. It doesn't matter. She'll bin the T-shirt when they get home. He'll never know. She blinks purposefully a few times, then forces her eyes away, concentrating on the menu instead.

Across from them, a young couple lean in close, doughy-eyed and all smiles. A middle-aged couple at another table sit in silence, smartly dressed, solemn-faced, their hands touching on the tabletop. The muffled sounds cut by a toddler giggling somewhere behind her. She doesn't turn, but there's a twinkle in Pasha's eyes, his grin instinctive. A room filled with happiness, contentment, togetherness. Smothering her. Her sense of solitude invaded by other's desires. She lifts the menu higher, shutting out everything else.

'Still nothing in the news, no U-turn, no grace period,' she says from behind the menu, matter-of-factly.

'It's the weekend. I'm sure by Monday they'll confirm something.'

She puts the menu back on the table and looks at his jaw set in a resolute line, his chest inflated, like he's brimming with assuredness. Like this is a war he's already won.

'We need a plan, Pasha. Just saying everything will be fine isn't going to cut it.'

He squares his shoulders, lifts his chin, striking an alpha pose, as if that will fend off her concerns. 'It just will be. Whatever it takes. I don't want you to worry. I'll think of something.'

'I already have. What about speaking to your Uncle Charlie?'

'Dear God, why? That man is the worst.' The mention of his uncle is enough to cave in the alpha pose, and he cowers. 'We promised we'd never visit him again after his last rant.'

'He might want putting out of his misery.'

His face pinches, and he folds his arms. 'You can't say such things.'

'We have to say such things. That's exactly what we have to do. Anyway, the man is the most miserable person alive. Can't hurt to ask.'

'Let's just wait and see next week.' He gets up, then kisses her forehead. 'Your usual?'

The thought of eggs Benedict twists her insides in knots. 'Just some granola and an orange juice.'

'Seriously? That's it?'

She nods, and he shrugs, then makes his way to the counter, light on his feet, almost skipping. No doubt he'll still order her a side of hash browns or pancakes just in case, acting like he's looking after her when all she wants is less fuss, more planning. He leans into the server and grins his too-easy grin, laughing as they converse, like he has no worries in the world. She's always loved that about him. His carefreeness, his self-assuredness, his unrelenting cheer. Such a contrast to herself and her never-ending gripes and cusses. They're like a Chinese menu, she'd say in one of her own light-hearted moments, sweet and sour. Right now, though, his joviality feels like a slap in the face.

A familiar voice hits her, the voice that always makes her neck stiffen and forehead tense. The husky projected voice of Aliya and her whining daughter, Candice. Aliya asks for a skinny oat kombucha with extra bubbles, loudly apologising to the server that it has to be takeaway, as she is simply too busy to sit and stay. Aliya is from spinning class and delights in telling everyone her BMI while parading around the changing room afterwards, saying how the class was too easy for the likes of her, how expensive her new kitchen is, and how Candice is the most amazing child that ever lived. Mae clenches her fists whenever she sees her. Aliya makes out her Life Score must be in the eight hundreds, yet she goes to a sub-four hundred gym. Just to feel superior.

Mae squeezes her eyes shut. *Please don't see us, please don't see us!*

'Oh, Mae. Is that you? Your red hair stands out so much, it's impossible to miss you.'

Mae's insides coil up. *Dammit.* 'Hi Aliya, nice to bump into you.'

'Bump being the most appropriate word.' She smiles a toothy smile and smooths her hands over her small tummy, thrusting her midriff forward right under Mae's nose.

'Oh, you're expecting again. How wonderful.'

Candice finds a pen in her mother's handbag, then doodles on the tabletop.

'Yes. Bump was fully registered before the cut-off.'

'Congratulations,' Mae says through gritted teeth, sure the temperature in the room has turned up a notch.

'So expensive, children are. I'm not sure we'll manage.' She wraps the end of her glossy plait around her finger. 'Candice here is such an excellent dancer, top of her ballet class. I'm sure she's going to be on the stage one day. Isn't that right, Candice?'

Candice continues to stand hunched over the table, then kicks over an empty chair.

Across the café, the bare brick wall is covered in framed photographs and artworks. Twenty-six of them, Mae counts. Eight of them are at a crooked angle, so obvious against the line of brick. She imagines straightening them all. Ah, the satisfaction.

'Computers, designer dresses, musical instruments,' Aliya continues, oblivious to Mae's blank stare. 'All these things really add up. Luckily Candice looks good in any colour and any cut dress, so it's at least a quick job buying her clothes. But the music lessons, the dance lessons, all of her books — she is such a good reader, very advanced for her age — all of it takes time. It's a wonder I even have time to let the cleaner in. And now with another one on the way.' She sighs so theatrically Mae can see her holding an Oscar. 'Well, it'll be quite the challenge.'

'How dedicated you are.' Every muscle in Mae's body is tight to bursting, her temples ready to rupture.

'Hi, Aliya.' Pasha returns from ordering, and Aliya points her stomach at him instead, pouting her plump lips. 'Oh, you're expecting. You and Mae will have a lot to talk about.'

She raises her eyebrows and looks at Mae, the corners of her mouth dipping slightly. 'You too?'

Mae's tight lips attempt a smile, and she nods.

'Well. . .' Aliya retracts her stomach and places her hands on her hips. 'I hope you got your registration done on time.'

'No, a few minutes late,' Pasha says and Mae shoots him a look. 'I think there will be more of a grace period or something. The website crashed.'

'I certainly hope there is not a "grace period"!' Aliya makes air quotes, her husky voice breaking into a squeak. 'You heard what the government said. There are too many people. Everyone needs to do their bit. I conceived nearly four months ago. I certainly don't think it's right to be trying for a baby now that the world has hit twenty billion. But you have elder family members, don't you?'

'Well, yes, but—'

'So, you're sorted then.' She dismisses Pasha with the wave of a hand. 'That's not so bad. And if you crave old people time, feel free to spend time with one of my grandparents. They're all awful, and it would save me having to entertain them,' she says as she snorts a laugh.

'Great. Thanks,' Pasha says.

'Well, congratulations, I guess. Shame for the planet, but at least your baby can be neutralised. And I'm sure it'll be very nice for you.'

Aliya collects her takeaway, then leaves, Candice kicking over another chair on her way out. The open door lets in a welcome icy breeze, carrying some street debris with it: a chocolate bar wrapper, some foil, which rustles across the floor, and a small swirl of dirt. Autumn has finally arrived, Mae realises. November 26th. She counts on her fingers eight months from now. She'll be due at the end of July. In June, she could be forced to have an abortion or would have signed up one of the Society's elders to die. Eight months ago, they were on holiday in Aldermaston. She'd been angry that the early spring sun had given her tan lines across her shoulders that would still be visible at Moira and Rolan's wedding. Pasha had told her they'd fade by then; that fake tan would cover it up. He was wrong, and of course, Moira had noticed and said she spoiled her bridesmaid's pictures.

Eight months have passed in a blink of an eye, yet it seems like a lifetime ago now. Such trivialities plagued her then, ate away at her, variables she couldn't control making her feel like she was drowning. Over tan lines and a disgruntled bride. How much worse will things be in another eight months? Will today's problems turn into mere frivolities as yesterday's had?

'What was the population when she conceived? Nineteen billion and a half?' Pasha says with a huff, sitting back so firmly in his chair it creaks.

'Why'd you have to tell her?'

'What? I thought it would be nice for you to have a pregnant friend.'

'She is not a friend. She's hideous.'

'Yeah, she does seem like a bit of a bitch.'

Their drinks arrive, and Mae appraises her orange juice. It smells off; the pulp reminding her of vomit. She swills it around in the glass, then pushes it away.

'What if there is no grace period?' she asks with a shiver of panic. 'What are we going to do?'

'We'll think of something. Let's just enjoy this weekend. It'll all seem better on Monday.'

His dark eyes glow with elation instead of apprehension. She wishes his joy were contagious, like she could feed off his spark. She catches him stealing glances at her waist, then happy peeks at the toddler still giggling behind, enthralled in his delight and oblivious to their troubles. His 'we'll think of something' does nothing to quell her concerns of 'we have to do something.' He looks at her like a kid waiting for Christmas. As if she were the wrapping and all he wants is what's inside.

Their food arrives, her granola no more appetising than the orange juice, banal yoghurt coating gravel and desiccated ex-fruit. The waiter places a pile of hash browns next to her.

'Just in case you were still hungry,' Pasha says.

So predictable. Mae doesn't grumble. She pushes her granola around, the slopping noise it makes against the side of the bowl enough to quash her hunger.

'Oh, look, the news is on the telly. Turn it up please,' he calls to the server.

Before the volume is turned up, Mae takes in the scene. Her head throbs across her forehead and temples. Despite their stiffness, her shoulders slump. The newsreader wears a tweed style jacket buttoned all the way up to her neck, her hair scraped back so tightly Mae's headache worsens just looking at her. An attempt to smooth out her forehead, she assumes. That newsreader has been on TV for so long, she must have had some Pres-X to keep her looking that young, and Mae's sure she can see some bright pink complexion showing through her makeup. The Preserved skin always goes bright pink during their regression years. Her forehead can't be naturally that smooth. There's only so much skin stretching a ponytail can accomplish.

Central London looks like some festival, with banners and flags flying, people beating drums in the background. Real police — Mae can't remember when she last saw real police — present on horseback and bikes. One man stands on a car and lights a flare. Pink smoke erupts into the air before he is carried off by three police in full riot gear. Proper police, not just Society Police. Reservists called up for times of disquiet only. The rest of the nation's security has been left to the general public for years now. Everyone's a snitch. *All Eyes Are Our Eyes,* so the government's slogan goes. But for this new law change, they've called in the cavalry.

The server turns the volume up, and the full din of it fills the café. Incoherent yelling and noise come from the drums rather than music, the newsreader yelling over the racket.

'Protests are beginning on both sides of the argument. The main group opposing the measures, Pro Grow, are here with me now.'

The Pro Grow group on camera are all young, maybe in their twenties, a mix of genders, but all with bleak faces, tense and serious. Some in the front look professional, Mae thinks, sensible. Not like the rainbow-haired reprobates in the background. No elders, she notes. Or at least, no obvious elders. Pres-X takers can be indistinguishable from the young.

'These new laws came totally out of the blue. The current restrictions were not given enough time. There is a lot more that could have been done. Reducing waste and consumption would have had a much more significant impact than govern-ment-sanctioned murder.'

'It's not really murder though, is it? The nation has had a pro end-of-life choice stance for decades now. The only eligible donors are those who would be eligible for end-of-life treatment, anyway.'

'The government are denying medicines, so they're forcing their end of life, anyway. And it's only the lower Life Scorers. The wealthy are taking Pres-X, so they're hardly going to volunteer. Let's call a spade a spade, shall we? This is a cull.'

Mae grabs Pasha's hand. Suddenly his affections are lacking rather than suffocating. His reassurances not enough rather than excessive. The pulse of his thumb beats on the back of her hand. She counts the beats as she squeezes and he reciprocates, a clammy bond forming between them.

'A cull is an aggressive term. All donors will be volunteers, giving themselves to the greater cause that is our planet's survival.'

'It's government sanctioned murder.'

'Back to the studio.'

'See?' Pasha places his other hand on hers as well. 'There are protests planned and all sorts. Trust me, this won't affect us. Can we just be happy and excited for a moment?'

She looks down at her granola, at her insipid orange juice, then breathes in the stench of fried food and bitter coffee, the world making her stomach churn but his hands doing the opposite.

She meets his gaze, his deep eyes burning into hers, his happiness hinging on her. 'Sure,' she says. 'We can be happy.'

Chapter 3

On Sunday, Mae throws up as soon as she gets out of bed, the relief it brings not worth the feeling prior. She washes her flushed face, the famous glow she is supposed to have definitely not delivering. Her red hair is greasier than normal and her freckled skin blotchy. She reaches for creams, lotions, all cosmetics claiming to brighten and rejuvenate someone sleep deprived and stressed. Pots promising miracles, yet delivering a meagre improvement. Her eyes are so puffy and bloodshot from retching that, despite applying the stuff generously, she still looks like she hasn't slept in days. No doubt Moira will look perfect as always. Immune to the stress her job brings, as well as age and anything else that causes skin to be displeased. And she knows it.

Placing her tubs of creams back, she knocks over Pasha's medicine packets from the cabinet. She picks them up, then arranges them as they were, morning and evening pills in order, the little green ones and the larger white ones on display, the days of the week on the blister packs visible to remind him. Sunday morning's pill hasn't been taken yet.

She finds Pasha flicking through the channels on the TV, cooking shows reminding her of what she just flushed down the toilet with soundtracks of what she can only assume are cats wailing. She smirks. He's so easily amused.

'You haven't had your Sunday morning pill yet.'

'I will after breakfast,' he says without looking her way.

She stands in the doorway, fidgeting on her feet, lips twitching as she finds her words. 'Is it hereditary?' she eventually asks.

'What?'

'Your motor neurone disease.'

'Nope. And even if it were, two pills a day, and it's no bother.'

'What if they cancel your medications too?'

'Hey! I'm two years older than you, nowhere near ninety.'

His sarcasm only serves to wind her up, and she huffs. 'You know what I mean.'

He turns to face her now, his complexion healthier than hers, eyes bright, muscles defined, not even a single tooth cavity. Hard to believe he has such a condition. His brain ticks over at a normal speed. He's as sharp as anyone, none of the sluggishness the medication warns about.

'Don't worry, Mae-bug, I am a productive member of society,' he says with a smile. 'You've read what they're saying. The world's demographics are off kilter. Offing thirty-somethings is hardly the way they want to play it.'

She returns his smile. The labour shortage of physiotherapists is widely reported. Killing off productive healthcare professionals is not a sensible approach, she was sure. Then again, is culling the Society's elders sensible, terminating knowledge, families, and experience? Sensible doesn't seem to be a priority for the Eyes Forward. Pasha's reassurances, as usual, do little to alleviate her fears.

'Can I get you anything?' he asks. 'How you feeling? You look gorgeous. Glowing.'

He'd say that even if she were covered in dirt and had warts. She's nothing special, not as special as Pasha thinks, anyway. But the little beauty she has is transient, a moment in time, that's all. Everyone is beautiful at some point. The impermanence of perfection makes such a compliment brittle and flawed, yet it's what everyone says. Why not compliment her brain, her personality, something else? Still, she can't help but notice how outrageously fuckable Pasha looks this morning. His vest shows off his defined shoulders, the sun beaming through the window highlighting his jawline, his earthy scent beckoning her. Perhaps they can stay in the flat a while longer.

'Feeling a little better, thanks,' she says. 'What time are they expecting us?'

'One-ish. Listen, there is one thing.' He elongates 'one thing' like it's actually a million things. Or one really big thing.

'Right. . .?'

'Well, I think Moira is expecting too. In fact, I know she is.'

Mae's neck bows, her head heavy. 'Great. One more bitchy pregnant woman.'

'She's not that bad.'

She definitely is that bad. 'How is she expecting? Rolan can't father children, unless they've done something remarkable with trans surgery now. Did they get some backstreet sperm or something?'

'No, not exactly.' His face gets redder. For once, he's the one looking at the floor.

'Pasha, tell me.'

'I may have helped out. I gave them a cup of my. . .you know. My stuff.'

Mae cups her face in her hands, takes a moment to process exactly what Pasha means by *stuff*. As obvious as it is, not wanting to believe it trumps the truth.

He stands up and takes her hands in his. 'We talked about this. A while ago—'

'Yes. And we decided it was so dangerous. Way too dangerous for you. Society Police are all over that. What if you get found out?'

'I was careful. Really careful. I know we decided it was too risky, but I didn't want you stressing about it. I wanted to help Rolan so much. He had it shit growing up. I was a crap brother. I never helped him out when our parents turned their back on him. I want to be a better brother now.'

'By impregnating his wife?'

'You're making it sound worse than it is. Ours is the only baby that's mine. Theirs is theirs. Only, well, the thing is. . .'

Her eyes blaze below her lowered brow as she waits for him to find his words.

'. . .It's totally illegal now. It's illegal enough donating sperm in the first place, but doubly illegal to have created two off-spring.'

'Aliya is expecting her second.'

'She's further along though. And an eight hundred plus. Even Moira's six hundred plus isn't enough to make the child legal. And ours being the latter could be, well, contraband.'

'That's an appalling term for this pregnancy.'

He looks at her, his eyebrows half-raised in that apologetic way he does, like a puppy who's just chewed a table leg. He's missed a patch with his beard trimmer. On his right-side jawline, a few hairs are longer. She can fix that, just a pair of scissors and it'll all be all right again.

'We just need to keep it quiet, okay?' he says, all softly-softly, the kind of voice he whispers in her ear in the mornings. 'No one has to know. It doesn't leave the family. It'll be so nice, don't you think, for our baby to have a cousin? Rolan will make a great dad.'

'Yeah,' she says. 'He will.'

Pasha's heart is too big to allow him to quantify risk. His desire to help leaves little room for caution and self-preserva-tion. It's one of the things Mae finds both loveable and infu-riating. She walks to the kitchenette to get the scissors. At least Pasha being a dumbass neutralises some of her own guilt. When that feeling that niggles at her, a little voice that tells her she shouldn't be loved, that she should rid him of the burden of her.

'They'd better not ask your Nan to be a donor.'

'They won't. They registered on time.'

She slouches over the kitchenette counter, her legs too weak to be supportive. 'Great. Fucking great.'

***

The ride to Moira's and Rolan's takes them across Reading town centre, down the hill to the river, on the slower pavements for once. 'Precious cargo,' Pasha says, justifying the cautious route. Delivery drones fly overhead, their off-white lacquer less foreboding than the Eyes Forward obsidian obscenities. Their hum less intimidating; a soft sound that dissolves into the background, masked by voices and traffic.

They take the shared path along the Thames, and the picnic area alongside is filled with families enjoying the couple of hours of sunshine the break in the clouds promise. Pushing kids on bikes, feeding babies, nursing grazed knees, and trying to get kids to wear coats. Screams, giggles, and cries fill the air, disgruntled geese chase off brazen children and scavenge for sandwich crusts. Pasha gushes at the happy children, while she winces at every cry and scream. Her legs are sluggish, like her bike weighs more than it used to. Every pedal stroke is an effort.

A child runs in front of her bike, and she slams on the brakes. He looks up at her, the bluest of eyes staring straight at her, like he knows her. He sees through her charade. The father comes and pulls the kid off with an array of apologies and words of caution to the child. Mae pedals away, a shiver inching across her shoulders.

Pasha fills in Mae's blanks, says the words she fails to find. 'No problem. Hope the kid's okay, not to worry,' or something to that effect. His words are punctuated with smiles and sparkly eyes. How has she never noticed that about him before, his paternal instinct? His compassion extends to more than just her, she reminds herself. She's never even held a baby, let alone spent time with children, yet for a few seconds she imagines what their child would look like, her red hair, his dark eyes, maybe. She squeezes her eyes shut, then pays attention to the tarmac instead. Being pregnant and having a baby are not the same thing. Not anymore.

They weave through hordes of tourists near the train station. All from Oxfordshire, clearly. Their slick-straight bobs, partings on the left side and tan satchels serve as a neon sign above their heads. Their accents are more subtle than Mae imagined, though. From their voices alone, she might not know they're outsiders. They walk differently; bunch closer yet seem to spread out more. She lifts the collar of her Berkshire peacoat, then pulls her Berkshire plait over her shoulder, like a bird fluffing up its feathers, or a dog pissing to mark his territory. Pasha straightens his back. Despite the chilly breeze, he undoes the top button on his jacket, presenting himself in the proper Berkshire way. They both ding their bike bells as they get close and the tourists sidestep out the way, phone cameras held up all around, creating more of a spectacle of themselves. Not Society Police, clearly. They wobble their phones too much, speak over the top of the video with excited voices, and put their own faces in the photos.

Outside the station, old CCTV cameras still hang. Smashed up and vandalised, their only function to remind people of how things used to be. Before most of the police were disbanded and the nation's security was handed over to the public, before everyone was blasted with messages that staying in their own county is best. Criminals don't shit where they eat, so the ethos goes. If no one travels too far, the nation will be safer. Monitored. Eyes forward, the government call themselves. Eyes forward, but snoops are all around. *All Eyes Are Our Eyes* is written underneath the Eyes Forward logo that's displayed on every bus stop in town. And with a nation of informants, all with camera phones, eager to up their Life Score, who needs the cost of the real police? In the Society, where your prospects are determined by a number you're assigned at the age of twenty-eight, one based on your parents' income and where you went to school, it pays to be a snitch.

They cycle past posters that remind them they are in Berkshire, as if the sea of peacoats and plaits aren't clear enough. *Keep your money in Berkshire. Boost Berkshire economy! There's no place like Berkshire. Berkshire: the best county to live in! Want an adventure? Explore Berkshire.* Words set against idyllic backgrounds populated with friendly places. More eight hundred pluses than any other county thanks to people keeping their spending limited to their own little devolved economy. A happy side effect of crossing county borders becoming taboo.

'Why would anyone want to go somewhere they stand out so much?' Mae asks.

'God knows.' Pasha re-buttons his jacket. 'Curiosity besting common sense and community spirit, I suppose. As long as they don't spend any money here, though, I guess they're not doing any harm to their own county.'

'Seems daft to go somewhere just to be scrutinised and gawped at. Look at all those Society Police checking them out.'

It's easy to spot the local Society Police from the tourists, not just from the clothes and hair, but from the way they slink around. The tourists look at the buildings and the space, but the Society Police's attention is solely on the people. Such places are prime Society Police hunting grounds. Tourists stick out, even if they're not doing anything wrong besides supporting economies outside their own county. The keenest of Society Police aren't even in it for the Life Score points. They're in it for the thrill of being a snitch. Those face shot IDs will be uploaded. Anyone checking in their home county database will be able to see who's travelled. How many tuts and eyebrow raises can anyone handle?

Now that they're away from the station, Mae flicks her plait off her shoulder and adjusts her coat back to where it was.

'Oxfordshire is big enough,' she says. 'Dumb to go so far from home.'

'Tell that to Moira. She thinks visiting other counties is something we should aspire to do.'

Mae groans. 'I adore your brother, I really do. But Moira? *Eurgh.* What does he see in her? Sure, she's pretty, but that really is it. Besides her Life Score, and there's no way Ro is that shallow.'

'Well, they're having a baby, so I guess we'll just have to put up with her.'

They ride in silence for a few minutes, the sun now obscured by clouds and the grey sky casting shadows. They pause a moment to turn their bike lights on.

'Want to play bingo?' asks Pasha.

'Moira bingo?'

'Yep.' He laughs.

'Sure, okay.' She thinks for a few moments, grinning. Their regular game making the prospect of seeing Moira a lot more entertaining. 'Full house when. . .' she thinks for a few more seconds. 'She makes some passive aggressive comment about us missing her, what was it, kitchen colour reveal party?'

'Maybe furniture reveal? But yeah, that's one.'

'Brags about her Life Score. Refers to something that is so simple "even I could do it".' Mae lists off the bingo items on her hand. 'Makes a show about cleaning up after us or implies we're going to make a mess. . .and. . .name-drops some designer or celebrity she's met.'

'That's five. That's a full house.' He laughs and shakes his head. 'Reckon that'll be easy too.'

They arrive at Rolan and Moira's building, then park their bikes in the shadow of its twenty storeys. Only a few years old, but faux timber beams cut across the façade, designed to make it look like some restored relic with a mishmash of reflective glass and gaudy curved iron window bars to add 'a sense of culture,' Moira had said. The Berkshire flag of the wilting holly tree hangs over the door and in several of the windows. Mae smooths down her helmet-hair frizz, then pulls her plait back over her shoulder. Her T-shirt clings unpleasantly and she wafts it away from her, the synthetic fibres more flammable than breathable.

Moira greets them at the door with exuberant welcomes and exaggerated hugs, air kissing loudly, the distance of her neck just enough to reveal her perfume to Mae. She looks immaculate, as always. Her curvy figure snuggly buttoned into a green dress, not a hair or hem out of place. Mae adjusts her jeans, tucks in her T-shirt, then fans the sweat from her face.

Rolan follows, hugs Pasha, and Mae also receives a two-armed hug, Rolan pulling her in close as if she's also family. In the second she reciprocates, Mae receives a lungful of his after-shave. It's intensely masculine and entirely overwhelming. His desire to overcompensate is unnecessary, Mae always thinks. He's taller and broader than Pasha, has designer stubble that accentuates his defined jawline, and has a depth to his voice that makes most women blush. He's always a gentleman, and this time is no different as he offers to take Mae's coat to hang up. Moira snatches it and checks the label, then scrunches her nose at the sight of the budget brand.

The entrance to the apartment smells like roasting herbs and pastry. Perfectly delicious, of course. The table is set with measured precision, each place with identically laid cutlery, a perfectly folded napkin, all atop a pristine white tablecloth that Mae dares not even breathe near. She'd think the clean surfaces, the meticulously straight tableware would make her comfortable, give her one less thing to stress about. But instead of being at ease among the orderliness, she feels she is invading, her mind too messy to relax in somewhere so gratuitously neat. It's too unsullied, too methodical, makes her feel like an eyesore. A pile of rubble.

Mae walks through the hallway three steps before Moira reminds her she still has her shoes on, then points towards the guest slippers. Pasha makes eye contact with her, winks, and holds up one finger. One bingo point down, four to go. Mae's unsocked feet, complete with raggedy broken toenails and cracked skin slip inside, and she squeezes her toes around the plush fleece lining. She takes Pasha by the hand as they walk through, their footsteps soft on the oak floor.

'Smells lovely, Moira.'

'Thank you. It's a simple recipe. Even you could manage it. I'll email it to you, if you like?'

'Great. Ta.' Mae looks over and Pasha, then mouths, 'Two.'

'The dining room will be a surprise for you, since you missed our new furniture reveal party.'

'Yeah, sorry about that. Think we had the flu.' *Three.*

Pasha takes a breadstick from the table, then eats it, paying no attention to Moira's tuts. 'How's work, Ro?'

'Oh, you know, too many hours, as always. But the bonus makes it all worth it. Got my Score up to 550 now.'

'Wow,' Pasha says as some crumbs spill to the floor. 'That's good going.'

'Not quite at my 650, but he's catching up,' Moira says through thin lips, eyeing the little mess Pasha makes. 'What's yours now?'

Mae looks at her feet, mostly to hide her smile, and counts the fourth bingo point. '370.'

'Aw, well, almost at that 400 milestone.' Moira sounds like she is addressing a kitten.

'I've made it,' Pasha says. '410.'

'Really?' Mae's voice screeches, her heart stuttering as she wraps her brain around what he just said. 'When were you going to tell me?'

He bites his bottom lip and shrugs. 'I was thinking a surprise dinner at that 400 plus Thai place on Church Street. But the cat's out of the bag now.'

'410,' Mae says, a few times, as if repeating it will make sense of it. 'How'd you manage that?'

He gives her a peck on the cheek. 'I'll tell you later.'

A disjointed silence sits over them for a moment as Mae is totally flabbergasted at how Pasha could have pulled off such an increase. Rolan looks impressed, though, and Moira squints through her approval.

Moira gestures for them to sit and winces as Mae and Pasha drag their chairs across the floor instead of lifting them. Rolan doesn't notice. He fills their glasses with alcohol-free red wine, its rich colour against the white tablecloth making Mae's heart race. She sits on her hands, not risking any movement.

Pasha strokes her knee under the table, like he's trying to rub away her anxieties. He picks up his glass, then drinks without a care that the soft furnishings likely cost more than their annual salaries combined. He and his brother exchange smiles and cheers, relaxed, content. Mae bites the inside of her cheek, now not only an eyesore but rude as well as she has not yet had a drink, not yet partaken in the customary cheers that risks a spillage and chipping of a glass. She eyes the room, nothing out of place. She counts the pieces of cutlery on the table, twenty. Eight forks, eight knives, four spoons, plus four serving spoons.

'You okay, Mae?' Rolan asks in a genuine way, not in the squeaky voice patronising way that Moira reserves for her.

She nods, takes a breath, then picks up her glass. 'Cheers,' she says, and they clink without losing a drop. She sips. It tastes divine.

'Oh, don't worry about the tablecloth,' Moira says as she returns. 'We got the cheap one out for you.'

Mae's jaw clenches, but Pasha's fingertips push into her knee.

'Thanks, Moira,' he says, as Mae feels his fingernails dig in.

Moira brings trays from the kitchen, silver platters of roasted vegetables and overstuffed pastry bursting with sauce. For the first time that weekend, the smell of food doesn't make Mae gag, yet she fails to feel hungry, her mind still reeling. As Moira piles delicate slices of thick-crust wellington on her plate, Mae just stares at her food, the numbers 410 turning over in her head. Pasha is a physiotherapist for the elderly. Crap money, but he loves it. How the hell did he increase his Score to 410? She's an accountant, earns more than him, and is still sub 400. She started on a lower Score, with no family Score to inherit. But she wasn't *that* far behind.

'It's the new building in zone two,' Rolan says, as if her surprise was for his Score, not Pasha's. 'I was assistant architect at designing it. All sold instantly, some residential, some hotel, some office space. Ridiculously expensive, but the views. . .you can see the whole city.'

'You still planning on moving to London?' asks Pasha.

'Not now. Not with the little one on the way,' says Moira as she takes her seat, lifting it to move it back, Mae notes.

'Oh yeah, congratulations,' Mae says.

'We are so grateful to you both,' Rolan says. 'You're giving us the family we've always dreamed of.'

Pasha squeezes Mae's hand and she glances over to see his teary smile.

'We're really excited about it,' Moira says. 'Got in well before all this donor stuff, too, luckily.'

'Good for you,' says Mae through her teeth.

'Well, we have some news too,' Pasha says. 'We're also expecting.'

The silence that follows fills the space quicker than light, is more intense than the smell of the food. All their breath is sucked from them. The news hangs in the air until it becomes weighed down with tension. Moira's smile fades, and Rolan's fork pings from his hand onto his plate.

'We had no idea you guys wanted kids,' says Rolan, when the conversation vacuum becomes nail-bitingly awkward.

'Of course we do,' Pasha says. 'It's all we've ever wanted. Isn't that right, Mae?'

Mae searches for her voice. She's never been able to lie. 'Well—'

'But. . . You can't,' says Moira. 'I mean, if they find out, your baby will be illegal.'

'Erm, why our baby and not yours?' Mae says.

'Ours was conceived first,' says Moira, over articulating every consonant and vowel.

'By illegal methods.'

'You are not implying that if one baby is to be terminated, it should be ours? We were first, you hear me?'

'I just don't see why your baby is any more valid than ours.'

'Listen,' Rolan lifts his hands like he is physically separating them. 'Both of you, it won't come to that. I'm not going to tell anyone that we used a sperm donor.'

'Well, where the hell do you think the authorities will think the sperm came from?' says Mae, alarmed at the harshness in her voice.

'I've been registered as a man for fifteen years. My passport says male, all my ID does. Why would anyone investigate further?'

'Plus, well, you know,' Moira says. 'Whose baby are they really going to take away? The one from the couple with our combined Life Score or yours?'

Mae stands, her chair squeaking along the floor behind her. She entertains the pleasant fantasy of it leaving deep scratches the whole way. 'Right, you—'

'Come on, Mae. Why don't we go home?' Pasha places both hands on her forearms, like he thinks she's about to pounce. 'You ladies don't need to be stressed right now.'

Mae yanks free from his grip, then turns to face him with narrowed eyes. *Patronising arse.*

'Moira, how could you?' Rolan's voice of disapproval at least sounds genuine.

'It's fine, Rolan,' Pasha says, 'just hormones, I'm sure.'

Mae stamps her foot. 'Moira being a bitch is not just fucking hormones! And no, it is not okay. I can speak for myself.'

'Let's just go,' Pasha says. So calm. So damned cool. 'Come on.'

They leave the apartment without the usual air kisses and farewells, the food virtually untouched. Mae kicks off the slippers, then puts her shoes on, walking three times up and down the hallway in them for no reason except to make Moira's blood boil. After, she slams the front door behind her so hard, she hopes it breaks the stupid designer handle.

The first few minutes of the journey home, they ride without saying a word, Mae gripping the handlebars so tightly, her knuckles blanch. She takes in Pasha beside her, his grin wider than ever.

'What are you smiling about?'

He looks at her, still smiling, like he's just won the lottery.

'Seriously? That was awful. We didn't even get a full house at bingo. She never name-dropped a celebrity.'

'I'm smiling because of you.'

'What about me?'

'You called it our baby. Not just pregnant. Baby.'

Her pedalling slows, and she replays the row in her head. Her defensiveness, her rage, her baby. *Baby.*

'Yeah,' she says. 'I suppose I did.'

Chapter 4

Mae's loneliness comes to her the most at night, when Pasha is asleep, and she has only creaking pipes and the goings on outside for company, when the wind whips past the windowpanes and the local fox screeches. It's only her ears that hear it. The drunks don't take notice, the late-night café dwellers keep their headphones in. She has too many memories to sleep. Too many years playing over and over. She stares up at the ceiling, in all the corners where the shadows rarely leave. The cold light of the moon fingers its way through the crack in the curtains and casts shapes in the gloom, the creeping familiarity of silhouetted nothingness like old comrades. Just her and the darkness.

It's never quiet. Even at night, buses frequently drive past. Mae doesn't mind the noise. It helps keep track of her sleeplessness. Count the hours away. She can tell what time it is by the bus. One pauses for a second, and the air ejecting tells her it's stopped at the bus stop in front of the 600 plus café close by. A late-night café that serves every drink with bubbles and every food item with a side of antioxidant molasses. The bus waits a moment before driving off, turning right just past their building. That must mean it's the number twenty-six, which means it's 12.30. The headlights shine a moving beam across the ceiling as it drives past before leaving her with just the dusky glow of the streetlights again. The sound of the takeaways kicking out their last customers, shutters pulling down, and some guy throwing up all resound.

That night, Pasha sleeps with his hand lying on her stomach, a show of togetherness not only for her but for what's growing inside of her. His soft eyes and wicked smile, he accepts her for all her 'quirks' as he calls it. 'Who wants normal, anyway? You're exceptional,' he had said on one of their first dates, when she'd had to leave the bar as the décor all clashed and the waiter was too shouty.

Years ago, she vowed never to fall in love. For reasons that seem hard to fathom now. Too complicated, too undeserving, too many questions. There's no instruction book, no formula to solve. Yet, for someone who doesn't know how to love, falling for him was as easy as curling up on a squashy sofa. Accepting, forgiving, comforting. He doesn't only love her; he is devoted to her. This she knows in her bones. And Pasha isn't one to pry. He's happy with the titbits of information she gives him about her former life. He never questions why she has no friends, that much is obvious. 'What does the past matter,' he'd say. 'It's you and me, here and now.'

How will she love her child? When, besides Pasha, she's never loved anyone, not really. A heart is just a muscle, isn't it? Unused, it withers away. For someone so hard to love, how can she think for a moment that the child will love her? It's impossible to explain this to Pasha. How can he understand such brutal doubts? The change is too great, and the discomfort of the upheaval makes her want to shed her skin like a snake. She's not ready to share. She doesn't know how.

Even when she retreats into her darkest self, the place where her mind builds walls out of solid steel, soundproof and cold to the touch, Pasha can break through. He can reach her through the endless oceans of her sadness that wash over her when, for no reason, the memories of her previous years submerge her, hitting her like waves. She doesn't have the words to tell him she needs him, but he sees it in her face, her hands, her entire body. His touch is her lifeboat. Only now, it's not just her he's trying to save.

As she lies awake, staring at the ceiling, the warmth of Pasha's sleepy touch can't thaw her chill. This is one wall he cannot break through. She shivers and buries herself deeper under the covers. Despite her promise to be happy, despite her calling the pregnancy a baby, she fears she is the loneliest she's ever been.

***

Waiting at the bus stop Monday morning, her nose sifts through the aroma of damp concrete, dredges up notes of bike lubricants, rubbery bus brakes, cheap aftershave from the man standing next to her, and Pasha's scent that lingers on her skin.

She's always had an acute sense of smell. Now, being pregnant, it's bionic.

Most of the buildings on Mae and Pasha's street are terraces built nearly two hundred years ago. Old buildings divided up lengthways and widthways to squash in more people, couples, families, homes a fraction of the size they used to be. Across the pavements outside, in the pedestrian fast and slow lanes, parents walk hurriedly with their offspring tied to their fronts, not with the pushchairs of the old days that Mae remembers. Such things haven't been around for half a century at least. The ankle-clipping devices and the space they take up long strewn into landfill. The streets have no room for such contraptions.

A mother consoles a crying toddler, blocking the slow lane with her fuss. Mardy people step over the crouched woman, verbalising profanities as they do. Yet the mother maintains delicate affection and patience. She's not flustered and barely notices the commotion she's causing. Her attention is solely on the child.

Could Mae be such a mother? Her own mother's affections were limited to a cold plate of food left on the side and a cry of 'help yourself' as she closed the door on her way out. Her work was always more important than looking after Mae. She'd had her too young, she always said. Extending the life of the living was her mother's mission. Creating more, well, that was irresponsible. Mae was unnecessary, one of life's excesses that should be cast aside like some impulse purchase. And in the end, a guinea pig.

Mae's thought spiral as she attempts to stand unnoticed, to blend in. An old woman concealed as a younger is hard on the senses. The world is loud, too loud. Mae's never adapted to the glare, the brightness of everything. Even the grey dazzles.

She keeps her hands to her sides and gazes at the floor, sleeves pulled down. A dark navy shirt today, the colour of trust. Monday, Pasha had said, will be the day the government announces some grace period, a rethink, some news to make her feel less like some conspirator, murderer, contaminator.

'Trust me,' he had said almost a hundred times.

She pulls her sleeves down further, then scrunches her cuffs in her fists. Navy blue, the colour of trust.

Society Police reminders plaster the bus stop, the government's Eyes Forward symbol with the words *All Eyes Are Our Eyes* written across them. As if anyone needs reminding. Phones in everyone's hand, nearly a hundred per cent of people have the app. Even Pasha has it.

'Just in case we see something awful,' he'd said, suggesting she should download it too. 'In case we can help a victim.'

Only for most, using the app isn't about helping victims, unless you count those with a low Life Score as victims. Sometimes it feels that way. Petty rule breaking is by far the most commonly reported among crimes. It works, the government say. Stemming the minor offences stops the major. The entire Society is comprised of snitches. There's nowhere to hide. And that's all Mae wants to do sometimes. Hide.

Flashing through the bus schedule announcement was the usual daily update: *Over one million Life Score points awarded to successful Society Police this month. Doing our county proud! Keep up the good work, Berkshire. All eyes are our eyes.*

Nothing's changed, not really. The announcements, the updates and reminders are the same as always. Yet Mae feels more conspicuous than ever. The red bump from the drone must seem so obvious, like an extra limb poking through her clothes. Surely, it must glow through her coat. She's brushed her teeth twice and eaten half a packet of ginger biscuits to keep her nausea at bay. Does she smell like ginger? Maybe that will be her giveaway.

She turns, briefly, wide scared eyes scanning the sea of faces around her. The dense mob of people waiting for the bus must be thick with keen Society Police, eyeing the arms of all the women just in case they have a red mark. Ready to judge. Poised to report any false move. Her quick glimpse proves inconclusive, so she braves another. They're all looking at their phones, or down the street, or the ground. No eyes on her. . .yet, no one noticing the red mark through her clothes. She puts her hands behind her back to hide it more and holds her hands together there, then realises this posture pushes her waist out. Not that she's showing but trying to make it look like she is seems worse, somehow. She fidgets back to standing straight, shakes out her arms. How awkward it is to stand naturally when forcing yourself to? She takes a breath, stretches her neck, then counts the kerb slabs between the bus stop shelters, although there's no need. She already knows there's eleven.

Feeling on-show, like a tourist in her own town, she curses for not cycling to work. Clouds loom overhead, the heavy air turning harsh as autumn licks its way up the street. Society Police seemed like less of a threat than the weather when she left for work this morning. Now, paranoia penetrating every inch of her, she's not so sure. Being pregnant isn't illegal, she reminds herself. Currently, they'd have nothing to report. But she knows how these things go. Once labelled and known, she won't be able to go anywhere without people photographing her hungrily, like their lives depend on finding fault with her. For some of them with the worst Life Scores, it probably does.

The bus is rammed, its air thick and stale, old mushrooms and yeast the predominant odours. She squashes up against a man with limited personal hygiene, his Berkshire fringe hanging in thick greasy tendrils sticking to his forehead. Angling her head away to avoid a full face-plant into his armpit, she's faced with a woman alighting behind her. Obviously pregnant. No one moves. The woman squeezes through the throng to the echo of tuts and scoffs. The woman's face tinges an insipid yellow and the dampness across her brow glimmers in the sunshine.

'Give the woman a seat, will you?' Mae says to some of the passengers that sit closest to her.

No one obliges. They lift their phones higher, blocking their view of her. No doubt they are logging onto the Society Police app, ready for a ruckus.

'Hey, come on! She's obviously not feeling great.' Mae's cheeks heat while she uses her tongue to search for remnants of ginger biscuit around her teeth. She lifts her hand to shield her face from the cameras. Nine phones face her from the minimal view she has, not risking peering around to count more.

'She shouldn't have gotten pregnant then,' one man says, as nonchalantly as that.

Mae's breath catches in her throat, and she rasps, 'Excuse me?'

The man leans in closer, crosses his legs over his expensive-looking suit, then folds his arms, revealing bejewelled cufflinks and a hologram watch. 'Why should I give up my seat for a woman reproducing in an overpopulated world? Fuck her. With any luck, she'll have a miscarriage right here.'

Mae gasps and instinctively places her hands on her stomach as a round of agreement sings from the other passengers. Mae's shoulders drop and hunch over as her head hangs low. She squeezes her eyes shut, wishing she were smaller, tiny, a speck instead of a normal-sized human with a big mouth. Why did she have to speak up? Everyone is looking at her. Even through closed eyes she can feel it. Her heart tells her so as it raps against her chest, like it's knocking on a door, seeing if she's in. She holds her breath, then counts to ten. She's not in, and soon she'll disappear. Soon no one will notice her anymore.

'Here, love. Take my seat.'

Mae opens her eyes as one man gets up, slowly, his frail back bent almost double, his shaking hand grabbing for the handle. The pregnant woman hesitates for a moment, then sits, mutters a thank you and covers her face with her hands.

'Polluter sympathiser!' Cufflinks man yells.

No one joins in his heckles. The woman wipes a tear away, then holds her swollen belly. Defensive, protective. The colour in her cheeks brightens, and her sweat dries as she leans her cheek against the cool window. Mae's heart stills, her shuddering breath surrendering to normality.

There is still some compassion left in the world.

As the woman settles in her seat, the cameras go away. Disappointment rather than relief hangs in the air. No ruckus and a pregnant woman accommodated. Nothing to see here.

Mae looks down at her own flat stomach. How long before she starts to show? A couple of months, maybe. How many mornings can she keep the sickness at bay? She can't hide her condition forever, especially now that the queen of gossip, Aliya, knows.

She gets off the bus a stop early, the extra few minutes' walk more appealing than the oppressive ambience of the bus. The clouds start releasing their promised shower, causing a mucky spray from the pedestrian traffic. Her shoes soak through quickly. It's not heavy rain but the kind of fine drizzle that finds its way under an umbrella and round the side of her hood. With her lack of caffeine, it's refreshing at least, more so than the arduous bus air.

She checks her watch and walks in the slow lane, shuffling along with the Society's elders and those too lazy to walk fast, just revelling in the cool autumn air, blowing the memory of the bus ride away. No rush, she has plenty of time. Twenty-three minutes for a seventeen-minute walk. She passes brick buildings with graffiti scrawled on the side: *Enough is Enough!* is the most common, followed by *no more,* and *Times Up!* Apostrophe missing, she notes, as she tries to maintain a blank expression while she walks past. Emotionless, irrelevant.

A glance around at those in her lane shows her to look by far the youngest. Would that raise suspicion? Make people think that she has a condition that's making her walk slow. Paranoia hits again, filling her mind with questions and doubt. She lifts her head, pushes her shoulders back, and tries to look natural, strong, healthy. Whatever she does makes her stand out, she's sure of it. She's like a pregnancy beacon with a neon sign above her head. She probably smells pregnant too. Her body isn't hers anymore, not private. She's exposed, accountable. As her heart races with each thought, she moves too quickly for the slow lane and migrates to the fast, heat rising up, almost jogging. Weird how, in her mild panic, she looks more normal, fits in more with the other commuters than when she was trying to relax.

Her phone pings with messages from Pasha. *Are you ok* messages. *I love you* messages. *How was the journey* messages. Not, *I've figured it out and it's all definitely okay* messages. She wipes her clammy hand on her jacket and replies with: *fine. Love you. Xxx*

She pockets her phone and continues the walk to work. She's still reeling from lunch at Rolan and Moira's and hasn't said much more than one-word responses since. Pasha's actions, as well as his secrecy and carelessness, grate on her, although surprise is lacking. He'd jump under a bus if his brother asked him to. Moira was right though. A combined Life Score of 1200 versus Mae and Pasha's of less than 800 would always shine them in a better light if the authorities had to choose. Until now, she'd forgotten the news of Pasha's Life Score. Too mad at Moira to think of anything else, stressing about the pregnancy, she'd put it out of her mind. It was a lie, most likely. An attempt to brag away Moira's condescending attitude. No way would Pasha go all Society Police special agent to increase his Score. No way. It was a lie. It must be a lie. Or there's some other reason.

A little tingle of dread fizzes through her as she tries to think what that reason could be. Again and again she asks herself: what dumbass thing has he done now?

Chapter 5

Mae's office is sandwiched between betting shops on Friar Street. She always wonders if that was meant as some sort of joke, to stick an accountancy business between two gambling houses. Her clients often think the same, in jest only. The company's reputation makes it clear they're not just a bookies.

She arrives at her desk as Sadie, efficient and punctual as always, brings her a coffee, which she accepts but pushes away. Did coffee always smell so strong? It's like she's swimming in a cup of the stuff.

'You okay, you look a little peaky?' Sadie asks.

Anyone would look peaky next to Sadie. And tired. And dishevelled. Her plait is silky smooth as always, like she'd arrived at work in some hermetically sealed container to avoid the humidity. It drapes across her shoulder, thick and long, and Mae suspects, ninety-nine per cent artificial. She reckons she could scale a building with that plait. At the top of that building would be Sadie's soft and forever caring face, military-style organisation, and a whole cosmetic's counter of makeup.

Mae hides her own spindly plait behind her. 'I'm fine,' she says with a wave. It's a rhetorical question anyway. 'What's on the agenda today?'

'Demand has been crazy this morning. I've been here half an hour and my inbox is full of people wanting appointments. They think their accountant can somehow change the law for them.'

'Law?'

'You not seen the news this morning?'

Mae shakes her head. She's been ignoring the national news since Friday night. There's only so many life-destroying updates she can take. Pasha will tell her when there's good news. Until then, she plans to do her best to avoid it.

'New inheritance tax law,' Sadie says. 'To save the Society's finances with all the elders being massacred.'

'None have actually been killed yet, though. I'm sure they'll do some sort of U-turn.'

'Unlikely. As many Pro Grow protesters as there are, there's twice as many holding rallies for support. Those Enough campaigners are loud.'

Mae bites her lip, remembering her commute. It seems no amount of rain and autumn breezes can keep bad mornings permanently barricaded from memory.

'Anyway,' Sadie continues, Mae's cluelessness too obvious to disguise. 'Inheritance tax is now set at ninety-five per cent.'

The cough she was holding back from the coffee stench now erupts. 'Wow! Really?'

'Yep. And every Society elder and their offspring are now in panic mode, scrambling to figure out how to keep their family jewels. It's not even Life Score dependent either. The whole of the Society is included in the law. Finally, the Society model is fully inclusive.'

Inclusive? Mae grits her teeth. If the government are to be believed, the point of the Life Score system was to make everyone feel included, to provide a census, to inspire social mobility. Not some scheme drawn up by a maths genius a generation ago as a way of labelling people and sifting the haves from the have-nots. Mae knows the truth; she sees those numbers for what they are. Not encouragement, but exclusion. Not representative, but prejudice. Such complex algorithms usually make her feel as balanced as the equation, but the Life Score algorithm is ugly in its simplicity. Some people buy into the model, think it's good for citizens to understand their place, Sadie being one of them. When she turned twenty-eight, she was awarded a Life Score of 500 due to her family's money, and has increased that to 600 by maxing out and paying off credit. That's it. She works a lower paid job than Mae, is a hell of a lot less qualified but reaps more reward due to her advantageous start. And feels the system is largely fair. As much as Mae likes Sadie as a colleague, they come from different planets.

The bitter coffee to her left starts to look more appealing as Mae scans her email list update. 'Right, well, don't actually book me any appointments this morning. I need a few hours to read through the details.'

'Sure thing.' Sadie smiles and goes to leave before turning back. 'Saw Aliya at Beanies café this morning. Congratulations, by the way.'

Mae struggles to smile. 'Thanks.' But when Sadie's face drops, her false lashes flickering over misty eyes, her skin paling even through the fake tan, she adds, 'What about you and Chrissy?'

She shrugs. 'Not sure. Chrissy is still keen. But I don't see how it would be feasible. It was bad enough trying to source a sperm donor before, now we need a life donor too. And I don't want some elder to die because of me.'

Sadie and her partner may have escaped the worst of the Society Police stakeouts but haven't been free of them entirely. Lesbian couples' doors everywhere are staked out, the keenest of Society Police hoping to get lucky and find evidence of illegal sperm donation. Of course, such crimes have been discovered plenty of times, 'all eyes' being impossible to avoid. That Pasha got away with it seems like too much of a fluke. The risk was too great.

'It's hard to imagine,' Mae says. 'I'm sure something will come up.'

'Sure. Anyway, I've emailed you all the deets. I've had a quick look through, seems watertight. No trusts. No offshore loopholes. Reckon they've been sitting on this for a while. No way did they draft this up since the population conference.'

'Set up an automated response. If anyone emails or calls to do with the new inheritance tax laws, they'll have to wait until I've digested it all.'

'Already done it. Of course, Katlyn's fuming. She said she'd stay home today though. Quite a relief. Don't worry, I didn't tell her you're pregnant.'

'Great. Thanks, Sadie.'

Sadie makes her way back to her desk, taking long strides in her perfectly fitted trouser suit, bossing it in heels in a way Mae can't even imagine. Her functional flats hurt her feet even when sitting. Sadie's feet, like the rest of her, work hard and never grumble. She can likely run a marathon in heels without a blister if it means getting some paperwork done on time.

Mae minimises her email screen, trusting Sadie to take care of that and focuses instead on the new regulations PDF. Four hundred and fifty-six pages of new tax laws and regulations released just a few hours ago. The press is typically told before the accountants and solicitors and anyone else who needs to oversee such things. From the reception desk, Sadie answers the continuous stream of phone calls and repeats, 'the accountants need more time,' and 'no, we have no comment to the press at this time. Try the accountants on Broad Street.' The replies of tuts and rage are loud enough to echo through to her office, anger and disapproval bouncing down the line again and again. In the end, Mae shuts the door. Impersonal and rude, she thinks, when she doesn't have a client in the office. But four hundred and fifty-six pages require most of her brain capacity.

And right now, her brain feels like it's made of cotton wool and chewing gum. She swallows a gulp of coffee, gags, then gets to work.

She skims through it first of all, making notes, highlighting, then starting again. 'Elder protection,' they're calling it, which makes Mae laugh. They want to ensure people aren't getting pregnant to inherit the family fortune earlier. Can't kill your granny and take her money. That's the state's job. She groans, then attempts another sip of now cold coffee. The bitterness sharpens her senses before the caffeine hits.

Even on mute, her computer is nagging at her, her inbox total now reading three digits, Sadie's automated reply clearly not making the point. Nearly all her clients are Society elders, and it seems the phrase *Don't shoot the messenger* doesn't apply when the messenger is your accountant. She scrolls through her emails and regrets it instantly. *There must be something we can do* is written time and time again. As well as, *I worked all my life for this*. As much as her sympathy is genuine, her real worries are more personal. If she loses all of her business to this, and her boss is unhappy, her hours will be docked, and her own Life Score will suffer.

She emails old colleagues and reads emails from others. Paragraphs of expletives, mostly. Fellow accountants pull their hair out, all with long lists of irate clients who refuse to believe this is happening. Her colleagues can't keep up. They're all in the same boat. This piece of new tax legislation is the most watertight document ever produced. The only saving grace for the wealthy is that Life Scores can still be inherited, just not the cash. And everyone knows it's easy to accumulate more wealth with a higher Life Score. That won't be enough to quell the rage of the most disgruntled, but it likely softens the blow just enough to keep the masses appeased.

Where Mae normally finds solace and solutions in numbers, as numbers can be utilised to help and empower people, now she has to use words, and words that are too blunt to be polite. She can't sugarcoat it. She drafts a standard reply to all enquiries, knowing that Sadie will add the required level of sympathy and pity. *This is the law now. 95% tax rate applies to everything. Life Score is still inherited,* is all she writes, then forwards it to Sadie.

Through her closed office door, the coffee machine grinds for the eighth time that morning, the fridge opens then closes, and Sadie sighs, slamming her fingers on the keys. She's clearly muted the phone, thank God. The shrill, incessant ringing that morning is maddening. No wonder Katlyn stayed at home.

Mae sits quite still for a moment after sending the email and wonders if she has no accountancy clients, how are they ever going to provide for a baby? Pasha's Life Score and wages aren't enough, even with his recent surprise increase. Still convinced he was lying just for bravado, she puts it to the back of her mind again.

Reading through her client list, she realises she'll have to retrain, maybe do business taxes and property, more self-assessments. Elder clients make up the bulk of almost everyone's industry, hers included. Cut that, and she'll lose eighty per cent of her work. She'll need to get ahead of the game, find a field that AI hasn't dominated. Accountancy software coding perhaps. Teaching, maybe. She messages Pasha and receives his usual *it will be fine* reply.

How can he always be so sure, like some kid, not a worry in the world? If the Society runs on positive mental attitude and hope, they'll be fine for sure. But it doesn't work like that. How on earth will it be fine? *Trust me,* would be his next line. Like he's some omnipotent being and has ultimate power. Buzzwords and motivational jargon are like gummy juice to him, kryptonite to her. But she does trust him, if she's being honest, however much it maddens her to think it. Those two little words are sometimes all she needs to hear. That he is taking the burden.

'I'm sorry, ma'am, but it's appointments only,' Sadie says loudly, a warning to Mae as much as a statement to whoever is on the other side of the door.

'She'll see me. I know she will,' the breathy voice replies.

Mae knows that breathy voice, or at least has a short list of who it can be. Whoever it is sounds like the walk into the practice has edged them closer to death's door. Muffling a groan, Mae gets up and opens her door. Mrs Osborne last came to see her on her ninetieth birthday, armed with cake as well as her investment portfolio. She looks like she's aged another ninety years since then. Her back rounds over like a wilted flower, her wise old head too heavy on her thin neck.

'It's okay, Sadie,' Mae says and opens her door wider. 'I could do with a break from staring at my screen anyway. Hi, Mrs Osborne. Come on through.'

Mrs Osborne hobbles in, her lungs loudly searching for breath. 'Dreading when my medication runs out.'

'Lots of awful news today, I know,' Mae says, as loudly as she can politely speak.

'Well, needs must.' She reaches for the chair behind her as Mae guides her hand to the rest. 'How are you, dear?'

'As well as can be. Thank you. Can I get you a glass of water? Cup of tea?'

Mrs Osborne shakes her head and holds her chest as her breathing settles. Mae studies her hands, the crisscross of papery lines a fragile map of memories and time.

'Now, I know you must be very busy, so I won't take too much time.' Mrs Osbourne pauses for breath again, pushes her glasses up her nose, then loosens her scarf. Her deep pink lipstick has been meticulously applied, only the thinnest sliver of grey roots showing at her scalp. Her plait looks tidier than Mae's. Thinner, for sure, and shorter. But she grooms herself in a way Mae can never find the energy to do. Even her scarf appears ironed. 'I want to know if there is a way someone can pay me a large sum of money, or rather, if they can pay my family a sum of money, for my life donation.'

Mae cannot hide her surprise. 'You want to sell your life?'

'I'm dying. Might as well put that to good use. I thought about taking that Pres-X medication, live longer and hope for this all to blow over by then. But I'm not well enough apparently. And anyway, I'm not sure that's the right way to approach the situation. Not that I'm getting behind the Time's Up movement. You've seen them on TV?'

Mae shakes her head.

'They shout a lot at the cameras. They're all so angry. Think us oldies should go willingly, that we've had our time. All these people growing younger with that drug, it doesn't seem quite right really. Don't you think?'

'It's a strange world.'

'Anyway, since my family can't inherit my money, can they be paid some other way?'

'I mean, well. . .' Mae sits back in her chair and ponders. 'Anyone can gift money. I assume you're talking about a large sum?'

'I think a million is a fair price. That's in line with what they would have received from my estate anyway.'

'So, your family doesn't want to use you as a donor themselves?'

'No. They're not planning families. Some of them have even signed up to the Enough rallies. You've seen those I assume?'

'I have.'

'I don't think they're hooligans like some of them.' There's a tremor in her voice, casting a hint of doubt. 'They just think that there are enough people. It's funny, isn't it? At my age, I should have opinions really. But I think they all make good points.' She clears her throat. 'I do want to be clear though. This payment idea is my idea. My family does not know that I am here.' Her speech shakes with volume and oath.

'Okay. Well, I'd say it's an ethically grey area—'

'I think we're past the point where ethics come into it.'

Mae nods slowly, her head awash with percentages and calculations. 'Well, a gift would be the most sensible thing. They'd still be taxed on it, but that would be in line with income tax instead of the ninety-five per cent inheritance tax. It's closer to what inheritance tax used to be, so I guess that would work out the same. As for how to tie it together so they know you're legit and the money is safe, that's a job for a solicitor.'

One million pounds. She continues doing the maths in her head. Could she and Pasha afford that? They could take equity out of their flat and source a little that way. They have some savings. She has shares in the company . . . *No!* She scalds herself. She isn't some bounty hunter. How could she even contemplate such a thing?

'Thank you for your help,' Mrs Osbourne says and prepares to stand. 'I shall make an appointment with my solicitor.'

Mae helps her up, then escorts her to the door. The autumn wind rushes in and Mrs Osbourne buttons up the top of her peacoat.

'I always loved autumn,' she says. 'Glad I get to see this one. There's something quite tranquil in knowing it'll be my last one, that the pain is almost over.' She smiles now, a contented smile that leaves Mae's jaw hanging open.

'You go careful now, Mrs Osbourne. Let me know how you get on.' Mae shuts the door behind her, then leans on it a moment, the conversation still sinking in.

'Was she for real?' Sadie says. 'Sorry, I couldn't help but hear. She does shout.'

'Yeah, she's quite deaf. And yes, she's actually considering getting paid to die.'

Mae stands in front of Sadie's desk, her own office too far of a walk in her shocked state. One million pounds. Getting paid to die. Her head throbs and she rubs her temples.

'This is crazy. Just crazy,' Sadie says, tilting back in her chair. 'Have you seen the rallies on social media? So much love for the government over this.'

Sadie's computer screen is showing the news, the delighted government saying how successful the scheme is already, four thousand donors found, creating two billion pounds in revenue. And it's only been a few days since the announcement. How can anyone argue with that? The newsreader lists off how many doctors and teachers that money will buy, how many roads it will fix. Like that is what Mrs Osborne surmounts to. Some pothole filler.

'The people on the bus were giving a pregnant woman a hard time this morning,' Mae says.

'Seriously? Shit, this is bad.'

'It was horrible. The poor woman.'

'You worried?'

'Yeah.' Mae fidgets on the spot a while as Sadie stares into her coffee cup before returning to her office.

Having a heart-to-heart with Sadie was not going to change anything or get her work done. She sits at her desk and gets a calculator out. She isn't going to pay one of Society's elders, of course she isn't. But if, *if* someone is willing, maybe. She logs in to their joint savings account. Their monthly additions should be getting healthier by now. She spends her life calculating her clients' net worth but rarely checks her own. It won't be much, but they live modestly and save.

As her bank loads up, she scrolls through property prices. Even a little apartment like theirs is worth a fair bit. A lot actually. Taking out some equity shouldn't be an issue. They could probably get a loan. A few more clicks to load up her savings account info and. . . Five grand. That's all? That can't be right. She refreshes the screen, but the amount doesn't change. *What the hell?* She can't understand it. She blinks a few times, rubs her eyes, yet the figure remains the same. It should be over four times that! Where's the rest gone? She scrolls through the statement and notices a large withdrawal just a month ago — into Pasha's personal account.

It's all going to be fine, trust me. His words echo in her head. Were they meant for just him? Is he running off with their money? *He's* going to be fine, not *them?* No. He's devoted to her. She's the one who finds it hard to love. For him, it comes easy, like everything. But unless he's paid for them to move to some remote location where the government can't find them, she can't fathom what spunking over fifteen grand could have done to make it 'fine'.

Her computer pings, despite being on mute. Certain emails ignore any silencing settings. Public service announcements, emergency warnings, and the police. She reads and her stomach drops. The police. A final warning about disturbing the peace before Life Score points are deducted. Someone uploaded a video of her from the bus this morning to the Society Police app. The software IDd her face, and now, for trying to help a pregnant woman, she gets a warning.

She thumps her forehead and covers her ears, her head ringing with sirens of denial and reason. Shutting out the quietness of her office, she lets her pulse ground her. Disturbing the peace? For trying to do a good thing? She grinds her teeth, squeezes her ears harder, trying to crush away madness.

Her stapler is at a crooked angle on her desk, her pad of post-its also askew. She straightens them, counts her pens, takes some breaths and swaps the post-its and pens around. A better arrangement. Not like Moira who pointlessly places things in certain positions just to be pretentious. Mae arranges things in a methodical way, sensible. She sets the phone at a slight angle for optimal use, then straightens it again, better straight for sure.

Her pulse calms, the ringing in her head dissipates, and her thoughts process. It's only a warning. Her conscience is clear. At least it isn't points deducted. Pasha is what she needs to focus on. Pasha and his dishonesty are more of a worry right now.

Chapter 6

The poster across the room in Mae's office shows an elder couple holding hands. 'Take control of your finances,' it says, with some quoted customer reviews underneath. Control is a slippery thing, hard to grab hold of, even harder to keep. The top of the poster is frayed, hardly surprising, it's been there years. She's always hated it. The background is some putrid cream set against her off-white wall. The colour combination meant to look sophisticated when really it looks washed-out. She takes a strip of Sellotape and sticks down the frayed edge. It's not a marked improvement, but at least she's more comfortable looking at it. When she starts doing a stock take of the teaspoons, sugar packets, and coffee pods, Sadie tells her to go home.

'There are eight teaspoons,' Sadie says. 'You know how I know that? Because you counted them and told me a few months back when Katlyn was on the warpath about the software upgrade not going to plan. You also told me there are eight teaspoons a few months before that when Mr Singh came in ranting about his fine from the inland revenue. They don't need counting again.'

Mae doesn't verbalise a reply, but her cheeks flush as Sadie's pity stares shame her bad habits. A small office space is like a magnifying glass for weirdness. Her desire to live unnoticed, like a speck of dust, is impossible in the workplace. Does she count out loud? Maybe. And she's sure there are only seven teaspoons now. She resists the urge to count again. Maybe one is on a desk somewhere. She scans the office, forgetting Sadie's scrutinising gaze.

'You're no good to anyone like this,' Sadie says, with more care in her tone than her words offer. 'Get some sleep. Speak to Pasha. It'll all seem better in the morning. You have appointments tomorrow, so might as well get your head clear.'

Defeated, Mae hangs her head and grabs her peacoat, making for the door with a mumble of thank yous and apologies and see you laters, pausing only for a second to note the missing teaspoon on the shelf in the waiting area. She'll put it away tomorrow.

A glance at her phone on the walk to the bus stop makes her kick herself. What's the point in reading more bad news? Pasha is going to need a magic wand to make this nonsense turn out okay. That, or a million pounds and a depressed pensioner. Even the celebrity pages are full of it, shaming actors and singers for being pregnant, their careers and PR image tanking at the hint of their good news. Awards nominations rescinded, sponsorship deals finished, posters defaced, *polluter* sprayed across them, *planet-killer*. Hot waves of nausea trickle up from Mae's insides to her throat and she slows her pace, moving from the fast lane to the slow lane again, the ninety-year-old shuffle the only speed her stomach can tolerate.

The area around the bus stop is cordoned off, police tape around it, and they direct her to walk to the next bus stop. She trudges down the streets, two hundred steps to the next bus stop, the autumn sun burning off the morning's cooling mist. Is it that hot, or is it her queasiness? She unbuttons her coat, which looks uncouth for this time of year, and the eye rolls and tuts from the fast lane striding past make her feel like a tramp. Still she feels hotter.

She eyes the deli, a fridge of cool drinks and snacks, but the seventeen-person queue forces her to reconsider. All she's had the entire day is half of a coffee, dry toast, a handful of ginger biscuits, and an apple. No wonder she's feeling faint. Just as she reaches the bus stop, her vision tinges a greenish-yellow, and the air closes in. How can outside air be so stale? She leans on the bus stop, not her rightful place in the queue, but she can worry about her rudeness later. Right now, she needs to not faint and to not dry heave. Not make a public display of being up the duff without a donor. Clouds immerse the sun and take some of the heat away, her broiling body simmering down as the air becomes thinner again, and her vision returns to normal.

'You pushed in, lady,' the woman from a few places back says, mercifully not until after Mae is mostly recovered. Such a small blessing is a win.

'Sure, sorry. I didn't realise.' Mae finds her feet again, then makes her way to the back. The crowd is lighter there anyway.

She counts the people in front of her. She'll make it on the second bus. Not so bad.

Murmurs of gossip ripple through the queue, busier than normal, with the other bus stop being closed. People moan about their aching feet, the longer walk, and the delay on their journey. A couple of women with firmly set fringes and thin, tight plaits stand shoulder-to-shoulder, as if they were whispering quietly to each other instead of announcing the news to the entire queue.

'Assault, apparently. That's why we've had to walk this far.'

'They beat up some pregnant woman.'

'The Enough group are beating women all over the Society, any woman that's pregnant, to make her lose the baby.'

'It's true. I read it in the news. About thirty women have been beaten up. Two died. No arrests yet.'

'The police can't get near the group. There's so many of them.'

'I've heard they're approved by the government.'

Mae covers her mouth to hide her gasp as sweat collects in her hairline again. She takes a step away from them, her legs wobbling before her feet find purchase. Behind, the rumours don't stop. A group of men now, from the sounds of it, though she doesn't turn her head to look.

'I've heard it's pensioners hiring thugs. Kill the women instead of making them become donors.'

'No one is making them. They have to volunteer.'

'Yeah, now. But who knows what will happen in a year? The Time's Up group are probably going to start on the old folk next. Some retaliation, I reckon.'

'It's probably the Preserved. Those hundred-year-olds on Pres-X won't be happy until the world is populated by people over a hundred who look like they're under thirty. That's what the world will come to soon. They say they're monitoring its use, but they won't make it illegal. The rich people in power want to live another seventy years too. Sweet deal for those with a Score of 900 plus.'

'When I get to 900, I'll never do that.'

'*When!* Don't make me laugh, Sid. You're stuck in the sub 400 club forever.'

'You're one to talk.'

Mae takes a step away from them too. Pensioners killing off women, the government trying to do the same, and pregnant women being beaten to death. Rumours, she reminds herself, still not daring to look at the news on her phone. It's just rumours. The world hasn't gone that crazy yet. With her head spinning, she has to check, and takes out her phone.

Across her screen are thirteen messages from Pasha, all reading more or less the same: '*Are you okay?*'

Yes, I'm fine, she replies. She doesn't mention that she is chewing back mini-sicks and is acutely stressed that he's drained their savings account without telling her. That her colleague sent her home for being too weird, and she may lose a huge chunk of her income. 'Fine' seems pretty far from the truth. But it's what he always says.

His reply comes quickly. *Be careful. I think you should work from home from now on.*

She thinks about her tiny flat, on that lumpy sofa, her back arching over her crappy laptop. And she'd still have to go into the office to see clients some days anyway. Mae needs to be proving her worth now, not shying away from the little work she's likely to have left.

She replies, *No need yet, maybe in a couple of months.*

She looks down at her flat stomach. Not yet. She's fine at the moment. Something will change. The world hasn't gone that crazy yet.

Then she checks the news.

Shit.

Chapter 7

Pasha is still at work when she arrives home. The apartment is clean, organised, so she has nothing to busy her mind with. Switching on the TV, she sees the news articles, same as she read on her phone but in video, which is far more horrific. Headshots of women, before they were beaten to death, social media posts of people celebrating the end of their life, Pres-X use rocketing as old people want to live longer until inheritance tax laws change, adverts for life sales, and Time's Up groups beating up Society's elders. It's been three days since the announcement, Mae tells herself. Just three days. And she has eight months of pregnancy to get through yet.

So many pregnant women being beaten up across the Society, many more than the gossiping people at the bus stop said. Society Police aren't reporting it when they see it, it's like some lawless coup. And the few real police that do exist are not able — or are unwilling — to make arrests. The Enough group are too numerous, too vociferous, too correct, according to the newsreaders tone. Is Mae imagining that? The newsreader's ambivalence towards such crimes? There should be outrage, demands for justice, but the anchor reads off the victims like she's reading a dull shopping list. Not a hint of care. She even smiles.

The Pro Grow rallies are being pushed aside by the Enough movement. In the crowds that march through the major cities, men, women, young, those that look young, old, a range of demographics, all cheer support across the globe for the new harsh measures to curb the population from the bottom. The Time's Up movement in contrast seems disorganised, no rallies, just a few social media posts and acts of violence. Vengeful young people and jealous elders who don't have the Life Score to finance Pres-X, the newsreader says.

Another two thousand donors signed up this afternoon alone. When their inheritance tax comes in, that'll be a few billion more quid in the coffers. Cheers from the news studio at the results, delight where Mae feels dismay. A few less mouths to feed, they say. More room for the rest of us.

Guilt inches over Mae as they show video footage of endless queues, overflowing landfill sites, bare ground where forests used to be, dried up water reservoirs. Reducing greenhouse gases wasn't enough, the newsreader says. Flesh footprint is the new carbon footprint. There are simply too many people across the globe. The camera pans out again to children with blurred out faces, so many children the world over. In the newsroom, they scoff and hiss at the sight of a parent with multiple offspring. Parent, why does Mae think that? It's never any old parent they show. It's mothers. Every footage shows mothers at the heart of the world's problem. As if men have no contribution to the matter.

The newsroom's rage and discontent grow louder when they show same-sex couples. Aghast that women must have facilitated male couples to have a baby, comparing renting out their womb to some greedy landlord. Two women in a relationship doubles the birthing capacity. *What have we done?* the newsreaders ask. *How did we not see this coming?*

Mae turns the TV off, dropping the remote as she slams her finger down on the standby button. She kicks off her shoes, drags her feet to the bathroom, then takes a shower. She exfoliates all over, angrily scrubbing, like she can cleanse her troubles away, rubbing off the old. If only she could begin anew. Dead skin cells are not all she feels like shedding. She wants to scrub years away, to go back to a time when the world wasn't like this, to long-lost years when life was simple, calculable. When she could just be, when her body was her own business. Just as she is drying herself, the door clicks open and Pasha's voice fills the living room.

'I'm home. How are you feeling? Crazy stuff on the news. I applied for our exemption. We stand a good chance, but it takes a while to find out.'

She steps out of the bathroom wrapped in an oversized towel, hair hanging in sodden locks down her front, still kinked from her plait. He walks over, then kisses her, the tenderness of which does nothing to calm her anger. The residue of this touch is one more thing she wants to wash away.

'What's happened to our savings account, Pasha? Fifteen grand. Fifteen thousand pounds have gone.'

He takes a step back, smiling, despite his taut body. 'Listen, it's a good thing.'

'A good thing? I'm an accountant, Pasha. I can't imagine what you've done that could be a good thing.' She tightens her towel, holding it up with crossed arms and tight fists.

'Have a seat. Calm down, I'll explain.'

'Piss off, telling me to calm down.'

'Okay. Okay. I didn't tell you because it's better you don't know. I didn't want you getting in trouble. I didn't want you to worry.'

'Oh, God. Shit, Pasha. You've done something really stupid, haven't you?' She sits then, her towel soaking through the sofa.

He sits next to her, facing her, then tries to take her hand, but she snaps it away.

'It's clever. Just listen. We were saying we need to up our Score and I said I'd try and think of something. So, I paid some extra tax, that's all. I did a tax return, saying I've got my own business on top of my job. I declared a fair bit of extra income, paid the tax on that, and it bumped my Life Score up forty points. Made my Score over 400. It's clever, like I said. A good thing.'

She rubs her forehead. Had he really just handed over their savings to the inland revenue? 'Jesus Christ. That's not clever. That's fraud.'

'Why would the authorities care about fraud when they're getting more money? Everyone tries to dodge tax, not pay more. This sort of thing won't even be on their radar.'

'If it gets found out, I'll lose my job. They'll assume it was me that gave you such stupid advice.' She shuffles further along the sofa, away from him, creating a distance between herself and his recklessness. Her wet skin pimples, cold and exposed.

He leans in, inching nearer, like an ambush hunter, she thinks. 'They can't prove a thing. No one will know I'm not seeing patients privately. Lots of physios do it anyway. I've considered it for real. It won't raise any eyebrows. Savings count for almost nothing towards Life Score unless it's millions, you know that. We went to shit schools, so we're always having to play catch up with no family wealth to speak of. I just gave myself a fifty grand a year pay rise. This gives us a couple of years to figure it out.'

Her shoulders stiffen and her jaw clenches. A couple of years seems like an eternity when the government can implement such drastic changes so rapidly. She rubs her temples. Why doesn't he see that? No buffer left, no 'just in case' money.

'With the inheritance tax law change, I'm likely to lose my job and lower my Life Score, not improve it,' she says, not making eye contact. She faces the wall, but his eyes burn into the back of her head. 'We have a baby coming. Hardly any savings. Shit, Pasha. You should have spoken to me. It's my money too. That was stupid. Really stupid.'

'We can get whatever we want on credit now. New sofa, baby furniture. But most importantly, we can even get the baby into a better nursery for the over 400s. The sub 400 nurseries are crap.'

This makes her sit a little straighter, her shoulders loosen slightly, and tears that were on the verge of falling dry up. He has a point about that, she has to admit. There's a sub 400 nursery on the way to her gym. Thirty kids per adult and the staff all chain smoke outside. The 400 plus nursery has half the ratio and a smoking ban, according to the women at her gym. They're even more flexible with their pickup and drop-off times. Fifteen grand extra in fees wouldn't be enough to buy their way into the better nursery. Everything is Life Score dependent.

'We can even try that restaurant on the corner of South Street now, if you like,' he says, gently, like she was about to shatter. 'That's a 400 plus. And it smells amazing.'

'With what money?'

'I'm sorry. I should have spoken to you first, but I didn't want you to stress about it. You know it wasn't the worst idea.' He leans in closer as she resists less. 'Everything I do is for you, Mae-bug. For us.'

He pulls her in for a hug, her wet hair soaking his shirt. She doesn't reciprocate and keeps her elbows to herself, but allows his contact to take some of her frostiness away.

'There was no U-turn today,' she says into the crook of his neck.

'I know. There's still time.'

'Maybe two months before I start to show. So that's two months before I'll be in danger.'

'You reckon we'll find a donor by then?'

She pulls away, searches his face for the truth in his reassurances, finding only a blank expression, impossible to read and not in the least bit comforting. All talk. No plan. 'I thought you said you'd come up with something else? You think being over 400 they're just going to let us off?'

'They asked for Life Scores on the exemption application. It won't hurt. But just in case. I guess they don't want to anger those Enough thugs any more.'

'Well, we'll just have to see what the next couple of months brings.' It's the most pragmatic thing she can think of to say, but it makes her lungs shrivel as she does so. Their plan is to have no plan. To wait. To watch the weeks slip by into a black hole of the unknown.

Pain thumps on her head like a heavy hat as she goes to the kitchenette, then puts the kettle on, making sure the washing machine is finished first so as not to trip the power. Pasha's Life Score will need to be a little higher still before they get allowed a more generous electricity package.

Pasha flicks the TV back on, then mutes it when the same, excitable newsreader announces the latest stats. They're updating them every hour, it seems.

'Nan phoned,' he says.

'You didn't tell her, did you?'

'No, no, of course not. She'll know though. She has that intuition.'

'If you call hacking every computer in town "intuition". I'd hate for her to think we're going to ask her to be a donor.'

'She didn't mention anything of the sort. Just asked us round for dinner tomorrow evening. She said she'll cook vegetable pie.'

Mae smiles. 'Sure. I love Nan.'

***

She lies awake that night, listening to Pasha's gentle snores, counting his breaths, feeling his fingers twitch. His love and devotion aren't just for her anymore. It's shared. How selfish of her, to be jealous, to want to keep him all for herself. But then, isn't that only fair, that for someone so deprived of love her whole life she'd want it all for herself? Bad mother, she tells herself. Bad mother, bad mother. And she's not even a mother yet. She's a foetus harbourer, an oven, cooking up a storm.

Her therapist, Donald, would tell her that she has to let it go, the dark feelings inside. That's pretty much all he says. A 700 plus therapist offering sub 400 therapy, trying to mansplain away her problems. That's all you get for her Life Score, the better therapy reserved for those with the Life Score who require it. It was Pasha's idea to see him, anyway. Mae was never fussed. The skeletons can stay locked away and crumble to ash for all she cares. Modern life is hard enough without dragging the past into it. But Pasha thinks it's good to face past trauma, that it'll help her cope with her anxieties now.

Whatever.

Donald, the shrink, became a shrink just so he can feel important and lord wisdom over people, she's sure. He's about as innately caring as the obscenely large desk he sits behind. He's Preserved, she's sure of it. Sometimes it's so obvious, they might as well smell like pickle juice and sugar. He uses phrases like 'it wasn't always this way,' and 'you would have been happier years ago when the streets were quieter.' Mae wonders if he knows how unhelpful such comments are, like he's telling Mae she's not equipped to deal with the world now. *No shit.* She might as well have spent that two hundred quid on a fortune cookie.

Donald seems upset he doesn't look older. If he did, then Mae might take him a bit more seriously. Sometimes she thinks he might stamp his foot or pout his bottom lip like a child, other times she thinks he'll crack open a brandy and suck her blood like a vampire. She plays along with the bare minimum that is required, telling him what he expects to hear to keep his childish old man tantrums at bay. He's heard all about her parents, that the crowds suffocate her, that she knows exactly how many steps it is from the bus stop to his office, and that if she didn't count the steps, she'd be sitting there trying to calculate how many. That his picture frame on the wall is about two degrees tilted, and the colour of his shirt clashes with the wall paint so badly, it makes her teeth itch. Thinking about it, she's surprised he hasn't put a straitjacket on her and locked her up.

Snap a band on your wrist, he says, when she's feeling overwhelmed. Tell Pasha your secret. He'll still love you.

Will he? Mae's not so sure.

Why is she thinking about Donald now? Late night loneliness dredges up useless therapy sessions, filling her mind with junk thoughts instead of useful ones. Distractions come in many forms. She looks over at Pasha, his bushy eyebrows, his mop of hair, the curve of his bicep against his side. She considers waking him but thinks better of it. Let him sleep. One of them should, at least.

Chapter 8

Mae opts to cycle her commute the next day. The fine drizzle is more appealing than arguing with other passengers. Their flat is located on a busy road lined with takeaways and cafés. The pedestrian traffic is a continuous train. Segmented speed lanes form during the busiest times, spilling out onto the puddle-lined roads, which Mae swerves to avoid. The bike traffic is equally as claustrophobic as the pedestrian, but it at least tends to move at a steadier pace.

A homeless shelter and off-licence bookend the street. The buses stop at neither, instead positioning their stops at the highest Life Score eateries. She frequently slams on the brakes behind the bus, waiting to move forward again when it departs. In the brief pause, she's bombarded with the aromas from the cafés. Fresh coffee that smells scorched, combined with overly yeasty pastries and bread.

Her ride takes her past Pasha's old school, ironically called, Oak High. The comprehensive hasn't a single tree on site and sits in a ditch. And it's crap. Way down the league tables and is attended solely by kids from sub 400 backgrounds — maybe the odd pupil with a parent nudging 500. Whatever degree you study after, however good your grades and first job contract are, no one who leaves there starts with a Life Score above 300. Pasha tried to justify it to her, to explain his childhood and say it's all his parents could manage. Their second-generation immigrant status made climbing the Life Score ladder near on impossible. No British lineage to speak of and an accent that made it hard to plead their case. He didn't need to justify it to Mae. As if she'd judge him for having a shitty start at life. His parents were loving at least. Just not wealthy. He had it pretty good, Mae thinks.

Life Score results day was when Mae and Pasha first met. Rolan and Mae collected their Life Score envelopes on the same day from that school. Rolan had been surrounded by family and old school friends, some he'd kept in touch with for the ten years since, some he hadn't but they still recognised him instantly. Mae stood alone, eyes to the floor, shoulders rounded forwards, taking up as little space as possible.

It was Rolan's twenty-eighth birthday, too, making his family even prouder. Mae watched from a shadowy corner as they all stood by as he opened his envelope, gave a little cheer and plenty of hugs when he achieved his 300, besting Pasha's Score of 280 that he'd been allocated three years earlier. Rolan's latest achievement will get sent out in the school alumni press, most likely. Rolan being an example of what can be achieved after leaving the shit pile. If you work seventy-hour weeks, kiss ass for a decade, and most importantly, date someone with a 200 point lead.

Mae was alone on results day, of course. She never went to that school and had no friends or family to speak of for a while by then. She always wonders if Pasha coming to talk to her was an act of mercy. As the room filled with excitable relations and camaraderie, Mae was quiet, clutching the envelope, daring herself to open it. All alone. Nothing out of the ordinary, she thought. But in hindsight, she must have looked odd. Odder than usual, anyway.

Pasha stood with her when she opened it, revealing her 240. He approached her, later telling her he thought she was stunning, that he couldn't resist. She'd smiled when he said that, politely. Not flattered. Not really. There were far prettier girls there that day. Mae just stands out more. Annoyingly so, all awkward posture and flaming hair. It's either alluring or a warning, she's never even sure which. Not that she wasn't attracted to Pasha's good looks, she just knows that such laurels don't last. A nice face is finite. Time takes it away eventually.

Well done, he'd said when she saw her Score, and offered to buy her a celebratory drink. 240 was as best as she could have hoped for. Better than she imagined, really. No family wealth to declare, she had woeful chances of ever doing well. 'Pity score,' some said when they saw the poor orphan woman in unfashionable clothes and her hair tied all wrong with her not-so-terrible score. And she'd been slaving away to get that pity score higher ever since. Post grad qualifications, working all hours, maxing out credit, being active and pleasant on social media, showing support for big money companies, all the tricks.

Increasing over a hundred points in five years is no small feat. Part of her discontent towards Pasha, she has to admit, is that he cheated. It doesn't seem right. But then, everyone's cheating at life on some level. She is partly annoyed she didn't think of it herself. Why should his Score be improved and not hers?

Her day at work is just as she feared. Losing clients, having to explain that she can't change the law, sifting through pages of legislation, trying to find a way around it, also researching other jobs and qualifications she can explore to save her tanking career. By the end of the day, socialising with Pasha's nan does not sound all that appealing. But she rides over there nonetheless, meeting Pasha a few streets away. Even with his helmet sitting wonky and his face flushed from the ride, he looks so handsome. It's hard to be mad at him for long. Impossible.

'Rolan and Moira coming too?' she asks.

'Not as far as I know.'

'Good.'

'Want to play Nan bingo?'

Mae smiles. 'Sure. Okay.' She thinks for a moment. 'She'll mention her old hacking days, try to feed us too much, and say you're too thin.'

'Those last two are kind of the same thing.'

'Okay. She'll moan about Moira, tell us she's never felt better, and. . .'

'Remind us we agreed to take Hooper when she dies,' Pasha says with a groan.

'Morbid, but yes. That's five. Easy.'

They dismount their bikes at the block of flats. Flower boxes line most windows, many still in bloom. Fake, probably, Mae suspects. No one living there is young enough to maintain such a display. The bike rack out front houses several rusty bikes, never used from what they can tell. They're always there in the same spot, collecting dust, weeds growing up around the spokes.

'Come right up, dears,' Iris shouts from her window before they've even had a chance to buzz the door. Through the corridor on the way in, Mae gags at the sickly sweet scent of lavender and old biscuits.

'You okay?' Pasha asks.

'Fine. Just a bit warm.'

Iris is at the door, arms wide open, her whole face smiling, just like Pasha's does. 'Come in, come in. Pie is in the oven.'

Hooper doesn't let them in even one step before drooling on their shoes. He's the oldest dog in the world, Mae and Pasha believe. Pasha can't remember life before Hooper and Mae can't imagine anything being older than Hooper. Every step looks like it takes him a mountain of effort. He has the most judgemental face, and his skin hangs off his creaking bones like rags. Mae bends to pet him and he flinches, then backs away. Half blind and almost entirely deaf, she suspects his sense of smell is also depleted. Not that he'd welcome her scent. He's disliked her from the get-go. At least he doesn't growl this time.

'Be nice, Hooper,' Iris says. 'He'll warm to you when he's yours, after I'm gone.'

Mae holds one finger up at Pasha with a grin. Their agreement to inherit the ancient dog was out of kindness to Iris, not out of a desire to spend time with the mutt. It was to put her mind at ease, though the scruffy beast looks like he won't last another winter. Barely another week. He hobbles back to the sitting room, then makes a show of getting onto his bed, stepping around in a circle nine times before collapsing in a stinking heap.

Iris takes Mae's face in her hands. 'Let me just look at you.'

Mae stands on the spot and allows herself to be inspected, dodging eye contact.

'As beautiful as the day we met,' Iris says.

Mae smiles and takes Iris's hands gently. They're cold, delicate skin too easily bruised. 'You too, Iris.'

The heat from the flat hits Mae as soon as she steps into the sitting room. The smell of gravy coming from the kitchen is so strong, it's as if she is in the pie herself.

'Smells delicious, Iris,' Mae says politely as she hangs her coat.

The flat is as disordered as always. Clutter on clutter, dust bunnies collecting in ever-growing piles. Mae snaps at an elastic band on her wrist, distracting her urges as she notes more crooked photo frames than straight ones, books on the shelf put in upside down and backwards, lids off little ornament boxes, drawers and cupboards only half-closed. Perhaps the only non-wonky thing is the crucifix on the wall.

Pasha puts his arm around her and gives her a stern glare. One time she insisted on reorganising slightly, and it caused more offence than she'd intended. So, instead, now she tries as best she can to keep her gaze on the floor, to not notice the debris in the carpet, the sofa clearly at an odd angle as its old imprints in the carpet are visible. She tries looking out the window. Perhaps that's easier on the eye. Just a few smudges on it. Not so bad. Seven big smudges and three little ones.

'How are you, Nan?' Pasha asks.

'Oh, I'm okay. It's good, actually. I've stopped all my meds now, ahead of them being stopped, anyway. Thought I'd get ahead of the game.' Her voice has a wistful clarity always, like she's telling a story, laced with imagination. 'I can have as many painkillers as I like, which is nice. Everything is wonderful.'

'Not great to develop that sort of habit,' Pasha says.

'I think my time of life is the best time to develop that sort of habit.'

'But you've stopped your heart pills?'

'Yes, and I've never felt better. Wine?'

She doesn't wait for an answer, going on to pour three large glasses with a wobbly hand. By some miracle, she doesn't spill a drop.

Mae looks at her glass but doesn't drink, avoiding Iris's stare, her cheeks reddening. Iris's intuition is finely honed, and Mae finds lying impossible. A tricky combination when harbouring a secret. Ordinarily, Iris is the one person she's always felt comfortable with, been able to be open around. She can laugh without judgement and talk in a way long-lost friends do. No need to hide her awkwardness. Iris finds it endearing rather than off-putting. Mae's anxieties come from the cluttered apartment, not Iris herself. She has a way about her that is familiar to Mae. No nonsense, and the same dismay at the state of the world, with a hint of nostalgia in her eyes that Mae can appreciate.

Iris narrows her eyes, half-smiles, then sits back in her chair. 'I would have thought you would have been right round after the announcement.'

'Sorry,' Pasha says. 'Have you been worried or suffering?'

'Not about me, dear. About your. . .situation.'

Pasha and Mae exchanged glances.

'Congratulations, by the way,' Iris says. 'Were you ever planning on telling your old nan?'

'Rolan told you,' Pasha says through his teeth.

'Don't be mean about your brother. He has enough to put up with, what with that partner of his. Awful woman, don't you think? You know, she came round here and told me I need to redecorate, then put up that ghastly photo of her. See it there?' She points to a canvas dominating the wall behind them. 'All tits. Why on earth do I want her cleavage on my wall? And she's put it up so high, I can't even take it down. At least you've got a wonderful partner. Poor Rolan.'

'You want me to take the picture down for you?' asks Pasha.

'Don't change the subject. We're discussing you two and your need for a donor.'

'That's not why we're here,' Pasha says.

'Truly, Iris,' Mae says. 'We are not asking you to do that. We never will.'

'I know you wouldn't ask. I'm offering.'

'What?' Pasha's mouth drops. 'No. We refuse. Isn't that right, Mae?'

'Absolutely. Please Iris, we're not okay with what the government's doing.'

Iris's smile reaches her glazed eyes. She looks serene. Whatever painkillers she's on, Mae wouldn't mind a few. Iris gets up to lay out some plates.

'Please, let me help,' Pasha says.

She bats his hands away. 'Hands off. I can manage.' She lays the pie in front of them, which looks too heavy for her shaky arms, and then cuts, her trembling hand pushing the knife down way too close to her other hand.

Iris serves up thick, oozing slices and passes some buttery potatoes before sitting back with a humph. 'There's no green veg. The shops were out. Some trouble getting deliveries.'

'It looks great, Iris,' Mae says.

'We all have to die sometime,' Iris continues, as if they all want to carry on that conversation. 'I'm not going to be like one of those Preserved. No offence to those who make that choice, of course,' she looks at Mae. 'But God knows what's in that stuff to make such old people seem so young. Living another seventy years. It doesn't seem right, not for me. I've got my Angus waiting for me in heaven, God rest his soul, and I am looking forward to seeing him again. I couldn't afford it, anyway. It's a drug for the 750 pluses. I wish they'd just make a drug that gave us younger joints. My hips are shot. Anyway, we all have a sell-by date and I'm past mine. So I might as well make myself useful in my ancient state.'

'Nan, really, we don't want you to be our donor.'

'It's what I want, though,' she says so sternly Mae jumps.

'We don't though, Iris,' says Mae, her words catching in her throat. Don't they, though? Mae wonders. Iris looks her in the eye, the longing look of an old friend, and for the briefest of moments, Mae feels reassured that they have a plan. *No!* Mae tells herself, squeezing her eyes shut and angling her head away from Iris's gaze. *We can't contemplate such a thing. Never.*

'I have so many regrets,' Iris says. 'People say live without regrets, but that's impossible. Your grandfather Angus, did I ever tell you about how he nearly died? And where I got this locket from?'

'Many times,' Pasha says.

'Well, we'd just got engaged that day. I was thirty years old.'

'I know the story, Nan.'

'Humour an old woman.' She takes a mouthful of potato, then holds her hand up to silence Pasha before she continues. 'He proposed up on the bridge. You know, the old cycle bridge that crosses the river. It's still there, I think? Anyway, he was standing on the railing like some valiant idiot. I said yes and he fell backwards, hit his head and ended up in the river facedown. I was beside myself with panic, but this young woman on the bank jumped right in, no regard to her own safety or the currents — that bit of river is known for its currents. But she swam out and dragged him to the shore. She saved his life and gave me fifty-five years of happy marriage with the man of my dreams. And she had the most beautiful hair. Some of it was caught in Angus's buttons and I kept it forever in here, in this locket. My good luck charm.'

'Gramps was the best, Nan.'

'I knew that girl from when we were children, lived on the same street. We used to ride bikes together and swap toys. Sweet thing, she was. Always sad, though. We'd lost touch over the years, but when I saw her then, I promised my old friend that I'd repay the favour, one day, somehow.'

'Well,' Pasha says. 'That young girl would be a very old girl now, or Preserved. How exactly do you plan to repay her? By returning that lock of her hair?'

Iris clears her throat, stops fiddling with the necklace she always wears, and snaps back from her nostalgia. 'This is how. By being a donor. I'm doing my bit for the population.'

'Nan, that's ridiculous. It makes no sense at all,' Pasha says, pie crust spilling from his mouth down his front. 'I'm sorry, but no. We don't want you as a donor.'

Mae looks at Iris, she is so resolute it makes Mae's chest ache. This isn't what they want, isn't what Mae wants. She's more sure of that by the minute. Iris can't be serious? Wanting to die, just because Mae's pregnant? She's so full of energy still for her age, has so much still to give. Hooper groans from his bed, like he is protesting Iris's pleas too. Mae scrunches her nose at the mutt. If they hadn't agreed to take Hooper, she bets Iris would not be so willing to die then. Perhaps they can say they've changed their minds, or say they've developed a pet hair allergy. That would be easy enough. One whiff of the dog always makes Mae want to heave anyway. Maybe she really is allergic, she thinks.

'So, if you're refusing my offer, what are you going to do?' Iris says, passing them more potatoes.

'Something will come up,' Pasha says. Mae's shocked that she's actually lost count of how many times he's said that. 'I'm sure they'll back down.'

'They have backed down,' Iris says. 'The Enough movement is the stronger voice by far. That's who they've backed down to. They're not going to change their minds now.'

'It's human sacrifice,' Pasha says. 'They can't be serious. I still think it's just a big joke. A wake-up call. They won't actually go through with it.'

'You seen the latest stats?' Iris asks. 'Eighteen thousand have signed up to volunteer. Nine billion quid extra for the economy in inheritance tax. This isn't going away.' Pasha reaches to stroke her arm, but she waves his hand away. 'Anyway, I see no reason why I can't volunteer. I'm old. I've had a good life. My biggest mistake was having so many children—'

'Nan!' Pasha scowls at her.

'It's true! Three, I had. The only decent one of the lot was your mother, rest her soul. I'll look forward to seeing her in heaven too. I miss her smile. My sons are nothing but a burden. I should have stopped after her.'

'Uncle Theo and Uncle Linus aren't the best—'

'Drug addicts, adulterers, uncaring. I don't know where I went wrong. I couldn't have been the worst mother, since your mum turned out so well. Last time I saw Linus, he threw a plastic cup out on the street, just like that. He has no care. No conscience. Theo is even worse. They never visit, well, hardly ever. And now they won't inherit anything, so I doubt they'll visit at all. The small amount the government leaves after inheritance tax will go to you two, of course.'

Mae shakes her head. 'Iris, we don't need—'

'But it's what I want.' She looks offended now, like their care is a slap in the face. 'Rolan doesn't need the money. I've already told him the little left will go to you. Moira wasn't too impressed, but she's a greedy so-and-so. And donating myself to your future is also what I want.' She reaches over the table for the serving spoons, then heaps additional pie onto Pasha's plate. 'You need to eat more, the pair of you. You're too thin.'

Pasha almost doesn't notice the third bingo point until Mae elbows him in his ribs.

'This baby is going to need its grandma,' Pasha says. 'It's not like we have much other family. We need you.'

'No. You need each other and the baby. When are you due?'

'End of July,' Mae says.

'A summer baby.' Iris leans back and stares up at the ceiling. 'I've always liked the idea of dying in the summer. Slipping away outside, warm skin under a blue sky, the sound of water, some birds cheeping at their chicks. That's just how it was that day on the bridge. Sounds perfect.' She nods. 'Please, I'm old. I'm ready.'

Pasha talks with his mouth full, while Mae's eyes are on her plate, shutting out the sight of him. How he can eat so much when they're having such an awful conversation is beyond her.

'Exemptions are possible if we've no parents,' Pasha says. 'So we've applied for that. And there's still a chance the government will change its mind.'

'Well, sign me up for now,' Iris says. 'At least then we don't have to worry about you being attacked when you start to show.'

'No,' he half-says, half-spits. 'The nan-E is administered right away. You can't undo it.'

'Well, fine.' Iris goes to take a bite but stops with her fork halfway. 'You've a couple of months until you start to show. So, in two months I'll sign up as your donor. Promise me.'

'Nan—'

She puts her cutlery down, then grabs his hands, her grey eyes looking deep into his. 'Please, Pasha. I'm not going to last much longer, and I'll snuff it a lot happier if I know you are both okay. I want to die on my terms. Hearing my little great-grandchild cry, with a view of the sky and a fresh breeze, looking at the clouds one last time. Not in some hospital bed or alone here. No one wants to die alone. I want to die surrounded by family, holding a new baby. My life. My terms.'

Iris shifts her attention to Mae. 'You know, don't you? You understand what I'm saying? How I have a debt to repay. Of all people, you should understand.'

'I do,' Mae says with a lump in her throat. 'Of course. But we want you around the baby for more than an hour.'

'Just give us two months,' Pasha says. 'It'll be fine. We'll have a plan by then.'

Fine. Mae tenses at the sound of the word. That damned F word.

Chapter 9

Part 2

If you strive to Score, the Society will strive for you.
Manifesto pledge of the Eyes Forward.

***

'The bus took ages this morning. Did you see the traffic?'
Sadie's voice is flustered as she walks into the office, bringing
a cold wind with her through the doors, litter blowing in to
form eddies across the doormat. Mae glances at the time on her
computer screen. 9:02. For once, she isn't the late one.

'I was dodging it all on my ride in this morning. Crazy busy.'

'Can't believe you're still riding in now. It's not even March
yet. It's freezing.' Sadie shivers as she hangs her peacoat on a

hook. Somehow, despite the wind, her hair still looks immaculate.

Mae smooths her own hair down. Not that it's needed; her helmet from her ride in has squashed it pancake-flat. 'I really don't want to get the bus. It's the only time I feel sick. Everyone will know. Society Police are still rife since the announcement. Everyone is itching to find a pregnant woman.'

'It's not illegal to be pregnant.'

'But my face will be known. I'll get followed everywhere. They'll be cameras in my face all the time. You know what it's like.'

Sadie does, all too well. Her doorstep had been staked-out for months by Society Police trying to get a whiff of a sperm donor. Her partner had ten Life Score points deducted for punching one spy in the face after he tried to search her bags for signs of fertility aids.

Sadie gives a knowing nod. 'You're going to start showing soon. You got a plan yet?'

'No. Still waiting for our exemption. They're issuing wristbands too. You seen them? Metal bands, red, white, and blue with "neutralised pregnant woman" engraved on the side and a registration number, in case anyone wants to check you have a donor before beating you up. They might as well brand us.' She groans into her tea. It's cold and weak, the only way she can stand it at the moment. 'Once our exemption comes through, I'll get a wristband and it'll all be fine.' *Fine*. Pasha's phrases are rubbing off on her. His certainty is bordering on delusional, though he still insists her pessimism is the overreaction. Still. It's been over two months, and they still have no plan B.

'When you get your exemption? You mean if,' Sadie says.

'Thanks for the vote of confidence.'

'How long till you find out?'

'That's the issue. It could be a few months.'

'Well, at this rate, at least you won't have to come into the office.'

Mae looks mournfully at her empty inbox. No meetings on the calendar either. After the initial two weeks since the inheritance tax announcement calmed down, it was as she feared. No work. She has courses booked in and emailed her manager with ideas to take the business to new areas, which Katlyn agreed to explore. But it's going to take time to rebuild and rebrand the business. Redundancy hasn't been mentioned yet, but Mae can feel it. Sitting at her desk, she's as useful as the empty chairs. There's only so much chat about cosmetics and politics with Sadie she can stand. Sadie worries too, sending out courtesy emails almost daily, rearranging the filing cabinet with such meticulousness, even Mae has to agree it looks as organised as it can be. The office is clean, gleaming even. New posters on the wall, finally that God-awful cream one on Mae's wall has come down.

The tidiness and orderliness do nothing to take Mae's anxieties away. Part of her net worth is held in shares in the company. With their savings pitiful since Pasha's withdrawal, she has no buffer, no fallback option. And a baby on the way.

'The traffic was all minibuses, did you notice?' Sadie asks.

'Not really.'

Sadie sits and doesn't even bother turning her computer on, already resigned to having no work for the day. 'It's all the Society's elders. They're moving out the towns and cities and booking up caravan and holiday parks. All congregating together, pooling their money to hire security.'

Mae's mouth runs dry. 'No way.'

'It's true. My mum said so. My gran has gone. There're groups on social media who've organised it. You know they've hired armed guards to escort the convoys? My bus went past several tanks this morning. Actual tanks! So many elders have been kidnapped already and held for ransom. And once the nan-E is administered, you can't undo it. They agree under duress and then that's it. Screwed. They're tied to that womb whatever.'

Mae's cheeks flame. Her morning sickness has mostly abated, but that news brings the nausea back. The only time she really feels pregnant is when she thinks about how screwed her pregnancy is. She avoids the TV and barely reads the news. It's easier to keep her head buried in courses, cleaning the flat, or counting the cutlery than worrying. She gets up and searches for a packet of biscuits in the cabinet. They're eating too many these days. It's all there is to do.

'The Eyes Forward are happy enough about it,' Sadie continues, filling the silence. 'With everyone so panicked about staying alive, no one has the time or energy to protest about the inheritance tax laws. There was a protest last week. Did you see the footage?'

Mae shakes her head, not wanting to engage in the conversation. She'd rather hear anything else, actually.

'About twelve people there. Pointless.'

Mae lifts her eyebrows to convey the interest she was struggling to find. A practised micro-expression of engagement before her genuine vacant face takes over. Was Sadie always this talkative? Probably, but Mae used to have other tasks to distract her. Now it's just Sadie's voice and the grating sound of her teeth crunching biscuits.

'You have any plan if your exemption doesn't work out?'

'Go to prison at this rate,' Mae says and stares into her now empty teacup. 'Pasha wants to pay someone, but we have no money. Nowhere near enough. I'm thinking an abortion would be best.'

Sadie shakes her head. 'Sucks. I just can't imagine,' she says and gets up to put the kettle on.

'I've got less than a month before I start showing. Maybe a week or so, really. What are we going to do? I'm going to get stoned to death if I don't have a wristband.'

'Go into hiding.'

'Don't. You'll give Pasha ideas.'

Sadie rocks back on her chair, contemplative, like she just said something sensible. 'It's not the worst idea. It's either that or stay indoors in your tiny flat for six months. The drones patrol the countryside less than the towns and cities. Head west, you might do okay. Wait it out there until you hear about your exemption.'

Mae's toes curl at the thought of travelling. Leave Berkshire? How exposed she'd feel, standing out, an obvious outsider. A *pregnant* outsider. She'd have Society Police snapping her photo every minute. 'Cross county borders? We'd be spotted in seconds.'

'Nothing wrong with being a tourist.'

Wrong. There is everything wrong with being a tourist. Even the thought of it makes Mae's back clammy. She's seen it at Reading train station plenty of times. Such odd behaviour attracts attention, is food for gossip. Hardly anyone bothers leaving their own county. Why support the economy in a different area? Mae can't understand it. People in other counties look different, dress different, sound different. Mae is different enough without making herself a total freak show. How to explain this to Sadie, though, who wears her own skin like a cosy tracksuit. Mae itches at the thought of everyone looking at her, sizing her up, suspicious eyes and trigger-happy hands holding up their phones.

'Why does anyone want to travel to other counties?' Mae peels her shirt from her back. 'You look so out of place. I'd hate to stand out like that.'

'Escaping the monotony?' Sadie says, as if monotony is a bad thing. 'I visited Wiltshire once. The colours people wear there! You wouldn't believe. And they have their hair piled up so high. All genders. Weird.'

Of course Sadie has been to other counties. Mae isn't surprised at all. Her bright red lipstick makes her stand out anywhere, willingly. Sadie isn't afraid of being gawped at. She even varies the brand of coffee she buys, 'just for a change,' she says. She once even tried out a new toothpaste. Her teeth are lovely, so what was she expecting to achieve?

'Did you try to fit in?' Mae asks, not really wanting to know.

'No. Just stood out. Everyone stared.'

Even Mae's palms are itching now. She squirms. 'There's something comfortable in being predictable.'

'Well, you might have to get uncomfortable. You can't just cut the nano out. It's in your blood.'

'Perhaps we should take a page from the elders and hire armed guards to shoot down the drones and Enough rioters.'

'Or form a commune like them.'

'Ha! Don't be daft.'

Sadie sips her tea, her face lost in the steam for a moment. 'It's pretty remote out west. You could disappear for a few months.'

'Nowhere is that remote.'

Mae usually finds Sadie's bluntness and matter-of-factness calming. There was never any guessing needed with Sadie. Right now, though, a little restraint on Sadie's part would be welcome.

After all of two hours in the office, Mae packs up for the day, then leaves. Better to sit alone at home than feel forlorn in the office.

'Call me if there are any clients,' she says to Sadie on her way out.

Sadie nods and waves, not looking up from scrolling her social media.

The convoy of minibuses and army tanks is still rolling down the roads. Their windows are filled with grey heads, frayed luggage bags, and cushions pressed against the glass. The cafés she cycles past are empty, the usual hubbub of elders all gone, deserted. Outside the sheltered housing blocks, workmen are bordering up the windows with planks of wood and nails, fitting barbed wire to the fences, the gardens left to weeds. Mae shudders.

She stops by the pharmacy on the way home to get some vitamins, to find they, too, are closed. *Gone out of business* plastered in red letters across the windows. The next one she tries is the same. It seems accountancy isn't the only business drying up due to the new laws. No bother, Mae tells herself. She can order online.

The traffic gets worse from tanks and minibuses. The slow-moving exodus of elders and their guards clog up the larger roads, buses bottlenecked behind, angry horns beeping, air dense with anger and panic. Mae struggles to take in the sight of it all. Every vehicle headed away from town, fleeing, luggage loaded, and tanks chugging along, flanking the minibuses. It reminds her of an ancient war film, some scary mass evacuation. Berkshire wouldn't be right without its elders. It would feel strange, unmistakably altered. Like the world has shifted a degree or two.

She tries to dodge the worst of the traffic and takes the long way home, along the river for a while and then up the back streets, avoiding tailbacks and puddle spray. The traffic thins slightly as she gets north of the river. She has elbow room on her bike, at least.

Rounding the corner up Gosbrook Road, young people dressed in black hoods pulled up and shoulders back to accentuate their swagger, roam the streets. Mae sucks her stomach in. Unnecessary with her current physique and not that easy while cycling, but she's guided by instincts. Still unsure if she even wants the baby, but that would be on her terms, not theirs. After a few pedal strokes, it's clear that patrolling for pregnant women is not their aim. For lining up down the alley is a queue of Society's elders, wielding cash and bank cards.

Mae slows, just slightly, rubbernecking down the road. One hooded youth approaches the queue with a bag of pills, then exchanges them for money. Not their usual customers, Mae is sure. The laws haven't only served to shut pharmacies, they're fuelling backstreet dealings in blood pressure pills, diabetes medication, and cancer drugs. She'd read a little about this in the papers, Sadie had filled in the blanks. Reports of elders being mugged for their cash, fake medication, cashing in their life savings for peppermints and Smarties. Mae recognises Mr Tubbs from the block next to hers. He grows herbs in his window box, real plants, not fake ones. He walks with a stick now, but she's sure he never used to. Swollen feet protrude from his sandals while he uses his free hand to feel his way across the wall. It's barely above freezing, and his coat looks threadbare.

She faces the road again and keeps cycling. Nothing she can do. She has her own problems.

Pasha is in when she arrives home, sitting on the sofa watching TV.

'Hey,' he says. 'You're home early.'

'As are you. Dare I ask why?'

'Well. . .' He turns off the TV, then gets up to give her a kiss. 'Four of my patients today are unable to leave their houses now. Stroke, heart attack, blind, and dead.' He lists them off on his fingers. 'Their lack of medication has either killed them or made them housebound and beyond my help. The others are either too scared to leave their homes, or they've moved to some elders' commune with armed security. You seen the convoys?'

'Yeah. Shit, this is bad.'

He gets a beer from the fridge. It's not even midday. 'Yep. And same tomorrow. And the next. How long before they get rid of me?'

A pang of envy takes hold of Mae as he glugs back the cold beer, icy condensation dripping down the can. Something to take the edge off would be welcome right now.

'I'm in the same boat,' she says, voice husky from her dry throat. 'No clients now. Not until the business expands into new areas.'

Pasha sits back on the sofa and continues to drink. The can is gone in seconds. Mae hides her disapproval, but the sour smell makes her cringe. She backs away and hangs her coat up.

'If only we had some savings to fall back on,' she says, as smarmy as intended.

'Yeah, yeah. All right.' He turns the TV back on, louder now. 'Nan is coming round in a bit. Rolan and Moira too,' he shouts over the adverts.

Mae bristles at the thought of Moira. 'Really? Why?'

'It was their idea. I dunno. I think Nan wanted to come, but Ro doesn't want her travelling alone. Me neither, really.'

'They're not at work either?'

'Apparently not.'

The news blares from the speakers now. The latest statistics updates: how many billions banked from the government's genius. Smug politicians rubbing their hands together, salivating at their success. Not much about the attacks on the elders, the kidnappings, or dodgy medication deals. That'll be a minor feature, after the ego stoking for the government and the sports, most likely.

'Shut that up, will you?' Mae says. 'I can't bear it.'

He clicks it off, then shuffles to her edge of the sofa. He still wears his pale grey work polo-neck and joggers. A comforting colour, like a duvet. She'd look washed-out in that colour, insipid, like Moira's carpet. Who will their baby look like? She hopes him, through and through. There's nothing of herself she hopes the baby will inherit. Maths ability, if she really has to choose one. Otherwise, her genes are a collection of mismatched rejects. Nothing has ever really fit. A jigsaw missing some pieces. Pasha would say otherwise. Where she sees skin that would camouflage against hallway paint and hair that would give most people a headache, he sees porcelain and fire. She knows she lacks the personality to match such an idiom. That porcelain would have to be brittle and the fire lukewarm. Again, Pasha would say otherwise.

Studying him now, relaxed on the sofa, messy fringe curling over his forehead, thick brows serving to make his expression more understandable, wanting to talk instead of hiding in a corner, it's clear. Far better the baby takes all its genes from him. Sun damaged versus sun kissed. Sepia versus full colour. Awkward versus easy-going. Easy to love versus, well, her.

Baby. She shouldn't be thinking in such ways, like having a baby is part of their future. She's pregnant. There's a difference.

'Shall we go see Uncle Charlie tomorrow?' he says. 'Before he legs it to some camp?'

'You actually want to ask him?'

'No. But like you said, he's the most miserable man alive. And he's old enough. Gramps always hated him too. He won't begrudge us offing his brother.'

Mae sits next to him now, staring at the blank wall ahead. How is it she can feel so cold next to such warmth? 'We have no savings, maybe no jobs, and no donor. Pasha, this isn't right—'

'Don't even say it. We'll figure it out. Your job is going to be fine. I'm going to apply for sports physio jobs, treat athletes instead of just elders. We need to branch out. We don't need savings, and we aren't getting rid of this baby. It's going to be fine.'

She squirms at that damn F word again. 'I need a plan, Pasha. I really do.'

The door buzzes and Pasha jumps up to let them in, leaving Mae still in limbo, needing answers, a plan, some certainty. But later. For now, they have to entertain.

Moira is starting to show, her midriff protruding just slightly. From her wrist dangles a metal bracelet, legitimising her pregnancy. Mae's body tenses at the thought that Moira's baby is more tolerable than hers. She hasn't seen them since their dinner argument and despite her intentions to let it go, the bracelet gets her back up straight away.

'Hi, Nan. How you doing?' Pasha gives Iris a hug, then a kiss on the cheek.

Eighty-nine years old and she's just walked up three flights of stairs. Puffing but still standing, the exertion merely adding colour to her cheeks. Mae gets off the sofa, then helps Iris sit.

'Lovely to see you, dear,' Iris says as she finds her breath.

'Have a seat, Moira,' Pasha says and gestures to the sofa.

Moira recoils her nose at the sofa and backs away. 'I'll stand, thanks.'

She looks strange, Mae thinks. Her hair not plaited but in long waves over her shoulders, makeup bolder, heels higher.

'How's it going, Ro?' Mae asks. His hair is different too. Swept back, no fringe, makes him look taller. Exposed and uncovered, his face is forlorn, not the upbeat uber positive guy she was used to. He's sapped of his usual pride and energy. His shoulders hang, his eyes are dull. 'We can't stay long. The taxi's going to wait for us. We just popped over to say goodbye.'

Pasha's head snaps up. 'Goodbye?'

'We have to leave,' Moira says. 'I'm starting to show. It's not safe for us here.'

'But you have a bracelet,' Mae says, the envy clear in her tone.

'Too many people here know us. They know the baby can't be biologically Rolan's. Society Police are after every point they can get. We've had cameras in our faces all week.'

'We're moving to Edinburgh,' Rolan says, almost with a cough.

Pasha's eyes bulge. 'Edinburgh! As in, Scotland?'

'Flat's already sold, actually. It got snapped up straight away.'

'Well, it obviously would. Such a nice place,' Moira says. 'The look in Edinburgh is acceptable, nice, actually. A little more varied than here. They wear their hair more relaxed, you see.' She flicks her hair up to demonstrate her perfect waves. 'The clothes, well, we'll get used to their taste. We'll pick up new coats and bags when we get there.'

'We have a B&B sorted in Edinburgh, some properties to view to buy, and I've got a job contract there,' Rolan says, like he's been planning this bombshell for months. 'It all came through today and we thought, what the hell, before things get too bad for us here.'

'Blimey.' Pasha perches on the sofa armrest, and Iris gives his hand a squeeze. 'Here I was imagining our babies knowing their cousins. This all seems so rushed.'

Rolan leans against the wall, mimicking Pasha's posture. 'I know. Maybe in a few years we can come back.' His head still hangs low and moisture glints in his dark eyes.

'Shit, Ro. I'm really sorry. I feel like I've helped screw things up for you.' Pasha's eyes glint in the same way Rolan's do.

Pasha looks so similar to his brother when he's sad, Mae realises. So different when elated, but right now, their faces are mirrored in pain.

'Not at all,' Rolan says, lifting his head like some bid to reassure. 'It's a fresh start, that's all. We're excited about it. New place, new challenges.'

Mae twitches on her feet and leans against the door frame, the word *new* making her insides curl. The ridged doorframe digs into her back, familiar, cool, sturdy, with paint peeling in all the right places.

'You know what you're going to do then?' Rolan addresses them both. Mae twitches some more, picks at the cuticle on her thumbnail, then looks at Pasha, who avoids her hard stare.

'No. Don't worry,' he says, as resolute as ever. 'And we're not going to murder Nan.'

'I can hear you, you know,' Iris says.

Mae steps forward, feet dragging as if they weigh a ton, looking at the floor. 'Guess this is goodbye, Moira.'

'It's a shame. I was really looking forward to helping you sort out your wardrobe one day.'

'Something for the future, maybe.'

'I was going to bring round some of my Berkshire pieces for you, but they obviously wouldn't fit. You don't have my curves.'

Mae attempts a smile. 'Thanks for the thought.'

They hug, for the few microseconds that Mae can stand it, saving all her hugging tolerance for Rolan. He embraces her with all the warmth family should. No air kisses. Just wrapped up in sadness.

'Keep in touch, yeah?' he says as she pulls away and nods.

'We'll come visit,' Pasha says.

'Look after Nan.'

And they leave. As sudden as that. Mae feels for the door-frame again, something she's acquainted with, as Pasha in pain is too alien. Pasha runs his fingers through his hair and leans next to her, his arm touching hers, his hand reaching for hers.

'It's not forever, I'm sure,' she says, quite unsure whether or not that's true. How far away is Edinburgh, anyway? Not that that's important. If it's out of Berkshire, it might as well be the moon.

Pasha's never had to be alone. Mae's always envied him for that. His parents died in a bike accident after he'd already left home. He'd enjoyed a childhood of parental affection and fa-milial closeness. His brother has always been a short cycle away, his nan just across town. Such a contrast to Mae's desolate years, opting to lock herself away with maths problems than to have any relationship with her family.

His charmed childhood has allowed him a lifetime of conversing effortlessly. He has plenty of friends. Mae could be in a room with a hundred people and still be alone. No siblings. Parents who never cared. Growing up she never knew human touch. Her tears were never dried. They just stopped falling. An unhugged child grew into an awkward adult, finding solace in enumerating her life rather than embracing anyone.

But she's used to it. The intimacy of solitude. The cold grasp of loneliness that lingers even when someone tells you they love you. For Pasha, though, this is all new. For someone who speaks his mind so well, saying goodbye doesn't roll off his tongue. Mae looks at him with pity and concern. Is her love enough? She feels it but struggles to show it. He's always understood this before, when he had his brother to prop him up. Can she learn to be better? To play partner and sibling? Perhaps their baby will fill some void. Suddenly, an abortion seems abhorrent. The thought of taking another member of Pasha's family away would be too cruel.

'I. . .' Pasha for once struggles to find his words. 'I haven't had a brother long enough. Not really. He wasn't Ro when we were kids. I know he has been for ages, but those years need making up, you know?'

Mae nods. It doesn't work like that, though. That much she does know. No matter how long you live, there's no second chance. Those lost years stay lost.

'I should have been a better brother.' Pasha wipes his eye. 'When we were kids. When mum and dad were around. I should have had his back then.'

'He's not dead, Pasha. And he understands.'

'You two need to consider leaving too,' Iris says, without a hint of doubt.

'Nan!'

'I mean it. Run for the hills. You need to hide somewhere until your exemption comes through.'

'*If* our exemption comes through,' Mae corrects.

'You've seen the news,' Iris ignores Mae's quip. 'Pregnant women are being beaten up all around the Society, the world even. What are you going to do when you start showing?'

'Breathe in?'

'I'm serious, sweetheart. You're not the Royals. You can't get away with this.'

'Don't tell me you've been watching that dreadful TV show?' Pasha says.

'Of course I have! I'm almost ninety years old, I haven't got much else to do. In my hacking days with the SAS—'

'Nan, you never worked for the SAS,' Pasha says, his jibe briefly turning his frown into a smile.

Iris scoffs. 'Not the one you're thinking of. Not some government group. Sisters And Spies, we called ourselves. Top-notch hackers, we were. Anyway, that's another story. But when I was in my hacking heyday with the SAS, I was always busy. Listening to all sorts of conversations, spying on people, unravelling their firmware, and you wouldn't believe the stuff I found out. They'd assassinate me if I told you.'

'I'm sure, I'm sure.'

Pasha's sarcasm is lost on Iris. Maybe she doesn't hear, Mae wonders, or chooses not to.

'It gets a bit dull being old. So yes, that Royals show has been quite entertaining. All those stupid people, lining up to be sacrifices, begging to be, just because it's a new prince or princess. Like other babies aren't as precious.'

'At least the Royals have options,' Mae says.

The TV show has been the highest ranking in years, according to the reports. The gossip from the show had been rippling through every café and walking queue for the last few weeks. As much as Mae refused to watch it, it's been hard to escape the gossip. The phone votes generate more money than the adverts. The premium phone-in tariff money goes to, well, the Royals most likely, though no one has actually said so. A talent show of elder citizens, pleading their eligibility, all lining up, begging to sacrifice themselves for the next royal baby. No prize money, no point in throwing cash at a corpse. But the association their relatives would receive, by having a family member linked to the Royals, would do wonders for their Life Score, undoubtedly. That has not been spoken of much, of course. Why tarnish the fun with the truth? Just the cynical minds and the realists ponder such thoughts. The nan-E medication is the same whoever they sacrifice for, and shrouds don't have pockets.

'I'm praying for you both,' Iris says.

'Yeah, thanks,' Pasha says without earnest.

Iris ignores his lack of gratitude. 'You'll figure this out, the pair of you. It's all going to be fine.'

Mae scowls. 'You sound like Pasha.'

Chapter 10

Uncle Charlie's home is in the bad end of town. The sort of end that Mae would never usually venture to alone. A seedy section where graffiti adorns every building and the pedestrian traffic walks quicker, warier, keen not to dawdle. The pubs serve more broken noses than pints, and the sport showing on TV results in more fights than cheers. They steer their bikes around a litter of broken glass and general detritus, dogs baring teeth in windows, graffiti that could be mistaken for patriotism if it was spelled correctly and contained fewer curse words. They pedal quickly on hired bikes, not risking their own.

Sunshine Care Home is within a high metal fence with a buzzer on the gate. Usually the door hangs open, screws loose on their hinges, but it's locked today. Mae leans over to press the intercom.

A curt voice answers so loudly, Mae and Pasha both jump.

'Yes?'

'We're here to see Charlie Taylor,' Pasha says.

A crackle replaces the voice for a moment, followed by static, then a security guard appears in the garden, pacing up and down the fence as he keeps his eyes on them.

'He hasn't got any guests on his list today,' the voice says.

'We didn't call ahead,' Pasha says. 'Didn't know we were meant to.'

'Hang on.'

The intercom goes crackly again, then quiet for another minute and Mae and Pasha wait, looking at each other, a silent conversation taking place as the security guard edges closer, taser hanging from his belt on one side, a baton on the other, hands hovering over both.

'I didn't know your uncle is now in prison,' Mae says.

'Sh.'

'What?' she says with a shrug. 'Security guy will be pleased to be likened to a prison guard. Old people minder is hardly as good.'

The intercom screeches and the voice returns, more tired now than rude.

'You can come in.'

The security guard walks to the gate, then closes it swiftly behind them before patting them down and escorting them to the front door. Mae grabs Pasha's hand as they walk in.

'What the fuck do you want?' Uncle Charlie's at the front door, thin grey hair in disarray and slippers on the wrong feet.

'Hi Uncle Charlie,' says Pasha, then goes to give him a hug, which Charlie backs away from, not even offering a handshake instead.

'Didn't think I'd be seeing you again since the inheritance tax laws changed.'

'You have no money to leave behind, anyway.'

'I've got a house. A nice one. Yet for some reason, you lock me up in here like some felon.'

Pasha exhales loudly. 'Your house was sold years ago to pay for your care here, Charlie.'

'Yeah. That's what they want you to think.'

They follow him through to the living room area. The dinner things are being cleared away and most of the other residents are dozing. The ones that are awake look up at Pasha and Mae with big longing eyes and not a hint of recognition.

Uncle Charlie points to the busy care staff. 'He's foreign, she's foreign, he's foreign. She looks like she isn't but is definitely foreign. It's like being on some shit holiday in here.'

'You keeping well, Uncle Charlie?' Pasha says.

'Don't you patronise me, young man. You look foreign too, you know.'

'Well, I'm still a quarter Greek.'

'And who's this woman with you? Is she foreign? No one in Berkshire has hair that red.'

Mae purses her lips and sits on her hands, keeping her eyes locked on the floor.

'This is Mae, remember?' Pasha says, stroking Mae's arm. 'My girlfriend of five years.'

'Girlfriend?' Charlie scoffs. 'Well, at least you're not all queer like your sister.'

'Brother. Ro is my brother.'

'Don't be daft. So, girlfriend, eh? Well, at least you haven't married her. She'll be after all you've got. She's got a greedy face. Needs a decent meal.'

'Uncle!'

'Oh, shut it. At my age, I can say what I like. You fucking youngsters are so bloody precious. Oh! My feelings! Pah! And now, because of your lot and all your spawn, we're locked up in here like a bunch of criminals. Young people trying to kidnap us, steal our medicines to sell, thinking our lives are less important than more bloody babies. Well, I'll be damned if they're kidnapping me. I'll kill myself before signing up to donate my life for a fucking baby. Your generation's taken all my money. You're not taking my life too.'

A woman dressed in a carers uniform comes over, treading meek footsteps with a tray of teas and biscuits, placing it on the coffee table in front of them.

'Thank you,' says Mae and Pasha.

'Don't speak to that one,' says Uncle Charlie. 'Probably poisoned it, knowing her. Slipping that nan-E drug in everyone's tea. She was pregnant last year. She'll be after another kid for sure. Dying to screw the planet up, is that one. She went to check on Ester a few days ago and lo-and-behold! Ester died. Nothing wrong with her, a fit and well hundred-and-two-year-old. Then this one gets her unaccompanied and whoops! She's dead. Just like that.' He attempts to click his finger but manages just a scuff. 'Stole my glasses too. I'm sure of it. Trying to stop me seeing, that's what she's up to. Look at her, she looks like the sort. Probably a lesbian.'

'Uncle!'

Mae winces from the volume of Pasha's voice and tries to sink deeper into the sofa, wishing it would swallow her and take her away from the stifling awfulness.

'What?' says Charlie with feigned innocence. Pallid, watery blue eyes stare like some lost bunny. 'You don't think she's a lesbian?'

'I just don't think it's relevant,' Pasha says.

'Course it's fucking relevant. Wipes arses and fannies, doesn't she? No idea how to wipe a man's arse properly. Way too rough. Calluses on her hands like she's better off plastering walls than looking after the pride of this community. They should check their CVs properly before they employ these people. Cheap labour, that's all they care about. Cheap staff with rough hands. Foreign lesbians. All of them. Even him.' He points at the male staff member cleaning up empty teacups. 'All slipping that death drug into our food. I watch the others eat theirs first. See if they choke. Luckily, I never ate what Ester ate. She never ate anything anyway. This new-fangled government wants to cull all its elders so you bloody youngsters can breed humankind into oblivion. Ridiculous. No more babies, that's what I say. Humans have had their turn. Let's go out with a bang! Fuck the lot of ya.'

Mae sits silently, wishing she could close her ears like she can her eyes. Pasha puts his teacup down on the table, having not drunk a sip. 'Well, it was lovely to see you, Uncle Charlie. We'll pop by again soon.'

'Yeah, sure you will. You've dumped me in here and left me to rot. Your grandad would have done the same. Never gave a shit about anyone but you and your sister. Selfish prick, he was.'

'Good to see you again, Charlie,' says Pasha as he and Mae stand to leave, pleased they never bothered taking their coats off.

'Bye Uncle Charlie,' Mae says, and the two of them bolt for the door, shouting thank you to the staff on their way out.

After they retrieve their bikes and are safely on the other side of the gate, they relax enough to breathe again and get over their stunned silence.

'Well,' Pasha says. 'So much for that idea.'

They burst out laughing, holding their sides, tears streaming, cackling like witches. Laughing at how appalling Uncle Charlie is, at how they could've ever even thought he would say yes. They laugh until their stomachs cramp and their noses run. Until the impossibility of their situation overtakes the hilarity.

When their laughter subsides enough for them to ride, they cycle swiftly through the neighbourhood, past the guys taking a piss on the pavement, past the pedestrian traffic causing some puddle water to spray and wet the walker's shoes, a cacophony of swear words behind them, past the youths selling drugs to elders on the corner. They don't pause for a moment until they make it to the river path. It's almost dark, but they slow, not trying to beat the sunset home.

Pasha rides alongside Mae, and she looks over, squinting in the glare, the settling sun bronzing his face.

'When Ro and I were kids, we wanted to make play dough. You know play dough? The stuff kids make models with?'

'I know.'

'Well, the recipe said cream of tartar. We didn't know what that was, so we used tartar sauce.'

Mae laughs. 'The white fish sauce goo?'

'Yeah. Uncle Charlie was babysitting us, and we'd made a mess. Not that he cared about that, but he was always calling Ro stupid and all sorts. So, we ended up making balls of snot. We played with it all afternoon, just to stop Uncle Charlie thinking we'd made a mistake.'

'Oh, Pasha. See, you weren't a bad brother.'

'Maybe not. He was a shit uncle, though. He's my great-uncle, but I can never call him great.'

It doesn't really hit her until they get home. When they step into their tiny apartment, when all their normal things remind her of how alien the world is. The one option they had is gone. The hopelessness is real, too real.

She opens the fridge to learn how little food they have. Society-wide shortages of everything have pushed prices up, so they've been shopping frugally. The Pro Grow group has commandeered shipments, blocking ports and roads, stopping deliveries until everyone learns to live on less. She finds a carton of soup and enough bits to make a salad. No beer left, to Pasha's disappointment, though she fails to muster any sympathy.

'What were your folks like?' he asks as they tuck in. 'I know you don't like talking about it. But anything you want to share?'

'They were brilliant,' she says, between spoonfuls of soup. 'At their jobs, anyway. They just had me too young. I got in the way. Dad was a mathematician. I get my knack for numbers from him, probably. Mum was a scientist. That's all there is to know.'

'What sort of scientist? Who'd she work for?'

'You're prying.'

'Sorry.'

He shuts up then, eats his food, and doesn't push it. He clears their plates, then does the dishes without another word about it. One day he'll bring it up again, Mae's sure. He won't ask for much, just a tiny morsel more each time it comes up. One day he'll figure it all out, or she'll have to come clean and tell him who—or what—she really is. That thought keeps her awake at night and robs her of the youth that's meant to be restored. Brilliance isn't all glory. There's shame in it. The shame Mae has kept inside for so long. Donald would tell her to let it out. Be honest, be proud.

Donald sits there with his eighty-year-old smooth skin and blackest hair, feeling not an ounce of disgrace. The Time's Up movement wouldn't rattle him. He stands so high and will continue to do so for another sixty years. Mae shrivels when she thinks of it, of them, of the damage her parents have done. A single generation of brilliance and they've turned the world inside out. Be honest? Be proud?

No chance.

XL Medico discrediting her mother was the only thing that took her down from her high horse. Elderly, frail and bitter, her life's work stolen from her by XL Medico, she never received any credit for it. She lived long enough to watch her name be erased, her bright pink skin turning crimson with anger. She's never mentioned; her name turned to dust long before her bones. Lucky for Mae. She never had to bother changing her identity completely. No one remembers Joan Porter.

Mae only rekindled her relationship with her mother to watch her mind slip away under the influence of alcohol and pharmaceuticals. Quite fitting, really, that a once renowned chemist found solace in such things. When Mae re-emerged to say goodbye, to gain some closure, her mother looked at her with recognition but little kindness. Any words of love were slurred and stank of cheap gin. If the drug hadn't reacted so badly for her mother, maybe they would have had the chance to live new lives together and salvage their relationship from the ashes. Maybe Mae wouldn't have spent her regression years so utterly alone.

Her father's name was equally obliterated. They never went to the right schools and lacked the correct allegiances. He may have invented the Life Score algorithm, but in doing so, gave himself a Score of almost zilch. For someone so clever, he was quite stupid not to see that coming. Forgotten geniuses, not worthy of accolade. No one wants a nobody in the history books.

Thinking of them makes Mae irritated and angry. She comforts herself in the only way she knows how. She leans on Pasha, her body against his. Breathing in his scent, the only scent she can enjoy these days. Where emotional intimacy is hard for her, physical is not, or not with Pasha at least. She can forget the years she spent locking herself away untouched, writing off any such desires as shallow wants. Skin-deep. Pasha's arms are escapism. Those times between the sheets, she is gone, elsewhere, more alive and adventurous. She knows for Pasha that isn't the case. He is utterly present, with her, there for her and her body. Still, the pleasure is shared. Ironic, really, she thinks that evening as they both lie exhausted on the bed, that her yearning for escapism a few months back has left her so entirely stuck.

Chapter 11

Saturday morning Mae's morning sickness is back and worse than ever. Perhaps it's worry: no money, no plan, and maybe having to run for the hills. Or perhaps it's Pasha's lousy cooking from the day before and still only three months gone. Still, after heaving into the toilet bowl for half an hour, she manages to keep down some dry toast and juice, then scrubs the sweat off in the shower and somehow leaves for the train station on time.

'It'll be fun,' Pasha says for the hundredth time. 'London is the one place in the entire Society where it's impossible to judge where someone is from. No specific clothing, all different haircuts. Everyone looks different.'

'But I don't want to look different.'

'I mean, you'll look the same as everyone because there's so much variety. We couldn't even play bingo in London, everyone is unique.'

She eyes him, his fringe pushed back, his coat unbuttoned despite the morning chill. His T-shirt peeks out from underneath, some gaudy orange thing he hasn't worn in years. It gives her a headache.

Mae went to London once for a school trip years ago. In the middle of thirty kids and several adults to supervise, she could just about handle it. Camouflaged behind the wall of other excited youngsters, her uneasiness passed unnoticed. Looking at the ground, everywhere is the same. Her feet are always her feet. Changes in tarmac aren't as alarming as changes in the whole world. She remembers how busy it was. The slow lanes were faster than they are in Berkshire, the noises louder. It was manageable, but just. Now, with only Pasha as a shield between her and the rest of a big city, no Berkshire crowd to hide behind, she's not so sure.

She cycles slowly, her queasiness a good excuse. If they miss their train, she won't be disappointed.

'Maybe we shouldn't go,' she says, trying to sound practical rather than pleading. 'The expense. We really need to watch our money.'

'We need to enjoy ourselves a bit. Unwind. And it's a cheap day out. It's just a train ticket. Roger has done the food, and you know how good Roger's food is, so we don't even have to spend money out of county.'

'Still—'

'You seen the adverts now?' he says, not giving her the chance to protest more. 'Some for just four hundred grand. We could afford that if we took some equity out of the flat.'

Four hundred grand. Pasha says the number like it's loose change, like taking money out the flat is easy to do and easier to repay. 'We definitely shouldn't be wasting money on train tickets,' Mae says.

They pass a boarded-up sheltered housing block, the words 'no cull' painted on the boards in spidery letters. Written over the top in capitals 'Enough is Enough!'

Pasha pushes his slipping bag back over his shoulder with a shudder.

'You taking your tablets?' she asks.

'I forgot yesterday. Takes a while to kick in if I miss a day.'

'Fuck's sake, Pasha. Don't forget, we need you.'

'We. That sounds nice.' He looks her way and smiles. 'Anyway, four hundred grand.'

'No. That's a ton of money. And I'm not buying someone's murder. What sort of parents does that make us?'

'The kind that would do anything for their baby.'

She shakes her head. They pass another boarded-up sheltered housing block, a care home left to ruin, and more closed pharmacies. Hard to believe there's enough space anywhere to house everyone who's deserted the town. Specialist companies promoting their 'relocation services' have been advertising during daytime TV. 'Get to safety,' they say. 'Security guaranteed.' They pass another row of empty bungalows, and a chill slides down her spine.

'Sadie is doing it,' Mae says. 'They're not even pregnant yet, but have a pensioner all lined up.'

'Well, if Sadie is doing it—'

'I'm disgusted with her, not proud of her.'

It wasn't Sadie's idea, Mae reminds herself. Her partner, Chrissy, has a biological clock with gongs louder than Big Ben. The handful of times Mae's met her, it's all she's gone on about. What babies she saw on the way, what cute little clothes she saw in the shop, new names she's thought of. Mae never understood, still doesn't. Pregnancy is not some magical time. Another stress and inconvenience etched with nausea and bras that don't fit. A situation that forces change, something she can hardly process. No one understands that view though. The spectrum of reactions runs from being delighted to appalled. There doesn't seem to be a middle-ground of apathetic and scared. She doesn't dare to Google if such feelings are normal. The government is so anti-baby they're probably looking for excuses to rid expectant mothers of the source of their worry.

Pasha's attentiveness and excitement is so intense and passionate, it only isolates her further. Locked in her mind of doubt and shame. She is, as always, utterly alone. At least that's one thing that never seems to change. She takes some consolation in that.

The train station is an assault on her senses. The aroma from the eateries is far stronger than the ones outside her flat and too sweet, like burned syrup. Announcements sound out constantly and are so loud they're barely understandable. Everyone is more angry and more impatient than when she walks down the street. The ticket machines don't work properly, and the turnstiles are too quick. She's too slow for everything, annoying everyone. It's not like there's some instruction manual at the entrance telling you the etiquette and rules.

She bumps into people walking the other way, has people barge past her, then gets accosted by staff as her ticket doesn't scan properly. But they make it onto the train. Sort of. The sub 400 carriage is so busy, they have to shove their way on. Pasha's 400 plus Life Score could get him into a quieter carriage up the tracks, but couple's privileges don't count on trains. From the commotion at the train doors, it's clear that many partners are not as gracious.

It doesn't smell like a bus. Different cleaning agent, Mae assumes, or likely just less of them. It's busy, too busy. They stand squashed by the door as breath from a stranger behind licks at her neck. It's warm, too warm, and the smell of crisps and coffee remind her of her morning's nausea. Pasha's hand holds hers, as always. Her index finger searches for his pulse and she counts the beats. Sixty-five beats per minute versus her eighty-two. Something to aim for, she thinks. Fifteen people share the crammed space, from what she can see, all Berkshire. Maybe people from other counties are in the carriages. Inspecting eyes scan the vestibule, and she keeps her ticket held up in plain sight, in case any Society Police dare to question. She can't handle a confrontation right now.

'Who do you think will win?' someone behind her says, their hushed voice resonating through the area.

'That sweet old lady from the West Midlands. She's adorable,' a high-pitched voice says.

A few grunts come from over Mae's shoulder, a couple of murmurs of agreement. Hard to count how many exactly.

'I like that old guy from Devon. He has a real charm.' A man's voice now, deep and assured.

'His Life Score though. A sub 300 is hardly the worthy kind to be sacrificed for the Royals. I think they only included him for diversity.' The high-pitched voice again, only slower this time, like a stamp of authority.

'The connections would mean more to his family, though.'

'Doesn't mean they deserve it more.'

Over and over, Mae wonders why they're going. The winner (they're actually calling it a winner) of the TV show to decide which pensioner gets the honour of dying for the new royal baby is to be announced in front of a live crowd outside Buckingham Palace. Bookies have closed now, having taken more money than they ever have, and Mae feels like she's the only one without an opinion. Who thinks the charade is barbaric nonsense? Even Sadie has her favourite. Twelve very elderly people are left to be paraded and judged, the general public all voting on premium phone lines, which one they think should die.

'It's given me an idea,' Pasha says, leaning close to her ear.

She looks at him for an answer, and he holds a finger to his lips.

'I'll tell you later,' he says.

When the train arrives in London, it stalls for a moment. The warm early spring sun beams through the window, casting its light right on Mae's head, as if she needs to feel even less comfortable. She unbuttons her coat but lacks the elbow room to remove it. All around, people adjust their hair, turning Berkshire fringes into quiffs, relaxing their plaits or even untying them completely. One woman removes her peacoat to reveal a denim jacket underneath. Pasha's hand tightens around hers, while his other goes to his head to ruffle his own hair. Her plait sits limp on her shoulder, frizzy and dull. The briefest thought enters her mind, but she dismisses it instantly. She'll leave her hair as it is. Changing it seems a step too far.

They alight the train and she manages the turnstiles without too much trouble this time, then comes to a standstill. A dense bottleneck of pedestrian traffic. She's sandwiched between a man with excessive aftershave and a woman with a laugh that would make an argumentative cat sound like a lullaby. She fans herself with the little room she has, flaps her coat, then tries to count the heads around her. They move, just one step. Everywhere around, people discuss the royal sacrifice, their favourite to win, and who's most deserving. It seems everyone in the Society has come to London for this.

They move another step.

Conversations change from excited to annoyed, the exhilaration morphing into frustration as the temperature rises a couple of degrees and the food stall smell becomes stronger. Mae takes a breath, then attempts to calm herself by listing prime numbers. A man, a few people away, screams at his neighbour — misplaced elbow, by the sounds of it, then another row about a woman's dislike of the smell. The level of hostility out of proportion, Mae thinks. The place smells bad, but not *that* bad. Worse than Reading station, for sure. Why restaurants think serving raw fish in such a condensed space is a good idea is beyond Mae's comprehension.

A small gap opens up to their right, and Pasha drags her through the crowds towards the exit of the station. 'Fresh air and you'll feel right at home,' he says over his shoulder, yanking one of her arms straight, while the other she holds up to shield herself from the spittle flying from mouths of people screaming down their phones and cursing each other. Most of the anger of the crowd seems to bear no origin except towards life and the world in general. She has little time to listen and wonder as they make it to the exit.

The fresh air never comes. Instead, they exit the station and enter a cloud of soot, a torrent of screaming bikes and vehicles and disorientating lights. More people shout on their phones, and somewhere a security officer yells instructions through a megaphone.

'Pasha, we don't need to be here. Let's go home.'

'Come on, trust me. It'll be fun.'

Fun? She winces at the word, then looks around at the fumes, the traffic, the enmity, and hurriedness. Since when did panic and antagonism constitute as fun? Fun would be staying at home with a book, getting a takeaway, a cosy duvet day together. What part of a ridiculously busy city is fun? They can't dawdle for long. Already shoves in the back are becoming frequent, passive aggressive tuts becoming less passive as people step around them. She looks down at her feet. Her same old feet, in her same old shoes. It all looks the same if she just watches her feet.

'Spare any change, love?' The throaty voice comes with the fetor of alcohol.

'Anything I can do for you? Pills? Powders?' Another one, just as hoarse and eye-wateringly foul.

'Got a needle of incurable hepatitis, if you fancy?'

Pasha stops, his arm slackens. 'What the. . .? Why are you selling a needle of disease, you sicko?'

'High demand these days. Make someone sick and they become eligible to volunteer.' He smiles, his teeth green stumps. 'Eyes Forward don't want healthy sacrifices. They want to cull the sick, understand?'

Pasha recoils. 'That's wrong. Just wrong.'

'We've all got to make a living. I've sold eight doses this week. They had some smack off Jimmy over there too. So they can enjoy their final months. We're not cruel.'

Pasha drags Mae away, her legs taking a while to catch up because she's frozen stiff. Did they really just offer her a disease?

He heaves Mae all the way to the bike station without a word, not that she would hear him over the noise anyway. There are four bikes left and Pasha unlocks two with the hire app. 'Follow me,' he says, as they ride away and make it onto the bike lane. Instantly on the bike, she feels more at ease. The bike lanes are more orderly than the pavement, less chaotic than the roads. The wind in her ears blurs out the rest of the din. She cools off, in her own zone, focussing on Pasha's back wheel instead of being hauled around like luggage. After a few minutes, the bike lanes thin out and she has space on either side of her as she rides alongside him.

It's a mild and sunny Saturday, the perfect weather for the live final. Union jacks flying, bunting lining every street, mock crowns and masks, merchandise being worn by almost everyone. Pasha was right, no one even looks her way. She doesn't stand out as overly Berkshire. Among the racket, she doesn't stand out at all. Her tight face eases into a smile, the cooling breeze flowing past and taking her agitation with it.

'Can't believe they're still together,' she says. 'I love Roger, really. But Tim is just an awful snob.'

'Just think of the sandwiches. Roger's picnics are the stuff of legend. They said they'd meet us on the east side of the Lido. They said we won't be able to miss them.'

'When have we ever been able to miss Roger?'

A circle of flags and bunting give away their spot where Roger stands on a cool box, shouting them over.

'Pash! Mae! Over here!'

'Long time no see guys,' Pasha says as they dismount their bikes. 'You Royalist weirdos.'

Roger pulls them in for a hug. 'Weirdos? The whole bloody Society is here. We wanted to go to the Mall, but it was way too busy. So we thought the big screen would do. The atmosphere is great, isn't it?'

Mae eyes him up and down, then laughs. She and Pasha haven't seen Roger since he moved to London with Tim over a year ago, and he's as eccentric as he always was. Bedecked in royal paraphernalia, face painted red, white, and blue, it's clear London hasn't changed him a bit.

'It's certainly lively,' Pasha says. 'Where's Tim?'

'Gone to get us coffees. Hey, sorry to hear about Ro moving north. Strange times, right?'

Pasha nods and sits on the blanket, dead leaves underneath crunching. Mae curls in next to him, tightening her coat around her. Only a metre away from the adjacent picnic, but that small bit of space feels like acres. No rancid breath on her neck, no gossip to overhear, the takeaway food stalls far enough away that she can smell earth instead of grease. Only her friends to invade her senses.

'So,' she says, 'where are the finalists, anyway?'

'To the side, there.' Roger points to the big screen TV. Every picnic group faces that way. The balcony of the Palace is the main view. Then the camera pans out to a high up seating area, twelve smartly dressed elders dozing in plastic chairs, the type they give school children. 'You see the seats? That's them. What an honour. The TV show was great. Did you watch it?'

'God, no,' says Pasha, although Mae is sure he's watched at least one episode. 'Watching a load of elders and infirm compete to die for the next royal baby? Sounds like car crash TV.'

'No. It was really good,' says Roger, his voice as animated as his gestures. 'See that woman there in the green hat? Emmie. She's my favourite. Ninety-two years old and can still tap dance.'

'Roger has poor taste.' Tim's voice comes up behind them. He's beaming, carrying a tray of coffees. His tailored jacket is pristine white, his hair slick, not a strand out of place. Mae can't fathom how it's possible to stay so spotless in such a busy city. She hasn't even had a coffee yet, and speckles of brown dot her coat, her ankles splattered from road grime.

'Lovely to see you all,' Tim says. 'Glad you found your way out of Berkshire, in body, if not in spirit.' He eyes Mae's plait, and for the first time, she feels like she has a beacon on her head screaming, *Outsider!*

'I like the old guy there, in the striped shirt,' Tim continues. 'Marcel. He was hot in his younger days. A pilot. Life Score over 800. He was the mayor of his town once too. He really deserves this.'

'Deserves to die?' says Mae, with a calibrated smile she hopes can pass off as charming.

'Deserves to be immortalised by the Royals,' Tim says, lifting his nose in the air. 'The princess is pregnant now, but no doubt she'll need another and the princes will need donors too. I reckon they'll announce a line of succession. And it's not just that. The Royal baby will have the middle name of the donor. The winner's family also get five annual unlimited entry visitor tickets to Buckingham Palace.'

'Lucky them,' Mae says.

'Well, we came for the food,' Pasha says. 'I assume that cool box is full of delights?'

Roger grins and opens it. 'My world-famous sandwiches, of course. Fillings' a little sparse, given the shortages, but all made with my special sauces.'

Mae makes a face at him. 'How special?'

'Girl, you have no idea.'

On the screen, the balcony fills. Silently parading out is the princess with her slightly swollen stomach, holding hands with the prince, their family filing in behind. They smile and wave until a marching band belts through the speakers playing the national anthem. Then, the world falls silent. Mae's only unwrapped a small section of her sandwich, but even the slight rustling pierces the sudden hush. She's sure she can hear her heartbeat. After a few seconds, a breeze blows over, carrying with it the distant sound of a protest, or cheers. It's hard to tell. Roger and Tim are too engrossed in the big screen to notice. Wide, unblinking eyes, hands held to their chests.

The game show host is on the speakers, introducing the family one by one as they smile down at the camera. The crowd around the palace erupts with a cheer as each royal's name is announced and they step forward to wave once more.

And here we have the finalists. Twelve brave patriots, ready to serve their Society in the most noble of ways.

The game show host's usually high-squeaky voice stays respectfully dulcet as he introduces the finalists, calling out the name of each. The camera zooms in on them in the seating area again where they're all stood, those that can. They too wave as they hear their name to the background noise of cheering and whistling. Then the camera pans out and shows the crowd around, lower down than the finalists stand.

And here below are the hundreds of people who applied for the show. Some made it on to the programme, most did not. But a special thank you must go to all those who put themselves forward as donors. The Society thanks you and your service.

On the pavement below are rows and rows of Society's elders, standing or sitting on fold-out chairs. Mae gasps, quite shocked at how many offered themselves up for donation. The cheers are more subdued for their introduction, and the camera doesn't linger for long, preferring to scan the crowd and zoom in on their banners and flags and face paints. Mae unwraps the rest of her sandwich and tucks in, sure it's the only delicious thing she's smelled in weeks.

The camera focuses on the Royals again as more extended family joins them. Mae recognises some faces from the news but can only name the main ones, the ones standing in front, the ones that seem the most jubilant. As the main couple stand forward again, they reach their hands up and the air fills with a deafening roar from the crowd that lasts long enough for Mae to eat half her sandwich. Once it's quieted down, the faint hum of boos wafts over. Mae pauses her chewing to listen. It's distant, but unmistakable. Despite the excited and cheery faces everywhere, some people are angry. Angry at what, Mae can't be sure. She swallows a bite of her sandwich and looks at Pasha. If he's worried, he doesn't show it. He shrugs, doesn't dare say the

F word. The boos trickle through the crowd again, with a word
distinguishable now.

Just one.

Enough!

Chapter 12

Mae looks around again, yet there's no one but supporters in sight. No protests on the big screen either, just thousands and thousands of cheery supporters.

Tim and Roger shake their head at the boos along with most of the picnickers in the park.

Once the Royals finish their waving and the crowd settles, the family leave the balcony and the doors close behind them. Roger and Tim look wholly disappointed, the brief glimpse not enough to scratch that itch. Their hands drop to their sides as they share a mournful exchange. Mae drips some sauce on the blanket as she takes another bite of her sandwich. So engrossed in the TV, Tim and Roger don't notice.

'Who are you betting on?' Pasha asks in a hushed voice. Mae turns to him and rolls her eyes, shaking her head.

'So, here's my plan,' he says. 'There are hundreds of old people here, along the Mall, who all wanted to be a donor for the Royals. How about we go find one, tell them about our predicament?'

'*Predicament?* That's a nice word for it.'

'You know what I mean.'

'What happened to not killing people?'

Pasha shrugs and makes a childish sad face, sticking out his bottom lip before taking a bite of his sandwich, spilling more sauce than Mae.

In front of the seating area on the TV is the presenter. His dulcet voice is replaced with one of excitement, bordering on hysteria. His shiny bright purple suit dazzles the camera, blue hair as wide as his shoulders frame his very tanned face, and his grotesquely white teeth make his smile appear insane. He twirls as he enters the stage, and the crowd roars as lasers dart across the palace and glittery confetti rains down on the flag wielding crowd.

'Ladies and gentlemen.' The microphone screeches with his words. 'The Royal family wish for me to say that your attendance today is appreciated. They pass their thanks on to every single one of you. Especially our volunteers. Once again, give it up for the volunteers!'

More cheers and whistles, fog horns blaring, and coloured smoke from flares etching around the camera's view. Still, when that quietens down, the faintest whisper of heckles and boos carry on the wind.

The tired faces of the final twelve fill the screen once more as the camera focuses on them, some smile, some wipe tears, some carry on sleeping.

'The phones have been ringing off the hook for the final votes. Sixty million votes have been cast! You are all amazing. Thank you so much!' He raises his hands and waits for the cheers to quiet again. 'The results are in, and I think you will all be delighted.' His gaze pans across the crowd, side-to-side, as the hush comes over them again.

Mae doesn't give a hoot about which elder is selected, but even she feels the tension boring into her chest.

'The Royal Family have been in talks with Parliament.' He pauses again, absorbing the atmosphere. 'And I am thrilled to announce that *no* sacrifice need be made! The Royal family are exempt from the new legislation! God bless you all!' In a whirl of purple and glitter, he dashes from the stage, leaving the camera aimed at an empty stage followed by the dozen confused elders.

The most ear-splitting silence follows. Mae squints to hear anything. As she fidgets on the mat, the leaves crunching underneath seem as loud as the crowd was earlier. When the awkwardness of the calm dissolves, the crowd responds with a mixture of cheers and boos. Emmie, Malcolm, and the others sit back down, the camera zooming close on their faces. Blank is how Mae thinks they look. Pale and blank. Tim and Roger gasp and grab hold of each other as they realise it's not a joke. None of the finalists will be sacrificed.

The boos that had been whispered earlier, gain in volume, while some distant chanting edges closer.

'One rule for them, another for us,' Pasha says as Tim and Roger sit on the blanket.

'"Us?"' Roger says, eyebrows raised. 'Are you guys. . .?'

'Sh.' Mae puts her finger to her mouth. 'But yes.'

'Breeding these days. Bit irresponsible, isn't it?' Tim says, narrowing his eyes.

'Hey!' Pasha says, too loudly. 'You've literally just been gushing over the Princess's bump.'

'Yeah, but she's a Royal.'

'Leave it out, Tim.' Roger glances at Mae's wrist to note her lack of bracelet. 'Congratulations, guys. What are you going to do?'

Mae scans the closest people for any camera phones pointing their way. None that she can see. Still, what would the Society Police have to report? They still have time. Being pregnant isn't illegal. But she'd be logged by them and followed till her eighth month, stalked in the streets and beaten if seen. She peers around again, craning her neck to see past the nearest picnickers. No cameras point their way, and she lets her stomach muscles relax.

Pasha shrugs. 'We've applied for an exemption, since we've no parents. But haven't heard yet.'

'Exempt. Ha,' Tim says, sucking his teeth.

Roger waves him away, and Tim turns around, sullen and glowering.

'There is a crowd full of old people wanting to be donors down by the Mall. Maybe see if you can speak to some?' says Roger.

Pasha nods. 'That's what we were thinking.'

'*We?* I was not thinking anything of the sort. I'm not buying someone's death,' Mae says. 'Even if I wanted to, a million pounds is what most are asking. We haven't got that.'

'We could buy five annual Buckingham Palace tickets for their family and name the kid after them, like the Royals.'

Mae can't tell if Pasha is joking. His face looks it, but his voice sounds serious. And loud. Still too loud.

'Like the Royals? Yeah, right,' Tim says from over his shoulder.

'Worth a shot, guys,' says Roger. 'Get over there now, before the crowd gets too mixed up.'

'Come on, Mae,' says Pasha, grasping her hands. 'What have we got to lose?'

Mae's shoulders slouch. She groans but concedes with a hunched posture and a reluctant nod. Pasha helps her up, more attentive than he needs to be. She's hardly pregnant at all. They promise to return in an hour for more food as they grab the bikes and cycle away, weaving through the crowds that fill the streets. Thousands of people exit the Mall, and they're like fish trying to swim upstream. Constitution Hill is impassible, so they go the long way past Green Park station before turning down St James's Street.

'Hurry up, Mae.'

'Shut it. This is as fast as I can go without throwing up.'

Roger's sandwich is repeating on her. Whatever his special sauce is, the baby doesn't like it.

The Mall is still rammed. So many have exited, but thousands upon thousands remain. No fast or slow lanes, just a torrent of people with pointy elbows and loud voices. Pasha and Mae dump the city bikes at the nearest docking area, then walk against the crowd, bumping shoulders with thousands as they all file out, wading through the throng. The resounding sound of disappointment echoes over the furore, fusses, and anger, lost money at the bookies, cries of 'fix' and 'what a joke'. The odd mutter of gratitude, too, that those who volunteered would be saved. Mae listens with keen ears and a knotted stomach. It all feels so wrong, like her skin is on backwards.

Pasha's hand grips hers tightly, collecting clamminess in between as the density of people makes the air stifling. Hot anger and sizzling disappointment are all around. She flaps her coat and wipes her brow. They walk through St James's Park, mossy ground forgiving underfoot, food stalls shutting up early for the day to an exhalation of curse words and shaking heads. Their takings down as the queues have gone, the entire crowd leaving rather than ambling.

'Can you believe this?' one woman says as she's caught up in a bottleneck by Mae and Pasha. 'We came all the way from Southampton for this crap.'

Another woman grunts, then agrees. 'I've a good mind to go off one of the donors myself. Why should they get away with this?'

Pasha yanks Mae forwards until they reach the next bottleneck. The conversation much the same. The air as thick with disdain. Mae keeps looking at her feet rather than the red faces and puckered mouths.

As they inch closer to the palace, the crowd becomes less vociferous and frailer. The temperature cools to a frosty ambience. Who knew survival would bring such bitterness? The hundreds of donors who didn't make the final are filing out, walking sticks acting more as trip hazards than supports. Their pace is slow, so it's easier to move against, though every shoulder barge poses as more of a threat, ruder, like an ambush. Mae imagines purple bruises erupting on every limb.

Pasha pulls her in close and whispers in her ear, 'This is prime ground. Look around. Any one of these people could be a donor for us.'

'This is ridiculous though. If we start asking, people will know I'm pregnant.'

He pauses a moment. 'Good point.' He drags her through another knot of crowd towards a thick tree trunk. 'You stay here. Right here, don't move.'

'What?' Mae's heart jumps to her throat. 'Don't leave me!'

'You'll be fine.' He lifts her hands up to kiss them. 'Look. Why don't you see how many trees you can see—'

She scowls at his patronising suggestion. 'Over nine hundred so far.'

'Okay, well, see how many people wearing blue hats there are. By the time you've counted all of them, I'll be back. I promise.'

'Pasha, please. This is a really bad idea. How are you going to even suggest this to someone?'

'Don't worry about that. Just stay here. I'll be back soon.'

After the briefest of kisses, he leaves, slowly, cautiously side-stepping through the flow of elders all making their way out of the park. Mae backs into the tree until its rough bark presses into her back. Three blue hats so far. No, four.

The hobble of feet is a constant hum but above that now, and getting louder, that same chanting she could hear when they were on the picnic blanket. Words indistinguishable before are clearer now, consonants snapping each word in half, vowels rolling them together. She shakes the chanting from her head, but louder still it becomes. Standing on her tiptoes, she sees the crowd is not all moving one way. Past the slow waddle of vacating donors, a new crowd arrives. Stronger, heavier foot-steps, brasher sounds, hitting the departees like a solid wall. The collection of heads that stagnate against the wall looks like a wish wash of colours, some impressionist painting where all she can see is blobs for heads. Impossible to count the blue hats like that.

Enough is enough! No more Royals! Enough is enough! No more Royals! Louder and louder as the wall inches closer and closer.

Mae reaches for a drink in her bag, then takes a sip, scanning the thinner crowd to her left for Pasha. But the chant from the right grabs her attention. She's in the middle of it all, sand-wiched between the factions. She glances around for an easy exit, but there is none. She can file in with the elders leaving and likely hit the protest wall or go towards the palace where the protest is heading and try to get around the other side of

the palace. She checks her phone for the news. Warnings of unrest flash across the screen: Stay away. Head home immediately.
Mounted police on their way to keep the calm.

Dammit, dammit, dammit!

Chapter 13

Still no sign of Pasha. She finishes her drink, puts the empty bottle back in her bag, then checks her phone again. Roger has texted: *where are you guys? Getting crazy down here, heading home.*

She waits, watches, still by her tree. Another text from Roger: *Are you okay? Let me know when you make it out. Pop by ours if you like.*

She doesn't reply. What would she say? That she's stood by a tree and lost Pasha? She counts her pulse, blue hats not enough of a stimulus. Eighty-four beats per minute. Eighty-seven now. She bites her nails till her fingers bleed.

Enough is enough! No more Royals! No more babies!

They're not far away at all now. No sign of mounted police. She messages Pasha: *P, you ok?* Then shares her location in case he's forgotten. Pointless as that seems, he's like a homing pigeon.

No reply. Another bleeding finger bitten down to the skin. She texts again: *P, please let me know where you are. It's been ages.*

She smells the horses before she sees them. The musty aroma alerting her from behind, the clop of hooves creeping up unnoticed against the din of the protest. Relief sweeps over her when she sees the police, actual police, not Society Police. Twelve of them on horseback, another twelve on foot in front holding up riot shields, an armoured truck trundling along behind them all.

'We're clearing this area, ma'am,' one says as they approach her. 'The Enough protest is turning into a riot, and it's too close for you to be safe here.'

'I'm waiting for my partner.'

'Wait for him at home. Move it.' He gestures towards the edge of the park farthest from the protest.

'He said to wait for him here. If I could just stay here for five minutes—'

'Leave now or I'll put you in the truck,' he says as he nudges her from behind.

'Get your hands off her!' Pasha's voice, finally. 'You okay, babe?'

Her relief is short-lived when she sees his face. Swollen, blood blotted around his nose, holding tissue to a split lip, claret stains down his orange T-shirt.

'I'm fine,' she says, avoiding asking about the obvious with the police within earshot. 'Let's get out of here.'

They make their way to the far end of the park. By now, a police cordon is holding the protesters back, and they're shimmied around the edge. Their brief mingle with the protesters makes Mae hold her breath as they squeeze through. Keeping her head down, she eyes some hands wielding batons, mercifully not using them yet. Sucking her stomach in, looking as un-pregnant as possible, she dare not breathe in case some smell makes her nauseous. They make it to the back of the group with nothing but empty roads and space ahead of them. She inhales a long fresh breath that not even a wave of sickness manages to spoil.

'Pasha, what happened? Let me look at you.'

'Some of those old guys have a mean right hook.' He's still holding the tissue to his split lip.

'Some pensioner did this?' She tries not to laugh.

'I wasn't going to fight back. About seven of them surrounded me. What could I do?'

'You should have messaged me.'

He holds up his smashed phone and sticks his swollen bottom lip out.

'Oh, babe.' She hugs him. 'Come on, let's get you home.'

'You got a drink in your bag?'

Before she can answer, a surge of sound from the riot comes towards them. They are too close to the palace still, too far from the riot police. A rock lands inches from their feet.

'Shit.' They both say.

'What way should we go?' Mae asks.

'Back behind the police line?'

'We'll never get through. And they might break through that line. It sounds like there are thousands of them.'

Another rock lands as the sound of breaking glass gets closer.

Pasha ushers her in front of him. 'We just need to get to a station.'

They run down the Mall, but the protesters are coming from all directions. More rocks land at their feet, smashing glass from flying bottles, the cry of *enough* repeating as if stuck on a loop.

'Stay close, Mae.'

She tucks in behind him as they approach the roundabout. From all directions, the roads fill with approaching protesters, hitting batons together, chanting.

'We just need to cross the river,' Pasha says, scanning the roads. 'Waterloo station will do. It's so close.'

Northumberland Avenue has the smallest crowd, so they opt for that, walking straight towards a wall of people. Restaurants, shops, and cafés all lock their doors and close their shutters.

Mae and Pasha bang on one. 'Please!' they both beg. 'Can we come in?' The staff shake their heads and mouth *sorry* in return. *Shit.*

They back into a doorway, then huddle together as the protesters walk past. Windows smash from their right, shards of glass spraying down. Baseball bats swing at every surface as the protest walks by. One woman approaches with a cricket bat, about to smash the window right next to them. She sees them, crouching down and terrified. Mae holds the woman's gaze, her eyes screaming for her not to hurt them. The bat pauses in mid-air before the woman lets the bat fall to her side, then walks on. Mae's relief doesn't last. The woman is replaced by someone else, then another, and another. How long could Mae's pleading eyes last? Someone will know she's pregnant soon, and someone will be too angry to be compassionate.

'I'm so scared, Pasha.'

He tightens his grip around her, and they make a smaller ball. He shoves her into the corner, exposing only himself to the riot. Mae buries her head into his shoulder, but she lifts it to peek again. They're still marching past. A blanket of broken glass and rocks scatter the pavement behind Pasha's back. An impossibility of sharp weaponry is strewn everywhere. Fights break out among the rioters, blood mists the street, and there's the glint of metal in someone's hand just before he drives it into someone's chest. There's no scream of pain, just the thud of a hundred kilos of flesh landing on the tarmac.

'Pasha!' she whimpers for him, but he whispers soothing nonsense that she can't decipher.

The air fills with smoke, so thick she can't see anything now. Back into Pasha's shoulder she buries, her trembling accentuated by his. Hooves stomp the pavement, and her sweaty body is drizzled with water as the edge of the water cannon spray hits the buildings with an angry roar. Still, they wait.

Pasha's arms give her a quick squeeze and release. She lifts her head, and his face bores into hers. Does she look as scared as him? He's supposed to be the brave one, to tell her everything is going to be all right. Her trembling breath morphs into tears. They flow thick and fast, her words muffling around them.

'Is. . .it. . .fin. . .finished?'

He looks over his shoulder, behind at the jagged ground and settling mist. 'It's okay, Mae. You're okay. We're okay. Let's stand together.'

He takes both of her hands. Stiff knees and weak legs make standing an uncertain task. They turn together to face the street. The smoke grenade has thinned now. The water cannon moved on. A few mounted police are still patrolling down the road. Broken fragments of building, handbags, and glass are everywhere. The mini supermarket's goods are strewn across the pavement, looted and empty now, the staff being consoled. The body has gone, just a puddle of blood remaining.

'What are you two doing here?' One police officer shouts, baton ready.

'We. . .we. . .we were hiding in that doorway,' Pasha says when Mae fails to find her words. 'Is. . .is it safe?'

'You look like you've been rioting. What happened to your face?'

Another police officer joins her now, then a few more come out of the shadows.

'Please, we weren't rioting. I got hit trying to escape the madness. We hid there.' He points to the doorway.

The shop staff are still inside, still with barriers down, but they nod at the officers and give them a thumbs up.

'All right, then. Get away quickly. That way.' He points to the way they were heading. 'Quick now, God knows if more will come.'

And they run down the street, jumping over the litter and debris, dodging more blood and broken glass along the way. Some others still cower in doorways, and all shop fronts have their shutters down. All the way to Waterloo, the streets are a mess. The station is surrounded by police, patting people down for weapons, talking on radios, suspicious eyes worse than Society Police. After a frisking and a few questions, they show their tickets and are allowed into the station.

They find a seat on the train and check Mae's phone. The riot is all over the news. Nearly the whole of greater London has been affected. Shops are emptied, food mostly but clothing stores too, electricals, all of them relieved of their wares. The Royals have been helicoptered to some safe location, the disappointment at the ending to the game show as loud and unruly as the Enough protesters. The thick crowd of rioters had broken through the police riot shields and smashed up the palace. Tear gas can be seen leaking out of broken windows, while injured people scatter across streets, some limping away.

Roger messaged to say they made it back okay and is relieved to hear they're on the train.

It wasn't just London. Every major city in the Society has riots, shops raided, streets smashed, and pregnant women, even with wrist bands, beaten to a pulp.

Mae messages Rolan, who assures them they're fine in Edinburgh. The riots there are just as bad, but they're not leaving their B&B for a while, and they're safe there.

The video footage and photos of the carnage show what a lucky escape they had.

'What are we going to do, Pasha? Seriously?'

'Nan texted. Before my phone was smashed up. She says she has an idea.'

'Your Nan's idea was for her to be a donor.'

'Another idea. Apparently. That's all I know. There's some small riot going on in Reading too. Nothing major. Look.' He shows her on the phone, and though it's minor, carnage is still carnage. 'Let's go straight to Nan's when we get off the train. Hear what she has to say. Looking at where the trouble is, it should be a safer route.'

'Okay,' she says, too exhausted to explain she'd prefer her own bed, her own lumpy sofa. Down her top is a sauce stain, and her coat is covered in dust and damp patches from the riot. She needs a shower. Pasha, more so. He blots his lip with the last clean bit of tissue, his cheekbone getting more swollen.

Mae leans back in her seat, her heart rate slowing but panic still coursing through her. She mutters quietly to herself, 'What are we going to do?'

Chapter 14

'My boy, what has happened to you?' Iris says as she opens the door.

She puts her reading glasses on, then peers closer, her eyes not fooled by Pasha wearing his T-shirt backwards and wiping the blood from his face. His lip and cheekbone are swelling more and starting to turn purple, along with his nose.

'Don't worry, Nan. I'm okay.'

'Hi Iris.' Mae gives her a peck on the cheek. 'An elder hit him.'

'An elder?' Iris says, so high pitched, Mae can't tell if it's meant with surprise or laughter.

'Hey!' Pasha says. 'It was several elders, and those walking sticks are basically weapons. If it was just one, I could've taken him.'

'Come in, dears,' Iris says. 'I'll make us some tea.'

Hooper stands, slowly, as if obligated but not sincere, as they enter the living room. He takes a step towards them, shakes half-heartedly with just enough energy to release some excess fur and smells, then curls up back on his bed.

'Hooper's still alive then?' Pasha says.

'Yes. He's marvellous, isn't he?' Iris says from the kitchen. 'Like a puppy some days. He's delighted you're here. Look at his happy face.'

Hooper turns his head away from them, his string of drool detaching and sticking to the carpet before he scratches his ear, then starts snoring. The wall around his bed is stained brown, like his fur colour is leaching into the paintwork. His legs twitch as sleepy spittle meanders down the side of his bed and onto the floor. Mae hopes, really hopes, the old dog dies before Iris.

'So,' Iris says when she arrives back with tea, placing the tray on the table. 'Why did "several elders" hit you?' She actually makes air quotes, and Mae chuckles into her teacup.

Pasha clears his throat. 'We were in London for the royal reveal—'

'Never knew you two are fans of the show,' Iris says. 'Strange ending. Should have seen it coming.'

'We're not fans. We thought there might be someone there who could be our donor.'

Mae clears her throat. 'Excuse me, but *I* never thought such a thing. I thought we were going to London to see friends. Oh my God! That was your plan the entire time, wasn't it?'

'No! I swear, I only thought of it on the train.'

There's a neediness in his tone, his eyes sinking to the floor before he meets her gaze. She folds her arms and looks at him, biting her lip. His eyebrows are slightly raised, his lips pouting off to the side just a little, those big dark eyes so full of love there's no room left for malice. He's not lying, she knows he's not. However much of a dumbass he is, he's a well-intentioned dumbass.

'Come on, Mae. It wasn't the worst idea I've had.'

'Your bloody lip says otherwise,' she says. 'Wanting to kill someone in exchange for Buckingham Palace annual passes.' She shakes her head. 'Shame on you.' She should keep written records of Pasha's stupid ideas.

'Keep the tickets and I'll be your donor,' Iris says in earnest.

'Nan—'

'What? Look at the state of you. That was a silly thing to do.'

'I did try and tell him,' Mae says.

'I'm sure you did, dear. You are the wise one out of the two of you. I knew that as soon as I met you.' She sighs, then sips her tea. 'Well, if you really are going to refuse my offer, I have a plan B. I've been doing some research. Got some old hacking friends who owe me favours. I can see you rolling your eyes, young man, but you are in no position to be mocking me, so listen. Have you heard about the hippies who say they get sick from mobile phone signals, or electricity, or whatever?'

Pasha narrows his eyes. 'Yeah. . .'

'Well, where they live, the drones can't go. Not allowed, health reasons. I was reading about it, and SAS confirmed it's true. There are some small pockets of land with a covenant that bans the drones. It could be a safe haven for you.'

Pasha puts his teacup down, and his jaw drops so low, his lip almost re-splits. 'You want us to live out our lives with a bunch of incense-burning potheads?'

'No. But I think it's your only option right now if you refuse my offer. At least hang out there for a few months until you hear about your exemption. The violence isn't going to get under control for a while yet. Even women with bracelets are being targeted. The government needs to sort the situation out and until they do, you're not safe.'

'We couldn't work,' Mae says, remembering their lack of savings. Fat lot of good a high Life Score will be at some hippy camp.

'Here.' Iris digs around in the side of the sofa and pulls out a thick envelope, then hands it to Mae. She opens it and nearly drops it on the floor.

'What! That's a lot of cash, Iris.'

'It's just sitting here, collecting dust. You might as well take it.'

'You could pay it into your bank.' Mae tries to hand the envelope back.

Iris leans away, hands behind her back. 'The bank will take the lot for tax when I croak. You keep it. You'll need it more than me. Use it when you get there and for your journey. The drones can't trace you then.'

Pasha takes the envelope and shakes his head. 'Nan, this is too much. We can't accept this.'

'Deny an old woman some joy, would you? Don't be daft.'

'You could put this towards some Pres-X,' he says.

'No. I've told you I don't want that. It's so undignified. No offence to those who end up on that path, or chose it, but it's not for me. I remember when the Pres-X trials first came out, you would have been just a baby. The hordes of people queuing up to get it, cashing in everything they had to get their dose before they made it too expensive even for the moderately wealthy. I'm not doing that. I told you. I've had my time and I don't want you mentioning that again.'

Pasha hands the cash back to Mae, who blinks away some tears.

'Do one sensible thing today, at least,' Iris says. 'This is your best chance. Take the money and go.' She picks up her teacup, then sips, and as nonchalantly as that, as if she hasn't just handed them a wad of cash bigger than they've ever seen and told them to do something so ludicrous.

Pasha slouches back in his chair, licking the cut on his lip as Mae shifts in her seat, then rolls her shoulders back, her muscles tightening at the thought.

'She's right, Mae,' Pasha says.

A chill creeps from the base of Mae's skull to her tailbone. She can't be right. It's a crazy suggestion. Old Iris must be having a senile moment. 'We can't, Pasha. We just can't. Where even are such places? I've never seen one.'

'There's none in Berkshire, that's why,' Iris says. 'Cornwall is your best bet.'

'Cornwall!' Mae nearly drops her teacup. 'No, really. That's impossible,' says Mae, almost laughing at the absurdity. 'How many counties is that? A pregnant woman on the run would get spotted in a second. It's too far. We can't.'

'Mae, really. We don't have much choice,' Pasha says, his voice more authoritative than kind. 'This is the best way to keep you and the baby safe.'

'But Cornwall.' She takes out her phone, then loads up a map. 'We'd have to leave Berkshire, go through Hampshire, Wiltshire, Somerset, Gloucestershire, Devon. So many county borders. We'd get spotted as tourists everywhere. Society Police would be on to us. We'd be followed by drones the entire way.'

'We'll blend in,' says Pasha, seriously, in his stained T-shirt and beaten-up face. He'd blend in as well as a giant grapefruit.

'Oh, come on,' Mae says, her half-laughter turning to anguish. 'What do they even wear in these counties? How do they have their hair? The accent. . .don't tell me you can do a Gloucestershire accent! Of course you can't.'

'When I was your age, we used to travel to other counties all the time,' says Iris, which makes Mae's jaw clench.

'No offence, Iris, but that was decades ago,' Mae says. 'It doesn't work like that now. It's wrong to support other counties' economies. Such behaviours raise suspicions. Not to mention, it's a health hazard. And everything is devolved to counties. Who knows what laws we could break without even knowing it?'

Iris waves away Mae's concerns with a flick of her wrist. 'The train from Reading will take you all the way to Weston-Super-Mare. That will bypass quite a few borders. Then, it's not too far to Cornwall. The only county borders would be Somerset to Devon, and Devon to Cornwall.'

'Just two borders, Mae,' Pasha says. 'We could do this.'

'Three. The train is the first one.'

'Still, not so many. You made it to London.'

'That was just one train, one border, and look how well that little excursion turned out.'

Neither reply. They just stare at her, unblinking, unfaltering, resolute.

'You're serious,' Mae says. 'The two of you. You're actually serious?'

They're not giggling over the suggestion, their eyes are big and stern, and they're not even smiling.

'Rolan and Moira made it all the way to Edinburgh. That's much further. And you know what a snooty woman Moira is.'

Iris says this in such a way, that if Moira can do it, anyone can. But Moira oozes confidence and would probably be pleased if people notice her. And she has a bracelet.

'They got a direct train, which makes it just one border crossing. And Edinburgh is a big city, so they'll blend in a hell of a lot easier than we will out west,' Mae says.

Iris gets up, walks out of the room, then returns with an overstuffed gym bag. 'Here.' She dumps it on the floor next to Pasha. The loud thud tells Mae it's as heavy as it looks.

Pasha picks it up. 'Nan, what the. . .?'

He pulls out the contents, bit by bit. A couple of mobile phones, never used SIM cards still in their packets, more cash, a first aid kit, inflatable pillows, and most alarmingly — fake IDs.

Mae gawps at it all. 'Shit, Iris. What the hell?'

'I told you. My SAS friends owed me a favour. Now, those IDs won't hold up to proper scrutiny, but when you check into hotels or B&Bs, they should do the job. There's a bank cash card there too, with money on it, for the places that don't take cash. Same ID on that. Should be good enough for bike hire.'

'Are these night vision goggles?' Pasha holds up an alarmingly high-tech-looking pair of binoculars.

'You'll spot the drones then.'

'A tent?' Mae says as she pulls out a tightly wrapped canvas. 'A tiny, uncomfortable tent. Iris, why have you put this bag together?'

'I started a month ago. Just in case. There's power bars too. Solar chargers, and oh, just a few other bits and bobs. And that is a printout of the fashions in each county, so you really won't have any trouble blending in. There's a grooming kit in there too, in case you need to cut your hair. It's all very well looking a bit scruffy in Berkshire when you sound like you're from here. But in other counties, you'll need to be presentable to stave off those pesky Society Police. Though I hear some counties have more enthusiastic ones than others.'

'This is all great, Nan. Thank you.'

Mae stares at Pasha, lost for words. This isn't a gift they want or can even use. They can't be serious. It's hardly Christmas and they're receiving new socks. This implies that they're actually going to go on the run, with illegal IDs, ditching their jobs.

'You should leave now,' Iris says. 'As soon as you can. I mean it. After the riots today, I wouldn't be surprised if they shut down borders and public transport. It'll be martial law before you know it.'

Mae scoffs. 'I'm sure it won't come to that.' Leaving the county is worse than martial law anyway, she thinks, but doesn't dare say.

'We can't risk it, Mae,' Pasha says. 'She's right. If we could find somewhere to hide out until the exemption comes through—'

'If,' she snaps. '*If* it comes through. What do we do if it doesn't? The baby will be taken away and we'll be in prison.'

'Stay in the hippy place, I guess.'

'Forever? Pasha, I can't. I just can't. What about work, our apartment, our friends? Everything familiar about Berkshire?' Her voice cracks. How can they not understand how ridiculous this is?

He takes her hands, then holds them to his chest.

'Trust me, Mae. You trust me, don't you?'

She swallows back a lump in her throat. Of course, she trusts him. That isn't the issue. It's the rest of the Society she doesn't trust. The overzealous Society Police, the changing laws, and their lack of funds. Even with Iris's generosity, they still need an income. He squeezes her hands tighter, breaking down the wall between them with his warmth. His eyes bore into her even when she can't lift her chin to look at his. Trust him? Trusting people is for fools, she knows this. She looks up, her eyes meet his. They're sincere, protective, all the things she loves about him.

Yeah, she's a fool. She nods.

'Let's do this,' he says. 'It'll be fine.'

Chapter 15

Part 3

Devolved is evolved. Your county is your home. Citizens of the
Society must support their local economies.
Manifesto pledge of the Eyes Forward.

***

'Why do I feel like you and Iris planned this whole thing?'
Mae says as they sit in uncomfortable seats complete with
stuck-on old chewing gum and a smell of burning plastic.

'What?' Pasha says.

'The getaway. To force me out of Berkshire. You're hardly
some globetrotter.'

'We didn't plan anything,' he says with a shrug. 'Maybe it's
just the hormones.'

Her shoulders tighten. 'Don't dismiss my worries as "hormones." I am allowed to have feelings, doubts. I am allowed to question this madness.'

'I didn't plan anything. But listen, we're in this together, Mae. You and me. We'll get through this together. No lies, I promise.'

She gives him the side-eye and keeps her mouth shut.

The train is much quieter than the London one. Midday on a Monday isn't a busy time to travel, and heading west — who does that? They'd spent Sunday packing meagre possessions, Mae fretting about clothes, since her body is not the same now as it will be in a few months, and she has no idea how long they will be away. The most beneficial research they managed to do was on fashions of each area, and it seems that one type of clothing is passable anywhere: hiking clothes. In each county, doesn't matter where in the Society, people wear hiking clothes if going hiking. Pasha's face was like a revelation.

'This is perfect. We can blend in anywhere. We just have to look like we're going out for a countryside walk.'

'Which will be fine when we actually are, but what happens at night if we need to go to the supermarket? We'll look completely out of place. And do women five months pregnant go hiking?'

'It's only a few days, a week max till we make it to the drone-free village.'

'You're still assuming such a place exists. Your nan and her make-believe hacker contacts are our sole source of information.'

'She wouldn't send us on some wild goose chase. She wants us to be safe.'

He has a point. Iris may talk wistfully about days when she used to travel, before crossing counties became taboo, before economies were devolved to such small radiuses, when Britain was a country not the Society. But she wouldn't endanger them for the sake of nostalgia. 'Those were the days,' she'd say, her inner spark still burning for her younger days. 'Things just aren't the same anymore.'

Things not being the same is something Mae can relate to.

Out the window, countryside whizzes by, miles of fields covered in sheeting, a white expanse like some ghostly mask. It's nothing like the industrial units and old housing she's used to seeing.

Already she's nervous, tapping her foot, pinging that band around her wrist. 'What about drones?' she asks.

'What about them?'

'If an Eyes Forward drone sees us, they might scan us, and they'll know we're away from home.'

'It's not illegal to travel.'

'No, but it's not *normal*. They'll want to know why. What are we meant to say? We just fancied some west country air? Come on, Pasha. You know that won't cut it. I'm pregnant, remember?'

'It's not illegal to be pregnant.'

'And what if martial law does come in? What are we meant to do then?'

He puts a finger over her mouth, like children do when they're being quiet. He smiles his easy smile. 'We have to try. Don't worry about Society Police or anyone else. It's just you and me, Mae-bug. Just you and me.'

She feels calmer at this, his vague words reducing her hysteria. The inexplicable trust she feels slowing her heart rate and regulating her breath.

Pasha rummages in his rucksack, and Mae relaxes slightly as she hears the rattle of pill bottles. At least that's one thing he remembered to pack. He takes out their new IDs, then inspects them, forcing a smile.

'Holly and Christian Brown.'

'We're *married?*'

'I take it that if I get down on one knee, that's a firm no then?'

She eyes him for a minute, just to be sure he's joking. 'I would just prefer to be actually married before I'm fake married to a man who impregnated his brother's wife.'

'You're really not letting that go, are you?'

She snatches the ID off him and examines her picture. It's the same as her driving licence, almost. In mirror image, her hair is photoshopped to look tidier, less red, just enough changes to make it a unique image that wouldn't flag up as a duplicate on any system.

'Holly. Sounds like a name from Iris's era,' she says, biting her cheek. 'And Christian. . . *Christian?* Is she trying to tout some religious message?'

'Don't read too much into it. They're just names. At least our date of births are the same. One less thing to remember.'

Holly. She repeats the name in her head over and over, trying to make it sound natural, cocking her head in a way that Holly would, crossing her legs, smiling in a Holly kind of way. But she doesn't feel like a Holly. Or maybe she does. A prickly shrub with poisonous berries. It's hard not to read too much into that.

The sub 400 carriage has seats less comfortable than their apartment sofa and is less welcoming than a takeaway two minutes before closing. The sparse other passengers look up from their devices intermittently to view them with scrutiny. They definitely stand out as odd, Mae is convinced.

Without their own devices to keep their attention, engaging in conversation, she's half-surprised the passengers aren't loading up their Society Police apps already. The phones Iris gave them are 'for calls and texts only,' under her strict instructions. No internet, nothing that can trace them. As if she thinks drones will actually be tracking them down for the next few months. They have them just to let her know they arrive safely, and so she can message them any updates in the laws or when their exemption comes through.

Months ahead without internet, social media, or any contact with the outside world. Mae is on the fence. The thought of being somewhere so alien makes her squirm, but the isolation could be a little mental detox. Yet, with all the changes in the world, the anxiety of not knowing could also be too much.

The train's upholstery is weathered, worn down, and thread-bare, holding permanent arse imprints dating back thirty years by the look of it. She keeps her hands on her lap and tries to shut out the edges of her vision. Her seat is number twenty-two, Pasha's is twenty-three. She recites those numbers, counting the rows to the exit. The windows are grimy, probably for the best, thinks Mae. The endless view of plastic sheeting is more monotonous than the slow lane in Reading town centre. Every bump aggravates Mae's bladder, but the state of the toilets makes her seal up like a clam. The thinly stuffed seats are upholstered in red and orange, like that's a colour combination that worked years ago. Mae's eyes water just looking at it, makes it feel like her back is shedding skin. The promised train upgrades over the years never happened, the lack of investment clear from the sticky patches on the walls and erratic speed of the struggling engine. Fewer and fewer people travel out of county. These old trains useful for so few jobs that require such excursions.

Conversation keeps her thoughts on track, away from the mental discomfort of the migraine-inducing furnishings and the impossible distance they are from the safety of home. But conversation is limited to Pasha, and Pasha, as always, feels quite at home.

'I hear Somerset is really chic, photo opportunities every-where. Cute little bridges over little streams,' he says with a contemplative gaze.

'I think you're reading tourist articles from the last century. It's mostly flooded and has an even older demographic than Berkshire.'

'Well, I am looking forward to finding these quaint little gems. As a keen hiking couple, we should enjoy the great outdoors.'

She leans in close and whispers, 'Except you hate walking anywhere, and I hate walking anywhere that isn't necessary. Walking in the grubby countryside for no reason is a mad person's pastime.'

'Holly doesn't think so. Holly loves hiking.'

'Shut up, Pasha.'

'Well, we can take some photos. Make it look like we're enjoying it.'

'With what shall we take these wonderful photos?'

He bites his lip. 'Good point. These old phones definitely don't take photos.'

The train bumps along for two hours before they arrive at Weston-Super-Mare, half an hour behind schedule. Not that they're in a hurry, Mae reminds herself. She's hardly racing to join the hippy camp that worships the nineteenth century.

As they draw closer to the station, Mae checks the information Iris gave them. She takes down her plait and attempts to arrange it into a ponytail. Harder than it seems, the pictures don't come with instructions. Pasha tries to help but makes more of a mess of it than she does. In the end, she does her best and puts her hiking hat on.

'Beautiful,' Pasha says.

'Put your hat on too,' she says.

Alighting the train, the station boasts they have arrived at *The edge of Somerset, the county where no one needs to leave*. Yellow flags with a red dragon fly from the corners of the building, looking more menacing than welcoming, seeing off the people in the train station rather than convincing them to stay. Alongside are more posters boasting, *Where nature and culture become one*. Mae's morning sickness starts to kick in late as she reads that, whereas Pasha seems to think it's the most profound thing he's ever heard, much more so than Berkshire's *Where everyone can excel* sign that adorns all of their stations and county propaganda, along with its claim of having the highest average Life Score of any county.

Taking a brief glance around the few people at the station, Mae takes in the appearance of the population of Somerset. Duffel coats with large buttons, the hair in tight, low ponytails, exactly as Iris's pictures show. Mae fiddles with her raincoat and base layer underneath, straightening them out, trying to look tidy, wishing she had a duffel coat instead. Another hiker sits in a café sipping a coffee, wearing almost the exact same outfit as Pasha, which puts Mae a little more at ease. Still, she treads swiftly through the station, her walking poles make a tinny clang against the hard floor, Pasha's louder. They make their way to the exit, then step out into the new county.

Chapter 16

The town doesn't smell like Reading. It smells of stagnant water, and the din of screeching birds is the loudest she's known. The pavements are quieter but disorganised, no lanes to divide people, just a kerfuffle of mixed speeds, slower people in the way of faster ones trying to squeeze past. Inefficient and unpredictable. Delivery drones are less frequent and the ones that do fly past do so erratically, like they're older models, swerving with inefficiency. Mae and Pasha wait a moment, assess the etiquette, then file in behind a few medium-paced individuals.

'This is weird, Pasha.'

'Different, Mae, not weird.'

Every commercial window seems to sell chips and little else, and her sub 400 Score is welcome everywhere. She can't see anywhere that caters for the high Scores. This should make Mae feel more welcome, but instead, she feels like she is scurrying around a ditch. She's used to being one of the poorest and knowing her place. This feels like a disordered free for all. Her stomach growls, but the thought of a box of grease is not what she wants. Her bladder is screaming at her, though, so after a few minutes they stop at a café that is quiet enough, and of course, caters to their Life Score. Instinctively, Pasha reaches for his phone to check where they are, then remembers, they're on internet blackout.

'Not to worry,' he says. 'I checked the way before we left. We just need to follow the coast south. I guess it'll be obvious when we're at the coast, and then as long as we head southwest, we'll come to the edge of Somerset.'

She checks her watch, an old analogue style that Iris gave her. No heart rate sensor, no fitness data, nothing trackable, just a couple of hands walking their way round the face.

'It's one o'clock,' she says. 'I really, *really* don't want to stay in a tent. It's cold, I'm cold, and it looks like rain is coming. Maybe we can find a hotel or something?'

'Sure. There's bound to be hotels along the coast. Our parents took us to one when Ro and I were kids.'

'Really?' her eyes bulge. 'You went to the seaside?'

'Yeah. A holiday. Was fun. I remember our folks moaning about how dirty it was, and we got sunburned.'

'Sounds horrific.'

'We were kids. We had a great time. People weren't so weird about county borders then. It was just before the county lines were fenced. Anyway, it was ages ago. After that, all our holidays were in Berkshire.'

'Glad your folks saw sense eventually.'

He laughs at her, then goes to order some food. Beyond the grease and cheap disinfectant, she can smell it. The moisture, the mossy smell, but not like normal Berkshire, countryside moss. The dampness isn't like when it rains on the pavement back home. Somehow, dare she think, *fresher?* Less humid, maybe. Though fresher, not entirely more pleasant. Disagreeable undertones of fish make the fresher notes fusty and sour. And the noise is less of a hum and more of a choir of screeches. The vocal birds overhead land on a bollard right by her. They're massive. Unblinking eyes watching her like she's their lunch.

Everyone who walks past wears duffel coats, mostly navy blue with faux fur around the neckline and little badges of the local flag pinned to their lapel. It's cooler here than it was in Reading, the wind harsher. Through the glass of the café, people arch diagonally against the gale. No, she says to herself. We will definitely not be sleeping in a tent.

'So,' Pasha says when he returns, cups of tea in hand. 'I asked the waiter about places to stay, and he recommends a street a couple of miles from here. A few hotels and B&Bs there. How's that? Just a short walk today, a decent rest tonight, then we'll be all fresh tomorrow.'

'So, the waiter knows we're not from this county?'

'I told him we're from the other side of the county.'

'And he believed you? Your accent, though—'

'It was fine. He didn't seem to care. Look around, no Society Police here. No one is paying us any attention. We're okay, relax.'

No Society Police visible, sure, but the posters are everywhere. The Eyes Forward logo on every wall. The taboo of crossing a county border is so entrenched, she feels like a criminal. Still, the enthusiasm in his eyes makes it hard for her to be grumpy for long. Hot tea in her hands, and a warm bed not far away. They could shut themselves away in a private room, snuggle up, pretend whatever is outside doesn't matter. For the moments while she drinks her tea, she tries to believe this. Once inside, the outside will just melt away.

After Mae has used the toilet, they start the walk along the coast to the hotel. It's slow, cold, and smelly. Pasha convinces her to walk on the sand, but after a few minutes, her shoes turn gritty and her feet are sore. It smells like a clogged drain laced with a ton of salt. They stop a while and stare at the beach.

'I remember the beach being nicer when I was a kid,' Pasha says, sadness in his tone.

Mae struggles to imagine how it could ever look nice. The tide is long out, just a browny-orange sand swamp that goes on forever. His disappointment makes her feel sorry for him. Not much, just a little. Coming here was still his stupid idea, after all.

She loops her arm in his. 'Come on,' she says. 'Let's get to the hotel.'

The wind dies off, and the remainder of their walk isn't overly unpleasant. Birds seem less numerous next to the sea than they do a few streets inland, concentrating their numbers around the eateries and bins. The familiar *All Eyes Are Our Eyes* posters are plastered on every street corner, every bus stop, the blinkered eye symbol alongside. But that's all that is familiar about the town. The roads are more packed than Berkshire. Cars beeping and crawling along, even slower than the pedestrians often. A lack of bikes and buses, Mae thinks. Seems strange, to clog up the road so much with individual vehicles. The lack of Society Police is odd, but very welcome. People have their phones in hand, but they inspect each other less, not raising their cameras, keeping them by their sides. Old CCTV cameras hang off on their hinges. Only here, the Life Score points awarded for informants are not displayed.

'Maybe they don't award points here?' Pasha leans in, speaking quietly. 'Such laws are devolved. I'll bet no one bothers snitching if there are no points in it for them.'

'Or maybe there's no crime?'

The kicked over bins and graffiti on walls imply otherwise. The duffel coats they all wear look years old, re-stitched and mended. Along the seafront, commercial windows are boarded up and lined with newspaper, *closing down sale* still readable through the smudges and smears. Every eatery they pass still predominantly sells chips, some advertising different sauces, each saying they welcome all Life Scores.

The lack of aspiration sends a chill across Mae's shoulders. She looks down at her hiking clothes, feeling expensively out of place. Her meagre sub 400 Score here seems extravagant. The wind has messed up the ends of her hair and it itches her neck. A ponytail seems an inconvenient hairstyle of choice in a windy coastal town, not to mention unglamorous. She tries to imagine Sadie sporting such a style, her manicured nails tying her hair with just one simple band. It seems unornate, overly simple, and irritating. She flicks it off her shoulders for the hundredth time, her red locks tacky from salt deposits.

The slow shuffle of pavement traffic isn't too claustrophobic. People give them a wide berth, more so than they do each other. The oldest seem to be able to walk a bit quicker than they do in Berkshire, or maybe they're just running away from them? Mae's paranoia runs riot every time she tries to take in her surroundings. It's just different, she reminds herself. That's all. Just different.

Eventually they arrive at a road hosting several bed and break-fasts, *rooms available* signs swaying in the breeze on creaky hinges. The gardens out front wilt with neglect, and unpruned trees mingle with dead ones, weeds outnumbering flowers. They choose the one that appears the least awful, then walk down the pathway, peeling spiders' webs off their faces as they do.

Inside, the place smells similar to Uncle Charlie's care home, with dimmer lighting and more questionable carpet. The whole place is decorated in maroon, like the walls are angry with them. Mae's shoulders tense and she shivers.

'Can I help you?'

They hear the voice a long time before they see its owner. So tiny, she sneaks up on them, her head only just visible behind the reception desk.

'Erm, hi,' Pasha says to the frizzy grey hair. 'We'd like a room.'

'A room? You know it's not even holiday season.'

'I know. We thought it would be a nice, quiet time to come.'

She chokes on a laugh. 'Oh, we're always quiet, duckie. Just the weather is worse for you, that's all. Not many people come visiting this way anymore.'

'Oh, that's a shame. It's quite lovely.'

He sounds so genuine, even Mae believes him. How is it he can say such untruths so easily? She finds it easier to not speak at all than to embellish the truth.

'Aren't you a sweetie,' the voice from the hair says. 'Where you from, anyway?'

'Other end of the county,' he says quickly. Too quickly. 'Near Bath.'

'Well, lovely to have a nice young couple come down this way. Sign in here.'

She passes them a guest book of empty, yellowing pages. Mae takes the pen and signs *Holly Brown*. Well, she thinks, not all lies are that hard. Writing them is easier than saying them, anyway.

Pasha looks at her and nods before taking the pen. *Christian Brown*.

A crucifix hangs above the reception desk. The lady sees Pasha's name, and her forehead becomes visible as she tilts her head back to glance at it. 'Holly and Christian,' the woman says as she peers at the guest book through thick glasses, the folds of her skin keeping them in place. 'Nice names. I never forget names. Not so good with faces. My eyes don't work like they used to. But names I can do.' Her eyebrows raise and Mae assumes she's smiling. 'Nice to meet you. I'm Cynthia and this is Dudley.' She points to a large photo on the wall of a rotund man with a kind face.

'Nice to meet you, Cynthia,' Mae says, then swallows before addressing the photo. 'And nice to meet you, Dudley.'

'You be staying long?' Cynthia asks.

'Just one night.'

'Ah. That's a shame. Be nice if you stayed longer.' She steps around the reception desk and her whole head comes into view. Below the grey frizz is a face as wrinkled as a cabbage, with cloudy eyes the colour of her pale skin.

'Sorry. We can't stay longer, I'm afraid,' Pasha says. 'We're trying to walk around the whole county.'

'Well, you'll have a nice time here. Folks are friendly enough. Or they were. They might seem suspicious, but that's just because they don't want no one snatching them for this donation nonsense.' She looks them up and down slowly, examining every inch. Her accent lingers on the Rs and her vowels seem muddled up. 'You wouldn't be here for such things, would you?'

'No, of course not,' says Mae, speaking quietly, not daring to attempt the accent.

'Where'd you say you're from again?'

'Other end of the county, near Bath.' Pasha jumps in before Mae has time to slip-up.

'Esme, who runs the café over the road, nice lady, but a bit of a gossip. She's from Bath, originally. You know her?'

'Not that I can think of. It's quite a busy city.'

'Hm,' she says, twitching her thin lips. 'Well, here's your key. You can pay when you leave, in case you want to stay a bit longer. Nice to have some young folk round here. You hungry? I could do you some chips.'

'Oh, I think we're fine. Might just order a takeaway later,' says Mae, feeling hot now. The coolness of outside long dissipated and the stuffiness of the reception is suffocating. She fans her jacket, fidgets on the spot, rearranges her hat as beads of sweat collect at the rim.

'There's no takeaways.' Cynthia steps closer and shakes her head. 'Best you'll get is chips. And my chips are as good as any other. Or have you young folk gone all American and call them fries?'

'Chips would be fine. Okay, thanks.' Mae agrees and backs away, needing a window, some air, some space.

'Sauce?' the word sounds less like a word and more like a noise the birds were making.

'Excuse me?' Pasha says.

'You want sauce?'

'Sure. Thanks.'

'And what about your breakfast? Eggs?'

'Some toast would be fine,' says Mae, the thought of eggs making her want to heave. The place smells musty enough without eggs adding to the aroma.

'You need your energy,' Cynthia says, 'all that walking. Beans on toast? Tea or coffee?'

Mae nods and backs away further. 'Okay, beans. Yes, thanks. Have you Costa Rican coffee?'

'Cloths a reakin? What are you trying to mean?'

'Nothing!' Mae says. 'It's a coffee. But yeah, any coffee is fine.'

'Lovely, duckie. I'll bring your chips up in a few moments. Hot water's off. I'll turn it on now, but it'll take an hour. Your room is at the top of the stairs. Have a nice stay.'

Pasha takes the key, then carries their bags up the stairs. The frayed carpet snags on their shoes so they step gingerly. The floorboards are lumpy underfoot and a draft blows up from the skirting board. Mae counts the stairs, sixteen, eight first, then another eight around a corner. Another eight steps to the reception desk from the front door. She saw a documentary once that said in new places, it's best to count your steps in case there is a fire. She doesn't need more motivation to count anything, but if anyone ever catches her, it's a good excuse.

The maroon continues, garishly so, and on the landing the dim flickering bulbs are even less inviting than downstairs. Their door is directly opposite the stairs, luckily. Mae doesn't fancy a walk down the hallway that wouldn't look out of place in a horror movie. Pasha puts the key in the door and they both tense, bracing themselves for what room they're paying to stay in looks like.

The room is surprisingly pleasant, photo frames of rolling hill landscapes hanging from the walls, a chesterfield in the corner. It's fresher smelling than the dank reception. It faces the sea, and the last of the day's sun beams in through the window. To Mae's relief, the maroon has ended and the pale yellow walls are much more relaxing. She walks to the window and opens it, leaning her head out and breathing in some cool air. The birds are loud again, squawking their evening chorus. She can just about hear the waves lapping the shore in the distance. Not so bad. Maybe she can cope with new places. She sits on the edge of the bed and removes her walking boots, shakes out the sand, then lies back. It's as comfortable as a bed can be.

'Was going to charge these phones, but the batteries are full,' says Pasha, inspecting the blocky devices.

'Well, it's not like we can use them for anything.'

'Maybe I should call Nan? Let her know where we are.'

'She's definitely bugged us or put trackers on us somehow.'

Pasha laughs and lies on the bed next to her, one hand resting on her stomach, giving a gentle squeeze. 'The hotel owner was quite nosy.'

'Yeah. And I guess we're eating chips then.'

'With sauce,' he says, mimicking Cynthia, and they laugh.

Pasha gets up to unpack, while Mae pulls her knees into her chest to stretch her glutes. They've not walked far, but tomorrow, who knows? She tells her body to relax, but they haven't crossed a county border yet. Not on foot, anyway. On the walls of the room hang pictures of Somerset, the towns and countryside. On a cushion is embroidered in delicate stitching, *Somerset, the county where no one needs to leave*. However comfortable the room is, Mae can't feel at home.

There's a knock at the door and Cynthia doesn't wait for an answer before coming in.

'Got your chips. And I've bought three types of sauces, no extra. I'll just charge for the one. I'll lay them on the dresser here. Some forks there for you as well, one each. So you don't have to share.'

'That's great. Thanks Cynthia,' Mae says.

'Breakfast is at eight. Suit you both? I'll bring it up to you.'

'Perfect. We'll just be having an early night,' Pasha says, in a cheerful hint for her to leave.

Cynthia seems to understand, or was going to leave anyway, as she exits, not shutting the door behind her. Pasha gets up, closes it, then leans against it, letting all the breath he has in his lungs out before giggling.

'She is quite a character,' he says, walking over to the chips.

When Mae has stopped laughing, she joins him at the dresser. 'Taste one, they okay?'

'They're just chips. They're hot and salty.'

'Mmm. Sounds perfect,' Mae replies with a grin. She eats one but is hungrier than she thought and devours over half. 'It seems the baby likes chips then.'

Pasha looks at the TV in the corner of the room, wide framed like it was at least fifty years old, a thick layer of dust over the screen. He switches it on. 'I was just thinking about the weather.'

'How very British of you.'

He smirks. 'Be good to know if it's going to rain for our journey tomorrow.'

Mae eats the last chip, then lies back on the bed, touching her toes and stretching her hamstrings. 'How far is it tomorrow?'

'As far as we can get. We can hire bikes from this town and just see how far we manage. It's about sixty miles to the county line.'

'We're hikers, though. Wouldn't we walk?'

'We can say we are biking to the start of our walk,' he says with perfect confidence. 'We'll collect the bikes here, then dump them before we get to the next county and hike over the border.'

'I don't think I can do sixty miles tomorrow.'

'We don't have to. Just see how we go. Nice and easy.' He finds a weather channel and watches a moment. 'Look, at least it's going to be dry. And when we've had enough, we can find somewhere to stay. Or find somewhere to camp. Get all cosy next to a fire, snuggle up in the tent. . .' He wraps his arms around her and pulls her close. 'It'll be easy. I'm sure of it.'

Where she should be nervous and agitated with her new surroundings, she feels at ease in his embrace. She lets her wall down, not by force, it just melts away for a moment. The rigidity she normally feels loosens for a few moments. Tiredness, probably. Maybe her worries have just run out. Maybe being in new places can be more exciting than terrifying. She presses her cheek on his and breathes him in. Safe. That's how she feels right now. Safe.

Chapter 17

The following morning, Cynthia knocks and comes straight in again, punctual and impatient, a loaded tray jiggling along with her wobbly footsteps.

'Here's your lovely beans on toast and coffee, duckies.'

The coffee smells like scorched paper, but Mae thanks her as she puts it on the dresser.

'Now, when you're off exploring today, don't you mind those young lads in their black jumpers. They're not doing any harm. We don't want no Society Police snitching on what they're up to, understand? I hear about them Society Police in the cities, how everyone is on it, spying on each other, snitching on this and that, sticking their noses in. But we're a community here. We rely on them boys. Hard for city folk to understand, but those lads are doing us a service. Helping out the old timers, now that the pharmacies are all closed.'

'We understand,' Mae says. 'And it's fine, really—'

'We all liked the Eyes Forward bunch when they first came in,' Cynthia carries on. 'Although, only looking to the future seems a bit harsh on those of us who haven't got long left. But no more of that left and right nonsense,' she says, gesturing side-to-side, the wrong way, Mae notes. 'Seemed sensible, really. It seemed a great idea: no more babies. Or less babies, anyway. Too many people, that's the problem. But killing us elders to make room for babies is wrong if you ask me.'

'We couldn't agree more,' Pasha says. 'Really.'

'Here I am, talking your ears off again and you're probably hungry and want to get going. I've left your bill with your breakfast so you can pay cash, if that's all right? Prefer cash round these parts. I can take card if that's all you've got. The machine is downstairs, but cash is my preference.'

'We can do cash. Thanks,' Mae says.

'Jolly good. Just pay at the desk when you're ready. Nice to have you here. We don't get many young folk around here visiting anymore. Where'd you say you're from again?'

'Near Bath,' Pasha says.

'Ah, that's right. Well, pop in and see Esme. She's in the café over the road. She's from Bath originally.'

'Will do, if we have time.'

'Nice to have young folk. Funny really. When I was young, we used to get fed up with all the visitors. Thousands we used to get during the busy seasons, from all over the Society. Now it's so quiet. No one leaves their own turf anymore. Thought that would be a good thing at first. Keep the town nicer, bit more peaceful like. But locals don't need to stay here, do they? They drive in and out. So many businesses gone. You understand? Probably hard to fathom when you're from a big city with all them Life Score people over 400. Bet you even know some 600 or 700s? Probably know some of them Preserved too?'

'Not many, a few,' Mae says, shifting in her seat.

'Well, you won't find any of that round here. No one's got the Score for such things. Left to rot, we all are. Anyway, I'll leave you to your breakfast. And if you want to stay another night, you'd be more than welcome.'

She leaves without closing the door again. Mae walks over and inspects the beans on toast. It was probably hot when she brought it in, but now the food sits limp and soggy on the plate, as unappetising as the stale smelling coffee.

'If we don't eat here, we might end up eating at the café with Esme, quizzing us on our Bath knowledge,' says Pasha as he makes pitiful eyes at the breakfast. 'You feeling okay?'

'I was. Not sure now I've seen the food.'

'Few bites and see how it goes?'

'You practicing your fathering skills on me?'

He grins and puts his arm around her. 'It is exciting, isn't it? To think we'll have a whole new tiny person soon.'

'Sh. She didn't shut the door and is definitely the type to eavesdrop.'

He cuts a piece of toast, then eats it with some beans. 'Not so bad. Eat up.' He sips the coffee and winces. 'Maybe we can just pour that down the sink.'

When they've eaten and poured the coffee away, Pasha takes their bags down the stairs, trying but failing to avoid scuffing the paintwork as the bags brush along the walls, and they make their way to the reception desk, cash in hand, ready to leave.

'Breakfast all right, was it?' Cynthia asks.

'Delicious. Thank you.' Pasha hands her the cash.

'Can't tempt you to stay another night then?'

'No, thank you. Maybe some other time.'

'Oh, I hope you mean that. Not many visitors these days. My own kids and grandchildren don't even visit now, not since the inheritance tax law changed. Not that I've got much to leave besides this place, but they were hoping to cash-in, I guess. You know Esme, from Bath?'

'You've mentioned her.'

'Well, she says it's good. Now she knows her family are coming to see her because they want to see her, not just hovering over her waiting for her to die and making sure they stay in her will. But then, her family still visits. That's nice for her, though. She deserves it.'

'As you do, I'm sure,' Mae says.

'I suspect the oldies in the city all live a lot longer, all on that new-fangled drug, I assume. They have the Life Scores to pay for it. I know they say they're going to monitor it, but you can do what you want if your Score is high enough. Not natural, I don't think, living that long, looking thirty when you're a hundred, living to nearly two hundred. Not God's plan. I wouldn't want to live another seventy years, anyway. I don't want to be away from my Dudley that long. He'd be cross when I got to him, waiting decades and decades. Still, I wouldn't mind younger knees.'

'It really has been a pleasure, Cynthia,' Mae says, with the sort of authority in her voice she reserves for her most talkative clients at work.

'Yes, Cynthia, we must get going,' Pasha says as they walk towards the door. 'Thank you so much.'

They shut the door behind them and instantly relax. The sea air blows away the musty smell from the hotel, taking the stuffy heat with it. Across the road, they spot Esme's café and opt to walk quickly past it, and past the "black jumper wearing lads," as Cynthia had put it. The queue of people waiting for their exchange is longer than the ones Mae has seen in Reading, the people frailer. Her thoughts go to Iris, her lack of medication, her heart condition.

'Maybe we should call your nan,' she says. 'Make sure she's okay without her meds.'

'We will. In a few days. If we call too soon, she'll worry.'

The tide has changed completely to when they arrived and the gentlest of waves roll against the shore. The cloud-dappled morning sun casts feeble glints on the water. With the lack of wind, the rest of the sea is smooth and calm, reflecting the sky back, and the stagnant water smell has gone. Just a fresh saltiness remains. The birds are noisy as ever, but Mae can forgive that.

When Esme's café is out of sight, they pause for a moment and just stare at the water. A few birds bob on the surface as boats linger in the distance. Three of them, Mae counts, out of habit rather than necessity right then. Pasha's arm hangs at her hip, hers at his.

For a moment, she really believes that maybe going to strange places isn't the worst thing in the world.

Chapter 18

The hire bikes are different to their usual ones: heavier, firmer saddles, squeaky chains. The electric is less helpful than what Mae is used to as well. They strap their bags to the back racks and get going, the lack of wind at least giving them an easier job. As they ride away from the seafront and farther from town, the traffic thins, then runs out completely. For the first time that Mae can remember, they are alone. No other bikes, no cars or buses on their tail, no pedestrians to dodge. Without crowds of people around, she can breathe deeper, can think louder, go at her own pace. Although, despite their solitude, she feels more eyes on her than when she did in the crowd. At least with other people visible, she can see where the eyes are. Now, she can feel glances creeping up her back, making every hair on her body stand on end. She checks behind them every few seconds, glancing side-to-side always, relying on Pasha to watch the way ahead. Alone? How is that possible? Besides indoors, they're never really alone.

Despite some rolling hills, the electric on the bikes holds up and the miles slip away, Mae's legs coping well, Pasha taking the lion's share of the luggage. He checks the map rarely, relying on following the coast and sun for navigation. Road signs don't mention the next county ever. It's like the world ends at the county line. Maybe it does? They wouldn't know for sure. Could be a cliff edge or black hole at the border for all they know. The local council would see directing people to another county as betraying their own economy. But Pasha has memorised the border towns and villages and is sure they are heading more or less in the right direction.

Out here, where paving slabs outnumber people, there are no old CCTV cameras dangling from the brickwork, no Society Police reminders. Well, hardly any, anyway. There are still bus stops and advertising billboards adjacent, the blinkered eye displayed, *All Eyes Are Our Eyes* written underneath. Occasionally, the polished face of an Eyes Forward MP glares at them, smiling in what is supposed to be an authoritative way, but appears more menacing. Yet such displays and advertisements are occasional, not on every street corner like they are in a busy town.

With the beans repeating on her for part of the morning, Mae's mind is mostly distracted with keeping her nausea at bay. Breathing in the sea air certainly seems to help, but after they've been riding for over an hour, she's exhausted. Lack of nutritious food saps her energy, and her vitamin tablets aren't enough to make up the difference.

Their route takes them inland to avoid a river, and they arrive at the town of Bridgwater. Busy, the town appears to bustle and churn in the same way Reading does, only not really like Reading. Less orderly, more engine noise. The transition from quiet countryside to bustling town catches Mae off-guard. The change in volume makes her muscles stiffen, flinching at the sight of drones again.

'Just stuff, delivery drones,' says Pasha as he scans the sky.

Pedestrians stop and stare at them as they ride past; Mae's sure their hiking gear while cycling makes them stand out. That and their age. The local demographic makes Weston-Super-Mare look like a nursery. The traffic is busy, noisy, trails of tiny cars weaving through the odd bus, speed bumps ignored, horns blaring. Mae tucks in behind Pasha and only manages to talk to him while they stop at some traffic lights.

'Pasha, it's so loud. Everyone is staring.'

'Just keep looking ahead. Doesn't matter.'

Tricycles outnumber bicycles, tandems are even more common. But despite their number, the total is few. *Thank God*, Mae thinks. The sluggish speed they were travelling at would make more bikes seem almost stationary. Crawling along almost at walking pace gives everyone too long to gawp at them, confused eyes following as they try to sneak past. Mae ducks her head, Pasha looks to the side. But they both see it. The elbow nudges, the pointing. They hear the gasps and the curious whispers. Even the deafening racket of the cars isn't enough to drown out the gossip.

Pasha decides a busy town centre is a good place to dissolve into the masses on foot, and Mae is too tired and hungry to argue. They find the nearest bike charge station to deposit the bikes, then head to the café next door. The sun glaring on the window makes it impossible to see what it's like inside. *Perfect*. No one outside will notice them. Like in the previous town, all the eateries say any Life Score welcome.

Mae makes a beeline for the corner table next to the window. Inside is empty, the quiet hour between breakfast and lunch. In Reading, brunch can be the busiest time, certainly on the weekends. But on this Tuesday, everyone has somewhere else to be. Outside the window, the town centre consists of thrift stores and boarded-up pharmacies. The same jumble of people as the previous towns, no organised lanes, everyone weaving everywhere. Must be a Somerset thing, she thinks. Unlike Weston-Super-Mare, this town serves more than just chips. According to the chalk board hanging crooked above the counter, it also has some sausages and pies, as well as salads. Mae shivers as she acclimatises, then quickly turns overheated.

'Anything you like the look of?' Pasha says.

'Is it weird that I quite fancy chips?'

'Ha! Go for it. Maybe some other stuff too. Might as well fill up.'

They sit for some time without being served, pushing around the salt and pepper, tapping their hands on the table. No sound from the kitchen, no sign of any waiter. After twenty minutes, and some sorrowful looks from Mae, Pasha gets up and leans over the counter.

'Hello?'

He's greeted with silence, so he looks over at Mae.

'Maybe they're shut?' she says.

'Hello?' he calls again.

Some footsteps trudge closer and a door behind the counter opens. A middle-aged woman with tired eyes and stained tabard approaches, face full of bewilderment. 'What? You lost or something?'

'No, we'd like to order.'

'For your grandparent or someone, I assume? Or are you one of them? The bloody elders on that young drug?'

'What? No. We'd like some food.'

'Food!' She laughs for a while, then takes in Pasha's earnest face. 'Really? Oh. You're not from around here, are you?'

'No. Bath. Just seeing the sights of the county.'

She gasps and recoils, backing into the door. 'You're one of them, aren't you? Old folk kidnappers!'

'No! No, God no. We really just want some food. We're hikers, see?' He steps back so she can observe his clothes. 'We really are just visiting this town, from Bath, and just want some food.'

She bites her cheek, narrows her eyes. 'You got cash?'

'Yes.'

'Any meds to trade? Diabetic stuff, heart tablets?'

'What? No. Really, just food for normal cash payment.'

She narrows her eyes into the thinnest of slits, then looks him up and down. 'All right, fine. Oven's not on. I'll have to heat it. What do you want?'

'Chips, sausages, vegetable pie, salad, orange juice.'

'All I've got is chips and meat pie.'

'That'll be fine then. Great.'

Pasha sits back down, speechless for a moment. Mae watched the whole conversation cowering behind the chair. 'Are we actually sitting in a drug front café?'

'So it seems.'

'Maybe we should go.'

'No. I've ordered now. That would be rude. And who knows if everywhere is the same?'

Out the window are people with black hoodies pulled up, covering most of their faces, seven of them. They walk from café to café, bulging pockets when they go in, slimline when they leave. They all appear broad and walk with uncertain feet, not the lanky youths she expects to see. Hard to make out their faces, but it seems clear enough these are not young people dealing.

'Pasha, look.'

He watches for a moment, notices their limps and slow pace. 'They're all young enough to get their meds but are just selling them on.'

'Maybe trying to pay extra tax by starting fake businesses to up their Life Score,' says Mae, as smarmy as she intends.

'You're still mad at me about that?'

She shrugs in response, hunger testing her mood.

'Look around here.' He gestures out the window. 'Who wants to up their Life Score? Nowhere cares what your Score is.'

'Mortgages do, loans do. And I'll bet these folk all have children who would benefit from a higher Scoring parent. It's not all about bars and cafés.'

Pasha leans back in his chair, folds his arms, and nods, making his 'fair enough' face: an upside-down smile and eyebrows raised. Mae isn't smug when she makes a point. She'd spend her life ridiculing him if that were the case.

The smell of cooking oil and pastry wafts to them from the kitchen, her stomach ready for it, her brain not so. She's finding it hard to pinpoint what exactly she would like to eat. A risotto, maybe. A thick wedge of creamy potato gratin, perhaps. Pie. . .not so sure.

She distracts her nose by gazing out of the window some more. The architecture of the place they cycled through wasn't dissimilar to Reading, but this square is. Dare she think it more aesthetically pleasing? White render with an attractive circular entranceway to one building, and pillars like it's from some history programme. Dilapidated somewhat, but there's an authentic beauty in that. Buildings that embrace the passing of time. There's a statue in the centre of a man looking proud, instead of the displeased Queen Victoria that Reading town centre has to offer.

She fondly remembers the lion statue in the little park, though, or what's left of it. It was supposed to commemorate a war, she seems to remember from old school days. Someone at some point didn't like that idea and chopped off two legs and his manhood. . .lionhood . . .whichever, the meat and veg.

Veg, that's what she's missing. Not the manhood kind, but some green beans, carrots, maybe some peas. Is it a craving? Probably not. What pregnancy results in a craving for vegetables? Aliya had said when she was pregnant with Candice, she craved malted milks and raisins — and reminded everyone that despite this, she sprung back to a size eight after giving birth. A desire for vegetables is more likely a sign of malnourishment than a pregnancy craving.

The shuffle of pedestrian traffic outside condenses and thins periodically, like swirling soup, or watching a starling murmuration in slow motion. There is some order in the disorder, somehow. Mae watches elders with walking sticks and frames make their way to their preferred café with empty bags. It's so brazen. No Society Police, no one even noticing, really. Mae couldn't decide if it was a good thing or bad. It's only small crimes going undetected, but what bigger ones then slip through the net?

Their food arrives, and Mae is pleasantly surprised. The meat pie contains some vegetables, the grease on the chips is minimal, and the sauce doesn't look radioactive. The waitress slams the plates down with contempt instead of pride and grunts to highlight her displeasure.

'Enjoy,' she says with enough irony to make a sitcom audience applaud. 'There's not enough food around here even for ourselves, what with these dumb Pro Grow people stopping deliveries. And now the likes of you want to come and eat our food. I'm charging you double.'

'Fair enough,' says Pasha with a shrug.

Mae thanks her and they tuck in as she stays next to them, looming over, watching every bite.

'Where you headed next anyway?' she asks as they both have their mouths full.

Pasha holds up a hand to ask for a moment to swallow. 'Along the coast for a bit, then home.'

'Where's home?'

'Near Bath,' Mae says this time. The lie said so often now she almost feels it's true.

'Well, you'd better watch yourselves. Most of the villages around here have banned young people. No pre-menopausal women allowed.'

Mae almost chokes on her second mouthful. 'That's ridiculous. They can't do that!'

'Yeah?' the woman crouches and leers her face inches away from Mae's. 'And who's gonna stop them? Some out-of-town city folk? Society Police fans, are you? Old folk murderers, are you?'

'Listen,' Pasha says, waving his finger. 'My grandfather used to love this part of the county. If you must know our business, he requested in his will that his ashes be sprinkled here.' Pasha reaches into his bag and pulls out a simple urn. Mae knows that urn, though she had no idea it was in his bag. 'Lady, meet Grandpa Angus.'

The waitress steps away from him and stares at the urn for a while, as if she expects it to explode. 'It's illegal to go around sprinkling ashes anywhere. You get sprinkled where you live as that's the place you like best. That's the rule.'

'Well, I guess we're all rule-breakers. Going to call the Society Police, are you?'

'Psst,' she hisses, then walks back to the kitchen, scuffing her feet on the lino floor.

Pasha chops his pie and shoves a large piece into his mouth, smiling at Mae so widely, pastry mushes around his teeth.

'What are you doing with your grandpa's ashes?'

'Exactly what I said. It was Nan's idea.'

'But why didn't you tell me?'

'Because it's illegal, and I didn't want you to worry.'

She moves her food around her plate, pushing it this way and that, dividing it all evenly into four sections. He's right, she would worry. And now, she is worrying.

'It feels lawless out here,' she says.

'I know. Like the Wild West.' He bounces his eyebrows.

'Well, where are we going to sprinkle them?'

'We're not for a while. If having them works a charm like that, I'll keep them till our exemption comes through. Grandpa wouldn't mind. He'd think he's on an adventure with us.'

An adventure? Why would anyone think that's a good thing? She glances at her watch. Twenty-four hours since they left Reading, and already they've had an altercation with a local and found themselves in a drug front café.

Pasha continues to rattle on between mouthfuls, about his grandpa Angus and the next town they're aiming for. Mae doesn't listen to the words, just the sound of his voice, his Berkshire accent comforting its familiarity. Heavy on the Rs and soft on the Ts. She misses home, their usual cafés, serving their usual brunch. She totals the bill in her head: thirty pounds, on top of what they spent in the hotel. All that money is going to another county, supporting their economy instead of her own. It's not like anyone from this county will go to Berkshire to balance it out.

Mae glances out of the window again, at all the boarded-up shop fronts, the eateries allowing any Life Score. Bridgwater's varying shapes of impoverishment are such a contrast to Reading's abundance. Reading boasts more 800 pluses than anywhere else. Mae hadn't considered what that meant for other counties before. Cynthia said her town had been left to rot. Not everyone around here is as mean-spirited as the café owner, surely. There must be some welcoming people around. Suspicious, sure. Understandably. Perhaps giving a little bit to this economy isn't the worst thing, she tries to justify. She manages to put food on her fork then, a few chips and some pie filling. She eats it and swallows. Not so bad.

Chapter 19

Before they set off on the bikes again, Pasha pops into a newsagent and buys a local paper. An idea that Mae dismissed immediately, insisting that physical papers don't exist anymore.

When he comes out of the shop wielding the paper, she holds her hands to her cheeks in shock. 'No way!'

'Yep. Although, you might wish I hadn't succeeded.'

He shows her the front page. 'Young person bans spread across the west of the county.'

'Crap. Can we avoid them?'

'I don't know, really. It lists them but doesn't give a map. I think we'll just have to be on alert.'

'What are they doing to people they find?'

He scans the article. 'It doesn't say. I don't think it's happened, not yet anyway. Not far from here are some camps that city people fled to. Holiday home parks, bit like that place in Pangbourne with all those wooden huts, except with armed security.'

'So, as well as dodging banned villages, we also have to dodge armed guards?'

'That's the gist. Yep. And also, this is weird. Check it out.'

He hands her the paper and Mae skims an article, her reaction not matching the tone the article intends. 'They're tattooing babies?'

'That seems to be the plan. In case anyone manages to have one illegally, I guess. All legit babies will be marked, to show they've been neutralised.'

Legit babies. Did Pasha just say that? Mae reads on and realises that yes, he definitely said that. Because that's what the article says, in black and white. It's like the world's turned medieval and is classifying babies as illegitimate if they aren't birthed via approved means. Branding babies is set to be the new norm, to stop them being murdered at birth by Enough enthusiasts, whose vociferous hate has gained so much traction that babies are the new vermin. Rats, cockroaches, mice, locusts, and children. Human beings: the great plague of the twenty-first century. Likening the government to Saint George, ready to slay the dragon. How considerate of the Eyes Forward, the paper says. Putting children's safety first.

As Mae reads on, it's clear that the danger is coming from the scourge of adults and the hate speech of the Enough campaigners. Yet it's the babies who will be burned and branded for life. Mae looks away from the paper, no point in reading more. There's no avoiding it. Without an exemption or a donor, they'll be prisoners at some hippy camp forever with a child with unbranded skin.

Mae sighs and gets on her bike. They cycle away from town, making slow progress in heavy bike traffic. The lanes aren't all partitioned from the road, and with more cars than they've ever seen, weaving and dodging vehicles makes it a stop-start arduous few miles. Pasha insists Mae goes in front so he can keep an eye on her and shield her from any cars creeping up behind. Like her armour, he claims. As Mae considers this, her skin prickles with cold. They could run into armed security any minute. What sort of weapons would they have? Pasha wouldn't be much help then. His bravado would only serve to get them in trouble.

As they leave the town behind, the weight of traffic evens out. Signs with towns and villages on them have been defaced: *No young people allowed! Fertile women STAY AWAY! Armed security patrolling this village! No menopause, no entry!* Almost every village sign has warnings plastered across it.

They stick to back roads, farmland mostly, but civilisation is unavoidable. The occasional bus stop still shows the Eyes Forward symbol, but the county seems a law unto itself. Mae rides alongside Pasha, him scanning the signs and buildings to the left, her the right.

It's less than an hour before they pass a village that has a banner out the front saying, *No under sixties welcome.*

'Reckon we can pass for sixty?' Pasha asks.

She scowls at him, shaking her head.

They pause a way ahead of the signs but only consider it for a moment. They're not close enough to the village sign for anyone to see them. From what they can tell, there is no one on the street or in their gardens.

'How about we backtrack to that junction, take a right, and try to ride around?' Mae says.

Pasha inches forward, squinting his eyes to see further. 'Probably for the best. You never know, it might even be quicker.'

They take the right, then another, and continue until they reach another village. A similar but less polite sign hangs over the street.

'Dammit.'

'This could be the case all over,' Mae says. 'Maybe we could go and ask directions?'

'And say what? We're trying to cross the county border? We're so close here, that's literally all we could be doing.'

'We might not be that close. You can't know that for sure.'

He thinks for a moment, still craning his neck to see past the village sign. 'Screw it. Let's just go for it. We'll max the electric on the bikes and whizz through. There's virtually no traffic. No one will get a good look at us, and we won't give any impression that we're stopping.'

A few cars drive past, a bus, all crossing into the village. They can't be keeping tabs on everyone, surely? Just two people, out for a cycle. That's all. Mae's mental reassurances do little to quell her nerves. She leans forward and strains her eyes to look for armed security, signs for a holiday camp, anything that would imply that people are patrolling with weapons. They stop long enough for the cold to trickle its way through her body and she shivers.

'Sod it,' she says. 'Okay, let's go for it.'

'Great. We'll ride side-by-side. I'll be kerb side to protect you from any pedestrians.'

'You mean, because you look older and it's you they'll see more of?'

He snorts a laugh, then leans in for a kiss. 'If you like. Now, ready? We'll give it everything we've got for a few minutes. One, two, three!'

They cycle as fast as their legs can take them, the electric function doing its fair share. After a couple of minutes, the quiet outskirts of the village turn into a market town centre, busy with pedestrians spilling out onto the road, cars parked where they shouldn't, and market stalls taking up a lot of space. The furore of trading echoes through the crowd, rustling shopping bags, everyone busy. So busy, they're not paying Pasha and Mae the least bit of attention. Until—

'Who the bloody hell is that?'

'Young people! See that!'

'The bloody cheek! Get her out of our town!'

'Murderers! Kidnappers! Destroy that womb!'

The heckles get closer and closer as the crowd becomes denser and denser. Mae and Pasha skid and weave the bikes around shoppers and trolleys and vehicles and dogs.

'Go, go, go, Mae!' Pasha shouts, as if she wasn't pedalling like mad already.

Single file now, no room for side by side. Pasha forcing Mae to the front, shouting at her from behind to go faster, faster. By their wheels land tomatoes, eggs, onions, all being thrown by the locals. There are squelchy thuds around them as the projectiles land by their bikes and splatters across their ankles. More insults, followed by taunting angry fists raised in the air.

'Get the fuck out, you murderers! Get that womb away from us!'

'Dee, get my gun!'

Gun? Mae's heart rate escalates as she pedals as fast as she can, meandering with all the efficiency the space can offer. The power reading on her bike starts to drop off, the battery depleting.

'Pasha!'

'Keep going Mae.'

The first gunshot makes Mae jump so much she almost comes off her bike. She rights the wobble and hears Pasha call from behind, saying he's fine, to keep going, they'll be out of the village soon.

Cars rev behind them now, and Mae glances back just as one almost rubs its bumper on Pasha's rear wheel. She looks ahead again, clenches her jaw, eyes streaming. She must pedal faster and keep Pasha ahead of the car.

The second gunshot screams past her. Not warning shots anymore, not if they're that close. The passengers of the car lean out of the windows, banging on the roof, the words indistinguishable but the intent clear. Cars come towards them now, swerving and zigzagging across the road. The first one aims right for her. She looks to the right, to the left. There's no way out. High hedges line the road, a blind corner ahead. She tucks in as close to the hedge as she can, spiky branches catching her arms.

No time to look back and see if Pasha is okay. The car coming towards them is picking up speed, horn beeping, lights flashing. She closes her eyes, unable to look doom in the face.

When she opens them a couple of seconds later, the car has swerved back to its side, the scream of brakes, tyres leaving black streaks across the road. The end of village sign is up ahead, her bike battery now in the red. Flashing, angrily.

'Pasha!'

'Almost there, Mae. Keep going!'

Some rubble lands close to the bikes, hard, menacing things, meant to maim. Chunks of bricks, glass bottles, smashing and making Mae skid around to avoid a puncture. The jitter of bullets and projectiles is like heavy metal music. She can't think in the fog of noise. An entire brick clips her knee as it hurtles to the floor, almost knocking her off balance. There's no pain, there's no time for pain. She doesn't even notice the blood until they are at the other side of the village sign.

Her eyes blur from tears, cheeks stinging from the cold wind, knee throbbing now and wet with blood, but they're out of the village. The cars stop at the edge and throw a few more rocks, but they're far enough away to avoid them. Her burning lungs heave for breath and she looks back at Pasha, cuts down his arms, face ablaze from the effort, but he's okay. They're both okay.

As soon as they round the next corner, they stop, get off the bikes, then hug a sweaty hug. Mae cries into Pasha's chest, his trembling embrace full of relief.

'We're okay, Mae. We made it. We're okay.'

Chapter 20

The road is lined with trees, no houses. A stretch of woodland offers shade and camouflage. They push the bikes into the thicket, clear a patch of bracken, then sit on the forest floor. Their dark green hiking clothes blend in with the woods. The trees are different to what she's used to in Berkshire, spikier bark, smaller leaves. A few bugs fly around, iridescent creatures. Flies with papery wings land on her skin. She's never minded the odd bug. There were more when she was a girl. So few these days. In the woods are the most she's seen in years.

On the forest floor, Mae feels they belong. No crawling feeling of eyes on her, just the sound of leaves creeping up on them. The biting cold that was coming with the late afternoon is mostly spared in the woods, the trees insulating them from the harshness. Among the trees, the world feels calm, peaceful, sheltered.

'I think we should camp tonight,' Pasha says.

Too exhausted to argue, moving anywhere seems inconceivable. 'Yeah. I can't cycle anymore.'

'Here. . .' He knees close to her and takes her leg, massaging her throbbing muscles. 'Might as well put my physio skills to use.'

She smiles and watches him work, gentle but firm, rubbing away her aches and soothing her tired muscles. When he finds a muscle knot, he eases it away, bit by bit, determined but not forceful. Thick fingers from years of using his hands. Mae catches sight of him in the blades of light slicing through the trees. She kneels up to move around him, then peels his jacket away from his skin. Several gashes line his neck, grazes, and swollen lumps. She inspects his back, torn clothes with blood seeping through. 'Looks like you got hit a few times.'

'Told you I'd protect you. I'm your armour, Mae. Always.'

She's never felt safer than she does with him. He'd walk her to work if he could. Escort her every minute to make sure she isn't overwhelmed. She gets irritated by his overprotectiveness often, feels condescended, even though he's often right. But her impatience isn't with any lack of independence, it's fear of codependency. If she allows herself to be overly cared for, how would she ever manage without him? What if he finds out the truth about her and leaves? She'd lock herself away again with nothing but textbooks for company. Now with a baby on the way, how would she manage without his support? She wouldn't, is the truth she is all too aware of.

His face is so full of love, she can do nothing but fall into him and hold on. For a few moments, they stay like that, holding on, knees digging into the dirt.

'Grab the first aid kit,' she says as she pulls away. 'We should clean up.'

Mud stains are all down his hiking trousers, grimy brown on the dark green. But she fails to care like she usually would. The bit of mud on their clothes makes them hidden instead of exposed. Makes her feel like they are exactly where they should be.

Pasha dabs her knee with antiseptic before he'll let her treat his wounds. It's a little swollen already, but superficial. She studies his face as he tends to her and he does so with such care, it almost makes her think she's deserving of such attention. That's how he makes her feel. That she is worthy. With him, her past can fade away into nothingness, the present staying at the forefront. Those nasty secrets don't disappear. They're mummified, preserved to be unwrapped at a later date. Despair, anger, regret. All these feelings she keeps at bay and plasters over with her shyness and awkwardness, burying her real self. The blanket of love he provides usually keeps such feelings at bay, cushioning her from her internal demons. Her fear above all, is that motherhood will somehow unwrap those layers, exposing her bare bones. Who is she really? A display of a person. A constant show.

'All better,' he says and smiles. 'You okay?'

She nods and smiles too.

She can't lie, she never had the knack beyond ticking the *Have read the Ts and Cs* box on forms. But she can keep her mouth shut, and that is something entirely different.

After they are cleaned up, Pasha manages to light a fire and they fumble with the tent until it looks like it should stand the test of the night. They have some rations of noodles and dried fruit. The noodles simmer on the fire, then Pasha serves them up.

'Worms,' he says with a laugh.

'At least we had that pie,' Mae says as she pushes the food around her tin camping plate.

The sweetness from the fruit floods her mouth. Syrupy, sticky. Mae wishes she has her electric toothbrush instead of the crappy bamboo manual ones. It'd be nice to feel clean inside if not outside.

Occasionally they freeze, breath still in their lungs as they feel the tremble of a car thrum by on the road. Mae wants to close her eyes in the way she did as a child. If she can't see them, they can't see her. Pasha's muscles tense, ready to pounce, a predator. But she can read his face so well, and he's definitely more prey than predator. His deep eyes bore into hers, a glassy film developing as he dare not even blink. A bunny in the headlights. The trees are dense enough, the light low, and they stay undetected.

The fire keeps the chill off, the external cold, anyway. Mae's bones still feel like ice, an emptiness where warmth should be, fear filling every void. How many villages like that will they come across? They haven't even crossed a county line yet.

A fingernail of a moon rises above the canopy, its wan light casting an ethereal glow across the thicket. They snuggle in close, not discussing the latter part of the day. That memory can go with the rest, thinks Mae. One never to be talked about. A write-off memory. They can pretend, for a while, that everything will be okay. That they are on some romantic adventure, not running, not hiding. The red mark on her arm from the drone has faded now; it's invisible among her dusting of freckles. So there's nothing wrong. Nothing dark growing inside her. They're just exploring nature. For that's how it feels for that evening, when their wounds are patched up and their tummies a little fuller. Like Grandpa Angus would want.

Just an adventure.

Chapter 21

They sleep well, considering. The ground is uneven, and the dampness underneath soaks up through their thin mattresses. They spoon for warmth, something Mae normally dislikes, but in the small chilly space, necessity bests preference. The morning sun rises late and when it does, its heat is insubstantial but the light is blinding, and the inside of the tent feels like a magnifying glass of glare. They have a small breakfast of dried fruit before pushing through their tiredness and beginning their ride. With the bike's batteries depleted, every pedal stroke is an effort.

'An hour to the border, I reckon,' Pasha says.

Mae says nothing but grits her teeth and carries on. Looking down at her waist, her stomach is less flat than it used to be. A bit of bloating from the food, perhaps? She counts the weeks on her fingers. Eighteen weeks. She's starting to show.

She knew the exact date as soon as her cycle was late. Eighteen weeks ago was Rolan's anniversary. Fifteen years exactly since his operation. Pasha is sure to celebrate with him every year, his re-birth day, so Rolan calls it, and tries to claim it actually makes him a teenager. They laugh about that every time. They

went to the Mexican on Broad Street, Moira getting them in
with her 600 plus Score, which she reminded them of all night.
How none of them would be eating such good food if it weren't
for her, how they had to keep their voices down so as not to
show her up, how Pasha and Mae must admire her and her Score
so much. Moira is usually less of a cow when she's had a few
glasses of wine, but that night she remained her condemnatory
self, sober as a judge and looking down on anyone less so. Seems
obvious now why she wasn't drinking, though Mae never sus-
pected it back then. Mae ate the food, every delicious mouthful,
and washed it down with enough wine to make Moira a blur.
Mae passed out when they got home and Pasha removed her
bag and shoes for her, then left a sick bowl by the bed. But she
woke early, head swimming, hungover and horny. Pasha looked
insanely fuckable, naked with his hair scruffy, thick eyelashes
twitching with his dreams. They'd spent the whole Sunday in
bed, unshowered, feeling a mess. Getting themselves into a bigger mess.

She looks over at Pasha on his bike with his big hands holding
the handlebars, messy hair sticking out of his helmet, and a dark
green jacket that matches his tan skin.

She curses how fuckable he is, curses herself for letting her
guard down and falling for him. What an idiotic thing to do.
She should have known better, should have stayed away years
ago. She's been sleepwalking into this mess for the last five years.
Mess seems like a hard word, but it's how she feels. Chaotic,
confused. A tangled heap of a life. He's too easy to love and

loves her too easily. His innate desire to protect will make him a wonderful father. And her own reluctance to love will make her a shitty mother.

Yeah, she thinks. Mess sums it up pretty well.

The hour to the county border is more like two, and it becomes clear they're close as no more signs point that way and every town and village and road indicated tells them to U-turn. When the signs run out, the tarmac turns potholed and gravelly, grass growing through in patches, banks uncared for, trees overhanging the road. When they haven't seen a car or bus or even another bike for ten minutes, Pasha suggests it's time to go on foot.

'The county border could be any moment,' he says as they dismount their bikes, leaving them on the side of the road. They'll get charged for that, but such things don't matter anymore.

'How will we know when we've crossed?' she asks.

'I don't know. Don't know if they're patrolled, don't know what the fence is like, or if there is one. I guess we'll just start seeing road signs again.'

Mae's stomach grumbles. They hadn't risked stopping for food anywhere, not wanting to go into a village after last time. They'll find a shop when they get into Devon or a café.

'Things will be different in Devon,' Pasha says as he hands her a small bottle of water, which she stuffs in her back pocket. She's hungry, not thirsty.

As they walk the cracked tarmac, ducking under half-fallen down trees, no-man's-land feels exactly like that. Not an engine noise, not a voice, not a footstep. A few birds announcing their presence is all. The soft wind rustles the trees. The stillness does nothing to calm Mae's nerves; it heightens them. A hundred and fifty million people live in this Society, how is it possible there is no one here? Every muscle hardens, ridged, ready for an ambush.

After fifteen minutes, the tarmac disintegrates into a dirt track, and the overgrown flora thins out, giving them a view of further ahead. There's a fence, which is chicken wire, an absolute ramshackle that's collapsed in places. Is that it? Mae wonders. No lookout points. No *do not cross* signs, not even any barbed wire. They pause behind a bush and watch for a few minutes, sitting on grasses different from the parks in Reading, buzzing with insects they never see in Reading. All of it feeling so alien, too still and a million miles from home.

'That must be it,' Pasha says. 'And there's no one there. I guess we just walk over.'

'And if there are patrols? What do we say?'

'We're hikers, off to scatter Grandpa's ashes.'

'And if they don't let us cross?'

'Let's worry about that if it happens.'

They approach the fence with soft footsteps, like they're stalking prey. Mae hangs behind Pasha, his hand gripping hers like iron. The fence looks even more weather-beaten up close. It's not so much of a fence but a trip hazard in places, toppled over and bleeding rust into the dirt. Pasha's head moves back and forth as he scans their surroundings, Mae's going the opposite way, less smoothly, more frantic. A cold breeze makes the nervous sweat collecting in her hairline run dry and sends a chill across her shoulders. Pasha shivers in the same way. She bites her nails, forgetting she hasn't washed her hands properly today.

'Nearly at the fence, Mae. It's going to be—'

'Don't you dare say fine.'

That damned F word. She crushes his hand, his bullshit reassurances making her flinch. Pasha doesn't seem to notice. He drags her a little further forward, her shaking legs making the crunchy ground loud underfoot. She struggles to remember a time when she's ever heard her own footsteps when outside. The noise everywhere usually drowns out any clamour she ever makes. Now she feels as though every step is revealing her to the world. Every step strips away a layer. Now just a few metres away, she might as well be naked, alone, her secrets inscribed on her bare skin.

They get to the fence and walk a little way along it to a part that's trodden down. They half-wonder if it's electric, but the state of disrepair makes it clear it isn't. The opposite side looks the same as where they just were: a deserted wasteland, a track through the plants, and then they assume tarmac road. There's beauty in the decrepitude, Mae thinks. The lack of human involvement here. Left to nature, the trees hum with life. Brilliant green leaves untarnished with city soot smell of pollen rather than pollution. The grass is a mixture of plants, no uniformity, little white opportunistic flowers poking through.

Pasha steps over first, stamping the fence flatter as he does, then Mae. They pause a moment, quite shocked that they have done such a thing, crossing a county line, on foot. Not just getting a train somewhere, but stepping over a border into an actual alien county. They take a breath, then a step forward.

'Stop!'

The shout comes from nowhere, and they freeze.

'Shit!' they both say.

'You two! Don't move an inch.'

They don't, standing like they're glued to the ground, Mae's heart thumping in her throat, her temples, her stomach.

'Shit, Pasha. Shit, shit!'

'It's okay. Remember the urn,' he says in a whisper without moving his lips.

Out from the dirt track ahead, three people walk towards them, dressed in camouflage clothing and stab vests. Tasers and knives hang from their belts, binoculars from their necks. They hurry towards Mae and Pasha as the two of them remain still, obedient. Mae sucks her stomach in as much as she can, her empty belly making it easier. The people approaching are middle-aged, forties, fifties, maybe. Their faces look aged enough that it's unlikely they're Preserved, which relaxes her a little. Too young to be hunted by Time's Up, too old to be wanting children. They won't be victims of the law.

'Explain yourselves,' the largest one says. His ruddy face glistens with sweat from his exertion as his hand hovers over his taser.

'We don't want any trouble,' Pasha says.

'Then don't cross the county line.'

'It's not illegal,' says Mae, her voice meek and quiet, not attempting to mimic the accent. Similar to Somerset, she thinks. 'We're not doing anything wrong.'

'On the contrary. It may not be illegal, but it certainly requires some explanation. Isn't that right, lads?'

The men on either side of him grunt and nod.

Pasha reaches into his bag. 'If I can show you—'

'Not so fast! No sudden movements.'

'It's nothing dangerous,' says Pasha, holding his hands in the air. 'We mean no harm. Do you want to have a look?' He slowly reaches for his bag and hands it over to them. 'Please, just be careful. It's precious to me.'

The man hands the bag to the other and he rummages through it, lifting out the urn.

'Well, well, what do we have here?'

'I know it's against the law, but that's my grandpa. And he loved this county so much. He grew up here, years ago, obviously.'

'You're supposed to love your own county that much, the one you live in, the one you die in. Nostalgia for another county is against everything this Society stands for.'

Pasha nods and makes those sad puppy-dog eyes that are impossible to say no to. 'I know. He was old, though. He had old-fashioned values. And he was born here, before Britain was the Society. Please, we're just trying to grant an old man's dying wish.'

'Well,' the man says, inspecting the urn some more. 'Where abouts in Devon?'

'Dartmoor.'

'Dartmoor! That's forty miles from here.'

'I know. We're prepared to walk. He was such a dear man. Please, I beg you. Let us finish our journey.'

Mae sinks a little, imagining they're actually going to have to walk forty miles.

'Hang about, and what's all this then?' The other man carried on rifling through Pasha's bag and is now taking out packets of vitamins. 'Why would a young couple like you need vitamins? What are you, Preserved?'

'God, no,' Pasha replies, loudly, overly defensive Mae thinks. 'We just didn't know what healthy food we'd be able to get. My partner here, she gets tired so easily, and with immune systems different everywhere, we thought it best.'

'These aren't just any vitamins though, are they?' the man says, scrunching his nose. 'These are the sort that pregnant ladies take.'

'Vitamins are vitamins, aren't they?' Pasha says.

Mae's entire body is thumping with her heartbeat, her breath rasping in her dry throat.

'We've heard of such people, coming over here to steal our elders to use as a donor. Is that what you're here for?'

'No! of course not,' says Mae, her voice squeaking with strain. 'We're on foot. How would that even be possible?'

'You got the tests, Paul?' the largest one asks.

'Sure do.'

The slightest one of the three takes a rucksack from his shoulder, then opens it and hands a small box to the biggest man.

'Well, the lady here won't mind taking a pregnancy test, will she?'

Pasha's Adam's apple slides up and down as his eyes dart back and forth.

'No problem.' Mae takes the box, then spots a bush. 'A little privacy, please. I'm not peeing in front of you lot.'

'Mae—' Pasha calls after her.

'I'll be fine. I'll just be by that bush.'

She smiles at him, locks eye contact for a moment, trying to convey a message she can't say aloud. She walks to the bush, holding her head up, hoping her legs don't look too shaky. Behind the bush, she drops her trousers to her ankles, then crouches low and wets the stick. After, she redresses, gives the stick a little shake, then walks back over. Pasha looks a mess, shaking, face so red he could give the ruddy-faced guard a run for his money. She waves the stick in the air.

'I reckon that's a minute or so.' She shows them the stick.

'Good.' They nod and look satisfied. 'Well, what do you think, chaps? I can't see any real harm in these two making their way to Dartmoor.'

'Doesn't bother me, sir.'

'Me neither,' Paul says.

'Well,' the largest one says. 'All right then. You two stay out of trouble. Don't go into the smaller villages, you won't be welcome. And if anyone asks, we didn't see you.'

'Thank you,' Pasha says, voice still shaking. 'I think we'll sit here and rest a while before continuing, if that's all right with you?'

'Suit yourselves. Welcome to Devon.'

And the three of them walk off back into the thicket of trees. When they are over a hundred metres away, Pasha's knees give way and he collapses to the ground. 'Jesus Christ, Mae. Why are you not pregnant anymore? What the hell?'

She kneels next to him, rubs his back, then leans in to whisper. 'I used water. I still had that bottle. No pee. Just water.'

He lifts his head, face breaking into a smile, relief bringing some colour back to his cheeks. 'Clever girl.'

Chapter 22

It takes a while for their nerves to subside. Adrenalin dissipated, they start to walk again. The tarmac road is easy to find. New bikes are not. The route takes them zigzagging across the east of the county, avoiding small villages as the border guards said. The deserted peripheral streets soon fill again, visible eyes staring at them instead of concealed ones. Hardly crowds, but enough people are around to make them appear less out of place. The gentle hubbub at least disguises the sound of their footsteps and stops Mae from hearing her own heartbeat. Devon looks much the same as Somerset, to Mae's surprise. Quite unsure what she expected, new species of trees, different architecture, maybe. The only giveaway that they are in a different county is the buses. Red logos on the side rather than yellow. After two hours of walking, they've yet to find a café or a shop, and they're running on empty.

'We could try a bus?' Pasha says.

Hearing those words out loud is still a shock, even though Mae's been thinking them for at least an hour.

'Where would we go? We might end up in a small village and get stoned to death.'

'Exeter is the biggest city in the area. Look here.' He points to a timetable at the bus stop. 'Pretty much all the buses go to Exeter. How about it?'

Mae wriggles her blistered toes in her boots, then drops her bag on the floor and stretches out her tired shoulders. 'Sure. Why not?'

A group of people walk past them, middle-aged, prissy, re-coiling their noses at the sight of them. Mae's stinky armpits are likely the reason, she thinks, until she takes a proper look at her and Pasha. How is it they've been walking so long and she hasn't even realised how filthy they look? She picks bits of dead leaf from her hair, then brushes some dirt from Pasha's jacket. Their knees are almost entirely caked in dried mud, with their luggage bags not fairing much better. They look exactly like they had spent the night sleeping in the woods. No big surprise there.

Mae inspects the other people in their tidy parkas and pol-ished boots up to their shins, hair in sleek waves looking a whole lot more glamorous than Mae does in her grubby clothes and debris-filled hair. In the time they wait for the bus, they check Iris's instructions for the correct attire for Devon. Hair down for Mae. *Down?* Never has she worn her hair down in public, not for years, anyway. Even at home she avoids it as it itches her neck and annoys her face. And right now, it's frizzing out like the bush she just peed in. Her hat does little to make it look better as it erupts in tufts in every place it can. Pasha needs to do nothing, his hat being the only costume he requires. Mae scowls at him as he realises and smirks when he sees her.

'You look gorgeous, Mae.'

'Piss off.'

By the time the bus arrives, there are several people waiting, giving them suspicious glances and keeping their distance.

'Hikers don't get the bus, Pasha.'

'Hikers with sprained ankles do.'

She furrows her brow, but when the bus arrives and Pasha limps onto it, using Mae as a crutch, she gets the idea. A fall could explain the state of their clothing too. Suspicion morphs into pity from the other passengers and some people at the front move to the back to offer their seat. Pasha winces as he sits, putting on a show that would sell out a theatre. Mae helps him, as attentively as she can manage, feeling a fool but too aware his method is working. When they sit, he looks at her, winks, then gives her a kiss on the cheek.

They say nothing for the journey, silence their best veil. The voices they hear have strange accents, much like Somerset, but elongating parts of speech she isn't used to, shortening others. She practises the longer R sound in her head, dropping the ends of some words, mouthing some vowels to herself. The bus meanders in and out of small villages, unwelcoming signs and partial roadblocks much the same as in Somerset. She swallows hard whenever she sees one, while Pasha squirms from the discomfort in his back against the hard seat, each unwelcome sign a reminder. Mae cranes her head back, eavesdropping on the conversation behind.

'You see the news this morning? It's like civil war at the moment in some places.'

'All those women dead. Serves 'em right if you ask me.'

'Geoff!'

'What? They got themselves pregnant. Some of those women were even lesbians.'

'I think men got them pregnant. It takes two to tango.'

'So what, you gonna say all the sperm-makers should be killed? Nah. They're just doing what men do. Them women chose to have them pregnancies. They coulda stopped it, but they didn't. Women think they can do what they want. This oughta be a lesson to them.'

'Geoff, really!'

'Separate them, that's what I say. Keep all the fertile women away, on some island somewhere. That's what the elders are having to do to keep safe. Why should they? Lock the women up. They're the ones causing the trouble, them with their hormones. That'd be far more effective. There's less of them, too, so it would cost the economy less. Stick them all on the Isle of Mann or summit. Bring them back onto the mainland when they've had the menopause and aren't a danger anymore.'

'And how would you have liked it, huh? If we were separated for thirty years when we were young?'

'Not our problem, love. We're not the ones breeding in a world like this.'

'And what about Jane, and Angie and Beth, your three daughters? Would you like them sent away?'

'They're near enough the right age now, anyway.'

Mae pings the band on her wrist and counts the streetlights as they drive past. Pasha keeps his head straight. An hour on this bus, according to the timetable. An hour of listening to this. Mae's stomach churns in empty queasiness as she rests her head on Pasha's shoulder and her vision clouds over.

'You all right, Mae?'

'Just a little faint. Give me a minute.'

He finds a packet of raisins in his bag and hands them to her. She eats the entire packet and after a few minutes she can take the weight of her head again. The couple behind have gone, but she hadn't noticed them leave. The lack of gossip is a relief.

'How much longer?' she asks Pasha.

'About fifteen minutes, I think.'

When the bus stops, Pasha helps her up, takes her bags, forgetting his feigned injury for a moment. He limps off the bus, on the other leg, Mae realises, yet no one else seems as astute. She checks the time. Three o'clock.

'Perhaps we can just find a hotel or something, rest there, and order takeaway. We've come such a long way.'

Pasha's complexion is looking pale, and she's sure he's faring worse than he's letting on. He nods, and they join a pedestrian lane to enter the city.

The city centre is heaving, same as Reading on a busy day. Busier, even. Flags fly from every rooftop, green with a white cross, but that's almost all they can see above the hordes of people. They stick to the slow lane so they can take in their surroundings without being barged along. Even in their shattered state, it is slow, but it gives them time to get their bearings and blood flowing again. Bike hire stations are everywhere, eateries are plenty with various levels of low stock warnings, but they both agree: privacy, a bed, and takeaway is all they can cope with.

The waddle of pedestrian traffic takes them out of the city centre and to some side street with a boutique-looking hotel. It has a vertical sign that says vacancies, but the windows are dark, like it's unlit inside. *Exclusive rooms,* it says in the window in flashing neon pink letters. *Executive discount* on another sign.

'I don't even know what that means, Pasha.'

'It means it's probably way over budget. But I'm tired and so are you, and we stayed for free last night, so I reckon it's fine.'

He doesn't have to justify it to Mae. Her feet are rubbed raw and her back aches from the night in the woods. If it was a million pounds a night, she'd still be tempted. They walk in and approach the reception. Inside is decorated extensively with pink. Pink sofas and carpets. Not just pale pink, but pink that hits you like a slap in the face. Kitsch knock-off chandeliers hang from the ceiling with black and pink crystals, and black vases on the desk overflow with faux pink flowers. The place smells like rosewater, sickly sweet like old Pot-pourri. Such an aromatic invasion, Mae wonders what smells they're trying to mask.

'Welcome to sExeter hotel,' the receptionist says as they approach, exactly like that, with the subtlest of Ss. 'You two found yourselves in need of an urgent room, have you?'

'Yes, we're very tired,' Pasha says.

Mae's cheeks are burning, at where they are or Pasha's naivety, she's not sure. Either way, she bites her lip to suppress her giggles and allows her embarrassment to turn into hilarity.

'Great,' the receptionist says, pinging his leather braces. 'How many hours would you like to, er, sleep?'

Pasha looks taken aback, so Mae steps in. 'The whole night, please. We really are very tired.' She forgets all about her accent practice, but the receptionist doesn't seem to care.

'Very well,' the receptionist says with a wide grin. 'We have our cosy honeymoon room available. I think you two will love it.'

'Great,' Mae says. 'How much?'

'Forty pounds an hour for the first three, twenty an hour thereafter,' he says, jerking his eyebrows up and down.

'Okay,' says Mae as Pasha still makes his confused bunny staring at headlights face.

The receptionist looks at Pasha, then at Mae. 'The Pres-X not kicked in properly yet?'

'What? No. Just tired. Can you recommend a takeaway?'

'There's a folder with menus in the room, just next to the remote for the mood lighting and ambience control.'

'Perfect,' says Mae as she takes the key card.

'Quite the submissive this one, isn't he?' the receptionist says to Mae as she takes Pasha by the wrist and leads him away.

The sickly sweet rose smell intensifies down the corridor, and dim lighting makes the walls feel closer. Mae swipes the key card and bursts out laughing as they enter the room. There's a heart-shaped bed with a revolving function and silk sheets, furniture with plastic, wipeable wrapping, and a bowl of condoms on the table.

'Oh,' says Pasha, the reality dawning on him. 'Chargeable by the hour. Now I get it.'

Mae grabs the takeaway menu, then lies on the bed. 'Yeah, it's that sort of hotel.'

His eyes go to the floor, his mouth upturns. 'But I really am tired.'

'It's fine, Casanova. All I want to do is shower and sleep too. And eat. What do you fancy? Chinese?'

He collapses on the bed next to her and lets out a groan. 'Whatever you want. Just lots of it.'

Chapter 23

They order food from three different takeaways, each one explaining they have shortages, portions are smaller, please bear with them during this difficult time. Mae says they understand, and any food is better than no food. By the time the third delivery arrives, they are more than stuffed and have leftovers piled up. A little guilt washes over Mae, and she sees the same feeling in Pasha. Food shortages, being told to live more modestly, and they order enough food to feed six people. 'Eating for two' doesn't really justify their gluttony, however much Pasha uses that line. And no doubt they'll be hungry again in a few hours. She wishes they could be like lions and have one big meal, then sleep for a week.

With full bellies, they snuggle up on the plastic-wrapped sofa.

'That conversation on the bus, Pasha, did you hear?'

'Yeah.' He kisses her forehead. 'That guy probably always felt that way. Laws changing don't change people's views.'

'You're probably right,' she says, remembering not just the bus conversation but the newspaper article, the bricks being thrown at them, and the need to tattoo babies. Laws may not change people's views, but they certainly intensify them.

They sleep in until almost lunchtime, then finish the leftovers for brunch. After Mae showers, she tames her hair and puts on the only change of clothes she has. Clean and fresh, it almost starts to feel like a holiday. Inside that hotel room, they could be anywhere. No doubt Berkshire somewhere has rent by the hour hotels. She can fool herself that they're not so far from home. For a moment, anyway.

After washing, Pasha sleeps some more and she watches him doze, content, happy. She wants to lie next to him, but they can't stay. Her waist is poking out a little more than it was the day before, from all the food maybe? Either way, the perception is the same. She has no idea how far they still have to go, if they'll even find the place and if not, if they'll need to make it back to Reading before they get in real trouble. She wakes him up and he protests only for a moment, his desire to use the heart-shaped bed for its real purpose now strong and urging.

'No time,' she says. 'We can't waste a day. Come on.'

The same receptionist is at the desk as they exit, and his eyes light up when he sees Pasha's rejuvenated self.

'Works wonders, the Pres-X, doesn't it? I've seen such miracles.'

'Yeah,' Mae says. 'As does a good night's sleep.'

'You're off to the convention, I assume? That's why you're visiting Exeter?'

'Erm, yeah. Sure,' Pasha says.

'Oh, here they are,' the receptionist says, looking past Mae and Pasha. 'Nate, Zen, some more for you.'

Two men walk over hurriedly, clearly excited. Identical parkas, shin-high boots, and two-hundred-pound haircuts, they stop right in front of Pasha and Mae.

The receptionist smiles and introduces them. 'You might as well all go over together. All you Preserved together. Nature's miracles.'

Nate and Zen clasp their hands with the sort of glee a child has at Christmas. No matter how much rest they've had, Pasha and Mae are never that enthused.

'Wonderful,' says Zen, smiling to reveal perfect teeth, his grin creating no laughter lines in his collagen-rich skin, eyes sparkly and bright. 'Shall we?' He holds his arm out and Nate loops his through. Pasha and Mae file in behind, the receptionist giving them a double thumbs-up.

'Why did you say that?' says Mae to Pasha as quietly as she can.

'I don't know. Just seemed the easiest thing to say.'

'Maybe we'll lose them in the crowd.'

As soon as they leave, it becomes clear that'll be impossible. Zen and Nate are friendly, attentive, chatty, the perfect hosts if you desire any. But Mae and Pasha want to disappear and they struggle to converse. Nate and Zen notice them dragging their feet and loop their arms with theirs and pull them into the fast lane, their mouths moving quicker than their pace.

'We never used to consider the fast lane before Pres-X. But now, here we are, with the bones and muscles of a twenty-year-old,' Nate says, showing his biceps.

'I did it for the skin,' Zen says. 'I don't think mine was ever this smooth.'

'And I can stay up late! Oh, the parties we've had. Divine. You don't realise how much you miss being young. How did you two cope with the regression years?' Nate says, inspecting their faces.

'It took some getting used to,' Mae says.

'Didn't it! I wanted instant results. Ten years of anti-ageing seemed to go on forever. But actually, it was such a beautiful process, just getting a little younger day by day. We've definitely settled now, though. Don't you think so, Zen?'

'Oh, definitely. Any younger and I'll be back to wetting the bed again!'

'You two look like you've got a few years to go? You're still regressing, I assume? How'd you cover up the pink skin? Make-up?'

Nate peers a little closer to them. 'Or were you dosed early?'

'Early,' Mae says.

Nate and Zen both lift their eyebrows at this. 'Well,' Zen says. 'I hear they're considering second doses, for when we get past middle-aged again. They're just testing it now. I can't imagine it right now, but by then, who knows?'

'You get the haters, of course,' Nate says. 'You seen the news?'

'We try to avoid it,' Pasha says.

'Probably for the best. Those protests ridiculing us for look-ing young, for living such a long time. They just don't under-stand,' Nate says. 'Being gay was still stigmatised when we were young. We spent our twenties in the closet. I didn't come out till I was thirty-one, when that section 28 bill of Thatcher got repealed. Years of my youth wasted, denying who I was. And even after that, we were treated differently for ages. I was fifty before I felt safe in my own skin. Nearly half my life in hiding from my true self, and then by the time I was comfortable with that, I was too old to enjoy it properly.'

'You remember what things were like then?' Zen says to Mae.

'Sure,' she says, avoiding the stare from Pasha.

'And it's not like we caused the population catastrophe. We never had kids, so why shouldn't we live longer? You have kids?'

'No,' Mae says, her cheeks getting hot, Pasha's grip getting tighter.

'Exactly,' Nate says. 'See, we should be allowed a second chance. But these protests and Time's Up haters remind me of the gay bashing of the last century. There's always going to be haters, they just hate different things.'

'Pres-X should be celebrated,' Zen says. 'It really is a miracle. To get another shot at youth, at life. All that knowledge and wisdom before always died. And for what? To make room for new, stupid babies?'

'The only bad thing about Pres-X is that in making people young again. It restores fertility along with libido,' says Nate. 'Pretty young-again woman like you need to be careful.' He gives Mae a playful nudge, and she smiles back in such a way she hopes renders her charming.

'Well, that's why we're here,' Zen says. 'To show our support. None of this Pro Grow crap, trying to take our food and necessities off us. You know, I couldn't even buy shoe polish the other day.' He tuts and shakes his head. 'Like the bloody Stone Age.'

Across the crowds, the chanting gets louder. Bubbling up all around them the voices repeat, impassioned, Zen and Nate joining in, 'Preserve not procreate! Preserve not procreate!'

Pasha and Mae lock eyes for the briefest of moments and mumble along: 'Preserve not procreate. Preserve not procreate.'

Pasha's hand squeezes Mae's, and he gives her a playful shove, then whispers, 'I thought you were no good at lying. That was great.'

Mae relaxes slightly at his joviality, blushes, and reciprocates his hand squeeze, eyeing the crowd for a way out. The pedestrian traffic goes on forever, no roads, no bikes, just ordered lanes all headed the same way.

As they approach the centre of the city, the traffic gets denser and denser, fast lanes busier than the slow, so many young people keeping the tempo high. Mae's legs struggle, even in Reading the pace isn't this fast. The demographic is unlike she's ever seen before, not the influx of elders they've seen so far. Youthful faces everywhere, smooth skin and shiny hair. The odd patch of bright pink skin showing under thick make up makes her realise.

'Pasha. They're *all* Preserved.'

'I was just realising that. Have they all come for the convention?'

She shrugs and tries to keep pace. Zen and Nate seem to know everyone, smiling and waving at many as they walk past.

'Where you guys from anyway?' asks Zen.

'Bath,' Pasha says without thinking.

A sharp intake of breath as Zen looks them up and down slowly. 'Somerset! My, my. You are dedicated to the cause.' Zen's delighted voice doesn't match his expression. 'I thought your accent was odd. That explains it. Still, good to have support from all over the Society. Exeter is known for its vintage,' he says with a wink. 'It has the highest population of Preserved in the entire Society, so you should feel right at home.'

Over the lines of people, Mae can't take in her surroundings at all. Just the pointed tops of buildings are visible above all the heads, the sun beaming down above them. The smell of a café wafts over, and Mae gestures towards some buildings off to the side.

'We're going to get a bite to eat,' Pasha shouts over the racket to the two. 'We'll probably catch up with you later.'

'Sure thing,' Zen says. 'The rally starts at the shopping centre entrance. You see the glass over there? Head there for one o'clock!'

'Great,' says Pasha, and they cross the traffic, a few curse words from bumped shoulders, leaving Nate and Zen chanting 'Preserve not procreate' behind them.

Chapter 24

The only café they find suitable for their Life Score is full of elders. Actual elder-looking people, not Preserved. Makes sense, thinks Mae. The drug costs more than even a sub 700 would earn in a lifetime. They sit inside, out of the noise, the cold morning doing nothing to stifle the heat from the crowd, but the air feels fresher indoors. Mae removes her hat to tame her hair, but Pasha's face at the sight of it makes her put it back on straight away. The server comes to them, a young woman with a tired face. She smiles though, warmly, and they order their food.

'Load up while we can,' says Pasha, never knowing when they'll run out of options.

'We should find a shop too,' Mae says. 'Get some camping rations. Just in case.'

The server listens to their order, then says, 'No tomatoes and no orange juice. Shortages. With the shipments being held up. The Pro Grows haven't let a boat dock for a week now, so it's the same everywhere. Some internal deliveries, that's all. Lots of stuff is in low supply. They say we should learn to live on less. Reduce consumption, you know. That's how to cope with the population crisis.'

'Not to worry about the juice or tomatoes,' Pasha says. 'We're fine without.'

The server smiles and looks more than a little relieved. 'Glad to hear it. Seems sensible.'

From where they're sitting, only the top of the glass-walled shopping centre is visible above the crowd. There isn't an inch between the sea of heads and shoulders. They can make out the tops of parkas from those in the rows closest to them, their shin-high boots all stamping in unison. All those with long hair wear it down so it flows over their shoulders, silky, glossy. Like Pres-X boosts keratin too.

As their food arrives, the noise outside picks up, those stamping boots stamping harder. The plates rattle on the table.

'Quite a gathering, isn't there,' the man from the couple behind them says.

'Doesn't seem right to me. All these rich folk getting to be young again. We worked so hard all our lives and our hips hurt, our hair falls out, and my bladder is ridiculous. You get a high Life Score and all that goes away.'

'Don't you worry about them, Kate. We've had a good life. We've been happy. Haven't we?'

'I know. You're right.'

Pasha smiles at Mae. 'Old couples are the cutest, aren't they?'

'Sh,' she says.

'What? They won't be able to hear us.'

'I can, son!' the man behind yells. 'Nothing wrong with my ears. It's my back that's messed up.'

Pasha's face reddens as he waves an apology, then diverts his attention back towards his food. Mae picks at hers, still full from the leftovers they had for brunch but not wanting to waste a mouthful. The stamping outside continues, and it's hard to think of much else. In the café, a TV hangs on the wall, playing the news from the rally outside. There's an empty stage in front of the shopping centre, big speakers on either side. As the camera pans around to show the crowd, a never-ending display of young, waxen faces fills the screen, all eyes facing the stage.

Mae swallows some bites, then pushes the rest around her still-rattling plate, the vibrations in the floor even tingling her nose. Pasha spills some salad down his front from not paying attention. He's always been a messy eater; it's something she's had to learn to tolerate. She imagines he'll be wiping the baby's chin too.

Baby.

The thought is still so unnatural. Her empty arms are heavy enough without carrying extra. Such a yearning she's never had. Sadie has. Her wife, too, they longed for a baby. Still do, probably. Such an innate desire passed Mae by. The years she should have developed that itch, she was too alone for the inkling to develop. That's her theory, anyway. Mae doesn't even feel pregnant. Not sick anymore, belly not really showing, not noticeably, anyway. She's just scared. That's all.

Some people arrive on the stage. No one Mae recognises from TV, but the crowd clearly does as their stamping feet are drowned out by cheering. The five people stand, absorbing their

welcome for a few minutes before raising their arms to quieten
the crowd. Preserved, they must be. Their skin is plump and ra-
diant, teeth perfect, eyes twinkling. Two clearly haven't finished
regressing as they have their patchy bright pink complexion on
show. They each take a step forward and air-punch with strong
arms, taut muscles, not a bingo wing in sight. The crowd cheers
again and when they calm, the person in the centre speaks.

'Good morning, Exeter! What an amazing show of support
we have here today. And what does this show the Society —
No, the world? That we will not be silenced! We will not be
discarded in a corner, left out to pasture. We are a formidable
force, and we are here to stay!'

A cheer again, even louder, whistles, too.

'Governments around the world wish to condemn us, to
condemn our very way of life, to try to take away life from the
people. For that's what Pres-X is, it's life itself. Here on the stage
with me, I have doctor Miles Singh, professor Adu Morris, doctor Ted Blackman, and I think you all know Monique Lakeman
and Danny Don!'

Each of them take a bow in turn as confetti rains down on the
stage, flags wave, and screeches of, 'We love you' are louder than
the cheering.

'These five people represent the best the world has ever seen
in medicine, science, and the arts. Without Pres-X, these people
would simply be allowed to expire, like some old fruit or milk
left out in the sun. Death was around the corner for all of
them. A miserable death of pain, forgetfulness, sensory loss.

But now, thanks to the marvel of Pres-X, they can stay with us, to continue their good work, to make this world a better place. Look at nature. A herd of elephants without a matriarch falls apart, undisciplined, no wisdom to find food and water. Our matriarchs are the bones of knowledge, the foundations of wisdom. Society is rife with crime, with greed, arrogance, narcissism. All these are traits of young people that take decades for them to learn to rise above. Why waste humankind's precious years learning how to be a respectable member of Society, when our matriarchs already know how?

'Governments and people the world over condemn this. They say people need to die, to make room for more people. Ignorant babies whose life successes are a great unknown. Because that is the way it has always been. Well, my friends, the Society has evolved. Humankind has evolved. And I say, preserve, not procreate! Preserve not procreate!'

The crowd erupts with the chant, repeating over and over, 'Preserve not procreate! Preserve not procreate!'

Pasha's cheeks ripple over grinding teeth, his knuckles white as he grips the table. She swallows, bites her lip, then looks back to the TV.

The main speaker lifts his arms to hush them again. 'Of course, people are worried about how we plan to implement such a change, and we have a plan. A paper that we are presenting to Parliament today. These rallies being held up and down the Society show that we mean business. Our plan is simple. No more babies. None. We will create a vast embryo store from a range of demographics, embryos harvested from each Life Score. And when we have enjoyed fifty years without new babies, then, and only then, can we consider growing those embryos, if there is a need. It is a simple plan, but wouldn't you agree, effective? No more of the cancer that is youth! No more of the consumerism that goes along with creating new life! No more risk of breeding criminals and thugs! A society of wise, educated, respectable people!'

The camera shows rallies around the world, dense crowds of young faces cheering along to the same message. Mae's breath is stagnant in her lungs as she watches, Pasha's eyes wide and reddening.

'Together, the Preserved around the Society are pooling our money to buy XL Medico, the lab that creates Pres-X. We will control its supply. I know some MPs and their families are already poised to take their dose, but I promise you now, if they do not agree to our terms, they shall have none! It is a matter of time before we are in control of the Society. If you want to live, you will agree to our terms!'

Pasha reaches forward and grabs Mae's hand as they sit silently, in shock. On the big screens are photos of politicians from Eyes Forward, their ages underneath, all approaching their seventieth birthday — when Pres-X becomes an option. Then, the screens show more rallies across the big cities, London, especially, thousands of youthful faces cheering.

'Look now, look to the screen,' the speaker continues, pointing at the big screens behind them. 'These rallies around the

Society have evoked such passion. And now, I present to you our bonfire. This effigy is about to be lit in London, right outside the palace. This huge pile represents but a fraction of the stuff that our plan means will no longer be needed. Cribs, blankets, bottles, bibs, those bouncer things that hang in doorways, nursing equipment, archaic pushchairs that some people still insist on using. Baby clothes, food. Look at the pile! Look! All that stuff, all that consumerism! Now, watch it burn!'

The pile is huge, a mountain of paraphernalia. Doused in what Mae assumes is petrol, it ignites instantly. Great, billowing flames lick up the sides and jut out the top with coloured plumes of thick smoke, burning everything that babies represent, everything a baby needs. Everything that is on Mae and Pasha's list to buy.

The smoke on the TV isn't the only smoke. Small fires spring up in the crowd outside their café too. The acrid smell of burning plastic is almost instant. Burning much smaller piles of baby equipment. An 'it's a boy' balloon with the words crossed out and 'who cares' written instead, gets released, along with other baby themed balloons, their ribbons on fire dangling below. 'Preserve not procreate' sounds louder and louder, along with 'Enough is enough!' Angry chants, banging on the walls, smashing glass. It's all too loud, too much.

'Pasha.'

His eyes are wide, terrified, the smoke getting thicker outside, the smell seeping in through the glass front, people squashed up against the window of the café. They've no way out.

'It's all right,' he says, his face betraying his true thoughts. 'We'll stay in here. It's safe in here. The fires will go out. People will go home in a moment.'

On the fire on the big screen, people are throwing dolls, really lifelike dolls, images of babies to be burned with the bibs and bottles. The camera zooms in on a doll's face, scorched and melting, its plastic eyes clouding over.

'What if they win, Pasha? Their terms?' Mae's voice cracks with fear.

'We'll be fine. They might stop any more babies, but we're already pregnant, so it'll be fine.'

He was shouting to be heard over the din outside, hands on either side of his mouth to project his voice. A loud gasp comes from the couple behind.

'Pregnant!' the man with a bad back and acute hearing yells. 'I knew you weren't from around here! You haven't got a bracelet! You've come to kill us elders! To kidnap us!'

'No, no, we haven't!' Mae says. 'I promise.'

'You hear that, Kate. Pregnant.' A stream of spittle comes out as he enunciates the P.

'We really mean no harm,' Pasha says.

'I have a good mind to bump you off right now. Get rid of that thing inside you before you have the chance to kill us.'

Pasha jumps in front of Mae with his hands held in front of him. 'Really, we promise, we don't want any trouble.'

'What you here for then?' Kate says, putting her glasses on and stepping closer. 'Your accent isn't right. You're not from Devon.'

'We're just scattering my grandpa's ashes. He was born here. He loved it here.' Pasha's words come out quickly, tumbling over each other.

'Don't give me that crap, young man,' the man says. 'I can spot a liar!'

'Marv!' The waitress appears and stands between them. 'You've no right to be beating them up. If you do, you're as bad as those who are killing elders.'

Kate was at the door. She'd slipped across the café so quietly no one even notices until she's stood there, door ajar, and clears her throat.

'Ahem,' she says, theatrically loudly. 'I'm going to shout to this crowd that we have a pregnant woman in here. They can deal with it.'

Mae lets out a little whimper, Pasha pushes her further behind him.

'If they stampede in here, you'll get crushed too,' he says.

'At least that is a death for a good cause,' says Marv, holding his fist to his chest. 'You go for it, Kate.'

'Attention everyone!' she shouts, alarmingly loud for such a small woman.

'Come with me,' the waitress says to Pasha and Mae. 'Hurry!'

She leads them around the back, past the kitchen to a fire exit. Outside, there's a small yard with bins and a gate at the back.

'That alley, it takes you to the back of South Street. You'll see the cathedral. Go, go, go!'

They run straight away, with no time to consider any other option. Shouting thank yous over their shoulders as they leave, the alleyway delivers them to the back of the rally. Mae's legs are still tired and cramping, but Pasha drags her along. The stampede of footsteps behind them shakes her bones as they run, not daring to look back.

Chapter 25

The cathedral is as obvious as they hoped. On a normal day, they might like to take a moment to admire it and walk around. Smoke drifts up above the rooftops ahead, the din of fire engines screaming towards the rally, the thousands of Preserved still chanting their message, loud and clear. The rally is spreading out, closer, their message hammering through the streets and alleyways.

From just outside the cathedral, they find a bike stand, but all the bikes have dead batteries. They run to the other side of the cathedral, closer to the chanting, but there they find another bike stand with two left, mercifully fully charged, and speed off. The traffic is heavy, and they take dangerous lines, dodging buses and cars, shouting for other bikes to move out of their way, making spectacles of themselves when what they really need to do is blend in. In which direction they ride, they don't stop to check, just away. Away from the rally, away from people burning images of babies, away from people wishing them harm, away from the crowds, away from the woman calling their baby a cancer. Mae waits for the bricks to land, for the gunshots, for the stones to cut, but they never come. A few angry heckles from other road users they've annoyed, but that's all. The chanting becomes quieter. They slow enough for Mae's pulse to calm, for adrenalin to abate, and her breath to steady. She blinks away tears as she notices the chill in the air again.

Once they've crossed the river and feel safer, Pasha stops at a newsagent and grabs a paper, then they are on their way again.

'We need to head east,' he says, trying to gauge the sun. 'It's not far to Dartmoor. That's a big area of nature. We can hike across there without passing through any villages. Shouldn't see too many people.'

Mae's legs are burning, every muscle hurts. They pause a moment to tighten the luggage straps as their bags begin to wobble, then get going again, weak legs pushing heavy pedals, eyes streaming with the effort. After a few miles, they slow down more, sure they're away from the worst of it. They ride alongside each other in stunned silence for a while. With their exertion over, the cold air begins to bite. It's the coldest day they've had so far, a breeze coming from the north carrying with it a grim promise of rain.

'I don't think it's camping weather, Pasha.'

'You'd say that even on a perfect day.'

She can't argue with that.

They push on to the edge of the city, the sky above blackening not only with clouds but with smoke too. Fire engine sirens continue to rip through the air and speed past them, ambulances close behind. They check around, but no one chases them, so they maintain their slower pace. They can't even hear the rally anymore, but the smoke gets worse. A few hundred metres further and they arrive at the source. An apartment block is ablaze, flames jutting out of each window, walls already blackened and the roof crumbling. No screams for help, the ambulance sits idling, and the fire brigade marches forward slowly.

Pasha and Mae stop to watch, dread in their guts, hands over mouths. The sign outside still readable through the graffiti says *Golden Years retirement home.* The graffiti sprayed over it reads *Seventy new donors made.*

'Oh, my God, Pasha.'

'Shit, Mae.'

The raging flames make it clear: there will be no survivors. Paramedics stand with their heads in their hands for a few moments, then drive away, lights flashing, sirens silent as they glide down the empty roads. They can't waste time here as from the look of the fogging skyline another fire rages not far away. One fire truck follows. The bike and car traffic are all at a standstill, the smoke across the street making it impassable. A firefighter approaches.

'It's going to take a while for this road to be safe to cross,' he says. 'Where you headed?'

'Dartmoor. Hiking,' Pasha says.

'Rain's coming. Best go home.'

'We like hiking in the rain.'

The firefighter looks at their raincoats with suspicion, soot streaks collecting in his eye wrinkles. 'Well, you can wait here or go up Redhills. No point turning back. There's people throwing fireworks into that rally. Foolish if you ask me, all those Preserved gathering together, like prime targets. Also, no point trying Cowick Lane. There's another old folk's home fire there. Bigger than this one.'

'Another one?' Mae says.

'You not seen the news?'

'I try to avoid it.'

'Suit yourself. Well, a few fires a day at the moment, across the Society, every county being hit. All old folk's homes.'

'Why burn an old folk's home?' asks Pasha.

'You two really don't watch the news, do you?'

Pasha shakes his head.

'Well, they're trying to kill off the old folk, saying they've had their turn and it's the young folk's turn. Just trying to free up space, it seems. These Time's Up activists are nothing more than terrorists. Meanwhile, we've got the Enough group trying to stop all babies being born and killing women, and the Pro Grow hippies stopping deliveries of anything, saying we need to learn to live without stuff rather than people. It's a bloody nightmare.'

Pasha lets out a slow exhale. 'Sounds like it.'

'Reckon they'll be bringing back the proper police at this rate. The Society Police just aren't up to the job, and the few riot police there are can't cope with this carnage. Still, I hope they convert the homes back into flats when they're finished. My son needs his own place, but it's so hard to find a flat around here.'

'Redhills, you say? That way, isn't it?' Pasha points behind them.

'Yep, that's right. Go back on yourself and take the left.'

It's only half an hour before they arrive at Dartmoor. They turn onto a more minor road, a single track with a view of the moors ahead just as the clouds release their promised shower. They shelter under a tree, still without its full spring canopy, but it's the best they can find. Heavy drops find their way down the back of Mae's neck despite her raincoat and she squirms, Pasha's arm around her shoulders doing little to warm her.

They say nothing for some time, the rally like the elephant in the room. So many thoughts whizz round Mae's head as she stares into the gloomy distance and her mind plays over scenes of the day: the sight of the bonfire, the hate in the crowd, the people burned to death in the care home. She doesn't disagree with the points made on that stage, yet doesn't agree either. But the emotion she feels more than any other is guilt. Guilt that she is pregnant, guilt that she agrees there shouldn't be any more babies, or less, anyway. Guilt that she has lived so long. Her secret eating away at her more than ever. Guilt that she is bringing a baby into this world. Guilt that she doesn't love her unborn child. And then, even more guilt as the most evil of thoughts comes to mind. That, perhaps the nursing homes burning down really will mean they won't need donors anymore. If enough old people are massacred, the world may welcome her baby.

Terrible thought. Evil woman. Bad mother, she chastises herself silently, pinching her skin, a tiny amount of pain to stop her hurtful thoughts. Not daring to speak out loud in case she says these thoughts and Pasha is appalled. She rubs her temples, trying to rub her evil thoughts away, to stop her wishing such terrible things. How is it possible that she can secretly wish that someone else will mass murder elders to take the burden from her? Because that's what this pregnancy is, a burden. Then her guilt intensifies as mothers shouldn't feel this way. A good mother should feel her child is a blessing and nothing more. A good mother loves her baby from the moment it is conceived. She's a bad mother and a bad citizen. She is losing. Whatever she feels, whatever they do, it's a loss.

The tree pokes into her back, and the persistent drip down her neck becomes more so as the rain gains enthusiasm. Not just chubby drops now, but a blanket, and her hair hangs in rat tails. Mae yearns for home, for the familiar loose floorboard dipping underfoot, the creak in the bedroom door hinge. That tap that either sprays too fast or dribbles too slow. This place is too strange, too different. Back home, she's just one pebble on a stony beach. Here, that beach is made of sand.

The bushes around are just coming into bloom. Mae counts the petals and notes the Fibonacci sequence. She usually prefers algebra to ancient geometry, but she'll take what maths she can get when she's away from home, exposed. A bloom on a thorn bush, ripe for picking.

Pasha takes the paper from his bag, then unfolds the wet pages. The front page is dominated by the headline: *And they're STILL breeding!* Big bold letters shame celebrities who've announced pregnancies, unsolicited photos of swollen tummies, young women with blurred-out faces going into doctor's surgeries, women shamed for buying baby clothes, the outlets pelted with rotten food and spray paint. The article reels off stats, citing each pregnancy as an attack on the Society, on the planet. The carbon footprint of each child, the amount of land used to feed it. That women need to keep their body clocks in check, learn to control their desires and hormones. Selfish behaviours should be punished, it says. *The misdeeds of women's hormones will end us all.* The Pro Grow activities commandeering shipments is heavily criticised, threatening our way of life, terrorist activity, it says. A lack of fresh fruit, fresh fish, car parts, and fuel. All a threat to the existence of Society and that reducing consumption is the mindset of madness and criminals.

Articles on the following pages report on the murdered pregnant women, the tone of the articles ambivalent, more like reading a shopping list. Reports of worldwide mass murder of elders are also reported with the same emotionless timbre as the pregnant women murders. Mae and Pasha's jaws drop when they read the figures. Since the announcement, ten thousand extra murders. Life is expensive, death is cheap.

'It's just one paper,' Pasha says. 'They pick a side. Other papers choose the other side. The Pro Grow seem like they have a sensible message, don't you think?'

Mae shrugs. What can she say? They both read the words. And now they sit, hiding under a tree with most of the world meaning them harm. The Pro Grow message is being drowned out by the Enough movement. The Time's Up anarchists are catching up. Killing and sterilising are gaining more traction than moderation. Who wants to live more modestly when they can just stop others from living at all? Their logic is just one side of a coin.

What sort of world will their child be born into? One that doesn't want it, evidently. An outcast, and Mae knows how that feels. Unwanted, yep, she can tick that off her own list. She's harbouring a child destined to feel forever alone, just like her. The product of evil, of murder, of pollution and selfishness. Born to live in a world where it is deemed as superfluous and unnecessary, to hide from slaughter and hate. To constantly live on one side of a divide.

Pasha's hand is on her arm now, rubbing the chill from her. His face isn't etched with guilt. He looks resolute, caring. Worried, sure, a little. But his determination trumps that. Bad citizen? Maybe. But he's chosen his side. He's chosen his baby. Perhaps, at least, the baby won't be so alone.

Chapter 26

The expanse of moor ahead of them is grey and deserted. It looks less welcoming than the rally, dim light coating lifeless hills. The grassy ground pools from rain, now looking like a swamp and smelling like one too. The road that circumnavigates it is poorly tarmacked and now covered in water. Mae scans the sky above, the gloom dissolving into blue close to the horizon. The grey clouds have an end, at least. Blue sky encroaches on the horizon. She's always hated rain. Memories of poor clothing as a kid replay, parents never checking that she was warm enough, and she was left shivering out in the cold. She'd wait outside her house after school, too young to be alone, really, count the cars that drove past, count the seconds, waiting to be remembered. Donald would say that she's scarred from this, that her parents made her feel alone, but she doesn't have to feel that way anymore. Easy for him to say.

Pasha's arm is still draped over her shoulder. They say nothing for some time, listening to the heavy drops. Some people listen to such sounds to sleep. They're supposed to be soothing, Mae's heard. Another drip finds its way down her neck, and the sound makes her want to pee. Across the mossy grass around them, worms come to the surface. No creature wants to drown in the dirt. Doesn't seem like the worst way to go, she thinks just then. Hidden from view, suffering out of sight.

The rain calms to a drizzle, then the sun breaks through. There'll be a rainbow somewhere.

'There's going to be civil war, Pasha,' she says, 'if there's not already. Or no war. We're just going to get wiped out. The Enough has the Preserved on its side. We don't have a chance.'

'It's going to be—'

'If you say "fine" I'm getting up and going back to Reading right now. There is nothing "fine" about any of this.'

He grips her tighter, pulling her into the crook of his neck. 'We'll get to the drone-free camp. The rest of the Society, well, who knows. But we'll be safe. It's not even that far now.'

The moor ahead goes on forever. How can anything that is further than that not be that far?

'First hotel or B&B we find, we'll stop. Dry off, get some rest. We could even stay a couple of days. As long as it's not a charge by the hour one.' He smiles and nudges her with his elbow.

When the drizzle calms to a mist, they find motivation to leave. The wind behind them makes it less unpleasant, and they join the tarmac road that cuts through the middle of the moor, that seeming more sensible than attempting to cycle over soggy grass. Only a speckling of houses is visible. Sporadic buildings, farmhouses, lonely thatched cottages. No villages so far. No signs telling them to keep away. With every passing mile though, they dread coming across an unwelcoming village, but rolling countryside and sparsity of housing keeps them safe.

After an hour, the bike batteries are in the red and they come across a collection of houses in a tiny settlement called Potsbridge. A little stone bridge crosses the river and over the stream, a quaint-looking bed and breakfast looks like the most wonderful thing they've seen in a long time.

They slog away at the pedals for the final few minutes as the batteries run out, then park the bikes and enter the B&B. It's late afternoon, and the drizzle is getting heavier again. Mae's Mackintosh has failed to keep her dry. She's soaked to the skin and even her bones are cold. She grabs her bag from the bike rack and curses when she finds water has pooled on top and plenty has found its way in. Pasha's is much the same.

They walk up to the reception desk with squelching footsteps, water trailing down their faces from their hair, making them like a pair of drowned rodents. After dinging the little bell that sits on the desk, a woman greets them, smiling with a tired and toothless smile.

'How can I help you?'

As she greets them, Mae notices the sign above the desk telling them it's a 600 plus B&B. Her heart sinks. 'Oh, sorry,' she says. 'We don't have the required Score.'

'Oh, don't you worry about that,' the woman says. 'My husband's idea, that was. But he's not working here now, so I say it's fine. Inspectors are never going to turn up this time of year.'

Mae steps back in surprise. 'Okay. Well, if you're sure.'

'Sure, I'm sure. Not like we've got anyone else here at the moment. How long you staying?'

'One night, maybe two.'

'Lovely. Sign here.'

Holly and Christian Brown sign the register as the woman stares at Mae. Disconcertingly so. She's a kind face, but her eyes burn with scrutiny, and Mae's cold bones heat up. This woman sees her, Mae's sure. She has the kind of fierce intelligence you can measure from a distance, though her eyes tell more of a story of regret. Mae looks everywhere except in her direction, avoiding eye contact. But the woman isn't looking at Mae's face, she's looking at her waist. Mae sucks her stomach in. The wet fabric clings where it shouldn't, as unflattering as it is uncomfortable. Still, her bump is tiny, negligible. The woman can't think she's pregnant. But those eyes are locked on her.

'What brings you guys to Dartmoor?' she asks, still snatching glances at Mae's waist.

'Just exploring the county,' Pasha says.

'I see.' She snaps her attention away from Mae's midriff to look Pasha in the eye. 'Well, my name's Dawn. If you need anything, just ding the bell. Your room is up the stairs on the left.'

As Mae goes to lift her bag, Pasha takes it off her and carries it instead.

'Nice man, you are,' Dawn says. 'Helping her with her bags. Lovely to see. Only time my husband ever helped me was when I was expecting. The bastard he is, never thought to be chivalrous otherwise.'

Pasha and Mae both laugh off her comments, then scurry up the stairs, keeping their blushes hidden from view.

The room is decorated in deep green, an intense colour, dark and foreboding, matching the colour of the Devon flag that's painted on the picture frames. Pictures of Dartmoor decorate the walls, all bleak hills and ponies. It's comfortable enough, more so than the woods, anyway, with a large bed and enough furniture on which to hang their wet things. There's a small TV in the corner, and a vase of fake flowers next to it. Pasha finds the remote and turns on the news.

'God, Pasha. What do you want to know? How shit everything is? How screwed we are?'

'I just want to see.'

Bonfires. That's what's on the telly. Worldwide footage of bonfires burning baby things. Every continent, it's the same, more or less, the Preserved stating their power. Such a collection of 700 pluses is a formidable force. Most are 800 pluses. Their message is the same in every country. They will own Pres-X. They will control who lives and who dies. Preserve not procreate chanting in the background.

'Satisfied?' asks Mae.

'At least it's not as bad here as that country,' he says as the footage shows reports of mass shootings of the sick and elderly across Russia and Africa. Anyone deemed to not be of use to the country are being rounded up, then executed. Fertile women are collected and caged, forced sterilisations, and unconsented abortions.

'I don't think the Society feels a million miles from that at the moment,' she says and hangs her wet things.

Pasha's beard has grown unevenly, she notes, with too much stubble underneath. How is it she didn't realise before? It must have been like that for at least a day. Their grubby clothes and lack of routine have blinded her from her usual worries. She looks at him a while, side-view, he's still facing the telly. Dishevelled, unwashed, bruised, stripped down to his boxers, but the dirt went right through his clothes to his skin. She must be as bad. Her unclean skin itches and she scratches, shedding some dirt. She searches their luggage for their toiletry bag, sure to find some scissors in there, but they have none. Pasha's medication rattles at the bottom of the bag.

'You taken your pills?'

He takes one from her and swallows with some water. Lies back on the bed, hands behind his head. 'Well, we'll soon be somewhere they can't touch us. It's not far now, I'm sure of it.'

'Glad you're sure of something.'

He flicks through the channels. News programmes play on every station, interspersed with adverts for elder citizen relocations to camps with armed security. Ads asking for foetus donations are frequent and feature pictures of jars filled with foetuses and smiling scientists. The would-be parents look pleased with their mega-sized cheque. News bulletins feature Pro Grow actions are condemned by most channels, citing damage to the economy, that purchasing excess crap is what keeps the wheel of money rolling, how the Pro Grow are threatening to bring the world back to the Stone Age and twentieth century war era rations. The general public being interviewed express their outrage, that they couldn't buy their favourite cut of beef, that peach juice was nowhere to be found, that they needed a new outfit for some living room furniture reveal party, but the lack of viscose meant they had to wear something drab. Then, a face they recognise.

'Oh, my God, is that—'

'Yep,' Mae says. 'Aliya. Turn it up.'

Aliya's perfectly presented face, sculptured eyebrows and slick plait fill the screen. The top of her peacoat is visible, faux fur trim fluffed to perfection as she stands in front of one of the most exclusive cafés in Reading.

It's simply dreadful. My daughter Candice here needs a new outfit for her dance competitions. She competes at a high level for her age, but no sequins anywhere! Not even any face glitter. These Pro Grow terrorists are holding our way of life ransom. And for what? We have to make sacrifices so that the world can carry on breeding? The whole situation is ridiculous. People need to start thinking about the bigger picture. No orange juice anywhere. And vitamin C is so important. They're damaging our health, these Pro Grow Nazis.

'They're only showing her face and not her five-month pregnant stomach, then?' says Mae through her teeth.

Aliya. Fucking Aliya and her stupid fucking glitter. Like that is in any way important. As if Candice hasn't got a million dance costumes, as if she even needs a new one. Mae kicks the table leg. A bit of pain is what she needs to quell her anger, the band on her wrist not nearly snappy enough. *What crap. What utter crap.*

After flicking through the channels, Pasha is about to turn off the telly when he finds a little support. A hint of a rainbow after the rain. One news channel touts the benefits of long-term moderation in consumption. How, with or without population stagnation methods, consumption reduction seems sensible. Mae and Pasha watch with mouths agape as the channel condemns the new policies of sacrifice, referring to withdrawing medications for elder citizens while the richest can take Pres-X as a form of eugenics, and begs the government to consider their economic plan of encouraging people to spend, spend, spend to boost the economy. They call the new laws a knee-jerk reaction, offering instant but unsustainable results at a massive cost to the public instead of proper future planning.

The politician they interview is so Z list, Mae has no idea who she is. She simply quotes the successes of the new laws, the billions they have banked, and the need for urgent action globally. She says every country across the globe has agreed to the methods, so it's tough. Pres-X encourages people to live healthily, she says, it's not offered to unhealthy people. The elder citizens losing their medications are unhealthy. It's simple evolution, she claims, much to the journalist's dismay.

'Well, nice to know there are some people on our side, at least,' Pasha says.

Mae frowns, quite unsure as to what her side is, then continues hanging wet things over furniture. 'If you say so.'

'I wonder how Ro and Moira are,' he says.

'And your nan.'

'I'm going to call her, let her know we're okay. Make sure she's okay.'

Mae nods, then hands him a phone that somehow managed to stay dry. He turns it on, then dials the only number it has saved.

'Are you safe? Have you made it?' Iris asks before they've even had a chance to say hello.

'Yes, yes. We're fine,' Pasha says. 'We're in Dartmoor, Devon.'

'My, my! You've done so well! Are you enjoying your adventure? Tell me you're enjoying it? It must be lovely to be away from this busy town and somewhere new. All that lovely countryside, such a wonderful experience.'

'It's great, Nan.'

'It's Mae I was thinking of, really. Is she enjoying it?'

'It's certainly been eye-opening,' says Mae, as unable to lie as ever. 'We just wanted to make sure you're okay.'

'Of course I am. Why wouldn't I be?'

'Lack of medication, old folk's homes being burned down, and food shortages,' Pasha says.

'Oh, don't you worry about that. My hacker friends keep an eye on me and all the unrest. There's still some SAS around.

They'll let me know if any trouble comes my way. I'll eat whatever is available, and I don't need any medication. I've got all the painkillers I want. I feel wonderful. Hooper says hello. Say hello to Hooper.'

'Hi, Hooper,' they both say, stifling a laugh.

'He misses you, I can tell.'

'Great,' says Pasha as Mae rolls her eyes.

'I checked your emails. No news yet on your exemption. Mae, someone called Sadie says hello, something about they've paid five hundred grand and it's all going ahead.'

Mae's stomach knots, and she bites her lip. Sadie's actually going through with buying a life donation.

'And Ro?' asks Pasha. 'Ro and Moira?'

'Spoke to them yesterday. I was on a video call, and Moira told me my hair looked a mess. Can you believe it? She moaned a fair bit that they can't get something, what was it? Some sort of tea she likes, I forget now. No deliveries, apparently. Quite the drama. Anyway, they seem fine, and are moving out of their hotel and into a house next week. Oh, and they're having a boy.'

'A boy!' Pasha says, grabbing Mae's hand.

'Yes, they bought an at-home scanner and watched some online videos on how to use it, emailed the footage to an online doctor. Couldn't risk going to the doctors with all the trouble. Made me wonder about you two, you seeing a doctor? You starting to show?'

'A little, not really,' Mae says. 'And maybe we'll see a doctor when we get to the drone-free place. Not sure.'

'Well, people had babies before doctors were invented. I'm sure you'll be fine. We should go, anyway, save the batteries. Call me when you get to the hippy camp?'

'Will do,' Mae says. 'Say hi to your hacker friends for us.'

'Bloody cheek. I know you're making fun of me.'

'Bye, Nan.'

'God bless, you two. God bless.'

Pasha hangs up, then lies back on the bed, smiling, his eyes glistening. 'A boy. Can you believe it? Our little one is going to have a boy cousin.'

'At least they're all okay.'

'What do you think we're having?' asks Pasha.

'Right now, a lovely long sleep.'

Pasha folds his arms and sticks out his bottom lip, making his childish sulky face. For the briefest of moments, Mae wonders if their child will have the same expression. She blinks away the thought and ignores his sulk. A ton of stress and their lives turned upside down is what they're having. She can't think beyond that, about what they're having in future tense. Future planning is for those with the luxury of security in the here and now. She's struggling to not think about what just happened a few hours ago. The only hope for the future she had was escaping another riot. And right now, all she can think of is getting clean and sleeping. Months in the future after a pregnancy that no doctor will monitor in a world where so many want her and the baby dead?

That's inconceivable. Too far away.

Chapter 27

They stay three nights at the B&B as the rain continues. The grey skies outside their window go on for eternity, the briefest glimpses of blue being only a tease before the rain clouds engulf them again. In that room, it feels like they are the only two people in the entire world. No Society outside, nothing that needs counting or organising. They, like everything in the room, are in the correct place. Compartmentalised. For those few days Mae wishes they could stay like that forever, away from noise and prying eyes, from elbows and tuts. No one watching, no one judging, only dim lights and silence where Mae can fall softly into Pasha's arms and imagine her heart isn't calloused by time and politics. They can just be.

Dawn asks no questions, much to Mae's relief. She happily serves them up large portions at breakfast before they return once again to their room, only leaving to have another meal at the pub across the road. It's a typical countryside style pub, old wooden farming equipment, trinkets on shelves, pictures of livestock, local beers on tap. Lucky for Pasha, since any beer imports are now impossible to source, according to the locals.

The pub regulars say how lovely it is to have tourists visit outside of the main season. Pasha and Mae say they're from Exeter, in need of some fresh air. Whether the locals think they're Preserved or not, they don't say, but they're as welcoming as can be.

Mae doesn't feel out of place, not too much anyway. She wears a baggy jumper always, her tummy discreet. Her hair has stopped kinking from its years of being plaited and now hangs more naturally. She still hates the feel of it down the back of her neck, but it's a minor inconvenience that she hides well. They hand wash their dirty clothes, sleep in a comfortable bed, and avoid the news.

It's a few days of sanctuary. A tiny hideaway, quiet, where time is erased, away from the busy towns and cities. Sure, the people are a bit old-fashioned, say inappropriate terms, talk about the good old days, but Mae likes that; she feels less like an alien. Not at home, but not as odd as she thought she would. She had never realised before how much she detests crowds. Reading is her home, as it's where she grew up. Mae spent her life locked in small rooms, avoiding the crowds that come with the town, her nose in a book, learning algebra and equations. Accountancy is way below her competence level, but it is — or was — steady enough work. That's the thing about numbers. Over time, language changes, science learns, everything moves on. Except numbers. They are infinite and infinitely the same. There's safety in that regularity. She's never had to re-learn how to count. However much time has passed, the value of X in a given formula is the same.

They opt to leave on the fourth day as the sky finally clears, a few bubbly clouds dotting across the cyan blue, the sun beaming. The temperature is warming as Mae realises it's the 18th of February. Spring comes earlier and earlier these days, so much earlier than when she was a girl. Daffodils are opening and blowing merrily in the breeze along the path and roadside, birds singing their spring songs. She counts on her fingers, nearly nineteen weeks. There's no denying it. Her stomach is protruding. Pasha runs his hands over her waist and glows in the way she is meant to, takes joy in her body's changes where she tries to suck it in.

He cups her face, looks into her eyes, seeing her insides, she's sure of it. He notices people in the way she doesn't, understands their faces and actions, can read anyone like they have nothing to hide. Does he see her as well as she thinks, the inner workings of her mind, the darkest place she tries to ignore? When she looks at people, all she sees is their movement, the transition from A to B. He notices everything in between. If his stare is meant to reassure, he fails. Feeling inspected and examined instead, she looks away, face red with shame. She can't feel his excitement, his love for this great unknown. She just needs to get dressed and pack. Practical things. Distracting things. Planning, not thinking.

As she packs, Pasha pops out to a shop down the road to stock up on some food for the journey. Snacks of fruit and energy bars was his plan, but he comes back with crisps, dried fruit, and a small bag of nuts. It's all they have, apparently.

'It'll do,' he says.

Mae grabs a baggy T-shirt to wear to breakfast, then they head downstairs. Dawn has laid out croissants, toast, jams, muesli, and milk. No orange juice still. No fresh fruit. Not that Mae minds. The croissants smell delicious.

Dawn is looking more tired than usual and is walking around as fast as she can, which isn't very fast, seemingly playing catch-up on all the things that she wanted to get done.

'Leaving today still?' she asks.

'Yes,' Pasha says. 'Making the most of the good weather for hiking.'

'Sorry breakfast looks a bit disorderly. Bles had me up half the night.'

'Bles?'

'My husband. Tell you what, when you're done, why don't you come meet him?'

'Okay, sure,' says Pasha, being polite where Mae scowls at the thought.

They finish up, then follow Dawn along the hallway to a wooden framed door with frosted windows. It doesn't look heavy, but Dawn grunts as she pushes against it, her breath fogging the glass. Their own living space, Dawn says as they walk through, footsteps quieter on worn-down carpet rather than the laminate of the hallway. The smell of ammonia and unbrushed teeth makes Mae hesitate for a moment before collecting herself and following Dawn inside. In the corner of the living room, a hospital style bed with a man lying down, sleeping, groaning occasionally. Jerky movements.

'This is Bles,' says Dawn, recoiling her nose as she speaks. 'He's horrible. Nastiest man you'd ever meet. Treated me badly forever. Never said a nice word to me. Never bought me anything nice or took me anywhere. And he does me the final insult by having a major stroke and getting dementia, so he needs constant looking after. I'm up often in the night while he wanders around ranting and raving, getting lost and breaking stuff, being a dick like he always was. Then all day he just lies here, no good to anybody.'

'Well, I'm sure you had some happy times,' says Mae, as she tries not to stare.

'I'll be happy to be rid of him.'

Pasha and Mae look at each other with raised eyebrows, the stuffy room suddenly turning chilly.

'I can spot a pregnant woman a mile away,' says Dawn, looking at Mae's waist and raising her eyebrows. 'You don't have to be shy with me, love. I was pregnant six times myself, but none of them worked out. I wasn't meant to be a mum. Reckon the universe was just trying to stop his nasty genes from being passed on. Quite right, too. The old git.'

'Oh, I'm sorry, I really am,' Mae says.

'There's something wise about you,' Dawn says to Mae, putting her reading glasses on to peer at her. 'I see it in you.

Smart. Like you understand the way of things.' She eyes Pasha now with pressed lips. 'She's older than you, isn't she?'

'Two years younger, actually,' Pasha says.

'If you say so,' Dawn says with a shrug. 'Anyway, I notice you're not wearing a bracelet. So, five hundred grand and he's yours.'

'Excuse me?' Mae says.

'Five hundred grand, and I'll sign him up as a donor. I've got power of attorney. I can do it. Can haggle a bit, if you like. But I'm not giving him away for free. This is an honest sale. There's a lot of people willing to pay, loads online. I could put him on one of them auction sites, but you two seem so nice. I feel like fate has brought you here.'

Mae and Pasha clock eye contact, shifting on their feet. 'Thing is,' Pasha says. 'We really don't have any money.'

'Thing is, love, you really don't have any choice,' says Dawn as if she is explaining to a kid how to tie their shoelaces. 'You city kids always have so much more squirrelled away. You're not from Exeter, I know that much. You're from a richer city, London or somewhere. Reckon you've got a house worth a pretty penny.'

Mae truly takes in the house they're in, so much bigger than anyone has in Reading and worth about a tenth of the price, probably. Five hundred grand seemed possible a few weeks back, but now she can't fathom how they'd repay the extra hit on the mortgage. And that's even if the bank would let them take the money out of their house. She hadn't considered it before, the permanence of their decision to run. Their jobs were dicey, anyway, clients diminishing, what little savings they had would be eaten up with their current mortgage repayments over the next few months. Her heart races faster as doubt and fear start to shake inside her. This was a mistake. This whole getaway was a rash mistake. Perhaps this is a chance, a chance to turn back the clock, go back to the familiarity of home and work their way out of debt. Retrain, like they were planning to do before.

Pasha shakes his head and holds his hands up in the same way Iris does when showing Hooper she's no food for him. 'We've explored this and honestly, we can't. We just can't. We don't even have jobs right now. And anyway, we don't even agree with it. It's not right. It's just not right.'

'He's a miserable old dick. You'd be doing him a favour,' says Dawn, turning her nose up at the sight of her husband. 'It's not fair to let him carry on like this, trapped in his mind, no clue which year it is, doesn't even know me half the time. You'd be doing him a kindness. Plus, the money could help up my Life Score, give me a chance at getting some Pres-X. You'd be taking his life but giving me a whole new one. I'd get to live again, without this dickhead screwing things up for me.'

Mae jumps as next to her, Bles stirs and groans. A wraithlike sound, as if he's calling them from the beyond.

'Pasha,' says Mae, still staring at Bles. 'Maybe we should think about this.'

'I'm sorry. But we simply can't,' Pasha says. 'We just don't have that much money.'

'Three hundred grand,' Dawn says, holding her hand out to shake.

'Pasha—'

'Seriously, Mae?' He stares at her, shaking his head.

'You were the one wanting to find someone,' Mae says, switching her focus between Pasha and the man straining to speak from the bed, the whites of his eyes reddening from the effort, his breath like an old bin. 'Remember your split lip, Pasha? Like Dawn said, we'd be giving her a new life. We could go home.'

A desk chair sits in the corner of the room and Pasha wheels it over, then sits, leaving Mae standing next to Bles. She inspects Bles's face, fully awake now, staring past her, mouth slightly agape like nobody's home.

'He seems gone already,' Mae says.

'He basically is,' Dawn says. 'You'd be doing him a kindness. Not that he deserves it.'

'I think we need to have a think,' Mae says.

'Well, stay another night. Free of charge,' Dawn says, a little lighter. 'How does that sound? Mull it over.'

'The weather is good, Mae,' Pasha says. 'We should get going.'

'We need to think, Pasha.'

Dawn clears her throat. 'Forecast is decent for the next week. No need to rush.'

Mae and Pasha pause a moment, Pasha on the chair, rubbing his forehead, Mae backing away from the bed to take his hand, encouraging him to stand. They go back to their room, the cheap laminate flooring spongy under their heavy feet, the weight of their decision like a physical burden. Back in the room, they sit side by side on the bed, fingers just touching.

'I know I said before we should,' Pasha says. 'But actually seeing a person that old, still alive, knowing we'd be taking their life, it's all different. I didn't know how different it would feel. And it's not him saying so. It'd be different if it were, but it's not.'

Mae doesn't respond but intertwines her fingers with his, feels his warmth. Always too much warmth. Too compassionate, too kind. Why can't he be the ruthless and practical one? Why must such a decision be hers to make? She puts one hand on her stomach and imagines Pasha's warmth inside her. What sort of child would be born from someone forced to make such a cold decision? From a mother with no heart.

'We're waiting on our exemption,' he says. 'And the hippy camp might really work out. We have other options.'

'None are good options.'

'But still.'

She shuffles closer, then leans her head on his shoulder. 'The exemption said it depends how many apply. So us not using it means someone else gets to. The net effect is the same.'

'Did you really just turn this situation into a maths puzzle?'

She half-smiles as he groans and leans his head on top of hers. They stay like this for a while. Still, thinking. Every few seconds that pass, Mae stiffens slightly more, takes some of Pasha's warmth and locks it away. Unused and unreciprocated, dampening his affections. She sits up, rigid, being the cold person she needs to be.

'I'm going down to see him again,' she says. 'To look at his face again. To imagine being responsible. Get a feel for whether it would be an evil thing to do or a kindness, like Dawn says.'

'Okay. I'll come. Let's look together.'

They pad down the stairs and towards the back room, the door swinging silently open, Dawn nowhere in sight. Mae hadn't noticed the pictures on the walls earlier. Frames still with the stock photos they came with, none of Dawn and Bles. They hang at crooked angles, dust collecting on the top. Twelve of them all together. On the mantle are five chipped, dusty ornaments in mismatched colours and eclectic styles. Plastic plants. A broken clock that idles at 13:07. With the patterned carpet and discoloured painted walls, it seems like the room hasn't been touched in a century. There is no love in that room, not an ounce of care.

Bles is still in bed, lying on his back, eyes open yet unseeing, mouth open yet mute. Holding hands, they approach the bed. Somehow, Bles looks even more vacant than he did before, breaths coming out in raspy whispers, dark skin turned blotchy, lips cracked and raw.

'He doesn't look like he's got long, Pasha. Don't you think?'

Pasha leans in, his face inches away from Bles's. 'It's like he's empty inside. Poor chap.'

Pasha startles, then snaps away as Bles grunts, eyes focussing and looking straight at Pasha's. A jolt of recognition. He blinks, mouth moves, then breathes deeper. Words try to come, but they're inaudible.

'What's he saying?' asks Pasha.

Mae shakes her head and peers closer to the bed. 'I don't know.'

Bles's mouth continues to move, making the shapes of words in the absence of sound. On the side, a jug of water sits next to an empty glass and Mae pours some out, then lifts his head slightly so he can take a sip. The whole time his eyes don't leave hers. She doesn't stare at his face but at the crumbs and stains down his T-shirt and bed linen instead. Seventeen big crumbs and countless tiny ones. After he's had several sips, Mae takes the glass away. Pallid spittle attaches itself to the glass, leaving a semicircle of mush on the rim.

His breathing steadies, and he finds his voice, managing two simple words. 'Help me.'

Mae gasps, cocks her head. Surely she misheard?

He wheezes a breath, then says, 'Save me.'

Chapter 28

There's no mistaking it. He said save me. Mae's eyes widen, and she leans in closer.

'Dawn will kill me.'

Mae backs away, and Pasha grabs her wrist.

'Shit, Mae.'

'Oh, my God, Pasha.'

With a weak arm, Bles points to the bedside table. 'Look,' he says.

Mae opens the drawer and lets out a little yelp when she sees the bottles and bottles of tranquillisers. 'Pasha, what the hell?'

Pasha picks up bottle after bottle, inspecting the labels. 'This is beyond my physiotherapist knowledge, but five different tranquillisers. That's enough to knock him out for days.'

'Help me,' Bles rasps again, quieter than a whisper.

Mae's brain isn't working quickly enough. She struggles to think while Pasha just stares at the bottles.

'What do we do, Pasha?'

'We should call someone, tell someone,' he says.

'Tell someone what?'

The shrill voice rattles Mae's bones as much as the pills in the bottles, and they jump, then turn. Dawn is in the doorway, a forced smile dominating her face.

'The old git is due his next meds. He'll be ever so confused,' Dawn says as she approaches, taking slow footsteps. Mae steps in front of the bedside table, the drawer still open, Pasha's hands behind his back, still holding the bottles.

'Just got to get him dosed up. He'll be nice and calm then.'

She steps closer, the open drawer in her eye-line, and Mae and Pasha's faces redden.

Pasha places his hand in front now, holding the bottles of pills right under Dawn's nose. 'You're knocking him out. Why so many of these?'

'We just stocked up before they banned medicines for us elders. Have one if you like. They'll take all your worries away.'

'He said help me,' Pasha says. 'He says you're trying to kill him.'

'He's got dementia, love. He talks a load of nonsense. And I was thinking, two-fifty, how does that sound? Bargain, that is. You won't get a better offer than that.'

Mae recoils when Bles's hand touches hers, cold spindly fingers like a brush with a ghost.

'Please,' Bles says, the quietest voice yet, still riddled with fear.

Dawn steps further forward, still smiling. 'I've got your pictures, you know. I'll upload them onto the Society Police app. Just because I'm old doesn't mean I don't do these things. I know how, and I will.'

'It's not illegal to be pregnant,' Mae says.

'Yeah, but using fake IDs is. And you know what'll happen. Your face will get recognised everywhere. Your real names, too, not them fake ones you signed in with. And no bracelet? Them Enough people will mow you down in the street. Beat that baby out of you.'

Dawn is just a step or two away from them now, one hand in her pocket, grasping an object, something large, a wooden handle sticking out of the top.

'Who do you think you're fooling?' she says. 'You're out of options.'

Mae's heart bangs against her ribcage. She looks back at Bles, her vision hazing with tears. He's so ill and so scared. How can it be possible that someone can cause another so much fear?

'You're killing him,' Pasha says.

'He's on his way out anyway. I'm just stopping him being so much of a bother in the meantime. Two hundred grand, and that really is my final offer.'

'You're going to kill him, with or without us,' Mae says.

'Yeah, but I'd much rather be rid of him and be a couple of hundred grand richer. That nan-E is a nice way to go, they say. Too nice for the likes of him. Someone will want his donation. You should count yourselves lucky, being front of the queue like this.'

'Help me.' Bles's plea again, more substantial now, throaty and grating.

'We can't do this,' Pasha says. 'He doesn't consent.'

'He doesn't know what he's saying,' says Dawn, her smile faltering into a grimace. 'And you aren't leaving here without signing up.'

Dawn takes her hand out of her pocket, clutching a tack hammer.

'Whoa!' says Pasha as he pushes Mae behind him.

'Christ, Dawn,' Mae says. 'You're going to try and beat us up?' Dawn's tiny, brittle frame doesn't look like much of a threat, and she moves back around to Pasha's side. 'Seriously, that's a ridiculous idea.'

Dawn smirks, locking eyes with Mae, then hits herself in the forehead with the hammer.

'No!' cries Pasha. 'What the hell are you doing?'

'Fell off my bike years ago. Got a metal plate on my skull.' She smashes the hammer into her head again.

'You trying to dent it?' Mae says. 'Stop it, Dawn! This is stupid.'

She hits herself once more, blood trickling its way between her eyebrows and Pasha lunges forward, wrestling the hammer out of her hand before she can hit herself again. In her other hand is her phone. Mae recognises the orange glow of the camera filming with the Society Police app.

'They hit me!' Dawn cries down the camera. 'They're trying to steal me and my husband. They're old folk kidnappers!'

She turns the camera round to face Pasha, who's frozen, mouth hanging open, hammer still in his hand. He lets it go, and it clangs to the floor. 'I didn't hit you! I'd never!'

'Shit, Pasha,' says Mae, cowering behind him now, covering her face with her hands. 'We need to get out of here.'

'Two hundred grand, and I won't press charges,' says Dawn, her jumper wrapped round the camera now, muffling the microphone. 'Your fingerprints are on that hammer, and your faces on camera.'

'We're not going to be blackmailed into killing your husband,' Mae says, loudly, hoping the phone will pick up her voice.

'I didn't do anything,' says Pasha again, voice quivering, his obtuse stare boring into Dawn. 'How could you?'

The blood is dripping onto the carpet now, seven drops so far. Its stain blends in with the pattern, and Mae wonders what other secrets that pattern has disguised over the years.

'Just use an auction site,' Mae says. 'Like you said, you'll get a good price.'

'Knowing my luck, he'll be dead before anyone has time to declare and pay. He needs to register as a donor now. Today.' She rubs her eye to dislodge some blood, but only manages to smear it across her face more.

Mae looks at Bles once more, his mouth still forming the words he is again too weak to say. Maybe he was horrible to Dawn, a bad husband, bad citizen even. But right now he's a frail old man begging not to die. She can't. She knows she just can't.

'I'm sorry. But no. We can't. Come on, Pasha. Let's go.'

They make for the door, Dawn following as fast as she can. Pasha straps the bags to the bikes, unplugs the charge cable, Mae trying to help but getting in the way. She doesn't look back, but Dawn's voice is getting closer, shouting louder.

'You've been in our village, taking food out of our mouths when there isn't enough to go around. This is the least you can do. Bloody scroungers. Two hundred grand, final offer.'

Pasha loads the bikes on the rack, Mae checks they're zipped up, then puts her helmet on with unsteady hands.

'You'll be back. I'll give you two days. I'll wait that long to inform the Society Police, just because I know you'll be back. You won't get a better offer.'

Pasha tightens the final bag strap on Mae's bike rack, and she gets going first, adrenaline making her pedalling sporadic. At least the bike batteries are full, and she can use the turbo function. Pasha catches up after a few moments, while Dawn's cries diminish as they cycle away.

Chapter 29

Having the wind with them and the sun shining, they ride at a good pace for an hour, conserving the batteries, just using their rested legs. They don't speak and concentrate only on putting some distance between them and Dawn. Across the moor, spring flowers are in bloom. Mae sees the first butterfly she's seen in years, and Pasha says he's never seen one. Then another. A red and black one first, then a yellow one shortly after. They slow their pace intermittently to appreciate the sound of bees.

After a couple of hours, the road signs stop pointing the way they're going, all telling them to backtrack or turn another way.

'We must be close to the county border,' Pasha says. 'Maybe put a bottle of water in your pocket again, just in case.'

She does that and after a few minutes, they abandon the bikes along a crop field, long stalks swaying in the wind. They haven't seen a house for a few minutes and the road is more or less empty, the only sound the rustling plants and the distant hum of farm machinery.

'How far to the border, do you think?' asks Mae.

'Hard to say. Not too far, I reckon, judging by the signs. Your legs up for it?'

'I think so.'

They walk. Mostly in silence, waiting for someone to approach them or question them. They watch for scrutinising glances and brace for interrogation. Mae ties her hair back, the irritation on her neck seeming pointless when there's no one around. They eat small portions of their rations, then sip at water as the day warms up.

After a while, they take a left and head over some more remote land, rolling hills. At the top of one, they see the sea estuary coming inland. It's colder up on the cliff, the wind carrying an icy gale, no relief from land. They walk downhill some more, across grasslands, sandy, soft underfoot. The sort of ground that sucks the energy from your legs. Seabirds fly overhead, but they're not the noisy sort they saw before. They glide effortlessly in the wind.

The grassy sand becomes more like scrub, rough and pointy bushes nip at their legs and snag their clothes. Mae drinks the last of her water, and Pasha's bottle contains only a sip.

'Damn,' he says. 'I thought we had a bit more than that.' He inspects his bag and finds a wet patch where the bottle has been, then screws back on the mis-threaded lid of the bottle. Too late for that to be effective now.

'We should buy a bottle from somewhere,' Mae says.

Looking around, 'somewhere' seems like a very faraway place. Squinting in the late afternoon sun, Pasha eyes the landscape, scanning the horizon for a sign of a shop or café.

'That way,' he says after a long thought. 'There's a road, roads lead to shops, and it's not too far out of the way.'

Without a better idea or even a hunch to follow, Mae agrees, and they set off, walking towards the road.

'If we do see anyone, at least we really look like hikers now,' Pasha says.

'Great. Irony. That's just what we need.'

'It won't be far, Mae-bug. I'm sure.'

She can feel a toenail digging in, and the small of her back aches more than her calves. Nothing compared to thirst, she tells herself as she plods on several paces behind Pasha. It takes over an hour to find a shop, the sun now merely an afterglow, the clouds pink and purple overhead. Crickets are singing and already Mae can feel dew collecting on her head. The shop is open, to their relief. A small newsagent next door to a pub and another shop that once sold beach paraphernalia. Its windows boarded up, the panes collapsed in places, and a burned-out hole through the brickwork. Eight cars parked out front, all owners in the pub by the looks of it.

'I wonder if we can get a hot meal in the pub?' Pasha says.

Mae looks at her legs streaked with mud and dusted with foliage, wriggles her toes in her shoes, finding blisters and aches. A comfy chair would be nice.

'Okay,' she says. 'Let's get the water first, though.'

Mae waits outside as Pasha buys the water, feeling alone and exposed. She rocks on the balls of her feet, hands in pockets, waiting in a dark corner out of view of the pub windows. Hearty home cooking wafts from the pub, mingled with the comforting aroma of a wood-burning stove. The deep sound of masculine laughter is far more enticing than the mosquito screeching in her ear. When Pasha arrives with the water, Mae leads the way to the pub entrance, batting the dusk bugs away as they walk.

A bell chimes as the pub door opens, and the ten men inside all turn to stare. Pasha and Mae pause in the doorway. The unwelcoming glares freeze them to the spot. They take a step closer. The stares remain fixed. Harder than the stone walls, colder than the night air.

They take another step.

'Got a law-breaker in here, Jake,' says a man stood at the bar, without moving his gaze.

The barman appears, tea towel in one hand, glass in the other. 'What do you think you're doing in here? You know the law.'

'Erm, no?' Pasha says.

'Not you. Her.' He points his finger at Mae, the tea towel hanging underneath accentuating his gesture.

Mae says nothing, just stands still, face reddening with the heat and the attention.

'You not seen the news?' the barman asks with wide eyes, then tuts. 'Bloody youngsters. Too self-absorbed to care about the Society. Don't give a toss about their own county laws.'

'I'm sorry,' Pasha says. 'We've been hiking the county. Not really had access to the news.'

Mae purses her lips at his voice. Not the right accent. Not even close.

'Well, let me enlighten you,' the man who'd been called Jake takes a step forward, dim lights shining off his bald head. 'Girls, like her, fertile age, cannot come into pubs. They're not allowed alcohol. In case they become reckless and get in the mood, you understand? Such girls need to be in control of their urges and stop burdening the county. The whole bloody Society is rife with girls and their urges.'

'I assure you that will not happen,' says Mae, putting a little extra emphasis on her Rs.

'Gay, are you? Well, you still shouldn't be in public. Still got a womb, gay or not.'

'N-no,' Mae says, struggling for words. 'I mean, I am not going to drink alcohol or have any urges.'

The man steps right up to Mae now, his beer breath in her face like a misty stench. She swallows back some bile.

'Why no alcohol, huh? Up the duff, are you?'

'We just agree, completely,' Pasha says. 'Women being frivolous has ruined the Society. I keep my woman on a tight leash.'

Mae clenches her jaw, undecided if she is more relieved at Pasha's words or livid.

The man pats Pasha on the arm. 'Glad to hear it. Still, the law is the law. She can't come in.'

'We could do you a takeaway, if it's some food you're after?' says the barman. 'Not got a lot in. Those damned Pro Grows have made some meat and things hard to get hold of. But I could do you a chicken pie, no red meat, some potatoes. No desserts. Can't get the sugar.'

'Bloody terrorists, those Pro Grows,' another man stooped over the bar says. 'Not had any apple crumble in weeks. No steaks, either. They need locking up.'

The rest of the bar drink to that.

'Sounds great,' says Mae, her voice husky in her dry throat. 'We appreciate it.'

'Maybe a bottle of beer to go? Just for me, obviously,' Pasha says.

They wait outside as instructed. It's dark now, the pink glow of clouds replaced with blackness. The mosquitoes once again scream around Mae's ears. The light above the outdoor seating area flickers with the moths that flutter around it. Mae fidgets, her back and neck itching, then scrapes every hair she can off her shoulders. Pasha stands under the flickering bulb, half in light, half in shadow, his messy hair casting a striking shade across his forehead, his jawline accentuated in obscured dimness. Hard to imagine he just said those words. Those awful, misogynistic words.

'Those words you said were horrible,' says Mae, quieter than a whisper but, with all the hardness she can convey.

'You know I didn't mean it.'

'But it appeased them. It actually appeased them. This is the world we live in now.' She wants to scream rather than whisper, wants to be heard rather than silenced. For once, being ignored doesn't seem like the best thing. It's like the Society are granting her desires and shutting women away. Only now it seems wrong. Enforced. Her choices sucked out of her.

Pasha puts his arms around her and pulls her in close. 'It'll be nice at the hippy camp. None of these kinds of people.'

'You don't know that, Pasha.'

'We have to trust Nan. What else can we do? At least they didn't notice our accents. Yours was quite good, I thought.'

She laughs at this and shakes her head. 'Yours wasn't even close. Nowhere near.'

He holds his face in mock defence, then puts his arm around her again, though failing to keep the chill off. Mae shivers, her hiking clothes not warm enough for such exposure. Away from the pub, the expanse of scrubby land awaits them. An uncomfortable night camping on rough ground with a zillion bugs around is not in the least bit appealing.

When the food arrives, the takeaway box hot in her hands, they switch their torches on, then walk out into the scrub.

Chapter 30

After another hour of walking, picking at the food in the box and taking cautious sips of water, Mae's had enough.

'It's nearly eight-thirty, Pasha. I think we need to call it a day. Maybe have an early night?'

'We should get up early then. Really early. We can't be far. We should do the border in the dark, try to sneak over unseen.'

Mae has little patience to argue, and with no better plan she agrees, and they find a clear patch in the scrub to set up their tent, mostly out of the wind. In the night air, the chilly wind is bitterly cold, not a cloud above to insulate them. When they look up at the dark night sky, they see stars like they've never seen before. A whole streak of them cut through the sky like a great stain. No moon, no artificial light. The sky is dazzling. No wonder Mae always feels so alone when the universe is that big. She's a speck on a speck, less significant than she ever realised. There's something comforting in that, in knowing how tiny and immaterial one life is. However long that life, whatever other lives that life interacts with. Mistakes are fractions of a life, that's all. Goodness, too, is diluted in the never-ending emptiness. She sees it then, in the vastness of the sky. None of it really matters, after all.

Lying in the tent in the blackness, Pasha's arm and leg are draped over her. She's still, on her back, staring up at nothing, so far away from anywhere. When she was a girl, she had a bad dream, of what about she can't recall. But she woke crying, screaming for someone to come. No one did. She shared a wall with her parent's bedroom, so they would have heard. But they left the little girl to scream, so scared. Mae had thought the world outside her room had disappeared, burned away. There must be nothing left. For what other explanation was there for a terrified child screaming for help but left so alone? When she woke the next day, she stepped out of her room, expecting to see blackness where the world once was. But it was all the same. Her parents said nothing, not a word to console her. Her fears were ignored. Just another act from a nuisance child. She knew then she was alone. There was no one coming to help, to care. As much as Pasha tries, as much as she loves him and he means well, she is on an island, far from him always. Skin touching, souls apart.

Pasha wakes early and nudges Mae. Somehow, without an alarm or even a glimmer of light to wake him, he's managed to wake up early.

'Mae. It's five o'clock. Let's get moving.'

They're still in their clothes from the day before, too cold to change. The tent takes a long time to pack up in the darkness, but they manage and are on their way before there's even a hint of sun. In the dark morning, avoiding the thorns is impossible. After a while, Mae doesn't notice them anymore. She can't see the grazes, the scratching feeling now too normal to pay attention to.

The ground underfoot becomes boggy, soaking through their shoes in places, and they make a beeline for a rough road with crumbling edges and longstanding potholes. Ahead, they see the estuary again, glinting in some artificial lights, buoys bobbing alongside small boats, the faintest sound of them creaking and the water hitting the wood. They can't find a way to cross it.

'I think this is it,' Pasha says. 'It's the river. That's the border.'

It's still too dark to make out what's ahead. A few houses, only their outlines distinguishable, windows dark. The river is flowing gently, the sound masking any other.

'I can't see a bridge,' Mae says.

'There won't be if it's a county line.'

Of course there won't be. Why would anyone want to cross a county line? Mae scuffs her wet shoes into the ground. 'I guess we have to swim then. Great.'

'You're a great swimmer. And I don't think it's that deep.'

'Glad your night vision and depth goggles are working.' She doesn't apologise for her snarky comment. Pasha brushes it off.

'There're some boats there, see? Maybe we could use one. There're some little rowing ones there, look. We could manage that. It's stealing, though.'

'It's that or freeze. That water looks cold.'

'Glad your thermometer vision is working,' he says.

Mae scowls, and even in the darkness she's sure he sees it.

Across the path, a pontoon leads down to the water's edge where several simple rowboats lay abandoned. In the dark, Mae counts six, maybe more. Pasha pushes one into the water, its hull scraping against the concrete seeming like the loudest thing Mae's heard in ages. She glances around. No one in sight. He puts the bags inside, then takes Mae's hand, her ankles soaking from the river.

'Shit! That's cold,' she says as the icy water seeps through her shoes. 'Seems my thermometer eyes are accurate.'

Pasha chuckles, shakes his head and gets in, tentatively, the boat rocking to the side as he does. Mae grips the side with all her strength, as if that will stop the boat from tipping over. Once steady, with the ore, he pushes the boat away from the edge, and they're away.

It's calm, water lapping gently on the side of the boat, the mellow bobbing side-to-side. The sky is lightening to their right, bringing some relief from the blackness, the centre of the estuary darker than the edge. Mae looks at her sodden shoes, imagines her toes turning blue inside. It'll need to get a lot warmer for those to dry off.

Pasha is on the ores, the wood groaning against the force of the water. He tries to find a rhythm, with no experience of rowing besides the machines at the gym. But they get further out into the river, the current not too strong, and the metres creep away, slowly.

'Hey! They've stolen my boat!'

Voices carry across the river, echoing from the surrounding hills. The dark outline of houses is now visible with light shining through the windows. The man waves an angry fist from the bank, and Pasha picks up speed.

'Shit, Pasha!'

'I know. Crap!'

He rows with all his strength, gritting his teeth, face turning scarlet in the early sun, sweat streaming. Mae looks back, wishes she hadn't. Four men now, all big. She can't make out the detail in their faces, but their body language and voices make it clear. They're all getting into their own row boats. And they're coming.

Pasha rows, faster and faster. Mae sits, useless, trembling, terrified. The wind picks up, just a little, enough to make it harder for Pasha, enough to sway the boat some more.

'Come on, Pasha.'

'I'm trying!'

His words are barely audible through his strained neck. He pants, breathing heavily with each stroke. The men are gaining, still far enough away. They wouldn't chase them into Cornwall, surely not. Half this river must be Cornwall. Once they're halfway, they'll be safe.

Mae looks left and right, dazzled by the sun as it glares over the horizon. It's hard to tell, but they must be more than halfway across by now. Yet still the men are coming, shouting, livid, relentless. Maybe it's the bank, thinks Mae. The river is Devon; the land is Cornwall.

Maybe this isn't the border at all.

She can't outrun them. No way could she even try. They'd give up when they get their boat back. Surely. She looks behind again. The men are past halfway now, some rowing with one hand, phones up in the other. Society Police. *Great.* Mae shields her face from view. It's too dark anyway. They're too far away.

The bank is getting closer. Almost there now. Pasha's arms shake with each pull and he moans with the effort, then, with a bump, they hit the land. No time for gently gently this time. They both jump out of the boat, water splashing up their legs, already sodden boots more sodden, cuts and grazes stinging from the salt. Pasha grabs the bags, and they run, not looking back, not caring where they go. They just run. The men's voices are fainter behind now. They haven't followed them. They've made it. They're alone, until—

'You two just stole that boat!'

A woman stands in front of them, her truck parked across the road with its engine running. They could run either side, but they wouldn't get far. Pasha drops his bag, holds his chest, tries to catch his breath.

'Borrowed it,' Mae says. 'We left it there for them.'

The woman laughs. A friendly sort of laugh, like making a joke with an old friend. 'Well, I doubt they'll see it that way. Get in, I'll give you a lift.'

They haven't even checked their printout. Mae has no idea what hairstyle she's meant to have. Birds nest, she hopes, as that's how it must look. Even Pasha's is puffy and unkempt. He looks at her, waiting for her to okay the lift. What choice do they have? They jump in the truck, and the woman speeds off down a dirt track. She laughs some more and cheers as they drive away.

'Woop! Ha. Those old Devon guys will be going nuts. Don't worry, they won't follow you here. This is brilliant. I'll give them shit about this for years.'

'You know them?' asks Pasha.

'Course. We've all been arguing over the river forever. Blaming each other for finishing off all the fish. It was their fault, for sure, in case you're wondering.'

Pasha nods, while Mae just sits, words amiss.

'So,' she says. 'What kind of trouble are you guys in?'

Neither answer. Mae instinctively covers her stomach with her hands, and the woman catches her eye in the rear-view mirror.

'Oh,' she says. 'That sort of trouble.'

'We don't mean any harm,' Pasha says. 'We're not here to hurt anybody.'

'You're here for Bodmin, I assume then?' she says, a question but not a question. 'The place with no drones. Good plan, really. I figured we'd get some women trying to make it there, but I wasn't sure how widely known it is. How'd you hear about it?'

Pasha and Mae are stunned into silence for a minute, their plan exposed. Pasha finds his words. 'My nan told me.'

'Resourceful.' She gives an impressed nod. 'I don't reckon many know about it. My sister moved there two years ago. Had headaches forever. Load of nonsense, if you ask me. But she likes it there. I can drive you most of the way, but you'll have to walk the last couple of miles. Cars aren't allowed. It's at a lake, an old fishery. There's no fish left now, so they took over the site. Once you're on the track, you can't miss it.'

'I...we...' Mae's mouth hangs open, wet eyes and dry throat. 'I don't know what to say. Thank you. Thank you so much.'

'Don't mention it. I get to help a nice couple out and take the piss out of the Devon guys. Cracking morning if you ask me.'

The chill from the river disappears, and a warmth spreads over Mae. Kindness, that's what the feeling is. Alien, obscure kindness. It's too easy to forget what that feels like when the world is so harsh and unyielding. Mae can't remember exactly when people's hearts turned to stone. Sometime when she would lock herself away with her maths books, like she saw the emotional winter coming. Had the world turned kinder, slowly, imperceptibly, and she had failed to notice? More likely, kindness clings on in the corners of the Society. Nastiness starts from the inside and works its way out. Perhaps, then, the community they're headed to won't be the most awful place.

The drive isn't far, especially at the speed she's driving. Single track roads lined with tall bushes mostly. Mae shuts her eyes, feels her neck relax, then sways with the movement of the truck like she's floating away, far away. The truck comes to a sudden stop.

'Right. Here you are. This is as far as I can drive you. Just keep heading that way. You'll know when you're there. Half hour's walk. Maybe forty minutes if you're slow.'

'We really can't thank you enough,' says Pasha as he gathers their bags.

'Do me one favour?'

'Anything.'

'When you get there, tell Lottie Molly says hi. Tell her Nan and Gramps send their love, and they wish she'd come home for a visit sometime. And tell her Dusty ate her blanket. I'm not replacing it. Will you remember all of that?'

'Sure thing,' Mae says.

'Well, good luck to you. And, er, well, congratulations.'

They watch the truck speed away, a cloud of dust in its wake. The sun is high enough now. The road visible, a scorched line in the ground. Pasha checks the phones. A trace of a signal, that's all. Soon, they'll have none.

'Best call Iris then,' Mae says.

He nods and dials.

'Hello?'

'Nan! Hi, it's Pasha. We made it. Can you believe it? We made it. Well, almost. Got to turn the phones off here, I guess. It's just a half-hour walk away.'

The line crackles slightly from weak signal. 'I never doubted for a moment. How's Mae?'

'I'm here, Iris. All good.'

'Well, I miss you both. I've been keeping an eye on national security chatter and the Society Police. You've not been flagged up at all. I don't know how you've managed it, but you've not been detected. You sneaky, clever people. I checked your emails yesterday. No news on your exemption yet. I'm glad you're there now, just in time, it seems. Almost a million extra murders now. Can you believe it? Martial law is doing sod all to stop it. They don't want to stop it. I don't know why anyone worries about the population. You can always count on humankind to wipe itself out eventually. I'm just glad you're somewhere safe. So pleased you're out of populated areas and can be somewhere beautiful. Is it beautiful there? I bet it is. And Rolan and Moira are safe. All my family are safe.'

'Nan, you just stay safe. Stay at home. Don't worry about us.'

'I've got Hooper to protect me. I'll be fine. I guess you'll have to try to call when you can.'

'We will,' Pasha says, slowly and assured. 'We'll call once a week.'

'Take care, loves. Be safe. Be happy. God bless you both.'

He hangs up, checks the battery. It's still almost full, so he turns it off. They stand a moment longer, looking at the road ahead, then Pasha picks up his bag, and once again, they walk.

Chapter 31

'You nervous?' Pasha asks.

'Yeah,' Mae says, and she swallows. 'You?'

'A bit.' He puts the bags down for a minute, then stretches his back before they continue. 'Want to play hippy camp bingo?'

'Pasha! We're going to have to live with these people.'

'So? It's just a bit of fun.'

Mae thinks for just a few steps. 'Okay. Incense burning.'

'Obviously.'

'Tie-dye.'

'Easy.'

'I can't think of anymore,' she says after a pause. 'Why is this so much more nerve-racking than Nan bingo?'

'Because we know Nan. And because Nan bingo means we get to eat pie.'

They round a corner of the hedgerow lined road and see Molly was right. It's obvious when they arrive. The morning sun dances across bunting that hangs from two trees, saying, electromagnetic free zone! They step closer, cautiously, though they see no one. Twelve wooden huts are visible, likely more around the other side of the lake. The still water of the lake sparkles, a few ducks on the surface, their ripples catching the light. Some kid's playground toys litter the lawn, and spring flowers are shooting up everywhere. Chickens peck at the ground, there are fenced off areas with vegetables growing, and fruit trees in early blossom. They step a little closer still. Laughter and children's voices come from the biggest lodge.

'Hello?' calls Pasha.

'Shh!' says Mae, and she elbows him. 'That might be rude.'

'Don't be daft. We've got to say hello sometime. Hello?'

A door opens from the largest hut and a woman steps out, long hair trailing over her shoulders, an oversized jumper hanging past her knees, covering her swollen stomach, no bracelet on her wrist.

'And who are you?' she asks, accusatory, unwelcoming.

Mae wants to run; her heart races. They've overstepped the mark, somehow. They're not wanted here. She takes a step back, but Pasha steps forward.

'I'm Pasha, and this is Mae. We, um, well, we were hoping we could find refuge here.'

The woman pauses a moment to look them up and down. Mae freezes, keeping her eyes to the ground.

'Nick! We've got another couple of strays!'

Nick joins her, his hair as long and mingling with his beard. He takes a fraction of a second to size them up. 'We've got no room for strays. Sorry.'

'Please,' Mae says. Her voice surprising her, her pleading, her desperation coming from somewhere innate, primal. 'We've nowhere else to go.' She smooths her jacket over her small bump, making their need clear. 'Molly said you might be kind enough, she said Lottie—'

'My Molly?' says the woman, her voice etched with surprise. 'My sister?'

'Yeah.' Mae looks up now to meet her gaze. 'She says Dusty ate your blanket. Sorry.'

Lottie snorts a laugh, then doubles over in hysterics. 'That damned dog! I made that blanket when I was at school. Man, I hate that dog, stupid mutt. Cute but stupid. You like dogs?'

'Not really.'

Lottie smiles some more and beckons them over. 'Come on in. Let's get you cleaned up. We'll ask the boss.'

Pasha leaves the bags where they are, then grabs Mae's hand and they follow, taking their first steps into the little settlement that reminds Mae of life from long ago, when people had gardens, no Society Police posters, no Eyes Forward logos, no fast or slow lanes. Just space and greenery.

'This is Sue.' Lottie points to an older woman tending to the garden. Her face looks as rough as bark. 'She's the boss here. Her community. She's the founder. Sue. Got this couple, in a bit of trouble, it seems.'

Sue steps forward, smooths some stray hairs against her head, then cups Mae's face in her hands and peers in close. Mae's stomach knots. She knows Sue sees her, in the same way Iris sees her. 'So I see,' says Sue, her tone kind and assured. 'Well, we can't leave them out on the street now, can we? No one deserves that, especially not at her age.'

Mae's cheeks burn under Sue's cold hands, and she doesn't reply. She tries to smile but finds only tears. Pasha puts his arm around her, oblivious to Sue's comment, and Nick leads them to a hut, carrying their bags. He's bigger than Pasha, broader, the bags seeming like nothing to him. Inside the hut is dark, just a small window on one wall overlooking some trees. A shelving rack on the wall, a gas lamp, a mattress on the floor. It smells like freshly cut wood.

They have no time to themselves. With their bags deposited, Lottie gives them a tour, and introduces them to so many people, Mae forgets their names almost instantly. Inside the community, there's a washing area, laundry, a school for the kids, and a library with actual books. Mae can't quite believe it. There are candles in every room, a large fire pit, musical instruments, and gas heaters.

'You'll be safe here,' Lottie says, smoothing her jumper over her tummy. 'No drones to find you. Not many people even know we're here. Best place in the Society to have a baby right now.'

Pasha tells them he's a physio, and they delight in the thought of his skills being put to use. They ask how far along Mae is, and she answers without shame, without fear. No one asks if she has a donor or if she registered on time. They give them food, show them the gardens, then assign them jobs for when they're ready. They meet the children.

When their tour is done, Pasha and Mae unpack their things, Lottie giving them blankets and pillows for their bed. The mattress seems perfectly comfortable, their few possessions fit easily onto the shelves. And it's theirs, their own space.

'For as long as you like,' Lottie says.

When night falls, they gather around the fire under a starry sky. Nick plays the guitar for a while. They eat vegetable stew, all grown on site. They tell stories of their past but don't push Pasha and Mae for much, preferring to wax lyrical about the new laws, the government, the chaos of outside, and their disapproval at the harshness of the world. Even in this isolated community, they know what's happening outside. Old newspapers are used for kindling. They're on Mae and Pasha's side, all of them. The electromagnetic interference from the drones is just one reason they hide away, the other is because they don't like any interference at all. They have plenty of food, they say. Their trips to town are infrequent and becoming even less so. Sod the rest of the world, Sue says, with a bluntness that makes Pasha laugh. His face glows in the light of the fire, and Mae watches the curve of his smile, the colour clash of his clothes, the unevenness of his beard, and she doesn't even mind.

As the fire burns, Mae feels a movement inside her. The baby. For the first time, she feels it kick. She really is pregnant. What the emotion is she feels, she can't describe it. She has no words for such a sensation. She holds her belly and tears gather in her eyes, but she tells no one. It's her moment only. It's the first time in her life she doesn't feel truly alone.

Chapter 32

Part 4

No left, no right. We look forward. To the future. To the Society's future.
Manifesto pledge of the Eyes Forward.

***

Pasha and Mae learn everyone's names and over the weeks, they adapt to their way of life, Pasha faster than Mae. For Mae, the routine is strange, the lack of electricity stranger. Candle-light at night hides the world from her, the flaws of a space masked by darkness. But it hides her too. The way she pulls her chin back, the slightest flinches she hasn't yet learned to suppress. She can wipe a tear and no one needs to know. The campfire at night makes her clothes smell, she can never scrub it away. But they're safe. She can feel that. Safe in a way she hasn't felt since the start of the pregnancy. She can wear any clothes she likes without worrying about her bump, can talk about being pregnant without fear. They both help in any way they can, tending the garden, looking after the chickens. Mae wears her hair however she wants here, which is almost always in a plait, although looser than she used to tie it in Berkshire. She can't stand the feel of it on her shoulders still, the warming days making her neck itch.

Mae teaches the children maths, badly, she claims, since as good as she is at doing things herself, explaining it is a whole other skill. The children don't complain. They find her weirdness exciting, so she is told, and the parents are happy with her lessons. Mae learns to tolerate their loud noises and excitable ways. The textbooks are lacking and without any computers, she finds keeping up her own skills a challenge. A couple of calculators only to be used sparingly, an abacus for the tiny ones.

Pasha finds playing with the children comes much more naturally. He understands their mannerisms, lets them use him for a climbing frame, and laughs at their games. When needed, he rubs everyone's muscle aches away. The children all like to touch Mae's stomach. Where at first she backed away from their sticky fingers and mucky hands, after a while, she concedes and enjoys their curious faces and squeals of delight.

When the sun gives way to darkness, they retreat to their hut, just the two of them, and enjoy their privacy, limbs entangling, breath panting. For a few hours every night, she isn't there. She is anywhere else.

Lottie has her baby just two weeks after they arrive, a little boy, Felix, they call him. The birth is quick, and Mae is there throughout. It's as horrific and magical as she imagined and makes her think her own birth will be impossible. She's not as strong as Lottie, not as resilient, not by far. Mae holds the newborn. It's her first time holding a baby and as she does so, her own baby kicks. She looks into little Felix's eyes with such a fear she can't explain, and such a desire to hold her own. A terrifying impatience. It crept up on her, little by little. That desire, that need.

When it was exactly that she went from being pregnant to having a baby, she can't remember. When was it her sense of dread was replaced with a deep longing? As she tends to the garden, she daydreams of what their baby will look like. Is it a boy or a girl? She thinks about names, imagining a future with the baby, holding its hands as it takes its first steps, watching Pasha be a climbing frame to their own child. His dark mop of hair, his easiness around others. She can see so much that maybe they really are making the impossible possible. The others all ask questions about her, though infrequently. They sense her shyness. She doesn't push away Pasha's affections towards her tummy now. She smiles with him.

Two other women are there who fled when the laws were announced, both further along than Mae. Scarlet and her partner, Dipika, from Devon, much to the ridicule of everyone else. Friendly banter, always, they give as well as they take. Scarlet has hair redder than Mae's, which makes Mae not want to stand next to her, like she'll get bleached out. Dipika is loud, out-spoken, doting. Scarlet rivals her on all three. Their pregnancy was registered on time, but same-sex couples attract too much attention, too much hate, they said. A bracelet jingles from Scarlet's arm. The baby can get a tattoo as soon as it's born. There will be a man's name on its birth certificate. Dipika cracks her knuckles when they tell their story and says she feels cast aside, like she's never going to be the baby's mother. They can never be a family.

'We were going to the Isles of Scilly,' Dipika says one evening in front of the fire. She notices Mae and Pasha's blank faces. 'It's a group of islands, pretty far off the west coast of Cornwall.'

'Sounds tricky,' says Mae, unable to imagine being even further away.

'Less prejudice there, apparently. The population is low, with no working-age people anymore, so they want a few young families. They said the first hundred young families would be welcome.'

'Really?' Mae looks at Pasha, but he's looking straight ahead, not noticing her gaze.

'Yeah. But we stumbled across this community a few weeks ago and figured it was as good as anywhere.'

'Erm, better I'd say!' says Lottie with a laugh, feeding baby Felix.

Dipika and Scarlet smile back at her, contentment in their faces, Mae thinks. Despite only being a couple of weeks ahead in her pregnancy, Scarlet's tummy is much bigger than Mae's and she remarks on it often. Reckon she'll be birthing a toddler, she says with a grin.

Mae just worries. Perhaps her own baby is too small, or maybe it's not growing properly. Could she have worked out the weeks wrong? The thought of a miscalculation plagues her only for a moment, sure she's right. But the baby, is it healthy? It kicks like it is. Scarlet must be right. Babies come in different sizes.

There is also Juanita, who's alone, and a couple of months further along than Mae and Scarlet, her tummy the biggest. She has a pale face, looks exhausted always, eyes of bottomless sorrow, more lines than she should have for her age. She cries often.

'He wanted to donate the foetus to science,' she says. 'Bank the money. So, I ran.'

'All alone?' asks Pasha.

'Yeah. From the other end of Cornwall, so no border to cross. The Isles of Scilly only want couples. They might report me for being alone. In any case, he'd find me there. That's the first place he'd look. His dad works for our local MP and is a big supporter of the Eyes Forward. He'd probably beat me to death himself if he found out. So I walked over thirty miles in a day to get here, leaving long before sunrise, before anyone would realise I'd gone.'

She says this all with barely a breath. She looks so tired and mournful. But she walked all this way, all alone. She plods around the commune slowly like she's weak, but she's strong, thinks Mae. Juanita looks at the sky often, disbelieving the drones will really stay away.

'Don't worry, dear,' says Sue when she sees her. 'There's a covenant on the land. They can't come here. You and your baby are safe.'

Mae avoids Sue, her knowing smile too personal, invasive. She's too kind, considering. Sue talks in Mae's presence of the old world, when Britain was a country and not the Society. She remembers what life was like before Life Scores were invented. She says how much freer they all were once. And Mae nods but says nothing. She looks at the floor, bites the inside of her cheek, then swallows in her parched throat.

Soon after their arrival, Mae passes on Molly's message in full to Lottie. She sneers when her grandparents are mentioned.

'Did Molly tell you what they did?'

'No?'

'Preserved. The two of them. They must be a hundred and twenty or something by now. It's sick. Unnatural. It drove me mad, seeing them get younger and younger bit by bit. That bright pink skin reminding me, like a bloody neon sign. Took about ten years to stabilise and the pink to go completely, and I tell you, when your grandparents look younger than you, that's weird. I was thirty by then, and they looked about twenty. They said it's so they could keep helping with the farm, but that's nonsense. They cashed in every penny they had for that drug, taking money out of the farm, too. If help on the farm was what was needed, we could have hired staff for a lot less. We all lived together in that big farmhouse, my parents and my sister until she moved in with her partner, Faye, and that stupid dog. She got some new job, something secretive. She never told us what. Anyway, that took her away from the farm. Lucky cow. Then I met Nick, and we came here. I'd always had headaches. Maybe it was the electromagnetic sickness, maybe it was just living with family, who knows? All I know is here, my headaches went away.'

Mae listens to every word, stifling her winces and bristles. 'You ever see your family?' she asks.

'Molly comes over from time to time. I miss her. But whenever she comes, we end up arguing. She says I should come home, help with the farm. And I tell her that's what the Frankenstein grandparents are for.'

Mae likes Lottie, she can't help it. She speaks her mind and doesn't mince her words. Her accent is soft, gentle Rs and stresses on the vowels, soothing to listen to, and she doesn't need Mae to say anything. Lottie fills the silences.

Pasha and Mae are honest about where they're from and say all about their journey. They all listen with admiration and fascination. The children think they must be joking or from out of space. They ask what Berkshire is like, laugh and recoil when they mention the clothes, the hair, how busy it is. Even Mae can hardly believe it.

Is she happy in the community? Sometimes she thinks so. Is it happiness or mere distraction? It's easy to forget the world outside of the camp. Easy to pretend.

Berkshire seems so far away. She feels so far away.

Chapter 33

Life is quiet, friendly. Everyone says hello to Mae every day and asks how she is. It's nice, at first. But after a couple of months, Mae misses the busyness. In Reading town, the constant crowds gave her anonymity. She could walk the streets and get a bus, and no one gave her a glance. No one knew her name. She could hide in plain sight. Here, the forty-three people who live in the community all know her name, all want to talk, and all ask her how she is. There's nowhere to hide. She never imagined a place with so much room, so much space, she could feel smothered.

She starts spending days in her hut, shirking her duties, blaming pregnancy tiredness, swollen ankles and whatever she can think of to have some time alone. There are not many mirrors around the place, mercifully, Mae thinks. She can feel new pudge on her face, her chin and cheeks spongy to the touch. Will Pasha still like her looking like this? Pasha is so busy getting involved, he notices her sadness but has no words to console. Her belly grows, the baby moves more, the life inside her feeling like her only friend, the only one she can talk to. The only one who knows what she's feeling.

There are swings in the garden, meant for the children, but she sits on one to pass some time. It groans under her weight, the growing baby adding more than its fair share. She rocks back and forth, like she's caught in a current. Each time she goes forward she is free, floating away, then she rocks back, retreating to the confines of this life, and she is trapped again.

The book collection is not extensive, but it contains one thick-spined medical volume on women's bodies, childbirth included in all its gory detail. Mae can't bear to look at it. The pictures try to use artistry to take away both the horror and the joy. She takes some comfort in watching Pasha pore over it daily. He's never been one to shy away from the science behind bodily functions. His interest in biology extends beyond physiotherapy. He studies and learns every stage of pregnancy and labour.

'Best to be prepared,' he says to Mae.

She nods. Being prepared would involve doctors' appointments, scans, blood tests. However much he dresses it up, Mae knows they're winging it.

He attempts to show off his knowledge with the numbers. The articulation of regularity, of rules. His way of reassuring Mae, she's sure.

'The baby's heart is beating at a hundred and ten to a hundred and fifty beats per minute,' he says with animated enthusiasm. 'Your cervix will dilate to ten centimetres.'

Nice try.

Dutifully, every week, they walk half an hour down the road to call Iris. The walk is getting harder for Mae. Pasha offers to go without her, but that short time away from the community is a welcome relief. She tells them news of Rolan and Moira, that Hooper is still alive, and some sparse details of any unrest back home. From their distant county, they celebrate Iris's ninetieth birthday with her. Mae watches tears brighten his eyes before they spill over and trace rivers down his cheeks. He reveals none of this through his voice though, gives no indication of his regret to Iris that he can't be there to celebrate in person, can't even send a gift. A song down the phone and wishing her well an inadequate commemoration for such a great age. A sympathetic face and a reluctant hug from Mae an ineffective comfort to Pasha.

The ninth time they do the walk, Iris has the email.

'It came this morning. I haven't opened it,' she says, Pasha holding out the phone on loudspeaker.

'Okay,' he says. 'We're ready. Open it.'

There's a pause that lasts forever.

'Nan?'

'Just saying a quick prayer. Now, let me see. Ah, yes. Rejected. Oh my, that is a shame. They don't explain it, they just say your application is unsuccessful, and you have less than a month to register a donor.'

A lump forms in Mae's throat, and she grasps her tummy like the baby knows; that it senses it's doomed.

'It's okay, Nan,' Pasha says. 'We're happy here. We miss you so much. But we'll be fine here. We can make a nice life here.'

'My offer—'

'No, Nan,' he snaps before she can finish. 'We don't want you being our donor. Please, don't say so.'

'I checked the Society Police app the other day. You were noticed on your journey. Somewhere in Dartmoor.'

'Dawn,' says Mae through her teeth.

'I've asked my hacker friends to try to take it down. Not sure they can manage it. This Society Police app is a bit tricky. But we'll see.'

'It's all right, Nan,' Pasha says. 'Doesn't matter. No one is going to come looking for us here. Ro and Moira okay?'

'Yes, yes, they're quite all right. Moira's very big now. Their new house looks very fancy. And I'm just fine, before you ask. As is Hooper. You know, he chased a squirrel this morning. Such a puppy still.'

They say their goodbyes, then Pasha hangs up, his arms wrapping around Mae. 'It'll be okay, Mae. It's just pregnancy blues. You'll settle here. I know you will.'

Mae has no words of reassurance. She wants to go home. Not community home, as kind as they all are. She wants her flat, her textbooks, her computer, all the things they're going without. Some anonymity. To hide. To give birth here, no doctors, no medicine, she can't bear it. No. That can't be what's happening.

'What about the Isles of Scilly?' she says. 'We could go there.'

Pasha knits his brows. 'Why? By the sounds of it, it's just as remote, and it's further from home.' His face eases into a smile, his eyes now pleading. 'We can have a nice life here, Mae. It's safe and they're good people.'

This she knows. They're all lovely. Kind, attentive. But they're everywhere. They know her. They see her. She feels exposed and too visible. They're here to hide, but she's never felt so unconcealed, like she's wearing hi-viz on a gloomy day.

They walk back, and as they do, Mae makes up her mind to try harder. They're good people; she's not denying that. It's her own goodness that's the question. Sue looks at her always with such knowing eyes, like she can read Mae's mind and has figured out all of her secrets. Mae keeps quiet, speaks little, and barricades herself behind a silent wall. But the baby inside her knows everything, as she knows the baby. The fug of loneliness chased away by the movements inside. She can't explain it, this feeling, of knowing another being so acutely, like the baby would be born and tell everyone all she knows. She even knows it's a she. Pasha is unaware of this. She shrugs when he speculates and guards her knowledge. It's another secret she wants to keep.

Chapter 34

Scarlet disappears for a few hours one day. Down the path that leads to the road. Dipika waits behind, pacing, biting her nails.

'You can go too, if you like?' says Sue to Mae.

'Where?'

'A doctor's visiting. She has a mobile ultrasound scanner. They can use it at the end of the path. The old office building there still has an electrical feed. You can go too if you want to see your baby.'

Mae shakes her head. That sounds risky. Too risky. Scarlet has a bracelet. She won't likely be exposed. 'No. Thanks, but no.'

'It's a quiet road, and the office building isn't used for anything.'

'All the same,' Mae says.

'I should have gone with her,' says Dipika, still chewing on her thumbnail. 'What if she's not okay? What if there's something wrong with the baby?'

Sue puts a hand on each of Dipika's shoulders, then takes a deep breath as Dipika copies her. 'Scarlet needs you relaxed and strong, to be her calming influence. Trust me. Trust this place. She'll be fine.'

Dipika's tranquillity restores, like Sue really has some sort of control over the universe and the Eyes Forward legislation and the Enough movement mentality. Dipika does look more relaxed, though. Perhaps words are enough.

Annoyed by Dipika's pacing, her own nerves unsettling, Mae goes to the garden, tends the plants, then picks some vegetables. Anything to keep busy. Kill time. Sue joins her, scraping her hair back into a loose ponytail. That hair was dark once, the odd strand of brown escaping the onslaught of grey. She stands close to Mae, which spoils her mindfulness for a while.

'He doesn't know you well, does he?'

Mae's face goes as red as the tomato in her hand. 'No.'

'He loves you though.'

'I know. But he wouldn't if he knew.'

'You can't be sure of that.'

Sue's words fail to soothe Mae like they did Dipika, and she kneels back to thin the carrot seedlings. Mae says nothing more, only picks in the dirt while Sue trains the cucumbers, her last words hanging in the air. Those words linger, won't go away, like some nuisance bug. Mae shakes her head, trying to free her mind of Sue's chat. For she is sure. Of course she's sure.

'I'm going for a shower,' says Mae to Pasha when he comes to join her. 'I look a mess.'

He pulls her in close. 'You look gorgeous.'

She pushes him away. He always says that. It's meant as a compliment, but compliments shouldn't come with an expiry date, as that one does. And she knows her looks will go. In a few years, likely less this time around with motherhood taking its toll. She'll be aesthetically stunted, yet her mind will still be there. How will he compliment her then? His love for her is more than skin-deep; this she knows. But soon she'll be an empty vessel again. Chipped and broken. When time has withered her once again, will there be enough love left? Underneath, is she enough?

If he knew the truth, probably not.

Mae changes her clothes after her shower, a habit she's been sinking into more and more as she's begun to notice the grub and stains like every mark burns. She's worked her way through the box of hand-me-downs of this and that several times. There are always plenty of clothes drying on the line, always plenty yet to be washed.

Pasha sits on the bed, waiting for her. 'Your clothes weren't dirty, Mae. You can wear those if you like.'

She scowls and buttons up an oversized shirt that just about fits over her bump. In the half-light of the hut, she finds some scissors, then trims Pasha's beard. He's not paid enough attention to it of late. It's uneven and spreading down his neck. He stands patiently, watches her work, and asks if she's okay.

'Of course I'm okay. It's just your beard.'

When she's done, she folds and refolds their clothes on the shelf, failing to make them tidy enough. They don't sit neatly enough, however many times she tries.

'Nesting,' Pasha says. 'It's normal.'

She shoots him a look. He's never referred to her as normal before. It doesn't feel like the positive observation he intended.

An hour later, Dipika runs to meet Scarlet walking back down the path, all smiles.

'It's a boy,' Scarlet says, eyes glinting with tears.

One of Dipika's hands goes to her mouth, and the other reaches around Scarlet. 'A boy! We're having a boy.'

Mae smiles, bites the inside of her cheek, then rubs her hands over her own tummy. Her baby kicks, her baby girl. She's not jealous of Scarlet and Dipika's scan, she tells herself. How can she be? She knows her baby. She knows everything is okay right now. If that scan could predict the future, she might be interested.

They make lunch, a salad of things grown from the garden. Mae picks off a caterpillar from a lettuce leaf before plating it up. She hadn't seen a caterpillar in so long before she came here. Now she sees them most days. She flinched at first, but now she flicks them away like they're dust.

Little Micky comes to help, a seven-year-old that Mae's been trying to teach maths to. His mother brushes his hair several times a day, but it still looks wild, hanging in front of his eyes. He always has grazed knees.

'Got some more tomatoes,' Micky says.

'Thanks, Micky.'

He smiles, pleased with himself.

A pair of dragonflies soar past them, locked in copulation. A bug that Mae didn't even know the name of before they arrived. Now she even recognises their mating.

'What are they doing?' asks Micky. 'They're stuck together.'

'Mating,' Mae says. 'Making baby dragonflies.'

'Well, they should probably think about that a bit more carefully,' Micky says with an air of superiority as he washes the tomatoes.

Smart kid.

The afternoon is warm enough, and they sit outside. Everyone talks baby names and baby toys and more baby names. Mae's desire to retreat to a quiet place is subdued for now. She wants to share in their joy, to absorb their elation. She doesn't want to seem rude.

'I listened to the radio for a bit,' Scarlet says. 'And the doctor, she was saying how bad things are out there.'

'How bad?' asks Pasha. 'Do we want to know?'

Mae doesn't, but she keeps quiet.

'Bad. Like, really bad. The body count is in the millions now.'

'No!' several of them gasp.

'And no one cares,' Scarlet continues. 'The Eyes Forward don't, anyway. They think it's some achievement. Reducing population was their campaign pledge, and they're achieving it. Mostly elders, tons of women. Often women are beaten but not killed. The Enough and Time's Up have wiped out so many.'

'We're so lucky to be here,' says Dipika, holding Scarlet's hand.

'Those elder communes, loads of them have been bombed. The armed security isn't enough. The Time's Up threw petrol bombs over fences. Loads more care homes burned down. Maternity units at twenty-seven hospitals have been bombed. Nurseries are shut. Women too scared to go out alone. Not just pregnant women, all women. They're wearing T-shirts and branded clothes to say they don't want kids. Loads even have the Enough badge pinned to their clothes. They've signed up as fully fledged members just to stop them being beaten in the streets, some trying to make themselves look older with makeup. Post menopausal, you know. So they're not considered a risk. No one's even rioting about the inheritance tax, not according to the press, anyway. They're all too preoccupied with rioting about everything else.'

No one responds. Pasha's hand tightens around Mae's.

'We're lucky we've got food here. The shortages are making the violence worse. Every city has curfews now and food is all rationed, but looting is still happening. In broad daylight, it's happening. You need a Life Score of 500 just to go to a budget supermarket now, apparently.'

They eat their salad, chewing rather than speaking. Mae picks at her lettuce, then slices her tomatoes smaller. She's not hungry anymore.

'I'm worried about your nan,' she says to Pasha.

'We just spoke to her. She was fine.'

'She won't be, though. Reading will fall, like London and Manchester. She said she didn't want to die alone.'

'She has Hooper.'

Mae can't tell if he's joking.

'You're not thinking about her offer?' asks Pasha.

'No. God, no. Of course not. But how much worse would it be? Would it? I don't know. But it would be bad. If she dies alone and scared at the hands of some Time's Up hooligans.'

'It's Nan. She probably has hacker friends watching over her.'

'I'm serious.'

As she stops talking, the deafening sound of fighter planes rip through the sky. Lottie soothes Felix, though no one hears his wails over the din of the planes. The flimsy tables rattle, the vibrations tickling Mae's whole body from her feet to her nose. She counts seven of them flying in formation, all heading east. To the cities, to the unrest, to the bulk of the population.

She hasn't missed seeing the news on TV or reading about it online. Not until now. Now she wants to know more, to see images of her hometown, her favourite shops and café. Is their flat still standing? Reading is just a town. Surely it won't suffer as much as the big cities. Which cities are burning? Is Edinburgh okay? Her thoughts go to Ro and Moira, their friends in London. . . She fidgets and grinds her teeth. They feel softer than they used to. Is it too much grinding or is the baby taking her calcium? Another thing to add to the list of Google topics she wishes she could search. The tranquillity of the camp now feels anything but. A frustration, an isolated vacuum of knowledge. She stands, looks east to where the planes went. Carefully clambering up on a low wall, she can see out to the moors. Empty. No fires, no people, no houses, no town. A buffer of nothingness. Which city is closest to where they are? She wonders and kicks herself for not knowing something so simple. Exeter seems like a lifetime ago, a whole county ago. She takes a breath and looks around at their oasis, their safe community. Morbid curiosity, that's all her desires are.

That night they don't light a campfire. It's early summer, the evening is warm and light, the sun setting over the moors casts an orange glow, the westerly wind warm with its last rays. The breeze carries with it a smell. Subtle, but Mae's sensitive nose can pick it up. The smell of burning.

Somewhere, inland, the cities are burning.

Chapter 35

Sat around the fire the following evening, Juanita fidgets, then goes back to her lodge and gives it a clean, sweeping the dust from around the fire, then fidgets some more. Her swollen belly is uncomfortable in the early summer heat, and she lets out a moan.

'You okay, dear?' asks Sue.

'I think,' she says with a pant. 'I think today's the day.'

The night draws out with sporadic moments of discomfort for Juanita. No one sleeps except for the children. Mae watches mostly from the sidelines, Pasha rubbing her back as if she's the one in pain. Sue and Lottie tend to Juanita the most, bring her water, cool her off or warm her up. They all pace with her, circling the lake twelve times over night, gravity helps, Sue insists. At daybreak, her discomfort becomes the cyclical pain Lottie and Sue both know and understand so well. The labour progresses quickly, the minutes gap in between shrinking fast. As Juanita's screams resonate through the camp, a whole new and unexpected sound reverberates through the sky.

A drone.

'What? No! It can't be!' Sue says as she wipes Juanita's brow. 'They're not allowed here. There's a covenant on the land.'

But it is there. They all see it, all hear it. That black disc and those red laser eyes piercing the sky.

Sue stands over Juanita, keeping her in her shade. 'Get her hidden, now. Mae, Scarlet, hide. For God's sake, hide! Take the children!'

Mae and the others run to the nearest hut, shut the door, but there's no lock, so they prop anything they can against it, then close the curtains except for a tiny sliver where they peek through. Lottie has Felix strapped to her front with scarves as colourful as a butterfly, shining in the half light. He's asleep. Thank heavens he's asleep. The smaller children grizzle, and Pasha holds little Anabel tightly, his hand over her mouth. Mae puts her finger to her lips to tell them all to be quiet. 'Quiet as mice,' she whispers.

Nick and Sue attempt to lift Juanita as another contraction drops her to her knees and she screams. The drone is by her now, jet black surface shining in the morning sun, those red laser eyes like daggers. Mae holds her own hand to her mouth as her whimpers threaten to give them away.

Unregistered pregnancy detected.

'No!' Juanita cries.

This pregnancy must be terminated.

A telescopic arm comes out of the drone, a needle glinting at the end.

'You can't!' says Sue, shielding Juanita with her body. 'Go away. You're not allowed here!'

Permission from the mayor to be here. By order of the Eyes Forward.

'No!' Juanita cries again. 'He found me. The bastard found me!'

'She's too far gone,' Sue says. 'You can't terminate now. She's in labour.'

No baby may draw breath without sacrifice. By order of the Eyes Forward.

'No!' Juanita screams again, recoiling between contractions. 'Please don't. Please, don't kill my baby.'

The drone buzzes closer, and Mae holds her hand to her mouth to muffle her own cries. Juanita is pushing now. The baby is almost here. The needle edges closer to Juanita as she screams again.

'I volunteer,' Sue says as she arches her whole body over Juanita.

Nick gasps. 'What? Sue, no!'

'I have a chronic heart condition. I qualify. Please, I volunteer.'

Juanita's guttural scream is haunting, a banshee. She's pushing again.

Mae's whimper breaks through, as does Lottie's, tears streaming down her face, shaking her head. The drone spins on the spot, red eyes flashing as if in thought.

Donation accepted. Hold out your arm.

'No!' the hushed cry from the hut, from everyone.

Sue kisses Juanita's head. 'It's all right, dear. It's my honour.'

She holds out her arm, then the drone injects her. She collapses to the ground. Dead. In an instant.

Nick sinks to his knees. 'She's supposed to get an hour with the baby!'

Late donors get no such allowances. New law. Congratulations.
And it flies off.

Chapter 36

When the drone is out of sight, they leave the hut, Pasha first, silent as he can, listening for the hum of the drone. Juanita screams and cries through her final push as Lottie runs to help. With Sue's body lying still just a few feet away, Juanita pushes her baby out. Cries of anguish and joy, of despair and love. The little girl announces her arrival with bellowing lungs as Juanita holds her and sobs and sobs. Mae backs away. It's too much. It's all too much.

Pasha finds her in their hut, her bag packed, ready to leave.

'It's not safe here, Pasha.'

'I know. But the unrest—'

'I'd rather take my chances with the thugs than the drones. We can hide out there. In here, we're sitting ducks. Let's go now. We still have a few weeks to get to the Isles of Scilly. They're all busy. Let's just run away.' She can't think about goodbyes. She can't look at that baby when her own child's life hangs in the balance. They have to get away before their time to find a donor runs out. She needs to run, somewhere, anywhere but here.

'Okay,' Pasha says. As simple as that. And with the early summer sun kissing the lake, while everyone is mourning and celebrating, they leave. Just a note behind that says: thank you for everything.

'I studied some maps they had, just in case,' Pasha says. 'It's over sixty miles to the ferry port. I don't think you can cycle now, not this far along.'

They keep walking. Mae says nothing. What is there to say?

They walk all day, and Mae's legs hurt. They eat the meagre rations they pilfered on their way out. Their cash left is minimal and the early summer sun is severe. Mae can't comprehend their situation, can't imagine not having this baby now.

It's impossible to know how far they've walked. The traffic is constant on the roads, so they stick to farmers' fields mostly, woods when they find them, roughly in the right direction. They think so, anyway. When night comes, they set up camp. Well, Pasha does, treading down the jumble of bracken to make the ground softer underneath. Mae sits quietly, telling her tummy that it's okay, that they'll find a way to keep it safe. Her feet and ankles throb, she's not walked much the last few weeks, blisters are forming already, muscles knotting up. She has to pee, all the time she has to pee.

Pasha leaves her at their camp and goes to a local shop, his haircut Cornish style. No one notices him, he says. When he returns, he is out of breath. His red face tells her everything before he speaks.

'Saw a drone,' he says between panting breaths. 'A black one. Eyes Forward drone. I think it was just on its way somewhere.

Wasn't scanning anyone. Anyway, best you stay out of sight. Luckily, the dads never got nano-tagged.'

Yeah, thinks Mae. Luckily men can still do what they like.

Her bitter thoughts are unkind, she knows this. Too tired and hot to be reasonable, she keeps her mouth shut. The best way to avoid conflict is to stay silent.

They eat cold beans and fruit and plain bread. It's too hot to light a fire and too many mosquitoes to stay outside. In the tent, they lie separately, side by side, a million miles apart. The baby protests, knows something is wrong, Mae is sure. The baby knows all her secrets.

They stay at that camp for a while. Hidden from view, a shop close by. Seems like a good enough spot, they think. Mae's blisters harden, her swollen ankles reduce. They have to keep going. They know this, but they stay a while longer. Just waiting, listening.

Mae counts the birds, the trees, the days. They don't need a calendar when Mae can keep track so well. The tangy scent of their unwashed clothes bothers her less. She's given up noticing the stains and the dirt.

Most days are dry and hot. The trees above blot out the worst of the sun. When rain comes, it drizzles only. The staccato rhythm of it on the canopy is like counting the seconds. Pasha encourages her to move more, but her hips ache, her back bowing downwards, weighed down by her hanging belly. Pasha rubs her feet, but it tickles instead and Mae flinches, unimpressed, like he's lost some strength in his hands. Or she's just less receptive to his touch.

At night, she speaks to her bump, silently, yet she knows the baby hears. She gives it the reassurances that Pasha gives to her and tells the baby that it's all going to be okay, the sort of bullshit that makes her turn away from Pasha. She can't say it out loud, can't hear her own lies, but she passes them on, dutifully, telling her baby not to worry, that they'll be a family one day soon.

When Mae sleeps, she dreams of the baby. A toddler, running around their apartment. Toys litter the floor, but Mae doesn't care, doesn't even count them. All she notices is her daughter. Her laughter is all she hears. Sometimes she has Pasha's unruly dark hair, sometimes Mae's fiery red. Her daughter's face is never revealed. She always has her back to Mae, like she doesn't want to show herself. She doesn't want to show Mae what she may never be able to see.

Another time, she dreams she's a spider, like the plenty they've seen in the woods, sprawling legs dangling from brilliant green leaves. When the baby is born, it eats her and Pasha, fuelling itself, ridding the world of excess life. She knows no fear. It's just the way of things, she tells herself in her dream, to consume then be consumed.

Pasha calls Iris to keep her updated on their progress, or lack of. He makes the call away from Mae, yet she hears him tell Iris that Mae is resting, and he doesn't want to disturb her. Mae knows what he really means, that he can't trust Mae to play along, to tell Iris that they're fine. He can't even trust Mae to speak. It's been days since she's said a word. At least Iris is alive.

He returns to Mae from the call, his face twisted with emotions, but Mae can't read him.

'Moira and Ro, they've had their baby, their baby boy. Angus, after Grandpa.'

The urn is still in their bag. Mae looks at it, half expects it to come alive and cry like the baby. The baby Pasha helped create, one more reason why their own child is to be born illegal. Contraband. Mae imagines Moira parading her child around with its tattoo, legitimising its birth, bragging about its legal status, while they hide in the woods with their own baby. Forever to be banished.

'They're all okay,' he continues. 'All healthy. But the other news. Uncle Charlie, he died. His home was set on fire. They were locked in. They all died in there.'

He shakes as he says this, a nervous tic, or pent-up emotions? Mae can't tell for sure. She fails to care about Uncle Charlie. In that moment, as she's lying in the dirt, fearing for her own baby's life, Uncle Charlie's death seems like a waste. A life they could have used. She thinks Pasha feels the same, hopes he does. She can't be the only one thinking such dreadful things. Pasha doesn't seem sad. No tears, no change to the colour of his cheeks. The vibrato in his voice comes from something else, some other news he isn't telling her. Exhaustion. Muscle fatigue. She makes a mental note to check on his medication.

'Nan is all right, though. She says she's not seen much trouble. Can't get some food, but she has enough, she says. Say's Hooper will look after her.'

His joke fails to raise a smile from Mae. She gives a little nod, lets him know she's heard. If only dogs could be signed up to be donors.

'Our place is still standing, Nan says. North of the river hasn't really been touched yet.'

Yet. Exactly what Mae is thinking.

'The high street has been ransacked,' he carries on. 'Most cafés and shops are shut for now. There's curfew everywhere. Society Police having a field day if anyone is out after curfew, apparently. Nan says it's being kept under control, not like the big cities. Wish I could speak to Roger. At least Ro is okay. But still, Charlie's home burned down. He was at a bad end of town, though.'

The air still has the smell of burning, the leaves on the trees blackening from ash being carried on the wind. What city was that coming from? The last embers of civilisation. Would they have a town to return to? Were they destined to live in the woods? Perhaps the drones would be destroyed in the unrest. Perhaps the Eyes Forward would burn down.

No chance.

'I think we're going to be okay, Mae-bug. I think we're going to be okay.'

His words hang in the air like the smoky smell. There's a drop in his tone, so different from months ago. What she'd give to hear him say fine again, to mean it. To believe it.

They move little by little through the woods, edging further west, but at a snail's pace. A couple of miles a day is all Mae can manage, sometimes needing a couple of days' rest in between. Not enough food, iron, probably, her growing bump demanding more and more.

One day, Pasha brings a newspaper back with some supplies. It's blisteringly hot, the trees offering little relief. Mae looks at the paper like it's about to catch fire, but she reads over his shoulder, silently, only half disbelieving.

Almost four million people have been murdered in the Society since the announcement. Not enough though, the tone of the newspaper seems to be implying. Food and fuel shortages are still reported, the Pro Grow gaining momentum, fuelling the hate on the other side of the argument. The Enough and Time's Up show no sign of faltering. Billions have been banked from tax and saving from the cost of supporting the young and the old. What a success, the papers say. The economy is booming!

Chivalry is demonised as healthy fathers try to offer themselves for donation for their unborn child, being refused as they are well and of working age. The Society needs such men. They're not surplus to requirements like the babies and their grandparents. Mae's mind casts back to the man selling a syringe of disease. Is he the only one profiting from the chaos? However unsavoury the methods, the Eyes Forward are getting what they want. The Enough and Time's Up are bookending the population with murder. No more children, no more elders. The Society will be entirely made up of working age citizens. Keep that economic wheel turning. The never-ending march of earn and spend, earn and spend. Strive to score, the Society relies on it.

Curfews are enforced by the overzealous Society Police, county borders shut, properly shut, not just trampled chicken-wire shut. No access to public transport, working from home essential for most. Women have been demoted everywhere, equality laws ripped up, for their own protection, it says. *Women just aren't like men*, the paper quotes some Eyes Forward representative. They have urges and needs that must be controlled. They cause too much trouble.

It happened so fast, the promise of progress tipping into the degradation of the Society. Like everything that was good was balanced on a knife edge, it never had stable footing. It was never meant to last. How things were seems like both a lifetime ago and only yesterday. The world is so unrecognisable now.

Across the world, much the same is reported. The Preserved have so far failed in their bid to buy out XL Medico. One small bit of good news, Mae thinks, before she goes on to read the most devastating news. Nine thousand babies were aborted in the final weeks of pregnancy in the last month, the drones hot on the heels of anyone trying to avoid the law. Six thousand women have ended their own lives, much to the ambivalence of the newspaper.

Mae watches the sky, listens, and begs the universe to save her child, to let theirs be the one that escapes. To take her life instead. Lord knows, she's lived long enough. She feels eyes on her always, the creeping sensation up her spine, a tingle on the back of her neck.

What if, is Mae's thought constantly. What if a drone finds them and ends the baby before it's born? Life goes back to normal, before all of this mess, before they had to run and hide. Would that be so bad? They were happy then. Cosy days in under the sheets, laughing at some telly, food easy to come by. It's an imaginative muse only, for she knows the change has been too great. There's no returning to that life now. Perhaps the drone will take her life too. She was never meant to last this long. All those years alone, life just drags on and on. Bad mother, she tells herself. No good mother would give up so easily.

But she's not a mother. Not yet.

Chapter 37

Weeks pass and they walk little. Her legs can't stand it. Progress is painfully slow. Her ankles bleed always from bracken and thorns, her shoes no longer fit properly. A tangle of thick and thorny limbs of plants swat at her, trip her, suck what little energy she has. She wants a shower, a proper mattress, to piss in a real toilet. That flushing sound is the only noise of civilisation she actually misses. Pasha talks to Iris some more, the ancient phone batteries last ages. Iris says her Sisters And Spies hacker friends are helping her, which makes him laugh. Mae's blank expression remains steadfast. She can't find the joy in anything.

Then one stiflingly hot day, they arrive at a beach. The most perfect beach. Water a shade of blue the likes of which Mae's never seen, a cool breeze taking the worst of the heat away. The sea turns white as it licks the tide-line where sand turns to pebbles. The stones scream in their thousands as the sea sucks away. A pleasant scream, cheerful, hopeful, promising to return. Is this what beaches looked like when Pasha went on holiday years ago? She can picture it then, the joy of going away, of finding somewhere so unimaginably beautiful. Her lips curl into the smallest smile, pleased that she gets to see it. Now, before the world turns muffled and cloudy. Her enjoyment of now is forever thwarted by her knowledge of what is to come.

Pasha takes her hand as they walk down the badly carved steps to the sand below. He's shaking, wobbling with each step. More and more lately, he shakes. He should be stronger than that. She can't lean on his strength just then. Has his medication run out? No, they took plenty, Mae reminds herself. He's just tired, that's all.

They sleep on the beach, in a cave where the tide doesn't reach, among the seaweed and shells. The smell is something unique, the sound more soothing than she's ever known. She's uncomfortable however she sits, the baby pushing on bits that don't want pushing. Hungry but not wanting food, tired but unable to sleep. The expanse of forever on the horizon, lying to them, telling them they're not backed into a corner.

Mae pictures their old apartment, wonders with pain in her chest if they'll ever be able to return. She thinks of Sadie. Why does she think of Sadie, of her clients, if Katlyn is going mad without Mae? Her life from before, the life she must forget now. But she wants to hang onto it for a while longer. She whispers Sadie's name, letting the S linger on her tongue.

'What did you say?' asks Pasha.

Mae shakes her head. *Nothing. Doesn't matter now.*

During the day, they move deeper into the cave, seeking shade, her red hair and freckled skin intolerant of the July sun. Pasha sits in front of her, keeping her in his shadow when the cave is insufficient. Godrevy, Pasha says it's called, seeing a sign when he went to find some food. No boats, though. No fishing, no people. He's bought a paper map and shows her where they can get a boat from to the Isles of Scilly. It's far. Still too far. And she is too pregnant to move.

They stay a night, then another, just staring out at the blinding sea. She sees apparitions in the heat, smiling faces of people she misses, a cup of coffee, algebra formulae. When the sun gives way to night, the visions go, and the blanket of darkness makes her feel like a little girl. That the world outside has ended, there is nothing left.

'We have to leave soon,' Pasha says the next morning.

'Soon.'

'Can you walk?'

'A little.'

She stands, but as she does, a pain shoots through her pelvis and fluid spills from her. It's too late. They've no time left.

The labour takes hours, longer than hours. Mae screams and sobs and worries and curses. The sun sets and rises again before she's even nearly done. She searches the sky for drones always, waiting for the hum, dreading their arrival.

'It won't be long now,' Pasha says, his eyes also scanning the sky, listening for the buzz between Mae's cries and groans, his hands shaking.

She watches his shakes. His limbs tremble always now. When did they get that bad? He's supposed to be strong and brave, her sturdy rock in a rushing river. It's wrong. Everything is wrong.

'Listen, Mae,' he says when she cries for him, for the baby, for the pain to stop. 'You're going to be okay. You and the baby. I stopped my meds a while ago. If a drone comes, I can volunteer. I'm eligible.'

More pain comes, all over, inside and out. 'No. No, please. I can't do this on my own.'

'You can, Mae-bug. You know you can.'

But she can't. She knows she can't.

'I told you I'd think of something, Mae. I'd figure it out, and this is how. Truly, Mae, I'm happy. Our baby will live on. You'll be a wonderful mum, with or without me.'

'No, Pasha. Please, I can't. You and me, in this together, you said. No lies. You lied!'

He wraps his arm around her as she screams in agony, her nails digging into his shoulders. He can't be about to die. This isn't happening.

'Trust me, Mae. You trust me, don't you?'

She does. She trusts him to make stupid decisions with the best intentions. He smiles at her with his doughy smile, his tear-stricken face, as she feels her baby ripping its way out of her. Has it come down to this? The worst choice imaginable.

'I trust you, Mae. I trust you to raise our baby, to be the mum you were born to be.'

He trusts her, but he doesn't even know her. Not properly. Can she let him die without ever knowing the truth?

'I have to tell you something, Pasha.' Her words come out in pants, in brief interludes between the pain.

'I know, Mae. I love you too.'

'It's not that. . . I need to be honest with you. . .to tell you everything—'

'It's almost here, Mae. The baby is almost here.'

The sound comes. A distant hum, gently at first, then louder. Mae can feel it in her bones, vibrating the sand beneath. She tries to be silent, but it's impossible and pointless. There's no one else here. It can only be coming for them. The hum continues, louder and louder. Too loud for a drone. Louder than her screams. A hundred drones, that's what it sounds like, what it feels like.

A car pulls up, a great black 4x4 in the sand. She squints to see it, vision fogged with sweat and tears. Mae screams out another contraction.

'It's coming, Pasha,' Mae cries through her groans. 'The baby's coming now.'

'Looks like I made it just in time.'

Whose voice is that? Mae looks up towards the car. There's someone there, walking towards them.

'Nan?'

Iris. A silhouette against the sky. *It can't be. It can't be.*

'Come on, dear,' she says as she crouches beside Mae, her knees creaking. 'A couple more pushes.'

There's no time for questions. Mae can't think about anything but the pain, about her baby. She sees Pasha, willing her on. She has a hand in both of hers, she can't ask why. In the confusion and chaos, the baby comes.

The crying is the most beautiful thing she has ever heard. A scream, a healthy scream. Pasha holds the baby up, so impossibly tiny, as fragile as porcelain, blurred through her streaming eyes. 'It's a girl, he says, weeping. 'You did it, Mae. A baby girl.'

Her heart is filled with love.

But Mae can't look at her baby for more than a second. She searches the sky, listens for the hum over the baby's cries as Pasha swaddles the tiny girl.

'There are no drones coming, dear,' Iris says.

The words sound strange, foreign, far away, like Iris isn't really here. She can't be here. Mae's head is stuffy and ringing, then Pasha hands her the baby. Her baby. She's not crying anymore. She looks up at Mae with the bluest eyes, and Mae knows those eyes. Holding her close, her tears flow. Mae is holding her baby. Her own baby. Still, she listens. Her child has drawn breath, the one thing the drone says she wouldn't be permitted to do. Her desire to protect dwarfs any other feeling. She remembers Pasha and his medication. He kisses her forehead. She can't lose him. But her baby, the tiny baby staring up at her, she knows her. She must live.

Whatever the cost.

She understands this now, more than anything else, and has a pang of understanding for her mother's actions. As old as she was when she forced Mae to live, as old as Mae was then, her desire was the same. Giving her the medication was giving them both another chance at a life together. Mae thought it was a punishment, another lifetime in purgatory. Through her slurred words and ambiguous actions, Mae hadn't realised. Her mother's final actions, all those years ago, were intended as a kindness. A mother's love.

Iris's voice is distant, unreal. 'I've been tracking you, of course. The Sisters are still everywhere and given the current situation, they were more than happy to help. They gave me a lift here.'

Pasha and Mae don't mock this time. The car is parked just a little way away. People stand outside, leaning against the car, smiling faces of people they recognise. Molly. The waitress from Exeter. Sisters And Spies. Iris had been sincere.

'Now, I don't have long,' Iris says. 'Perhaps I can hold my great-granddaughter a while.'

'Oh, Nan,' says Pasha, hands over his mouth. 'No. you didn't.'

'Of course I did. Ages ago, as soon as your exemption was rejected. Now, no tears, you two. This was my choice. My life, my terms, remember? To say thank you to you, my dearest friend,' she says to Mae, cupping her face with her hands. 'I always said I'd pay you back. You gave me a lifetime with my Angus. And now I get to die alongside my family. Such an honour.'

Through her tears, Mae nods. She knows. She's always known. Pasha is at the edge of her vision, his confusion morphing into realisation. Iris removes from her neck the locket she's always worn, a Saint Christopher engraved on the front, then hands it to Pasha. He pauses before opening it, hands trembling more than ever, and stares at the lock of red hair inside.

Mae can't face him now. Her old friend needs her more. Mae hands Iris the baby, her precious little bundle.

Iris takes the baby, coos at her, kisses her cheek. 'You look just like your great grandpa. You have his ashes still?'

Pasha, still hands over his mouth, nods.

'Good, good. I'd like us to be together. I'm looking forward to seeing him now.'

'Nan—'

'I saw a priest yesterday, so don't you worry about me. I'll be in good hands. You've had a real adventure, you two? That's what I hoped for, to get you out of Berkshire. Do something besides straightening pictures and counting things.'

Mae wants to respond, but she has no words. Her baby will live. Pasha will live. That is all she wanted. This should be a happy day.

'Now, be quiet,' Iris says, before Pasha can protest more. 'Let me just enjoy the quiet. No sadness. Just some quiet.'

Mae says nothing but reaches for Pasha's hand as she grants her old friend her wish. Pasha's eyes are fixed on Mae, staring, but he keeps hold of her hand. Thank God he keeps holding her hand.

'Mae...' Her name rolls around the cave like a breeze. 'You're P... P...' The word is too strange to say, unpronounceable, lost in his throat.

She nods, biting her bottom lip, looking down at her lap. 'I wanted to tell you. I'm so sorry. I always meant to tell you.' A pathetic plea. Little more than a whimper.

He shuffles closer, leans right in, his forehead resting on hers. His breath heats her cheeks. 'You should have trusted me, Mae. You should have known that I love you enough.'

She looks up at him, his eyes so close. The barrier that has always separated her from him has gone. Everything she is, laid bare. 'There is so much I should tell you.'

He glances down at the locket in his hand, the strand of Mae's hair from a lifetime ago trapped inside. Then he puts it in his pocket and cups her head in his hand. 'We have our whole lives, Mae. Tell me whenever you're ready. It's you and me, Mae-bug. Here and now.' He kisses her on the mouth. Salty with tears of relief that spill out of her like a river. He leans back and wipes her cheek with his thumb, sturdy enough now that Mae can rest against him. His face wears that easy smile Mae loves so much.

'You two will be just fine,' Iris says as she steps out of the cave, bathed in sunlight. She sits on the sand, looking at the baby for a while, then out to sea. After a moment, Mae stands, weak legs wobbling, Pasha's hand gripping hers firmly, his other arm around her waist supporting her as they walk outside. Next to Iris, they sit silently, shoulders touching.

Blue skies ahead, a warm sun with a cool sea breeze. A few bubbly clouds. The rustle of trees, some birds cheeping at their chicks.

A note from Emma

Donate is the first book in the Eyes Forward Series. If you enjoyed it, please consider leaving a review on Amazon and Goodreads. Reviews are so vital for indie authors such as myself and knowing you enjoyed my work makes it all worthwhile. You can order the second book, Preserve, now. It's set ten years after Donate, and shows how the Society has adapted to appease the Enough, the Time's Up, and the Pro Grow factions. There are new characters to meet, and the story gets a whole lot darker. Check out my website and Facebook page for updates. Book 3, Rebel, is due for release January 2024, and can be pre-ordered now.

Subscribers to my website receive a FREE spin-off thriller novelette that features one of the characters in the next book, Preserve. Sign up via my website to get your copy.

If you are in the mood for some more twisted dystopian, my first series, The Raft Series, is available now.

Donate, if stripped down to its bare bones, is a story about love. The love between a parent and child, between partners, and family members. It's about how that love continues to persevere and struggle when everything else in the world is going so very, very wrong. I adore these characters. Mae and Pasha's bond is so raw and so flawed. You'll have to wait for the final book in the series, Rebel, to see how things pan out.

The Society came about from my own alternative way of living. I've been a nomad for a few years now, spending most of my time dawdling around the mountains and coastlines of Europe. Dystopian literature plays on our fears, our what ifs. I have lived all over Britain, including a fair chunk of time in Reading and Cornwall. The counties across Britain are all wonderfully unique and I love exploring them. If it became taboo to cross county borders, I think I'd go insane. There is so much to see in this little world. If you are not familiar with Godrevy beach, it is as beautiful as this book describes. More so. Words cannot do it justice. I can confidently say that the food is also a lot better than this work of fiction implies! Indulging in a cream tea in that part of the UK is one of my favourite things to do.

Acknowledgements

Donate would not be in print without the help of my wonderful betas and critique partners. Thank you to Maggie, Mitra, Danica, Emily and Chrissy. Their time and honest feedback made this book what it is today. Thank you also to my editor Shannon K. O'Brien, for being so incredibly thorough, and Natasja Smith for her proofreading skills.

Thanks especially to my partner, John, for giving me the space and time I need to write, for his support, patience, and encouragement.

And thank you for reading it.

Made in the USA
Monee, IL
02 May 2024

57875861R00218